MURDER
ON THE QUAI

MURDER
ON THE QUAI

CARA BLACK

Published by
Soho Press, Inc.
853 Broadway
New York, NY 10003

Library of Congress Cataloging-in-Publication Data

Black, Cara
Murder on the Quai / Cara Black.

ISBN 978-1-61695-808-4
eISBN 978-1-61695-679-0

1. Leduc, Aimee (Fictitious character)—Fiction. 2. Women private
investigators—France—Paris—Fiction. I. Title.
PS3552.L297 M88 2016   DDC 813.54—dc23   2016001949

Printed in the United States of America

10 9 8 7 6 5 4 3 2 1

Again, for the ghosts

"Every contact leaves a trace."

—Dr. Edmond Locard,
French criminologist, 1911

MURDER
ON THE QUAI

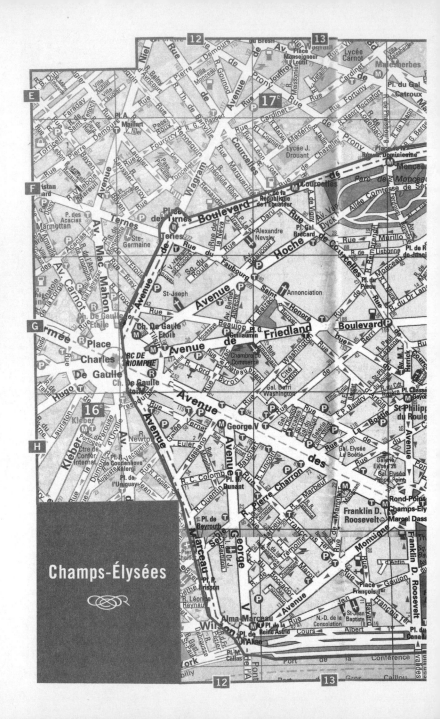

Champs-Élysées

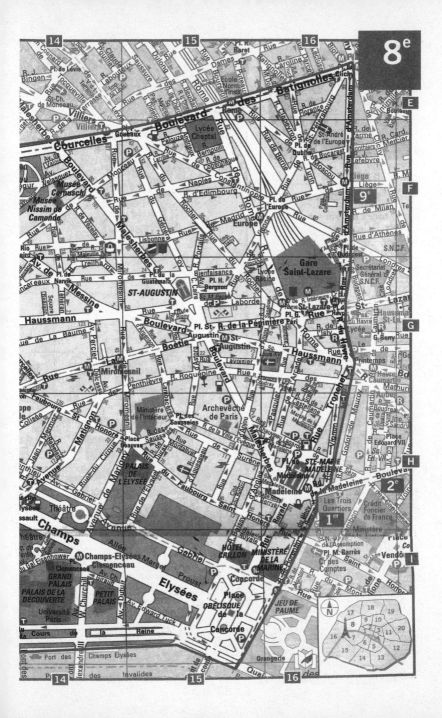

Paris · *November 9, 1989* · *Thursday Night*

STANDING OUTSIDE THE Michelin-starred restaurant, a stone's throw from the Champs-Élysées, the old man patted his stomach. The dark glass dome of the Grand Palais loomed ahead over the bare-branched trees. To his right, the circular nineteenth-century Théâtre Marigny.

"*Non, non,* if I don't walk home I'll regret it tomorrow." He waved off his two drunken friends, men he'd known since his childhood in the village, as they laughingly fell into a taxi. Course had followed course; remembering the caviar-dotted lobster in a rich velouté sauce topped off by Courvoisier brandy, he rubbed his stomach again as he waved goodnight to the departing taxi. His belly was taut with discomfort; he needed to stretch it out before bed. Besides, he always enjoyed the walk home to his place on Place François Premier. Even now, after all these years, pride swelled in his chest that he had secured himself an address in *le triangle d'or*, the golden triangle, the most exclusive quartier in Paris. The thrill of living among the mansions and *hôtels de luxe* between avenues Montaigne, George V, and the Champs-Élysées never got old to him.

He looped his silk scarf tight, took a deep breath of the piercing chill November night. Belched. The born farmer in him sensed tonight would bring frost—a crinkled frost that would melt on the grey cobbles like tears. In the village, it would have been a hoarfrost blanketing the earth like lace.

He looked over his shoulder—force of habit—with vigilance that hadn't diminished in forty years. They were always so careful, so scrupulous about the details, took precautions—yet Bruno's murder had scared them all. Made them wonder at the implications. Could it be . . . ? But a month passed and nothing. Were they safe?

Not totally safe, not until the final trust document was rubber-stamped tomorrow. But that was only a formality. Nothing would go wrong this late in the game. He knew that—they all did.

Yet why had he woken up shouting in his sleep last night? Why did Philbert's dentures grind so at dinner, and why did Alain drink a whole bottle of wine himself?

Brown leaves gusted against his ankles. On his right a blurred Arc de Triomphe glowed like a painting on a postage stamp farther down the Champs-Élysées. He kept a brisk pace, got his blood flowing, warmed up. He was fit as a fiddle, his doctor said, his heart like that of a man twenty years younger. A couple passed, huddling together in the cold.

Walking under the barren trees by the Grand Palais, he became aware of footsteps behind him. The footsteps stopped when he did. But as he turned at the intersection in front of the zebra crossing, he saw no one.

Nerves. The light turned green. He crossed. Midway down the next block he heard the footsteps again. Turned.

"Who's there?"

Only a dark hedgerow, shadows cast from trees. Unease prickled the hairs on his neck. He walked faster now, looking for a taxi. Silly, he lived two blocks away, but he never ignored a feeling like this. Each taxi passed with a red light crowning the roof: occupied.

Stupid—why hadn't he taken the taxi with the others? Kept to their protocol of precautions? His meal, rich in cream, sat in his stomach like a dead weight.

Every time he heard the footsteps, he turned and saw no one.

Paranoid, or was he losing his mind? Or was the brandy heightening sensations and dulling his reflexes?

Then a taxi with a green light slowed. He waved it down. Thank God.

"*Merci*," he said, shutting the taxi's door, breathing heavily.

"I'm only supposed to stop at the taxi stand, monsieur."

"Then I'll make it worth your while in appreciation."

He gave the address.

"But that's only two blocks from here."

"Consider your fare doubled, monsieur."

The taxi pulled away from the curb. He asked the driver to close his window.

But the driver ignored him. And turned toward the river. Not the way home at all.

Ahead, streetlamps rimmed the quai, their globes of light reflecting yellow shimmers on the moving Seine. His heavy insides curdled.

"You're going the wrong way."

The taxi accelerated, throwing him against the back of the seat.

"Stop." He tried the handle. Locked.

Afraid now, he pounded the plastic partition and tried reaching for the driver's shoulder. The wheels rumbled down a cobblestoned ramp.

"Let me out."

He didn't even realize where they were until the taxi

stopped. The taxi had lurched to a halt below the Pont des Invalides, nestled in the shadow of its arch support. Mist floated over the Seine, the gurgling water swollen by early November rain.

And then the door opened and before he could defend himself, his arms were pulled behind him. "Take my money, just take what you want."

"You know what's going to happen, don't you?" said a voice.

He gasped. "Please, let me go."

"Don't you remember the river?"

Panic flooded him. "*Non, non.* You must understand—it wasn't supposed to happen . . . We can make it right."

"Liar. Payback time."

A rag was stuffed into his screaming mouth. His bile rose and all the rich food lodged in his gullet, choking him.

"You remember, don't you? It's your turn now."

He was shoved to the edge of the quai and down into a squat. Through his blinding terror he saw one of his shoes fall into the water below. The lapping waves from a receding barge and the faint rhythm of faraway car horns masked his cry of pain. Even the lit globes of the sodium lamps faded into the mist on the cloud-blanketed night.

"How does it feel?" a voice hissed.

But he couldn't answer as the sour-tasting gag tightened across his mouth. His tied hands gripped and flailed. He couldn't breathe.

It wasn't supposed to happen that way.

The shot to the back of his head was muffled by the plastic Vichy bottle used as a silencer and the rumble of the traffic overhead.

Paris · November 10, 1989 · Friday Afternoon

AIMÉE LEDUC GAZED IN horror at the mess in her test tube in the *école de médecine* lab. Her experiment ruined. Again.

She held the tube to her nose and sniffed. Bleach. Someone had sabotaged her work. Probably one of her twelve fellow premed lab mates—all of them under twenty, like Aimée; all of them male.

The professor was heading her way.

"This is the second time this month, Serge," she said, panicked.

"Didn't I warn you?" said Serge, an upper-class lab assistant, lowering his voice. "Around here you have to guard your tubes and petri dishes with your life. It happens."

Yes, but that didn't make it fair. She wanted to shout, to accuse someone. It was well known that only 15 percent of students would be allowed back for the second year. The cutthroat competition led some students to sabotage others just to stay in the running.

"Don't forget this assignment goes toward your semester grade," Dr. Fabre, their instructor, was saying as the lab emptied.

What could she do?

She liked Dr. Fabre, an older man with tortoiseshell glasses and a slight stoop. His lectures had a strange but appealing energy. Now he asked, "A problem, Mademoiselle Leduc?"

"Someone poured bleach in my test tube . . ." *Merde*. She didn't want him to think she was the type to whine.

Dr. Fabre shook his head. "No other students had this issue. Do you expect special treatment? Instead of blaming your errors on others, check your notes."

"But Dr. Fabre, you can smell it . . ."

"So you say, Mademoiselle Leduc. But if it means so much, you should have watched your work more carefully. Perhaps slept here. I did in my premed days."

No sympathy here. They wanted to be doctors and help people—why not start with themselves?

She could cope with grueling exams, reports, and all-night studying. But this? She bit her lip, determined not to cry. "Professor, would you please let me redo the experiment? I'll have the results by tomorrow morning."

"I've got four classes to grade and my schedule's full. It's not fair to the others, mademoiselle."

Or to her, but it seemed that didn't matter.

"Let me warn you," he said. "We expect the best. Despite the promise you've shown, you're a candidate for the suspension list. Consider this a formal warning."

Her heart dropped. "There must be a mistake." She riffled through her bag and pulled out her notebook, where she kept duplicates of her assignments and grades. The same notebook with the surveillance case notes she'd been transcribing for her father. "Sir, I scored in the top ten percentile, and I turned in all my assignments."

Dr. Fabre shook his head. "As so have many others. I can't make exceptions."

She managed a nod before she humiliated herself further, and to refrain from kicking the door as he exited.

She rolled up her lab coat sleeves and cleaned the lab in

the coffee-colored light of the dank November afternoon. It was her turn to be the first-year grunt. At the faucet she scrubbed her hands with carbolic soap, trying to figure out what to do. The formaldehyde smell permeated everything. Her shoes, her clothes. She couldn't even shampoo the smell out of her hair at night. Another thing she'd chalked up to life in med school.

Serge came in, handed her a paper towel, then leaned against the counter where the surgical instruments dried.

"First year's the toughest. You'll get over it. Everyone does, Aimée." Serge had the beginnings of a beard, thick black hair and myopic eyes behind black-frame glasses. "I was a *carabin*, too." A stupid archaic term still used for med students, because their lab uniforms resembled those of *les carabines*, riflemen in Napoléon's army.

"I expected a grind, but backstabbing?" She wanted to spit. "You heard Dr. Fabre. I'm going to fail."

"Pah, you'll make it. It's all about the exam, no matter what he says. You work hard," Serge said. "Be patient."

Patient, her? It was all she could do to focus. From day one, the competitiveness, that feeling of never measuring up, had dogged her. Every morning she told herself she could do it—couldn't she? After all, she'd made it into med school.

Her gaze out the narrow lab window took in the gunmetal sky over the medieval wet courtyard of *l'école de médecine*. Students bent into the November wind. Nine more years of this if she passed. Maybe ten.

"You'll see it's worth it when you find your calling. I hated my first autopsy, threw up," said Serge. "Almost left medicine. But the next involved a homicide victim. The policeman asked the attending examiner questions. How he looked at the body for clues to solve the murder fascinated me." Serge shrugged. "That's when I learned that the dead talk. I'm learning how to listen."

"But it's the living I'd rather figure out," she said.

Serge took off his glasses, wiped them with the hem of his lab coat. "I've been accepted into Pathology after my rotation."

She smiled, happy for him. "Congrats, Serge."

Serge shrugged. "Take a walk. It will clear your head."

She hung up her lab coat with LEDUC stitched on the lapel. The old-style thirties script reminded her of the Leduc Detective sign hanging over her father's office on rue du Louvre. She kicked off her scuffed clogs and stepped into her worn Texan cowboy boots, put on her leather jacket, and shouldered her bag.

"Aimée, what about your late lunch? We're heating up the *croque-madame*."

"All yours. Knock yourself out."

She waved at Serge. She'd lost her appetite.

NEAR THE STUDY lounge where everyone hung out between lectures, she looked for tall, blond Florent. They'd met at the study group, almost two months now. She wanted to lean on his shoulder. No, face it—she wanted to do a lot more than that. Crawl under the duvet with him, like the other night. The morning after, brioches in bed, skipping study group to lick off the buttery crumbs. Murmurs of a weekend in Brittany at his aristocratic family's country home.

She didn't see Florent among the loitering undergraduates. Time for a pee.

After checking the whole row of bathroom stalls, at last she found one with toilet paper and latched the door.

The hall door opened—voices, footsteps. The squeal of the faucet.

"Why didn't you tell me before? I love clubbing at Queen," said the nasal voice she recognized as Mimi's. Florent's sister was a third year. Tall and big toothed, Mimi reminded her of a horse. Water gushed from the faucet and she heard snickers.

Aimée flushed, pulled up her agent provocateur tights and headed toward the sinks.

"I want to go with you, but Florent's engagement party is this weekend," said Mimi.

Aimée blinked. Florent's engagement party? She and Florent were supposed to be going to Brittany.

"I thought I recognized those cowboy boots," said Mimi, turning toward her. Her voice lowered as if in confidence. "I just felt it was right to tell you that I don't think your weekend plans with my brother are going to happen."

At the soap-splashed mirror Aimée finger-combed her spiky hair and dotted Chanel red on her trembling lips. Her mouth was dry. Mimi's friend, the Queen clubber, eyed Aimée with a predatory gaze.

"Why's that, Mimi?" Aimée said finally.

"He's getting engaged this weekend."

Breathe, she had to keep breathing. "Florent didn't tell me . . ."

"I'm telling you, *compris*? No idea what he was thinking leading you on, but this engagement has been in the works for eons." Mimi laughed. "Florent's inheriting a title. You think my family would let him get serious about . . . ?"

A knife twisted in her gut. Could it be true? He'd never mentioned an engagement.

"Don't take it hard. You'll get over it. Just don't kid your-self."

"And you're his messenger service?"

Mimi sighed as she drew in brows with an eyebrow pen-cil. "*Désolée*. He didn't want to hurt your feelings."

Was it that Mimi and her crowd hated her and were just being nasty? Or was Florent a gutless wonder who couldn't tell her face-to-face? Maybe both.

"*Non*, I need to see him." She turned and stared at Mimi. "He needs to tell me himself."

"Don't say you weren't warned." Mimi snapped her makeup case shut. Noises echoed in the corridor as she opened the bathroom door and left, followed by her friend. "Seriously, let's go clubbing," she was saying as the door closed behind her.

Out in the corridor Aimée had to pass by Mimi and her group of laughing sycophants, who were blocking her way and shooting her looks. Her face reddened. She wanted the creaking wood floor to open up and swallow her. A loser. She'd die if her friends heard, and they would—Florent was supposed to come to her best friend Martine's birthday party.

Waves of humiliation washed over her. She should have known that Florent, an aristo from the posh Neuilly sub-urb with *de* in his family name, had been slumming with her. She'd been naïve to trust him, the spoiled bastard. For God's sake, she'd slept with him. His feelings for her had probably been bogus like everything else about him. Except for his prospective title.

Furious and blinking back tears, she ran down the stairs and through the twisting medieval maze of the seventeenth-century building. The hallways were glacially cold, with dust in the corners. A dead quiet clung to the tall glass anatomy displays of skeletons and bones. She hated the whole damn place.

COMING INTO THE chilly cobbled courtyard, she zipped up her leather jacket, looped her scarf, and pulled on her gloves. Her pager erupted in her pocket. Florent with a kiss-off?

But it was from her father at Leduc Detective.

Strange, he never paged her.

His office was ten minutes away and she could use the walk. She passed the pillars enclosing the garden sculptures of École des Beaux-Arts, continued along the quai Malaquais, its misty banks burnished gold in the light of the streetlamps, and crossed the Pont des Arts, pushing aside the memory of sharing midnight Champagne here with Florent. The Seine swirled below, green, black, and turgid. The *bateaux-mouches* slid, twinkling, into the dusk. She hurried now, pulling her collar up against the chill, through the Louvre's shadowed Cour Carré.

By her father's office, she stepped into the warm corner café, whose windows were clouded with moisture, and nodded at Virginie, the proprietress. The staticky radio news channel blared, mixing with a whooshing of the milk steamer.

The local butcher, a rotund man wearing a white apron smeared with blood, set his *demi-pression de bière* on the counter. "Tell *le vieux* I've got that lamb shank he ordered." His *boucherie* was around the corner, its storefront crowned with the traditional horse busts.

"*Merci,*" she said.

Le vieux, her *grand-père,* had founded Leduc Detective

after years at the *Sûreté*. His private detective agency made use of his contacts and connections to specialize in missing persons. "One of the top five agencies," he'd always say. "I'm discreet and get results."

The butcher liked to talk. "He's quite the *gourmand* these days, eh, your *grand-père*?" He drew on his beer. "Semi-retirement? One like him never retires."

He'd got that right, according to her father, who'd taken over Leduc Detective after he left the Paris Police. *Grand-père* had run a one-man show at the detective agency until then. He had officially retired to make room for his son, but kept many fingers in the pie. Too many, Aimée's father often said.

"Tell him I'll save some beef cheeks. I know he likes them."

Sounded like the butcher missed her *grand-père* and his business.

"In the continuing historic news from Berlin," said the announcer's voice coming from the radio behind the chipped melamine counter, "on this cold afternoon, for the first time in twenty-eight years, crowds pass beyond Checkpoint Charlie after the Berlin Wall fell last night . . ." The rest was lost in crowd noises.

"Can you believe it?" said the butcher, rubbing his hands on his apron. "That's the end of Communism and I just paid my Party dues."

THE WIRE BIRDCAGE of an elevator in her father's building on rue du Louvre sported an OUT OF SERVICE sign. When was it ever in service? She picked up the mail from the concierge—bills. The winding stairs were redolent of beeswax polish. She was still trudging up to her father's office on the third floor when the timed light switched off, plunging the staircase in darkness, and she almost stumbled. Feeling her way up the smooth banister, she managed to reach the landing and hit the light. Leduc Detective's frosted-glass door was open. Odd.

"Papa?"

Stepping inside, she heard his muffled voice. Drawers closing. The old wood-paneled partition blocked her view.

She hung up her leather jacket but kept her scarf on. Her father's nineteenth-century office, with its high ceilings, carved wood *boiseries*, and nonfunctional marble fireplace, enjoyed nineteenth-century heating. She rubbed the goosebumps on her arms, then gave the radiator a good kick. Sputter, sputter . . . *et voilà.*

On the wall were old underground sewer maps that had fascinated her as a child. Still did. She set the bills below the old sepia photo of her grandfather during his *Sûreté* days, waxed mustache and all. Next to it on the wall was Leduc Detective's original business license.

"I kept my distance, as requested, Jean-Claude," a woman was saying. "I asked for nothing. But we're still family, and now I need your help."

Family?

Curious, Aimée peered around the screen. She saw a woman sitting across from her father at his mahogany desk. She was in her mid-forties, with broad cheekbones and short, brown hair. A mink-collared coat rested in her lap. Wide-set eyes blinking with unease, she reminded Aimée of a deer. A frightened deer.

Who was this woman?

Her father looked up at Aimée, his reading glasses riding

down his nose, his dark brown hair curling over his suit jacket collar. His expression was both irritated and quizzical.

"You paged me, Papa. Something come up?"

Her father sighed. "My daughter, Aimée, Mademoiselle Peltier."

"No need for the formality, Jean-Claude." The woman reached out to shake Aimée's hand. "I'm Elise, your father's second cousin. We met but you were small."

"We did?" Who knew she had this distant relative?

"You were a toddler." Elise gave a small smile.

Aimée's heart dropped. "Then you must have known my mother." Her American mother, who had disappeared when Aimée was only eight years old, leaving Jean-Claude to raise their daughter alone.

"That's not why Mademoiselle Peltier's here, Aimée," said her father. His mouth was tight with anger. "Elise, I'm packing," he said. "My train's in an hour. I know someone very good who can help you."

"*Mais* you're family," Elise said, insistent. "You're a former policeman. Without your help I'll never discover the truth."

Aimée shot her father a what-in-the-world look. He averted his gaze. Was he hiding something? She couldn't remember the last time she'd seen her father so uncomfortable.

Elise turned back to her. "As I was telling your father, my papa was murdered. He was found tied and bound, a bullet in the back of his head, under Pont des Invalides." Elise twisted her Hermès scarf between her fingers.

Aimée tried not to betray her shock. She'd followed the story in *Le Parisien*, every lurid detail. She knew the spot, the dock for the *bateaux-mouches*—a busy place. "Wasn't that a few weeks ago? Did the case get solved?"

Elise's lip quivered. "It's been a month and the police have discovered nothing. My mother's gone into a shell, won't speak or eat."

Aimée tried to catch her father's eye.

"Again, I'm sorry, but my field's missing persons, Elise." Her father slid files in his briefcase.

How could he act so cold—so businesslike—with his cousin?

"Papa still had money in his wallet, his keys."

"That's right, the article said nothing was missing," said Aimée. She remembered reading that a fisherman had found the body early the morning after. "He wasn't a robbery victim."

Elise nodded. "Why? That's what I want to know. Who'd do this?" Her voice cracked. "The police say they have explored all avenues. Even after I showed them this. I found it in Papa's coat pocket."

Curious, Aimée glanced over as Elise set an open matchbook on the desk. In it was written *SUZY* and a phone number.

"Can you find her, Jean-Claude?"

"Why do you want to find her?" her father asked. Aimée recognized that question he used to divert spouses from pursuing *un amour* best left alone.

"Who is Suzy?" said Aimée.

Elise rubbed her eyes. "You remember Papa, *non*, Jean-Claude? He's not the type to have a mistress, but now I've got my doubts. What if he got mixed up in shady business at a club, you know?"

Aimée picked up the matchbook. LE GOGO was emblazoned in gold on the cover.

"Le Gogo's off the Champs-Élysées on rue de Ponthieu, *non*?" said Aimée.

Elise nodded. "You know it?"

Aimée shrugged. "Know of it, *oui*."

A quartier of *boîtes de nuit*, discos and clubs like Queen, Rasputin, and Régine's for *la jet-set*, at least until a few years ago. Places Florent's sister, Mimi, clubbed at.

"Jean-Claude, I'll hire you to investigate. Do this for me, please? Find this Suzy and see if she had anything to do with his murder."

"Haven't you called this number yourself?"

Of course she had, Aimée thought, catching her father's eye.

"A man answered and I hung up." Elise looked beseechingly at Aimée's father. "The police have gotten nowhere. But one of the inspectors, a Morbier, told me you would help. Then I realized he was referring me to you, Jean-Claude. My own family."

Morbier was her father's first colleague on the beat, and Aimée's godfather. He must have felt sorry for Elise. What she didn't understand was why her father appeared so reluctant to help.

She opened her mouth to speak but caught her father's *be quiet* look and the slight shake of his head.

"Elise, pursuing this could lead to discovering something that might hurt your mother," said her father. "An indiscretion you wish you didn't know about."

Elise's eyes welled. "That's what the police say, what everyone says. But it's not right." She erupted into sobs. "Papa wasn't like that. Maybe everyone says that, but he really wasn't the type to go to these clubs."

But she was ignoring the evidence in her hand, Aimée thought. The man must have led a secret life.

"He was murdered in cold blood. Shot on the quai." Her

lip quivered. "But no one cares, they're indifferent, no one wants to help—not even you. It's like it never happened."

"The police have their procedures, Elise. They're not indifferent; they follow clues. Check evidence. This murder may have been random, the most difficult kind to solve. Morbier must have told you that." Jean-Claude passed her a box of tissues. "I'm sorry. Truly sorry."

"The *certificat de décès* came today." She blew her nose. "I don't know what's worse: seeing it in black and white and not being able to do anything, or seeing my mother wasting away to nothing."

Elise set the report on the pile on Aimée's father's desk. The radiator sputtered.

"Jean-Claude, I've written down everything I can remember. Plus there's a copy of the police statement. Please. It's all here."

Her father nodded. Scanned the statement.

"I'll do it the minute I get back," he said. "But only to find clues to turn over to the police, you understand?"

In answer Elise pulled out her checkbook.

"Will that do for a retainer?"

Five thousand francs. Aimée's eyes bulged.

Elise blew her nose, wiped her eyes, a mascaraed mess.

"Elise, there's a WC down the hall," said Aimée, shooting her father a look.

HER FATHER SLAPPED a report into his briefcase, buckled it closed. "Aimée, I know you go back to the lab on Friday nights," he said. "But Sylvie's still out with *la grippe*."

He gestured to his secretary's desk. Reports piled high around a wilting dahlia plant. Poor Sylvie, sick like *tout le monde*.

"Hate to ask, but could you put in an hour and organize things? Handle calls from the answering machine while I'm gone?"

This was the last thing she wanted to do. She had so much on her mind—she had her place in the premed program to save.

"That's why you paged me?"

Again he nodded. "Two clients haven't settled their accounts," he said with a sigh. "It's tight this month. That's why I'll take her case."

The curse of the business. As a private contractor, he was always the last to get paid. But how could she refuse to help?

"*Bien sûr.*" She tapped her boot heel, surveying his secretary's cluttered desk. But now there was something she needed to ask *him*. She swallowed hard. "Papa, Elise remembered me from when I was little. Did she know *Maman?*"

For a moment, pain shone in his eyes. "It's been fifteen years. Elise and I were never close."

And where her mother was concerned he ignored the question. As usual.

But she wouldn't let him off this time. "What about my mother?"

"We don't talk about the past, Aimée."

She steeled her nerves, aware this was painful for him, too. "It's time we do. I want to know if my mother's alive. I want to know about my relatives."

"Not now, Aimée. Leave it alone. Trust me on this."

"She's still family, Papa. A blood relation."

He glanced at his watch.

"Something come up all of a sudden?" she asked.

"You could say that. If I don't leave I'll miss my train."

"Train to where?"

He had packed an overnight bag, she saw.

"*Alors*, Gerhard called from Berlin."

Now Aimée remembered his contact there and the news bulletin on the radio. "Berlin? But the Wall's just come down. Why now? You think it's safe?"

"Safer than ever. I need to get hold of those Berlin files in person . . ."

Hadn't she transcribed his investigative notes on a German couple last week? "You mean the missing husband?"

"*Exactement.* Before the Stasi destroy all the records." He rubbed his forehead.

Elise would be back from the bathroom any moment. Aimée didn't want to let the woman get away without hearing what she had to say about Aimée's mother. On impulse she said, "Let me follow up on this Suzy. I read all about the case, Papa."

"Aren't you a first-year med student with exams coming up?"

Aimée pointed to the mink-collared coat draped over the back of the chair. "Didn't you say it's tight this month?"

His mouth pursed. "Not a good idea, Aimée."

Now he thought it wasn't a good idea for her to help— now that it was something interesting. He'd been happy to ask her to organize his files and answer his phone messages. "A piece of cake, Papa. Not even an evening's work. You always tell me to follow my instinct. I can do this in my sleep."

She'd been raised by two police detectives, her father and her grandfather. She'd spent her childhood dozing in the backseat of the car while her papa was running surveillance, and her teen years keeping the pot warm on the stove for him when he was out on all-night stakeouts.

"Remember last year when I helped you track down that *fille* at the disco because you were too old to go in?"

An aristo's underage daughter who'd run off with a Corsican gangster.

"This is different, Aimée."

"How? You're just saying that. Look, it's a simple job of asking around at this club and giving Elise some closure, *c'est tout.*" As she said it out loud, she wondered why the police hadn't just done the same thing—it sounded straightforward enough. "Did Morbier refer her because his hands are tied?"

"Something like that." He'd bent down to pick up his case and she couldn't see his expression. "Don't you have a lab write-up to do, Aimée?"

Changing the subject, as usual. "Not exactly," she said.

She felt like a six-year-old again—getting in trouble on the playground. How could she tell her father when he was running to catch a train? Face his disappointment?

Her papa cupped her chin in his warm hands. "What's up, *ma princesse?*"

Why did she always forget how well her father knew her? "My lab experiment was sabotaged, Papa. It's so cutthroat. I might get suspended even though I've done the work."

Her father snorted. "That's going to stop you? Nothing worth doing comes easy." He winked. "You'd let them intimidate you? Where's my fighter?"

That's all he could say? On top of it, her boyfriend was getting engaged. Her life had fallen apart.

"Don't disappoint me, Aimée," he said, his tone turned serious. "I want better things for you. To be a doctor—have a respected profession, meaningful work—that's so important."

Translation: It was important for him. He didn't want her to follow in his footsteps, and especially not those of her mother—an American free spirit who couldn't cope with being tied down to her family and who'd broken his heart. But Aimée's memories of her mother were warm and fuzzy—*chocolat chaud* and madeleines and stories at bedtime.

"How are we related to Elise and her family? Why didn't I know they existed?"

"We'll talk when I get back."

She let out a groan. "You mean I have to ask *Grand-père*, is that it?"

Her father shrugged.

Not again. "You're still not speaking to him?"

Her father reached for his wool scarf. "He's not speaking to me. But he's the one to ask about that side of the family."

Fine. She would. "Well, we can solve Elise's mystery for her and put the check in the bank. We both know her father had an affair—cut and dried. I'll check out this Suzy this weekend and then write up a report."

Simple. Then back to the grind of the textbooks.

"For once listen to me. You've got an exam coming up," said her father. "That's the priority. Concentrate on studying, that's your job."

"Papa . . ."

"Not now, Aimée." His expression was full of sadness, misgiving, and urgency, all at once. "There are some things you should know. We'll talk when I get back."

She hadn't seen that look on his face since that day when she was eight years old and she'd come home after school to find a note on the door in her mother's handwriting: *Stay with the neighbor.* It was the last she'd ever heard of her mother.

"What's wrong, Papa?"

He was about to speak, but the door's buzzer sounded and he glanced at his brown leather watch. "That's the taxi."

He gave Aimée a hug, enveloping her in the scent of his wool overcoat and pine cologne. Kissed her cheeks, leaving a warm imprint.

"I'll call you from Berlin."

She wished she'd had enough time to drag it out of him, whatever it was.

Halfway down the winding stairs, he called up. "Don't forget what I said. Hands off. And reserve the van for the Place Vendôme surveillance."

ELISE RETURNED FROM the bathroom, mascara and eyeliner carefully reapplied around her doe eyes.

"My father's left for Berlin," Aimée said. "He's sorry, he meant to say goodbye." She rushed on, "Elise, did you know my mother?"

Elise's eyes widened. "Yes, *l'Américaine*."

Aimée's pulse thumped.

"So you do remember her?"

"Yes, I think we have some photos."

Photos? Aimée didn't even have one—her father had burned them all. "I'd love to see them. Learn about my family."

The radiator sputtered.

"Of course. They're somewhere. I'll need to find them. Right now, I can't leave my mother. I'm afraid she'll hurt herself. She's talked of suicide, she hides her pills." Elise's mouth quivered. "My father's murder's taken over our life."

If Aimée found Suzy, distraught Elise would want to pay

her back by finding those photos. Give and take, do a favor and get one in return—didn't it work that way?

"I'll find Suzy, Elise."

Elise took her coat, then Aimée's hand. Her wide-set, red-rimmed eyes welled again. "*Merci* for your offer. So sweet. Your father's honorable and I'm sure that's true of you, too. But I need *his* help."

Aimée's heart fell. She smiled through the sting of her disappointment. "We're family, Elise. In case you need anything, here's my card."

SHE KICKED THE radiator until it sputtered to life. Then again for good measure.

She looked at Sylvie's desk—she should get started on that. It would take her mind off her looming academic suspension.

Her hand hovered over the phone as she debated whether to call Florent and ask him about this weekend. Maybe she'd misunderstood.

Fat chance.

No doubt his horse-faced sister had enjoyed following her into the bathroom and dropping the bad news—putting Aimée in her place. Meanwhile, Florent was taking the coward's way out.

Forget calling Florent. She'd make him deal with her face to face at next Tuesday's lab class. In the meantime, screw him.

In two hours she'd finished logging and sorting the inbox, followed up on the outbox, filed dossiers, and typed her father's notes. If only her father had let her computerize their system, she could have accomplished it all in under half an hour.

She wished she had time to go back to that computer course she'd taken over the summer.

Her eye caught on Elise's folder, the generous check. Could she tie that up tonight?

Didn't her father always say you can't make a goal unless you kick the ball?

She rooted around in the file cabinet until she found her father's notes from a similar case to Elise's—a widow who had been investigating her late husband's illicit affair. Aimée studied them. Simple.

She'd make a list of key points from Elise Peltier's notes—that was always the way her father built an investigation. Then add details from the police report to create a brief profile.

Bruno Peltier, aged sixty-seven, of 34 rue Lavoisier, retired, discovered in the early hours of October 10 on the quai under the Pont des Invalides. Gunshot wound to the back of his head. He'd last been seen leaving his residence on foot at 8 P.M. for a dinner with old friends at Laurent, a posh restaurant off the Champs-Élysées in the old Louis XIV hunting lodge.

When he hadn't returned home by 3 A.M., his wife called one of the friends he'd been dining with. The friend's name was not in the police report or in Elise's notes. Bruno Peltier had never shown up at the restaurant, the friend said to his wife: they'd figured he had the flu. The police were called to the quai after a fisherman found him at dawn with his wallet and ID.

Not much.

She called Suzy.

The number rang and rang.

"Oui?" said a man, breathing heavily as if he'd come up the stairs.

"Have I missed Suzy?"

"Who?"

Now what could she say? Think, she had to think. Come up with something plausible.

"*Excusez-moi*, monsieur, but Suzy gave me this number."

"*Et alors?*"

"I borrowed money from her on rue de Ponthieu a few weeks ago," said Aimée. "I want to return it."

"Ah, you mean . . ." Pause. "I see."

See what? "Is this a public phone?"

"What's that to you?"

Helpful, this man. "So where can I reach her?"

"Comes and goes. I don't monitor the tenants."

So Suzy rented. This was probably a public phone in the hallway. "What's her last name?"

"Don't you know it?"

She reached in the secretary's desk drawer for the petty cash box. She checked the amount—enough for a bribe? Her father would shoot her. She had no idea what he needed to pay his informers. Then again, she could replace the petty cash and then some with Elise's check.

She pulled a petty cash receipt off the pad and started filling it out. Eight hundred francs, more than a nice evening out with wine, should do the trick.

"Look, I'll just drop the money off, leave it with you. Give me the address . . ."

Money. According to her father, it worked most of the time. And saved a lot of standing around in the cold for hours. At least she hoped it would.

This could be fun, she thought, checking her mini surveillance tools, which she had fit into her makeup kit: lock-picking set (just in case), tweezers (always handy for a stray eyebrow or a sliver-sized piece of evidence), waxed thread (useful for stitching a hem or tying slingshots), nail polish (to stop a run or to mark territory), and, for key impressions, putty she hid in her blush compact. From her father's collection, she chose the palm-sized light-weight camera and extra film.

Gauze-like evening clouds zigzagged over the Louvre as she ran to the Métro. Shouldering her secondhand Vuitton carryall—a summer score from the flea market—she hopped on the second-class car, pulled out her anatomy textbook and highlighter, and tried to read. Five stops later she noticed the woman next to her, a sophisticate in a black YSL trench and pearls, had fallen asleep. Aimée nearly had, too.

A short walk under the bare-branched trees on the brightly lit Champs-Élysées, then a right past the tiny art cinema, Le Balzac, one of her premed Friday night haunts; down narrow, winding rue Lord Byron, named for the poet who, according to her *grand-père*, had never set foot here. Off rue Washington, she found Suzy's address by walking through a tall carriage entrance that led to Cité Odiot, a grassy enclave bordered by towering plane trees. An island of calm. She breathed in the damp leaves, heard twittering birds in the hedge. Such an oasis, three blocks from the jammed, busy, yet seductive Champs-Élysées and the death-trap roundabout of the Arc de Triomphe.

This quiet, dimly lit green enclave, surrounded on both sides by rose and cream buildings, extended half a block. Exclusive and hidden. At odds, she thought, with the peeling stucco of the leprous gatekeeper's loge.

A quick scan of the names on the row of mailboxes and she spotted a label that read S. KIMMERLAIN/R. VEZY.

Could that be Suzy? She reached in with pincered fingertips and came back with a France Telecom ad flyer addressed to Suzy Kimmerlain, #402. She pulled out the camera from her leather jacket pocket and snapped. *Always document everything*—her father's dictum ran through her head.

She felt like a secret agent in those old spy movies.

The gatekeeper poked his head out of the loge. She didn't need his help now. To avoid him she slipped behind a column and then ducked into the stairwell. The climb to the fourth floor—narrow winding stairs, like in a medieval tower—would give anyone a workout.

Neither door on the landing held a nameplate. No one answered at the first. At the second, a woman with her head wrapped in a towel cracked the door. A green gel mask covered her face.

"*Oui?*"

"Suzy?"

"If you're selling something, I don't want any."

"Please, Suzy . . ."

"She's gone to work," the woman interrupted.

Great.

"But I owe her money," said Aimée, sticking with her earlier improvisation. "She told me to bring it here."

"*Vraiment?*" A shrug of the pink bathrobe-clad shoulders. "Leave it with me."

Did she look stupid? Aimée shook her head. "In person, she said."

The kettle whistled. Over the woman's shoulder Aimée could see a narrow *chambre de bonne*. A bare-bones accommodation, a former maid's room, in a *quartier luxe*, only a few blocks from where the wealthy Monsieur Bruno Peltier had lived.

"Wait a minute. You're the one she talked about, *non?* You used to work together?"

Aimée nodded. "That's right."

"Then go find her at work." The woman started to close the door.

Merde. "But I went and she's not there," she lied.

The woman expelled a rush of air as if Aimée were slow. "Try the Alibaba."

The door shut in her face.

IF PAPA HAD said it once, he'd said it a thousand times: "Ninety percent of surveillance consists of tedious plodding and persistence." Find a name, a location, and follow up. Keep following up until you find a thread, a path leading somewhere. As he once said after a long night's surveillance, "Investigating is just not going away."

He tried to make his work sound boring, but she carried boredom in her rucksack in a biology book.

So far she'd found Suzy's full name, her address, and gotten the name of her current employer, all in exactly forty minutes. Now she needed to record it all, write it into a report and log billable hours.

Totally manageable.

Gare de l'Est, Paris · Friday Evening

"MESDAMES ET MESSIEURS, sehr geehrte Damen und Herren . . ."
the announcer droned in a nasal tone as the night train
to Berlin pulled out of Gare de l'Est. Jean-Claude Leduc
settled back against the leather seat in the dining car, a Stella
Artois in front of him, an unread copy of Le Monde boasting
photos of jubilant Berlin crowds pulling the Wall down.

He took a long sip, opened his briefcase to scan his
checklist for the Place Vendôme surveillance. His informer
had been contacted, the equipment was ready. He'd be
poised to go once he picked up the van Aimée reserved.
Bon. All done, he shoved the list back inside his briefcase.

Even his notes made him feel dirty. Under protest he'd
agreed to one last job. The damn thing stank to high heaven.
The nastiest of all and in the "defense of the country." That
catchall phrase meaning quite another "defense" but he'd be
paid not to make a fine distinction. The last one, he'd told
them, then I'm out.

If they didn't cut him loose . . . He put that out of his
mind.

Then he pulled out Gerhard's telegram. Reread the terse
message: Doctor's prescription ordered. Available 24 hours only.

Code from his contact that East German Stasi police
were about to bring to light Jean-Claude's missing wife's
records—secret and damning documents. That old longing
bubbled up inside him. Why couldn't he let go?

In his jacket pocket he fingered the locket containing a

snip of Aimée's baby hair—the one thing Sidonie—he never used Sydney, her American name—Leduc had taken with her when she'd left more than a decade ago. The locket arrived in an envelope last night, a signal that he and Aimée were in danger. A signal to make good his promise.

An old promise to the woman who'd ruined his career, put their daughter at risk, who'd left him, and who still made his heart pound. The love of his life, the woman he couldn't forget. The mother of his child.

He'd always known her Stasi files containing evidence, long under un-bribable key, could sooner or later get leaked—her arms deals, the terrorist cover-ups. He'd promised long ago he'd use his connections before that happened. A damn ticking time bomb, and now with the Wall down and the Stasi files opening, time was of the essence. The only protection now was the thing that had driven them apart.

Negotiating her prison release had got him drummed out of the force and driven him to the dark side, beholden to the Hand, a corrupt syndicate.

Sidonie was on the wanted list; sought by the Hague war-crime investigators, the Cypriot arms dealer, and Balkan gangs she'd double-crossed. He'd always had to think three steps ahead, knowing those types would do anything to control Sidonie with her past and make her work for them. He had to protect Aimée, her chance at a career, a life without the tentacles of her mother's crimes. Now was his only chance to erase her mother's past for good.

Over-reacting? Not when the secret services monitored him.

Another sip. The Stella went down smooth. The wheels clacked rhythmically; the outskirts of Paris passed by in a haze of misted lights. He loosened his tie, his shoelaces, and sat back. Sighed. Those thoughts he'd kept at bay for so long threatened to flood in.

You could only keep the past in the past when you weren't going to a city that held its secrets, he thought. And Sidonie's eyes, so like Aimée's—those big almond-shaped orbs—filled his mind. Would he ever be free of this woman, his first love? The only woman who'd taken his heart? But he was reminded of her every day by his Aimée, who, damn it, resembled her mother in so many ways. He couldn't control her, either.

His eyes closed. His thoughts drifted.

"That seat taken?"

He blinked and saw Soli Hecht, the old Nazi hunter, a bent man with a white beard and round glasses. Soli set down his overcoat, then his malacca cane. The diner car's lights reflected off his glasses so Jean-Claude couldn't read the expression in his eyes.

Jean-Claude shuffled the telegram into the file and closed the folder.

"And if I said it was?"

"That would look rude, Jean-Claude."

He sighed. Moved the file into his briefcase. The vultures were descending on Berlin to pick its carcass clean.

"So unlike you. You love company, *non*, Jean-Claude?"

"Don't start, Soli." Jean-Claude sipped his beer. "We finished that business last year."

"We did?"

Not again. Well, he wouldn't open himself up to allegations by this Nazi hunter, who'd accused him of bilking descendants of Jews lost in the Holocaust. He hadn't, but Soli Hecht had a lighting-rod sensitivity to those in his trade.

Finding missing persons had always been Leduc

Detective's bread and butter. Now, as the winters passed, the agency's cases concentrated on families looking for Jewish survivors, their property long lost and their inheritances often ground into dust.

Soli ordered a glass of Bordeaux. Settling back, his gaze took in the last Parisian suburbs fading in the mist.

"How did you get involved with someone like her?" said Soli.

Jean-Claude's hand tensed on the beer's cold frosted glass.

"What do you mean, Soli?"

"*L' Américaine*, the terrorist—your wife, Sidonie Leduc."

Stupid. He must have fallen asleep with the damn file open.

"It's none of your business."

"You're wrong there. She's linked to the Palestinians and Arafat." Soli sipped his wine. "We've had intel she trained in a Hezbollah cell in Syria. Of course she's got contacts in Hezbollah."

Jean-Claude stiffened. Was it true?

"Why didn't you ever tell me, Soli?"

"Tell you that I knew your wife's wanted?" said Soli.

Merde. Did everyone know?

"I mean tell me you're Mossad, Soli," said Jean-Claude.

Soli grinned. "You never asked."

"So she's on your hit list?"

"You know I can't talk about that."

"Stick to old Nazis, Soli. Argentina, the south of France— plenty to choose from." Jean-Claude rubbed his eyes. His mind was racing, turning Soli's words about Sidonie training in a Hezbollah camp over and over. What else did the Mossad know or suspect?

"So how did you become involved with her, Jean-Claude?"

Jean-Claude downed his beer. Set it down, leaving a ring on the dining table cloth. "A personal matter, *c'est tout.*"

Why had he said that? He was off his game.

"Jean-Claude, I know you're going after her records. Not a bad idea since lots of people are interested in Sidonie Leduc, aka Sydney Hartman."

Jean-Claude's heart thumped.

"We've got all night, Jean-Claude." Soli sipped his wine. "These things work in mysterious ways, as you're aware. I might know someone who might know someone who might have access to information, that kind of thing."

A bargaining tone in his voice. That unreadable gaze behind those thick-framed lenses.

"What do you want, Soli?"

"Maybe I can help you and you me. Tell me the story. Convince me she's small-fry, if you can."

Jean-Claude's fingertips traced the rim of the empty glass. "She's the mother of my daughter, Soli."

"*Oui*, but it's her Hezbollah contacts that interest me. A certain Abbas Musawi, a raid in the Bekaa Valley. Find him and we do business."

As if Jean-Claude could promise that?

"Deal," he lied.

"Call me a student of human nature," Soli said. "Fascinated to know how people connect. Tell me how you met, Jean-Claude."

He groaned inside. Hated to talk about the past.

Usually the hypnotic lull of the train, the rocking motion, the muffled whistle at the stations, put him to sleep. But tonight, across from Soli, he let it take him back to that first time he and Sidonie had met.

"It was the sixties. De Gaulle was back in power—the Fifth Republic—and I was policing a protest on the Left Bank."

Soli nodded. "Those days I remember. You were one of the Hirondelles, eh, wearing that cape?"

Jean-Claude nodded. "Capes weighted with lead. De Gaulle wanted them to lie flat from our shoulders."

Soli stretched. "I heard getting hit by a cape could knock a protester out."

"Not mine." Jean-Claude shrugged.

It all flowed back—that hot June day, protesters' tempers flaring on Boulevard Saint-Germain, him sweating in his wool uniform, the hissing crowd. He'd been assigned to march several protesters into the *panier à salad*, the salad spinner, as they called the paddy wagon.

He could never forget the long-haired young woman in black. She had been stunning, with bigger eyes than Juliette Gréco, if that was possible. But such a horrific French accent. A foreigner, *une Américaine*?

"She pushed a battered paperback in my face," Jean-Claude told Soli. "Kerouac's *On the Road*."

"*C'est quoi ça, On the Road?*" Soli asked, leaning forward. "A socialist manifesto?"

Jean-Claude shrugged. "Like some beatnik bible. She said, 'Read this, it's good for your soul. Then you'll understand our politics.'"

Their politics? He'd felt like a fool, yet he hadn't been able to move his eyes away from her. "I don't care much for politics."

The others laughed and hooted at him.

"But you should," she said.

Earnest, this one. Exquisite.

"I just do my job. Keep order, keep my quartier safe."

"You all have agendas, filthy *flics*," shouted the sweating, shirtless *mec* next to her. "You do the government's dirty work, repress free thinking!"

"*Alors*, why am I standing here letting you spout off and defending your right to do so?"

She grinned. Those intense eyes pulled him to her like a magnet. How could anyone have bigger eyes than Juliette Gréco?

Shouts echoed off the boulevard, the whine of a siren. A piercing whistle signaled him to round them up and move toward the truck.

"Why did you become a policeman?" she asked him.

"I fell into it, followed my old man."

"Where's your passion?" She tilted her head. "Don't you want to change things—stop injustice, protect people's freedom?"

"Blanket statements you people make." He shook his head. "What about those who have no time for lofty ideals, politics? Who struggle every day, eh? We're their only way to get justice, their line of defense. That's why I stay. If there's crime, I solve it. Like the shoemaker on that corner, who got robbed last week. I get redress, or try to prevent—"

"See, you do have passion," she interrupted.

Passion? He'd never looked at it that way. The girl fascinated him.

"So you're an artist?" he said, noting the sketchbook poking out of her bag. "That's not political."

"Art is political. Everything's political."

"And making love's political?"

She laughed. A clear, silver-toned laugh. "Only a Parisian *flic* would say that."

The chief's whistle blew again. "Get out of here," he said. "Take your book with you or I'll throw you in the wagon."

"Hey, that's not fair," someone shouted.

"Only if you meet me later." She pointed to the Café de Flore. "Tonight. I'll change your mind. Change your life."

She smiled with her eyes. And he was lost.

The clacking train wheels brought him back to the dark countryside flying by, and to Soli's long, myopic look. Soli nodded and handed him a card. "Don't forget our arrangement. Sunday I'll expect a call. My Berlin contact's very good."

Jean-Claude took it. "*Merci*. Mine's very good, too."

IF HE WASN'T careful, he'd drift more, relive that day yet again—that day, and the incredible week that followed, that turned into a lifelong obsession and a child they'd made together.

Non, don't get pulled down that hole again. Maintain self-control, responsibility for Aimée. Try to let her not get hurt. Again.

If he found Sidonie this time, Aimée would never know.

"SUZY?" THE TANK of a doorman had tattoos up his arm and plenty of attitude. "You're too early, *mon enfant*. Club doesn't get going until after midnight."

Mon enfant!

"Like I don't know that?" she said, putting her hands on her hips. "She lives in my building. Sap that I am, I told her roommate I'd drop off something she forgot at home . . ."

He waved her off, bored. "She's eating dinner with the rest."

"But where?"

"Leave it with me."

"It's personal," Aimée said. "You know, a necessary female item."

The bouncer shrugged. Stared at her, then pointed across the street. "Are you blind?"

She felt like an idiot—what was she missing?

"Don't you see her over there?"

A group of women were passing by on the opposite sidewalk.

Which one?

"Suzy?" she shouted, hoping one would react.

A head turned. Aimée waved and was rewarded with a blank stare from a woman with short black hair. She turned away and kept going.

Great.

"She's your friend?" the bouncer said.

"I've changed my hair. New color."

And with that Aimée ran across rue de Ponthieu, dodging a taxi who honked at her. She caught up with the group of women mid-block.

"Suzy, your roommate's sick . . ."

Suzy turned. "Romy looked fine an hour ago."

Think fast. Come up with something. "There's been an accident."

"*Quoi?*"

Why couldn't Suzy cooperate and stand still?

"Not on the street." Aimée gestured to the *café tabac* ahead.

"What's happened?" she said suspiciously. "Look, I don't have much time . . ."

"Two minutes."

In the café, Suzy stood at the counter and nodded to the waiter. "Joel, *un express.*"

"*Moi, aussi.*" Aimée said, realizing Suzy was a regular. Impatient, Suzy drummed her tomato-red lacquered nails on the zinc counter, then set down a pack of Gitanes. She wore leopard-print leggings, an oversized black sweater that slipped off her shoulder, revealing her bra strap, and minimal makeup. Give her a wig, go back several years, and she'd win a *Flashdance* look-alike contest. As kids, Aimée and Martine had snuck into the matinee three times to see it. She loved that movie.

"An accident, you said, involving Romy?"

"Romy's doing a facial, she's fine." Aimée slid fifty francs over the moisture-ringed counter under the cigarettes. She hoped that was enough. "I need information. I'll keep your answers quiet. At Le Gogo you gave an elder gentleman in his late sixties your number. Remember him?"

"You're joking, right?" Suzy's brown eyes narrowed. But she slipped the fifty in her bag. Aimée guessed she was in her thirties. Her makeup kit poked out of her bag. She definitely could use mascara for those thin lashes.

Their espressos arrived. Joel lingered, wiping the table, until Aimée handed him ten francs. "That's fine, Joel."

She turned to Suzy. "How long were you seeing Bruno?"

Suzy grinned. Unwrapped the sugar cube. "You're a kid, probably at the Sorbonne. What, nineteen or twenty?"

Damn, she wished she'd changed from her Sorbonne attire of boots, denim skirt, and black turtleneck. As if that would have helped. "Does that matter?"

"Too young for an undercover *flic*. I know all of them anyway."

"I can help you in a way they can't." Aimée set her bag on the zinc counter.

"How's that?" Suzy said, interested now.

Aimée pulled out her wallet; from behind her *carte d'étudiant*, took out the faux PI license she'd had made. She'd only used it on one occasion before. She also slid the camera behind her bag by the sugar bowl. "I freelance."

Sort of true. Now she'd go with the scenario her father used. "First we establish what you know about Bruno. The last time you saw him."

"*Désolée.*" Suzy dunked the sugar cubes, stirred. Looked out the window.

Aimée used that moment, with the camera behind her bag shielded by her hand, to snap a photo of Suzy. She cleared her throat to cover the click.

"I don't see how we can help each other. I'm an escort, not a hooker."

"Do I care? More to the point, do I look like vice, Suzy?"

"*Chérie*, I think you're late for class." Suzy laughed and gathered her bag. She stopped to make eyes at the little furry head poking out of the Dior bag of the woman next to her. "*C'est adorable.* What's its name?"

The woman told her.

"*J'adore* bichon frises."

Aimée had to get Suzy's attention back. So far she'd squandered a chunk of her budget and she had nothing.

"Suzy, please, think back about a month ago, a client at Le Gogo. Bruno, an older man, late sixties."

"A silver fox? Not too many when I worked at Le Gogo."

Aimée opened the matchbook, showing Suzy her name and number. "Didn't you give this to Bruno?"

Suzy glanced at it. Shrugged.

Aimée took out Elise's photo of Bruno Peltier: white-haired, wrinkles around smiling eyes, wide like his daughter's. He was trim in a jogging suit, on the short side. She slid it under Suzy's demitasse saucer.

Recognition showed in the escort's eyes. She gave Aimée a calculating look. "*Et alors*, how can you help me?"

Before Aimée could answer, the club bouncer stepped into the café and took Suzy's arm. "You're due at the club, Suzy."

The next moment, Suzy had gone. But Aimée had seen a flash of fear in her eyes. Suzy had been about to tell her something. *Merde.*

"Didn't even touch her espresso," said Joel.

"I'll drink it." Like Aimée needed another espresso. "He always like that? Rude, so protective of her?"

The café light reflected on Joel's rimless glasses. Aimée wished she could see his eyes. Always a good barometer, her father said.

"Depends."

"Why would our talking bother him?"

"The club keeps a tight rein on the girls," said Joel. "Maybe he thought you were recruiting her for another club."

"*Moi?*" She shook her head. Came up with a story. "My boss thinks Suzy witnessed an old man being assaulted, that's all. I wish I could have asked her a few more questions."

Joel lowered his voice and leaned forward. "Suzy works an after-after club, too."

Aimée nodded. These after-afters ran from 2 until 5 A.M. for the die-hards. Sounded like she might be pulling an all-nighter. Maybe she did need this espresso after all.

"Ever seen him around?" She showed Joel the photo Elise Peltier had left of her father.

"That's the man who was assaulted?"

"You could say that."

Joel shrugged. "Not a local in here. But the older guys like Régine's."

AIMÉE WALKED PAST the back of the Claridge, the elegant hotel, then by a *boîte de nuit*—no name—with quilted gold leather doors for an entrance, and reached the Pharmacie Optique du Docteur Athias, its name bright in green letters. Another architectural victim of the seventies, looking out of place among the glittering neon club marquees behind the Champs-Élysées.

It would still be a while before the night action got going. There was no point in surveilling Suzy now—that wouldn't bear fruit until later. What could she do for the next few hours? What would her father do?

He'd start at Régine's and work his way down the street. But how would she get these bouncers to talk to "a kid" like her?

She had an idea. She'd treat it like an experiment in the lab: she'd try out a hypothesis, then categorize what worked and didn't in two mental columns—one for positive trial outcomes, one for negative ones.

She sidled up to the bouncer who stood, arms crossed, in front of the black façade under the silver letters spelling out RÉGINE'S. The half-open door revealed a slice of the glitz factor inside.

"Have you seen my grandfather?" she asked innocently. "We live around the corner, but he wanders sometimes, forgets where he is. He hasn't come home, we're worried."

She showed him the photo. As he studied it, she considered how natural it felt to lie to someone to get information out of them.

"*Désolé.*" He shook his head.

She got the same response with varying degrees of sympathy from all the club bouncers. So far, her hypothesis was not testing well; several points in the minus column.

The last bouncer, whose hair glistened with gel, shook his head. "I'm substituting. Raoul, the regular, is sick. Check with the bartender."

In the deserted club, purple strobes flashed, "Love Shack" by the B-52s blared on the speakers. That song was everywhere. The smell of clove cigarettes tickled her nose.

"You're early, *ma chère*," said the bartender, an untied bow tie hanging down his pristine white shirt as he polished glasses.

"Sorry to bother you, but it's my *grand-père*. We live on

rue Washington but he wanders, you know, forgets where he is. Seen him?"

He didn't even look up. "A missing person, eh? Talk to the *flics*."

"That's my next step." She sighed. "He used to come to the clubs in the forties and sometimes he thinks he's still a young man."

"Don't they all?" said a middle-aged woman with bright red hair. She heaved an armload of account books on the black bar counter. "Accounts done," she said to the bartender, and then, turning to Aimée, "An old, lost gentleman? Let me have a look."

Aimée concealed her excitement. Showed her the photo.

The woman pulled her glasses down from her head.

"His name is Bruno Peltier. Look familiar?"

"Been a while. But he came in several times."

Ooh, the woman remembered him. Had Aimée hit pay dirt already? "Alone?"

She shook her head. "Can't remember. You sure he's as forgetful as you think?"

Aimée tried for a perplexed look. Then shock.

"*Mon Dieu*, did *Grand-père* run off with a girl?"

The redhead shot the bartender a quizzical look. From the corner of her eye Aimée saw him shake his head slightly.

"Not one of ours," the redheaded bookkeeper said. "Again, haven't seen him for a while. *Bonne chance*."

Glad to get out of the blaring music and clove smell, Aimée stepped into the cold street. Looks like Bruno had liked the nightlife. But she'd tracked down a Bruno sighting. Score one in the plus column.

She huddled in a doorway. With the windchill factor, she needed a down coat. What could she do now? She couldn't go home to change, didn't relish waiting hours in a café for Suzy.

Several shopping arcades from the Champs-Élysées connected to rue de Ponthieu. The Club Alibaba cornered one of them. She waited until the bouncer got involved in a conversation.

Could she slip by him?

Just then Suzy and two other women sashayed past him and into the Alibaba's door under the club marquee. She took a quick photo, but the bouncer looked up and saw her. Wagged his finger at her as if she'd been a bad girl.

Let him think he owned the street. He didn't own the arcade. At least she'd seen Suzy go inside.

As a truck passed, she ducked into the arcade—a dimly lit seventies steel-and-chrome affair with a bunch of shuttered boutiques and a small bar. Deserted on a cold autumn night. She saw what she took for the Alibaba's back delivery door. Tried the handle. Locked.

Sheltered from the wind, she kept an eye on Alibaba's back door. A waiter wearing a long white apron and black vest came out of the small bar and lit a cigarette. He exhaled, blowing smoke rings. She was about to cadge a cigarette when he glanced at his watch, pulled out a key chain, unlocked the Alibaba's back door and went inside. The staff must work in both establishments.

She ran and caught the door, pinching her fingertips in the gap before it shut. Somehow she wedged the door open and slid inside. Damn, she'd have a blood blister.

She needed to act quickly. A wall of thudding sound reverberated in the dim corridor; she felt the pounding of Duran Duran in the soles of her boots.

She found Suzy applying eye makeup in a communal

dressing area partitioned by curtains. A stale odor came from an empty box of chocolates.

"*Alors*, how did you get in here?" Suzy expelled air in annoyance. "Shouldn't you be in bed?"

Instead of rising to Suzy's bait, Aimée shrugged. She had to get something out of this woman.

"Wouldn't you like to make extra for just sitting on your *derrière*, Suzy?" She leaned toward the makeup-smudged mirror. "Me, I only get paid if I deliver. I'm in school and this is how I make my rent, *compris?* I live in a place smaller than yours and Romy's."

A slight exaggeration. Several of Suzy's *chambres de bonnes* could fit into Aimée's seventeenth-century townhouse apartment on the Ile Saint-Louis. Minor details.

"Does this jog your memory?" Aimée dropped a hundred francs and the matchbook into the chocolate box. If she didn't pace herself, she'd run out.

Suzy lit a cigarette. "Men on the verge of cardiac arrest aren't my type."

"Fine." Aimée reached to take back the note. The carrot-and-stick approach her father used. Too bad she didn't have a stick.

Suzy's hand stopped her. Offered her a cigarette. Aimée took one. And accepted a light.

Thupt went the flare of the match. The tobacco jolt hit her, as good a rush as the espresso.

"I only worked at Le Gogo maybe for a week and a half in October."

The date clicked into place. Bruno Peltier had died on October 9.

Aimée pulled out the photo again. Always make sure, her father said.

"And you know him, you're sure?"

Suzy nodded. "Saw him twice."

"Go on. What was he like?"

Suzy glanced around. Stabbed out her cigarette, stood and closed the door.

"Never flashed his money but appreciated good things," said Suzy.

"A typical old money type?"

Suzy thought, then shrugged. "Depends what you call typical."

"Loaded and *discrète*?"

"That's funny you say that. He's a provincial, like me—not old money. I went to meet him and his friends once for a drink on Avenue Gabriel."

Ooh, this was working. Aimée nodded in what she hoped looked like encouragement. "Which place?"

Suzy thought. "That chic spot, off the Champs-Élysées."

"Which one, Suzy?" She heard her own eagerness, tried to soften her voice and sound more encouraging. "Can you remember?"

"You know, the old hunting lodge . . . Laurent, that's right, it's called Laurent."

That fit with Elise's statement. Score this in the plus column.

"I drank champagne, then split. Not my crowd."

Now a minus.

She shook her head. "I don't understand. Why would you leave, Suzy?"

Suzy balled up a chocolate wrapper. Twisted it between her thumb and forefinger. "He wanted eye candy, *tu comprends?* To show off. But I got another booking. Left. Glad not to face a dinner with a bunch of old farts."

"The night of October ninth?"

Suzy shrugged.

Could she have been with him the night Bruno was murdered? What were the odds that his friends had gathered two nights that same week at Laurent? But hadn't his friends told Elise's mother that Bruno hadn't shown up for dinner?

Aimée pulled out her school pocket calendar, found the date and pointed to it. "A Monday, October ninth. Remember?"

Suzy's brows knit in thought. "My mother had a gallbladder operation the next day, I remember. Let's see. The operation was on Tuesday."

"You're sure?"

"Yes. I had to get up early the next day to get to my mother's. There are no direct trains from Gare de Lyon to Cantal."

Cantal, a town in the Auvergne region. "My grandmother's from near there. Whereabouts?"

Suzy made a face. "Aurillac, the land of old geezers—that's all that's left down there."

Aimée thought through what Suzy had just told her. People lied sometimes, her father always said, and sometimes they lied for reasons unrelated to an investigation.

If Suzy accompanied Bruno to Laurent, yet his friends said he'd never showed up, someone was lying.

Aimée's pulse sped up. Her father had told Elise Peltier that random murders were sometimes the hardest to solve—but if the people who had last seen Bruno Peltier alive were lying, it didn't seem like such a random murder after all. Why had the police declined to follow up?

Was Suzy part of the setup? But why had she admitted going there—implicated herself—if she was?

Aimée wished her father were here.

Suzy took her brush and applied eyeliner.

"Last time I saw him, kid. Never heard from him again. I've helped you now."

Aimée reached in her bag. What bonus could she give? "Tell me about his friends."

"We were in the bar. Like I said, got another booking and left before they came."

"Did he talk to anyone?"

"Maybe. The bartender? Look, I've got to go."

Aimée took out another hundred-franc bill and her card and left it on the table. Hoped that looked legitimate enough. "That's got both my numbers and my pager, if you remember something else."

She added the small bottle, part of a sample packet, of Chanel No. 5 she'd acquired at Galeries Lafayette when she'd splurged on Chanel lipstick.

"Chanel. Nice touch, kid. You're more professional than most."

A rush of pride surged through Aimée. Wow, she had gotten real information from this woman.

Suzy stood up, giving Aimée the full-length view of her micro silver mini and matching boots. "Bruno's wife's checking up on him?"

"Not anymore." Aimée shook her head. "Why's the bouncer so protective of you?"

Suzy didn't meet her eyes. Aimée saw a slight tremble as Suzy slid the cigarettes into her bag. "Jealous, maybe?" Suzy shrugged.

Instinct kicked in. Suzy was lying.

"What are you afraid of, Suzy?"

But Suzy vanished in a clinking shimmer behind the orange gauze curtain.

AIMÉE STOOD IN the crowded Métro car, with an accordion player and a young boy jingling coins in a coffee tin for a handout.

She held onto the greasy pole as the Métro swayed. Thank God for the warmth, although she could have done without the germ-laden mugginess. The burning smell of brakes was followed by a whoosh of cold air as the doors slid open.

She emerged from Cité, one of the deepest stations carved under the Seine, to face the Préfecture de Police, then turned right toward the Palais de la Justice, which hid the indigo stained glass of adjoining Sainte-Chapelle. The pavement bustled with passersby in wool overcoats. Lamplight filtered through the bare plane trees with their peeling-bark trunks. She passed the green cast-iron Wallace fountain, water trickling over its four caryatids, and parted the heavy velvet draft curtains of *café-bistro* Le Soleil d'Or, frequented by the *flics* from the *préfecture*. A lively crowd ate, talked, smoked, and drank.

Off-duty *flics* never strayed far from the umbilical cord, she thought, recognizing a few faces who'd worked with her father. The ones who'd sat by and watched when he'd been fingered for someone else's corruption. At least that's what she'd overheard. She'd like to spit in their drinks. Instead she ignored them and caught the owner Louis's attention.

"Mademoiselle Aimée," said Louis, kissing her on both cheeks. She'd known him since she'd come here to do her homework at the back banquette. "Any tips for arthritis, *docteur?*"

"*Alors*, Louis," she smiled. "I'm only first-year premed."

And for how long?

"Date night with your *grand-père?* Claude's with . . ."

His mistress. She waved the words away.

"You know he doesn't want me going up there," she said. *Grand-père* now spent more and more time with his mistress, a relative of Louis's who lived in the old family quarters above. Aimée's papa refused to acknowledge the relationship that had been going on for years.

"*Mais non*, he's over there." Louis pointed.

Claude, lush white hair curling over the collar of his sweater-vest, sat at the back banquette. He beckoned her over, a smile on his long-jowled, mustached face, and patted the banquette seat beside him. *Grand-père*'s hug was big and overwhelming—just like Papa's. Like father, like son.

A plate of half-eaten *steak frites* sat before him. The wafting aroma of the morel sauce made her realize she hadn't eaten.

"Hungry, *ma puce?*"

"Only time for *un chocolat chaud*," she said.

He motioned to Louis. "Her usual."

She gestured to the small, dirty white dog next to him. "And who's the fluff ball?"

He shrugged. "A stray." The little thing shivered, and the next second it was worming into her lap.

"*Et alors*, you think you can do surveillance with me?"

Her *grand-père* paused, his fork midair. "Your father sent you?"

"*Pas du tout.*" The dog licked Aimée's wrist.

"So he's got you working again." Her *grand-père* cut a

morsel of meat, took it between his fingers and let the dog smell it. Gone in an instant. "He should do it himself."

"Papa's on the night train to Berlin."

"Into that mess?" He sat back, pulled a cigar from his vest pocket, tapped it on the white paper tablecloth. "*Alors*, I'm retired. Why didn't he call me himself instead of sending you?"

If she reminded him that he wouldn't speak to his son, she'd be putting herself in the middle. Why couldn't her grandfather and father settle whatever it was between them?

"*Mais non*, it's me asking the favor, not him." She dipped a *frite* in the mustard pot. Then another. Couldn't help herself. "What's with you two anyway?"

He shrugged, as he always did when he wanted to avoid a subject, and twisted the end of his mustache. "What's he got you doing now?"

"Surveillance, *comme toujours*," she said. It wasn't entirely a lie. "I need your overcoat. Please, *Grand-père*."

"Aren't you supposed to be studying, *ma puce*?" He rubbed her cheek.

"And I'm not? It's a few hours' work, *c'est tout*."

He squinted his left eye, like he did when he was secretly pleased.

"Good thing I'm bored," he said. "What surveillance?"

She grinned. "I thought you'd never ask."

Over a steaming cup of *chocolat chaud* dolloped with *crème*, she pulled out her notebook.

He took a glance. "Your lab notes? Want me to lose my appetite?"

"*Mais non*, it's this part." She turned the pages and pointed to her scribbled case notes. "The victim is Bruno Peltier, *Grand-père*. He's family."

"That's a stretch," he said, shaking his head.

Surprised, Aimée related Elise's tearful explanation. "She said a second cousin. So how are we related?"

"Ask your father."

"Funny, he said the same thing—to ask you."

"Wrong side of the sheets. That kind of relative, *comprends?*"

An illegitimate child? "But whose?"

"That's all you need to know. We don't talk about him." He raised his thick-fingered hand. "So what have you got there?"

Still curious, she had to let that go. For now. She showed him Peltier's photo and his daughter's statement. "Don't you remember the murder on the quai a month ago?"

"That was Bruno Peltier?" Her *grand-père's* bushy eyebrow rose.

She talked him through her notes, telling him everything she knew. "Cause of death, according to the *certificat de décès*, a shot to the back of the head."

"*Et alors, ma petite* detective, what does that tell you?"

"He rubbed gangland the wrong way. Got in over his head. Gambling?"

Her grandfather leaned over to pet the dog still on Aimée's lap, who gave a little sigh of contentment. "Think, Aimée. How would they get their money back?"

"So scratch gambling. Okay. Suzy's pimp? Or her husband?"

"Take it step by step, Aimée." Her grandfather gave a little sigh. "Be methodical, like you would for anatomy. Looks like the man got a bullet to the head. Execution style. Of course you noticed the bullet, but with my eyes, I can't read that . . . a nine millimeter or twelve?"

"Not from a pistol," she said, knowing that much. "But a rifle?"

He made a face. "You should know better. I've got one myself."

Louis put down a second *chocolat* before her.

"*Merci,*" she said, smiling at him. She licked the rim of her cup. "You mean that old submachine gun in your armoire— the one that jammed all the time in the war?"

"Sten gun. Such *merde* the *Anglais* dropped," he said.

Aimée became aware of a buzzing of nervous energy taking over the bistro. She looked up. Out the windows, which overlooked the Seine, she could see the blue-lit Zodiac police boat speed by below.

"Another floater!" she heard someone at a table nearby say as he grabbed his coat.

"That's why's my beeper's going when I'm almost off duty," his table mate said, his chair scraping back.

Her *grand-père* pointed to her notes. "So Suzy drank with Bruno at his last known location."

"That's why I need to confirm with the bartender. Have a chat." She downed the last of her velvety *chocolat chaud*. "May I borrow your bike?"

"It's freezing, Aimée." Her grandfather handed her his motorcycle keys. "My helmet and jacket are on the coat rack."

She ruffled the dog's fur and kissed her grandfather. Her last image was of him puffing on his cigar and feeding the puppy bits of steak.

SHE THREW HER bag in her grandfather's motorcycle sidecar, adjusted the helmet's strap, and pulled on his big shearling-lined leather motorcycle jacket. Huge; she swam in it. Goggles on for protection against the biting wind, she eased his BSA into first and maneuvered past the *préfecture* along the quai. She weaved in traffic, glad of the jacket and the power of this machine between her legs. She just hoped her knees wouldn't freeze solid.

Bruno's last known location, Laurent, a chic resto, set back in the park, commanded a partial view of the Champs-Élysées under the bare, low-hanging branches. A few diners sat in the oval dining room and warm smells came from the kitchen. Impressive, *très sophistiqué* and out of her budget.

Her cowboy boots conflicted with the dress code. If only she'd thought this through and stuck a pair of heels in her bag. Too late now.

"Bonsoir," she said to the man at the bar, the helmet under her arm. Tall, olive-complected, and dark-haired in a white shirt and black jacket, he could grace the Dior Homme runway show. He nodded and slid a cocktail napkin in front of her.

Not the bribable type. Or if so, not one she could afford. How could she play this?

"We're serving a Sancerre, if you're interested. Smooth and subtle."

He imparted a touch of seduction as he smiled a second too long. His tone was smooth and not so subtle.

She gave a little pout. Regretted not applying mascara. "I wish. *Mais non, merci,*" she said, pulling out the photo of Bruno. "Can you help? I know the *flics* probably questioned you about this victim . . ."

"You're what, a *flic* from a special unit? Kinda young, *non?*"

Quick, too.

"Close." She smiled, showing her doctored PI license. But not for too long. "I'm Aimée and you're . . ."

"Marc." He set a coaster in front of her and poured her a Pellegrino. "On the house."

His warm fingers lingered a moment on hers as she took the glass. Like Florent's fingers. Stop. Focus, she had to focus.

"*Merci*, Marc. The victim's daughter's devastated. She's hired us."

"Why?"

Her father always said to control the questioning, don't let it get away from you.

"It's hit her mother hard," said Aimée, hoping to elicit his sympathy. "That's all I can say. You'll appreciate my discretion, I'm sure. But even after a month there's no closure in the investigation. Nothing." She shrugged. Needed to establish a baseline. "Did the *flics* question you about Bruno's visit here?"

Concern showed in Marc's face.

"*Pas du tout.* But I left for Sardinia the next day. Had no idea until I came back from holiday. They spoke with my boss. Shall I get him?"

"So no one has questioned you?"

Marc shook his head. Picked up a wine glass to dry with a towel. A piano tinkled in the background.

"So you do remember October ninth, Marc, because you left for holiday the next day, *non?*"

He nodded. "I've thought about it a lot, to tell you the truth."

Good, a thinker. She readied her camera behind her helmet.

"So tell me about Bruno and his companion."

"Such a crazy evening. We had a ministry bunch, then the . . ."

He liked to talk. She had to suppress her glee—she was so pleased with herself for finding another informative witness. After he had related what seemed a typical evening, he described Bruno's arrival. "With a woman. A looker, like you." Marc grinned. His charm probably worked on most of the female population, but not on her, not tonight.

Her heart was racing because she had just learned Suzy hadn't lied—which meant Bruno's friends had lied to Madame Peltier, and to the police. She needed to focus on her witness now, see what other information she could get from him. "So that struck you as unusual, Marc?" she asked, remembering to use his name. Add the personal touch, her father always said.

His eyes lifted from her sweater. "Eh, she looked bored. Left. Every month, Monsieur Peltier and his friends dine together. I get the feeling . . ." He paused.

Eager, she leaned on the bar. "Go on."

"Provincials." He'd lowered his voice.

"Eh, meaning . . . ?"

"Maybe they live here, but can't rub off the village dirt." Marc hesitated. "That's not the best way to say it, but you understand, *non?* Nice enough gentlemen."

Suzy said the same thing—she'd called Bruno Peltier a provincial.

"When's the last time you saw them?"

"Why, recently."

"Are they here now?"

He shook his head.

That would have been too easy.

"Did you see Bruno actually join them that evening?

He shrugged. "I didn't notice."

"Did you see him leave?"

He shrugged again. "But I saw them leave last night."

"Last night?"

"Two took a taxi and one walked."

"And you remember this why, Marc?"

"Three sheets to the wind, I'd say. One of them forgot his scarf, cashmere, came back in the taxi and left me a generous tip." He smiled. "They tip well."

She still didn't know if Bruno had joined the friends for dinner, or if he'd left for some reason before they all met up. Suzy had been afraid of something—did she know more? These old friends—were they in on it, or were they in danger, too? Wouldn't they be nervous about dining here again so soon after Bruno's murder?

"Look," Marc said, "I've got clients to serve. That's all I know."

But she couldn't give up. Never leave without a name, a contact, her father said.

"One more thing, Marc. Remember anyone here in the bar that night who Bruno talked to?"

Another shrug. "Regulars, I'd say."

"Any chance you can give me their names?"

"Not if I want to keep my job. I only helped you since it's hard for his family. And Bruno is—was—*un gentilhomme*."

Marc moved away to the end of the Art Nouveau bar. Put that in the tried and failed column, she thought. She'd pushed him too hard and he'd shut up. Lesson learned.

She felt eyes watching the back of her head. When she turned around, all she saw was a waiter arranging pots of hothouse orchids in the foyer.

So the rest depended on corroborating Bruno's dinner companions' story. Who were they?

On the foyer's right, the maître d's podium stood

unattended. Never leave a place without noting as much detail as possible, her father said, even if you discount it later. She sidled up close to scan the open reservation book, flipped to the previous night's reservations—so many names listed. *Merde.* No way she could remember a page of names.

Impossible to rip the page out. What would her father do? She reached in her bag, palming her camera as she saw the maître d' approaching. *Merde* again. She lifted her bag as a shield, aimed shots at what she hoped was the right angle.

"May I help you, mademoiselle?" The maître d' was polite but cold. "A reservation perhaps?"

She had to think quick. "*Merci*, maybe you can help me." She gave a small smile. "I think friends of my relative, Monsieur Peltier, dined here last night."

"Peltier?" He gave a quick scan. "But there's no reservation in that name."

She felt he deliberately misunderstood.

"Monsieur Peltier's deceased, but he used to meet his friends here every month. If I could get in touch with them—"

"We're closing soon, mademoiselle," he interrupted. His eyes had narrowed. "If you'll excuse me."

He put the reservation book under his arm and gestured her to the door.

Pah, she'd been thrown out of starred places better than this. Once.

She mentally put Marc in the plus column, and in the minus went the maître d'.

Bon, she'd write up her notes, craft a report with billable hours. Get the film developed to back up her report. Then return to studying.

She'd enjoyed the thrill of acting detective for a few

1820-2020

hours—the break from her books. And she wasn't half bad at it. Now with Elise in her debt, hopefully, she'd call in a favor and get those photos of her mother.

Yet, standing out in the crisp night under the blanket of stars fading into the fog, she couldn't ignore a hunch. It was telling her to go take it one step further—to retrace Bruno's route to the quai. View the spot at night. If she could make anything out in the drifting mist.

Her Tintin watch, a sixteenth-birthday present, read 10:30 P.M. Glad of her wool gloves, she shifted into first. The headlights wobbled as she drove over the cobbles and the sidecar bumped along Avenue Gabriel. On one side, she passed a palatial mix of Haussmann buildings and older *hôtels particuliers*; on the other, the Théâtre Marigny—how often her *grand-père* had taken her to the puppet theater there on Saturdays, treated her to *barbe à papa*, the sticky, pink spun sugar on a cone, strolled through the stamp market.

By the time she reached the Seine, the charcoal mist curled under the bridges like an outstretched hand—like the Greek sea sirens beckoning the unwary to a watery grave.

Think like the murderer, her father would say. How would he lure his victim down here unless he knew him? Or had him in a car? There had to be a driving ramp to the quai. No law against driving here, she hoped, but she didn't have a license, so if she got caught . . .

A perfect moment for the bike to stall. *Merde.*

Better to come tomorrow when she could see, take a better look.

But voices and the thrum of an outboard motor drifted up through the mist. She made out a faint blue, quivering glow—the distinctive light of the Zodiac police boat.

Those overheard words from the Le Soleil d'Or came back to her . . . "another floater"? A siren wailed. Could something be happening right now?

Restarting the bike, she popped into first and drove it up on the curb. Her headlight beam lingered and died yellow on the pavers as she switched off the ignition. She pulled the motorcycle up against the wall. From below, voices mingled with the gush and splash of the Seine.

As she made her way warily down the stairs, the wind was almost strong enough to knock her off her feet. The mist, thick as lentil soup, dampened her cheekbones, her hair, her grandfather's jacket, blanketed her freezing knees.

She navigated down the cold stone railing to pick her way across the cobbled quai. Water churned in the wake of a barge that had already disappeared downriver. Shadows filled the crevices, making the quai otherworldly. Her knees trembled. What was it about this place?

Why had she come down here? Stupid. About to turn around and retrace her steps, she heard a voice shouting from the boat.

"Shine it there!"

Ahead on the quai a spotlight clicked on, penetrating a layer of mist to illuminate the damp cobbles. She jumped back toward the wall, into the shadows. Cold droplets of rain pattered on her wrist.

Then, in the boat's light, she saw it—a figure floating in the water behind a docked *bateau-mouche*'s propeller. What looked like a man tangled in the ropes anchoring the boat to the quai's edge.

Good God. In the exact location Bruno Peltier was found shot.

She shivered with fear. *Go.* She had to get the hell out of here. This had nothing to do with her.

The police, yelling directions at each other, used a pole to free the body. It bobbed and turned sideways. In that moment of white light, she saw a man with his hands bound behind him, one bare, bloated foot banging the quai's edge.

Unlike the cadavers in med school, this one looked fresh. How long had he been in the water? The hair at the back of his head was dark and matted with what looked like blood— a bullet hole like Peltier's?

She pushed the fear and revulsion aside. Compartmentalize, they told them in med school. View the body as a study tool, not as the human it once was. Not as a person who lived, breathed, laughed, cried, and loved. She grabbed the camera from her pocket, focused the zoom, and started clicking.

The wail of a siren echoed off the stone bank. The red glow of a police car barreled up the quai. Rain beat down on her hair, catching in her eyelashes.

"You! Over there!"

She ran like hell up the stairs.

Chambly-sur-Cher, Sologne region, Vichy France
November 1942

COLD NEEDLES OF rain stung Gaubert's face and his arms ached. It was midnight, and the rising river was barely visible in the darkness, but they couldn't rest. Mud sucked at his ankles; his right leg, which was shorter than his left, fought for traction. There were four of them from the village—Gaubert, Bruno, Philbert, and Alain—fighting their fatigue to pack sandbags along the old *moulin's* bank in the rainstorm. Here, the broad river was the demarcation line, a border dividing German-occupied France from their village, Chambly-sur-Cher, on the Vichy side—free France, *la zone libre*, or so they said.

Just a meter behind them, the narrow road topping the embankment was washed out. Their attempts to stave off the river and prevent the flooding of the village wheat fields looked futile. They depended on the winter wheat sown in the fall to feed them next year.

"Any moment, the water will reach the bridge," shouted Alain. "Faster!"

Trees, their roots loosened, slipped and washed away. They needed a lot more sandbags and stone than they had left in the milk cart. The pair of sopping-wet draft horses pawed their hooves in the mud and neighed.

Thunder boomed and lightning crackled. Or was it the British planes bombing Vierzon station again? They had been attacking rail lines the past week.

Through the slanting sheets of rain, Gaubert saw a yellow glow. It came closer, within yards of them on the embankment road. Now he could make out a wobbling pair of headlights. He heard shouts in German.

Merde. A damn troop truck. Why couldn't they stay out of *la zone libre* and keep to their side of the river?

The truck's wheels spun in the mud. Gears ground and whined above the distant thudding of the bombing.

"*Achtung. Hilfe . . . uns verloren . . . am zug.*" Gaubert couldn't make out the German. A Wehrmacht soldier was trotting toward them, shouting, his gun over his shoulder. "*Wo ist die Brücke?*"

Bruno, Philbert, and Alain kept piling the sandbags, ignoring the soldier. "You speak Fritz, *non?*" Alain, dripping wet, said. "What's he saying?"

Not that the time Gaubert had spent wounded in a German POW camp after the Battle of the Somme made him fluent in German.

"They're lost. Something about the bridge," he said. "The railroad track's damaged by the bombing and . . ."

The roar of spitting mud, more grinding gears and barks in German came from the truck. Three soldiers jumped out in the pelting rain, pointing their rifles. They were gesturing toward the horses tethered to the farmer's cart. They wanted help pulling the truck out of the mud.

Gaubert noticed how young the German soldiers were. Boys. Like they'd all been in 1916. Now it was happening again.

The soldiers had stepped closer, were shouting in the Chambly men's faces.

"They're ordering us to use the sandbags to get them tire traction out of the mud. Hitch the horse to pull."

"Shouldn't we inform our great leader Maréchal Pétain," snorted Bruno, "that some damn *Boches*—"

"Halt!" One of the soldiers pointed his rifle at Bruno. *Boches*, a slur coined in the last war, was still a dirty word. Forbidden.

"Tell them we're a little busy and to get back to their own side."

Gaubert's sodden coat weighed on his shoulders. The rain and wind lashed his face. "Shut up, Bruno. If we don't, they'll—"

"Shoot us when they need us to get the damn truck out of the mud?" Bruno squinted, his black hair streaming with rain.

Another soldier jumped out of the truck, shielding his eyes from the rain. He slipped and fell back against the dark green siding. Wind gusted, lifting the truck's soaked canvas side panel aside, exposing the rear. No soldiers inside. It looked empty.

A yellow-white explosion burst in the direction of Vierzon. One of the horses, an old mare, her mane glistening with rain, neighed loudly in fright. Three of the soldiers had pulled out binoculars to look, the other two backed toward the truck, cocking their rifles.

Right then Gaubert knew they were going to die.

"Look, there're only five of them," said Alain, straightening up, something in his hand. "One for each of us. And a bonus one. Come on, we can take them." His eyes were narrow in the rain. "They're guarding something in the truck. Valuable. I smell it."

Crazy, that Alain. "*Et alors*, how can we attack armed soldiers? With sandbags?"

"Make no mistake, they're going to shoot us, Gaubert."

And what they feared would happen happened: a roll of river water overflowed the sandbags, gushing everywhere, splashing their legs, the truck's tires, like a tidal wave crashing into the fields. The soldiers grabbed onto the truck's side rope ties for balance.

"Now!" shouted Alain, barreling into a surprised soldier's torso, knocking him down. He raised a knife and slit the soldier's throat.

"Halt!" In the chaos of rushing water, only one soldier was still standing without hanging onto the truck for support. He was aiming his gun at Alain.

"Now, I said!" shouted Alain.

Maybe it was the relentless rain, his failure to stop the flash flood from ruining their farmland, the hopelessness of impending starvation—or maybe it was his aching leg, and the certainty he'd die in this muddy field after cheating the Somme. But Gaubert didn't care anymore.

He grabbed at the nearest soldier's rifle, knocking it away and fighting him down in the mud, slipping and sliding, rolling in the sludge. The others had also lunged into the fray. Gaubert heard a scream, then another as Alain twisted his knife into another soldier's ribs.

Gaubert struggled with his soldier, who was slippery as a river eel. He sputtered, gulping muck. His fist flailed and slapped mud. The German struggled until Gaubert's hands caught the epaulets of the jacket. Now if he could just grab the bastard's neck.

That's what it had come down to last time. Us or them, him or me—no different from 1916 except this was the next generation. A generation born after they'd fought in the war to end all wars. God, did it never end?

Gasping, spitting leaves from his mouth, he groped at the

man's neck, found the clammy skin, felt the ropy, pulsing muscles. He had forgotten how rudimentary it was, once he'd gotten two hands around the man's throat, to choke and strangle someone. The German's kicking and splashing dwindled until Gaubert had crushed his windpipe.

In the headlights' glow, Gaubert got a better look at his victim. The chubby-faced soldier looked eighteen.

"Quick, catch them!" shouted Bruno.

Gaubert looked up. One of the bodies was about to float away; the other's arms flailed and splashed in the light. On the pinky finger of his clenched fist was a gold signet ring. Still alive. And then he floated away. Two of the other bodies had lodged against the tires. Gaubert looked back down at the German he'd killed, at his dead blue eyes open to the rain.

What had they done?

Gaubert struggled to his feet, blinking, wiping the rain from his eyes and scanning what he could see of the horizon to see whether another truck followed. Crackling static issued from the truck's radio, interrupted by the occasional German word—eerie in the rainy night.

"What do we do now?" Alain asked, panting. "This truck could be part of a convoy."

They had to move fast.

"Grab the rope holding the canvas and tie the bodies before they—"

"*Non*, throw them in the back," said Philbert. He was the thinker among them, a lanky wheat farmer. "We'll use the mill's timbers to leverage the truck. Shove it in the river. Sink it here, by the mill wheel—the deepest part."

What seemed feasible in theory—they only had to push the truck a short distance—took time. Time in the driving, relentless rain. The field around them had sunk into the overflowing river.

The men worked silently. Unspoken among them lay the knowledge they'd be shot if they were discovered. What choice did they have?

Gaubert prayed to God the fifth soldier who had been swept downstream drowned before anyone discovered him.

Gaubert, Alain, and Philbert wedged wood under the wheels, and Bruno started the engine. They made slow progress, laying plank by plank under the truck's wheels with Bruno in the driver's seat, shifting gears and gunning the accelerator. For every meter or so gained, the truck slipped back half a meter, sometimes even more, on the submerged sandbags.

Soaked, shaking, and frozen to the bone, Gaubert collapsed on his bad leg as he carried the last plank.

"You want to die here, fine. Not me." Alain's chest heaved as the truck hovered by the bank's edge. Silt eddies swirled below. "Get up, Gaubert. Think of what will happen if we don't submerge this."

Gaubert couldn't think of anything else.

"For an empty truck it's damn heavy," Gaubert gasped. Panicked by what they'd done, they hadn't thought to look inside the wooden boxes in the back of the truck, or check the contents. "What if there're arms or mortars in there? We should give them to the Maquis."

"You want to check, be my guest," said Alain. He talked big, but Gaubert had no desire to go scrounge in the back of the truck where they'd piled the four German bodies.

"He's right," said Bruno, the chicken farmer, his wet sweater plastered to his stocky frame. "They must have been guarding something they couldn't leave behind. Come on, Alain, you started this. Your big idea."

Philbert had climbed in the back. "Give me that crowbar, Alain. Hurry up."

Gaubert shook with cold; the damp and wet seeped into his bones. His bad leg had gone numb. At forty-five, he was the oldest among them. This bunch of hayseeds who'd never seen the trenches thought they knew everything.

Thinking of his wife and small son, Gaubert was filled with mounting dread over what they'd done—this spontaneous stupidity. At the possible German reprisals.

They'd be found out. Shot.

"*Mon Dieu.*" Philbert shone a soldier's flashlight. "You won't believe it."

"Believe what?"

"Get the cart, Alain. Back it up to the truck's edge."

Lights bobbed on the opposite bank of the Occupied German side. The bridge's metal struts glistened in the light, beaded with rain. Rain and more rain. But the French sentry box was dark. Deserted.

"Forget it. There's activity across the river by the bridge . . ."

Gaubert's words died as he looked inside. Philbert's beam illuminated a small wood crate with leather handles, marked with a swastika. Inside were gold bars stamped with serial numbers and the word *Reichsbank*.

"Looks like fifteen or so crates like this," Philbert said. "Lend me a hand."

Scraping, then a loud thunk as Philbert heaved one of the small crates into the cart. Then another.

"Back the cart closer, Alain. They're damn heavy."

Gaubert climbed down and helped Alain grab the reins to back the horses up. Then he climbed into the cart bed and the four men worked in pairs, hefting and stacking the heavy little crates by the leather handles. Ignoring the bodies. When they were done, they jumped out, splashing in the swirling mud.

"Now," said Alain, "the truck goes down the bank into the river."

Gaubert ground his teeth. Remembered. "We've got to strip the bodies."

"Too late, we don't have time—"

"At least take off the uniform insignia."

"He's right," Bruno said, climbing back into the truck. He took over the unpleasant work of stripping away the murdered Germans' identification.

Finally, on the count of three, all four of them shoved the truck, grunting and cursing in the sheeting rain. Gaubert's leg, frozen and numb, caught in the sucking mud. At last the truck slid down and sank with a trail of bubbles below the surface.

"WE SHOULD HAVE dumped the gold in the river," Gaubert said, peeling off his sopping jacket, his shirt. Alain had driven the team and cart to Gaubert's barn, where the four men now stood. The silver light of incipient dawn peeped in through the barn's single, high window. "You're crazy, we can't keep this here."

"Just for now, Gaubert," said Alain. He seized a shovel and cleared a space by the hay rack, where he began to dig. There was gold lust in his narrow eyes.

The rain had erased the cart tracks, at least. Yet it would only be a matter of time until the truck was discovered missing. Until the fifth German washed up somewhere.

"What if that truck across the river was searching for them?" said Gaubert. "Or they saw us?"

He imagined his wife, Fanny, a widow, and five-year-old Gaby fatherless, hungry . . .

"*Alors*, we wouldn't be here in that case," said Philbert, who'd stripped off his overalls, grabbed a shovel, and was pitching in. "Who's to tell them, eh? We keep this between us. *D'accord?* A pact of silence."

"What if—?"

"If anyone outside our village knows, there will be reprisals, *comprends?* We can't share this. We've risked our lives."

"More like committed spontaneous idiocy," said Gaubert. "We can't eat gold bars."

"Not now. Not for a while. But wait till this hell of a war ends," Philbert said. "For now we contact your old comrade, the jeweler in Saint-Felice."

Baret, a man he'd fought with at Ypres. Baret had been gassed and lost his arm. "He's not much of a jeweler these days, in case you hadn't noticed. He works on his brother's farm."

"Why don't we have Minou melt part down into smaller bits we can use?" said Bruno.

The village blacksmith, who had the intelligence of a ten-year-old.

"And let Minou in on it?" said Alain.

Gaubert heard the greed in their voices. And only a few hours earlier, they had killed with their bare hands. "We don't do anything now," he said. "We wait, see if there's any reaction."

As if he hadn't heard Gaubert, Alain said, "Why should we offer Minou a cut when he didn't even—"

"Worry about that later," Philbert broke in. "Remember, flogging gold bars will lead right back to us."

"They'd never search the church," said Gaubert. "Let's move them there. I don't like it here on my land."

"Damn it, it's just for now," Alain said. "We can't move them again until it's dark."

Reluctant, he agreed. In the dim November dawn, they could do little without attracting attention.

"I wonder why the truck wasn't part of a convoy," Bruno said. "Seems strange."

Philbert scowled. "Not even the *Boches* are stupid enough to move gold in one truck without protection."

A German troop truck carrying fifteen crates full of gold bars vanished in a rainstorm. How could it be that no one knew or cared? Those broken German words Gaubert remembered hearing—*lost, train, bridge*—ran through his head.

Chilled to the bone, exhausted by having worked through the night, he stumbled into the kitchen. His Fanny looked up from the stove, rubbing her eyes. She wore her nightdress and Gaubert's thick wool socks. She smelled of sleep. Wisps of hair fell from her bun as he buried himself in her neck, her skin so warm he wanted to curl up beside her.

"You're as cold as ice," she said. She rubbed his frozen arms. "You're shaking."

He let Fanny sit him down by their large, open farmhouse fireplace. She wrapped a warmed brick in a blanket to thaw his numb leg. He was tired, so tired, and fear banged in his heart.

"We've got to talk, *ma chère*," he said.

"Papa, Papa." There was a tugging on his arm. "You're supposed to take me to school." His little son's big blue eyes stared into his. They were the same blue as those of the young soldier he'd strangled.

"Shh, Papa's tired," Fanny said.

"He's always tired." Gaby pouted. "Like a big bear."

Fanny grinned. "So mama bear will walk her little bear to school. We'll sniff for honey and berries."

Gaby's eyes gleamed. He loved to pretend.

Gaubert was asleep before they had left the room. He dreamed of river eels writhing around a gold treasure chest that turned into the soldier's blue eyes open to the rain.

"WAKE UP." FANNY was shaking him. "The Germans are shooting people in Givaray."

She handed him a bowl of steaming chicory, the ersatz substitute for coffee. How long had he been asleep? The weak afternoon light faded in the kitchen's corners.

"Why . . . ? I don't understand."

Her hands clasped his shoulder. Fear, he saw fear and sadness in her eyes. "The cheese maker, the priest's parents—they're rounding up anyone. They said they'll execute sixty more if no one confesses."

"Confessed to what?"

"Four *Boches* bodies. Soldiers. They found them in the water."

She told him how less than a kilometer away, across the river, four bloated bodies had washed up on the Givaray village bank.

Acid bile rose in his stomach. Why the hell hadn't they taken the extra step and stripped off the uniforms?

So the damn current had freed the bodies from the canvas. Would the Germans dredge the river and discover the truck? Would they realize the gold was missing? Outside the window there were gunshots in the pewter twilight. For a split second he was back in the trenches, the horror as fresh as it had been in 1916.

He tried to clear his head. People—innocent village

people—were dying because of their impulsive tussle last night. They'd been so distracted by the gold that they hadn't taken the care they should have in hiding the bodies. What would happen when the fifth body washed up? It could turn up here, on the Chambly-sur-Cher bank.

Gaubert leapt up and pulled their suitcase from under the armoire. "Take Gaby and go stay with your aunt."

Fanny's eyes, a pale topaz color, widened in fear. "Why, Gaubert? Is there something you're not telling me?"

He shared everything with her, always had. But he couldn't share this.

"Saddle up the draft mare. Forget the roads—they're impassable," he said, throwing an armful of sweaters into the case. "Use the south fields."

"I'm not leaving you, Gaubert. Who will feed the cows?" Stubborn as always and he loved her for it. But not now.

"Fanny, our village could be next." He took her warm hands. Squeezed. "It's not safe here."

"What do you mean, next?"

If he told her anything, he'd put both Fanny and Gaby in danger.

"There's no time to argue. Take what you can and I'll bring the rest."

Fanny stared. He felt her gaze plumbing his soul. She knew him so well.

He shivered. "For Gaby's sake and yours, don't ask me any more. Please."

"You had something to do with those dead German soldiers, n'est-ce pas?"

"I'm telegraphing your aunt from the post office, right now, that you're coming."

Loud knocking came from the farmhouse's front door.

He peeked through the lace kitchen curtains and saw Rouxel from the local *Parti Populaire Français*, the fascist political party. A rumored collaborator.

Terror-stricken, Gaubert looked around. Threw the suitcase back in the armoire. "You have to leave now." He thrust her coat into her arms. "Through the barn. Quick."

"But Gaubert . . ." Tears glistened in her eyes.

"Where's the woman I married, who promised to love and obey?"

He pushed her toward the back door. She clung to him. "And didn't you promise to have and hold me forever?" She wouldn't go.

Trembling with panic, he raised his hand at her—the first time he ever had.

"Hit me a thousand times, I'll still love you."

He turned away. His heart was bleeding. "If you love me, you'll take our son, keep him safe."

Gaubert waited until Fanny was gone before he answered the door.

Dresden · November 10, 1989 · Friday Evening

HEINZ FELSEN WAS irritated to see the teaching assistant waving to him from the back of Dresden University's full lecture hall. What now? Unless his granddaughter had gone into labor early, they knew not to disturb him during his evening lecture.

"*Entschuldigung,* Herr Felsen," the TA said, handing him an envelope. "This came priority for you. It's marked urgent."

Felsen took his glasses from the lectern and tore the strip on the yellow-and-red DHL envelope. Inside he found a slip of paper. On it: GO TO A SECURE PHONE. DIAL-IN PROCEDURE ACTIVATED.

Wasn't that all over now? He'd once been a low-level Stasi, a communist double agent, but he had been out of the field for years, done his time in a West German prison until he'd been traded. Now he just taught espionage techniques. Questions flitted through his mind. But habit and instinct died hard.

"Take over, finish up the class for me," he said to the TA, handing over his notes. "Make sure you hand out next week's assignment, *verstehen Sie?*"

Outside the lecture hall, he waved to his teaching colleagues, pointed to his watch and shook his head. No time for their usual evening beer after classes. Out in the *Universität*'s parking lot, he got in his Russian-made Trabant, drove it out onto the potholed road and past the Stalin-era concrete housing projects. Put Robert

Schumann's Sonata in D minor in the tape deck and tried not to overthink this.

He'd taken care of his files long ago. The old boys' network turned up loose cannons sometimes, an erstwhile informer needing money and thinking the world hadn't changed.

The Wall had fallen, for God's sake, and after the semester ended he'd be lucky to have a job. Who knew what this new era would bring.

Twenty kilometers away, he pulled into the *Gasthaus*. The phone cabin—a working one, so rare these days—was shielded from view from the road by the car-wash exit.

He dialed the number he remembered by heart. A number he hadn't called in ten or more years. Not since he'd been sent back to the East in a prisoner exchange.

"Take this number down," said a voice. The required three-second pause. "Ready?"

He was. Pencil and Nestlé chocolate wrapper in hand. Prepared as always, according to Stasi procedure.

He wrote the message down. Hung up. Read it slowly. Then again.

He felt tempted to call back for reconfirmation. Instead he called the number he'd written down with a Munich area code and used his alias.

"It's Willi," he said. "How are the reunion plans going?"

A woman answered. Standard procedure. Only his former handler from the old days would track him down like this to relay a message. Whatever it was, it was important or he wouldn't have gone through such machinations.

"The invitation from Marie got lost," she said. "She wants a reply."

His Paris informer needed to speak to him—his Paris informer from his SS days in occupied France.

After all these years. It would have to mean . . . He sucked in his breath. But no, it couldn't.

His brother.

Heinz twisted the worn gold signet ring on his pinkie. The ring matching the one worn by his brother Gottfried, who'd disappeared in France in 1942. *Gott im Himmel.* This was about Gottfried—she had information. He knew it. His pulse raced like it hadn't in years.

He drove to the storage facility to visit his locker and withdrew an alternate passport, French francs, and a carton of Ernte 23 cigarettes. At Dresden *Bahnhof*, he left the Trabant on a side street, purchased a ticket to Paris. In Leipzig, he disembarked, smoked a cigarette on the platform, and used the public phone to call his wife and tell her he wouldn't be home for a few days. The next call was a message for his Paris informer, whom he hadn't seen in forty-five years.

Paris · Friday, 11 P.M.

AIMÉE KNEW VORTEK, the photographer around the corner from Leduc Detective, kept late hours in his darkroom. She also knew she had to get her film developed right away.

She gave a quick glance behind her in case she'd been followed, but saw only a few taxis passing in the mist. She parked in the garage on rue Bailleul, the narrow street by Leduc Detective, in her *grand-père*'s spot. The damn sidecar filled up a whole space. She shook wet drops off her *grand-père*'s motorcycle jacket and nodded to the young attendant, safe and dry in his office, where he listened to the radio.

For a moment she stood below the overhang at the corner of rue de l'Arbre Sec, thinking. Hadn't she done the job—found Suzy and questioned her?

But there'd been another murder. This murder, with the same MO as the murder of Elise's father—how could they not connect? It wouldn't be right not to follow up.

Her hands were still shaking. She couldn't clear the image of the body bobbing in the quai, the old man's blood-matted hair.

What the hell was going on? Was a serial killer attacking old men—old men who met at that chic restaurant?

She wished her father were there, that she could ask him what to do—or, better yet, let him take over, make everything right. But he'd rushed off to Berlin with no explanation. She had no idea how to even reach him.

In the pouring rain she ran across the street and through the opening of a small courtyard. The shop was dark. A steady drip from the gutter beat a rhythm on the cobbles. Wet and shivering, she shouldered her bag and hurried under the passage to the shop's side door.

She knocked. Knocked again. "Vortek, it's Aimée. Please, I need your help." She pounded now. "It's important."

A window shutter on the top floor creaked open. "Quiet out there. We're trying to sleep."

The door cracked open a few centimeters.

"Please, Vortek—"

Then her wet sleeve was yanked forward so hard she almost tripped. "Shh, careful of the steps," said Vortek, "and be quiet."

The shop, which had been a warehouse, was stacked with turn-of-the-century magazines, old press photos, and newspapers halfway to the peaked glass ceiling. In addition to his photography business, Vortek collected and sold vintage photographs, newspapers, and magazines. The smell of newsprint made her sneeze. He guided her toward the door on the far wall, a small office full of index-card boxes whose dates went back to the seventeenth century.

"Call next time. You're lucky I opened the door." A Polish accent tinged his speech. He wore a dark wool sweater, corduroy pants, and slippers. Salt-and-pepper hair stuck out in thick tufts and a scarf was wrapped around his neck. "What's so important?" He lit a cigarette.

"Can I have this film developed?" She handed him the roll she'd taken out of the camera. "Please, as fast as possible."

"It's for your father?"

Her father brought Vortek work all the time. Leduc had

an account. Vortek made the best false papers this side of
Lodz, her father said.

"You could say that," she said, not wanting to lie.

His gaze hovered on the roll of film. "Then let's say that."

"Prints only. Three copies each. And I want the negatives
back." *Merde*, that sounded naïve. Vortek could make prints
anyway. She handed him three hundred francs. "We'll keep
this off the account for now. How long, Vortek?"

"That's it? And you want a rush order?"

She handed over another hundred-franc bill and nodded.

"I'll call you when it's done. You know the way out." He
let her out of the office and disappeared behind another
door, offering her a brief glimpse of a small room bathed
in red light and dripping photos hanging from a clothes-
line.

Even using her penlight, she stumbled in the warren of
dusty aisles, knocking into a stack of 1900 *Paris Illustrés*.
Back outside, she walked in the wet shadows through the
covered passage, then back into the downpour, through
the sliver of a courtyard and to the street.

She wished she had an umbrella and her boots weren't
soaked. She bolted down the narrow cobbled street. In
Leduc Detective she took off her wet clothes, kicked the
radiator into life, and put on her father's English Hobbs
electric kettle.

Wearing her father's oversized Breton sweater and her
old riding jodhpurs from her *lycée* days which she'd just
discovered in the back armoire, she scrounged in the secretary's desk drawers for the old-fashioned pair of Charentaise
felted wool slippers she hid in her desk. Now at least her
feet wouldn't freeze on the wood floor. She found a *tilleul*
sachet of lime flower tea, poured in the hot water, and

inhaled the steam. Always good prevention against a winter cold, her grandmother used to say. She'd been gone several years now—how Aimée missed her. Thinking of her grandmother made her wonder about her grandfather and the fluffy puppy he'd brought into the bistro. He had a knack for picking up strays; it used to make Aimée's grandmother shake her head in faux despair whenever ragged mutts followed him home.

Aimée blew her nose, wrote up her notes into a report. She would attach the photos once they were ready. She mulled over her situation. As much as she wanted to get her report to Elise so she could try to get those family photographs of her mother before her father came home, she decided she couldn't rush this anymore, now that she thought there was another related murder. She wanted to confer with her father and see the developed photos first. Her father had forbidden her to take any action on Elise's case, but God knows she needed his advice now. He'd understand, wouldn't he?

But her father wouldn't be in Berlin yet. She could leave a message at the hotel, but which damn hotel? Gerhard would know. Now what was Gerhard's last name?

She thumbed through her father's Rolodex. After five minutes she found KÖHLER, GERHARD in Berlin. Hoped it was the right guy.

She punched in the country code and listened to the ringing for what felt like a long time.

"*Ja?*" a sleepy voice answered.

"I'm Jean-Claude Leduc's daughter, Aimée."

"Do you know what time it is?"

"*Désolée*, Gerhard," she said, glancing at the clock. 11:30 P.M. *Oops.* "Forgive me for calling so late."

"A problem? Are you all right, *Fräulein*—I mean, *mademoiselle*?"

Finding a murdered man floating by the quai had altered her evening. No need to bring that up. "Fine."

"*Mein Gott*, when I get a call in the middle of the night—"

"No, I'm okay, it's just—*désolée*, but where's my father staying? I need to get in touch with him."

"Hotel Altdorf . . ." His voice faded. Came back. "I haven't found those files yet. My contact's gone incommunicado."

She wondered if the files had anything to do with the German couple and that missing husband he'd mentioned before he left.

"The Stasi center's . . . Si . . ." He fuzzed out.

"We've got a bad connection. Please repeat that, I'm writing it down." Not her business, but she should leave the info for her father.

"Sydney Hartman. His relative, he said."

Her breath caught. Her mother.

"Her Stasi file's thick," Gerhard was saying. "Already interest from the Americans. They're willing to pay."

Pay? Pay for files? The news hit her like a punch to the stomach.

"What files do you mean?" Her voice came out broken and small. "Wh . . . where is she?"

"It's . . . bad connection." The phone line or to do with her mother?

Think. Get information before he hung up.

"Who else's interested?"

"*Vas . . . ?*" His voice wavered.

"Who's interested in her files?"

"Mossad. Tell your father I'll know more tomorrow. *Auf Wiedersehen.*"

Gerhard hung up.

She clenched the phone, shaken. Her knuckles were white.

After her mother had left them when Aimée was eight, Jean-Claude had refused to speak of her, burned her things, acted as if she'd never existed. Had he known where she was all this time? Why had he hidden this from Aimée—why? What else had he lied about?

This gaping pit of sorrow and guilt and rage opened, the pain that never went away.

She rang Hotel Altdorf and left a message with the concierge, asking her father to call her at home as soon as he arrived in the morning.

Sunk in her dark thoughts, she jerked when the phone rang.

"I don't do snuff photos, Aimée," Vortek's voice rumbled with anger.

She'd forgotten to warn him. An amateur mistake. *Merde*, he'd tell her father. Her father, who'd lied to her.

"I'm sorry, Vortek," she said. "I meant to say those photos go to the police."

"Or to a tabloid or *Le Parisien*, who would pay a lot for something like this, eh? You skimming off your father now?"

"*Mais non*, Vortek. I wouldn't do that. I came on this accidentally. My cousin—"

"I don't care, Aimée. A child shouldn't have pictures like these."

Child?

He hung up.

SHE TOOK HER boots from the sputtering radiator. Still damp. Her grandfather's jacket was damp, too, but the sheepskin lining was soft and dry. She wrapped her father's wool scarf around her and trudged out in the wet street. Thank God the rain had stopped.

Vortek stood in the alley under the passage, smoking. She pulled out a fifty-franc note, almost the last of her stash, to keep him quiet and exchanged it for the envelope he held. Checked that the photos and negatives were inside.

Gruesome. She suppressed a shiver.

"My father was a partisan during the war," Vortek said, blowing a puff of smoke. "Fighting in the forest outside Lodz."

"*Et alors?*"

"The old man in your photo—that's the way they used to shoot *collabos* during the war. Tied up, bullet to the back of the head. A warning to anyone who thought about turning them in."

"But it's 1989. The war's been over for more than forty years." She tucked the envelope in her bag.

He flicked his cigarette into a puddle. "You think the past goes away?" said Vortek. "I see it every day, people rummaging through our stock looking for their history. Even on *télé* last night there was a movie about a man who takes revenge for an old war crime." He gave a twisted grin. "But you're the detective now."

At that moment, it struck her that nothing she had ever done in her life had gotten her blood rushing like her little surveillance job tonight had—nothing had ever made her feel this way before. And she wasn't half bad at it.

"You could say that, Vortek." Didn't she have a doctored PI license to prove it?

Chambly-sur-Cher · November 1942

"The commandant at Givaray has some questions, Gaubert." Rouxel, the reputed German informer, stood in the farmhouse doorway, his beret cocked. He'd always been the village bully; now he'd found his vocation as a Party fascist. A Citroën idled out front, the motor powered by a *gazogène* cylinder mounted on its hood.

Gaubert clutched his fist behind his back. Wished to God he could grab the German rifle they'd salvaged last night from the *Boches*. Shoot this damned collaborator.

"We're in Vichy, as you well know. I don't report to—"

"But Maréchal Pétain has called for cooperation, so bring your *Ausweis* and get moving."

"Why?"

"Ask the commandant. He said he wants to confer with the mayor."

If he didn't go, it would look suspicious.

Gaubert took his time finding dry boots and his wool coat, made a show of going through his drawers for his papers. He wanted to give Fanny as much time to escape as he could.

Gaubert avoided the barn, directing Rouxel to drive the Citroën toward the side road. But the tires stalled in the mud rifts, so the two men ended up walking five minutes to the bridge over the Cher River—the demarcation line dividing *la zone libre* from Occupied German territory.

"Some German soldiers washed up on the Givaray bank," said Rouxel as they walked. "Know anything about it?"

"Not my business," Gaubert said warily. "That's across the river."

"The commandant's in a tizzy. Can't figure out where they came from. Or why he wasn't notified of a convoy."

With the confusion of the bombing and rainstorm, maybe no one had followed up?

"Hitler didn't notify me either," said Gaubert. "What's it to do with us, anyway, in *la zone libre*? All that bombing last night . . ."

"Between you and me, as a Frenchman, do you see tears in my eyes?"

Just greed, Gaubert thought. The rat sensed something. He picked up his pace so Rouxel would be discouraged from further talk.

At the wooden sentry hut, Gaubert presented his *Ausweis*, printed in both languages, to the French customs official. The official studied it, nodded his braid-trimmed blue hat, and raised the bars to let them onto the bridge. Twilight had descended on the flowing river and the rain had stopped. The bone-chilling damp made Gaubert shiver. The scent of rotten leaves rose from underneath the bridge.

After they'd taken a few steps away from the customs official, Rouxel seized his arm. "You, Philbert, Alain, and Bruno were out last night piling sandbags."

So the rat knew.

"No secret. And with no help from you, Rouxel," Gaubert said, stopping in the middle of the bridge. "We could have used your muscle. Now that the fields have flooded, God knows what we'll eat."

Looking at the swollen, khaki-colored river, he felt mired

in guilt. As illogical as it would be to confide in the rat, part of him wanted to pour out the truth, confess so no more innocents would be shot. No more cheesemongers or elderly parents dying for their secret. Only he, Alain, Philbert, and Bruno deserved to die.

"The wheat fields are ruined," said Gaubert. "Cornfields, too. You, me, we'll all go hungry unless . . ."

Rouxel's eyes on him were calculating. Everyone knew he dealt on the black market. And as mayor, Gaubert had to come up with something, some plan for food.

"Unless what?"

An RAF formation droned overhead, drowning his answer. Then several planes broke off and swooped down. A burst of machine-gun fire clattered, strafing the German side of the bridge. Pings sounded off the metal. Gaubert dove in the mud. A cry as Rouxel grabbed his leg.

"I'm hit."

Rouxel was shouting, his voice high with pain. "Help me, don't leave me here."

Tempted, he was tempted. Gaubert grabbed him under the arms and dragged him back to the Chambly side. Rouxel, heavy and moaning, made it difficult. He called to the French sentry post for help, but the border guard had fled. The damn coward.

Once he'd gotten him off the bridge into the shelter of trees on the slippery bank, he tore Rouxel's sleeve and used it like a tourniquet to staunch his bleeding leg.

"Gaubert," Rouxel wheezed, "I can help you supply food to the village."

Gaubert snorted. "You mean via your German connections? What, you'll sell us their rations for double what you pay?"

"Say what you like," said Rouxel, anger and pain in his eyes. "The commandant's men saw you on the river last night. They're convinced you had something to do with those dead men."

So that's why they wanted him in their occupied zone, to interrogate him until he cracked. He remembered the lights he'd seen in the distance. They couldn't know for sure, though, could they? "So the *Boche* offered you a cut and you believe him?"

"I'm not stupid," Rouxel gasped. "*Boches* don't share. They do business. You need my help."

Business. Rouxel would sell him, the entire village, even his own mother out.

Farther down the river, the explosions and strafing continued. Dark smoke clouds billowed up into the sky.

Rouxel was bleeding like a stuck pig and clutching his jacket.

"Hiding something, Rouxel?"

Gaubert pulled Rouxel's jacket open and his hands came back sticky with blood. A bullet hole gaped in the man's chest. There was a blood-smeared letter folded and tucked into the jacket. Gaubert seized it, ignoring Rouxel's bleats of protest, and moved out of the man's reach to read it. In passable French, Commandant Niedhofer was offering Rouxel three hundred francs to bring Gaubert, the mayor, over to the German side. Rouxel had been selling him out.

"Gaubert?"

Alain's head popped up from the bushes. Where had he come from?

"Have you gone crazy? Crossing the bridge under fire?"

Alain crawled up the bank, tore more branches from the

bushes to cover them. "I saw that scum go to your door. What does he want?"

Gaubert thrust the note in Alain's hand. "Look."

"*Alors*, we'll work this out," Rouxel sputtered. "You think I believe the *Boches*. I'm on your side."

"Like hell you are." Continued strafing by the RAF on the other side of the bridge and the answering German anti-aircraft fire kept everyone inside. No one in their right mind would get near a window.

"They want to know who murdered these German soldiers," Rouxel said, gasping. "I can fix it with them, tell them—"

Alain shoved Rouxel further behind the bushes. He lifted his arm and brought it down on Rouxel's head—over and over, like one possessed. It took Gaubert too long to realize Alain was holding a rock, which was stained bright red with Rouxel's blood.

Horrified, Gaubert grabbed his arm. "What've you done now?"

Alain felt for Rouxel's pulse. "Dealt with a loose end." Alain dragged the corpse the rest of the way into the brush, arranged branches to hide it. "You should feel relieved."

Relief and guilt at the same time. And claustrophobia—he was stuck in a secret with this hothead, who'd get them all shot. Last night Gaubert had murdered a soldier, a boy. Robbed Nazi gold. Now he'd been separated from his wife, his child—he was trapped in a web of death and deceit.

"God knows who will come looking for him."

Alain's small eyes scanned the riverbank. "Tonight I'll come back and bury him so deep God won't find him."

Gaubert wanted this all to go away. Rouxel's sticky blood on his fingers, the mud, the bombing. And the damn gold.

A siren whooped in the village, rattling his nerves. At the checkpoint on the bridge, Gaubert saw the German guards. Their rifles rose.

"Don't you understand?" he said to Alain. "Rouxel wasn't a loose end. The Germans know."

Paris · Friday, Midnight

BACK AT LEDUC Detective, Vortek's words spun in Aimée's head—could the old men be executed in revenge for a past crime? But why now? she could hear her father ask.

Toujours le sceptique, he'd say, look at both sides. What other possible motive could she find?

She thumbed through the photos she'd taken a few hours ago: the brass mailboxes at Suzy's apartment building; Suzy at the café counter, her silhouette half obscured by Aimée's bag; under the Alibaba club marquee; a slice of the cute bartender Marc's shoulder; Laurent's reservation page at cockeyed angles.

The last several horrific shots of the man bobbing against the quai, a dark red hole in the back of his sopping wet head, blood-stained rag in his mouth, one bare foot. The tied hands.

Staring more closely, she noticed that the fingers on one hand had bloated like white sausages against the rope, but the other hand's fingers were smooth, slender, flesh-colored. She tried to recall her anatomy lectures and whether there might be any reason for one hand to bloat and not the other. The only thing she could think of was—could the arm be a prosthesis?

What should she do now, at this hour? It was late, she felt tired. And she wanted her father's advice before she did anything else. About to call it quits, she noticed the red light blinking on the answering machine. When had this been left and why hadn't she noticed it?

She hit play. "*Allô?* I'm sorry to call so late," said the voice she recognized as Elise's, "but I need to reach Jean-Claude as soon as possible. Can you let me know how to contact him? I'm at home. The police called me . . . I'm afraid." A loud click as the phone hung up.

Aimée's throat tightened. Had the *flics* recovered evidence tonight on the quai linking the new body to Elise's father's murder? Did the second murder put Elise in danger?

What had she gotten into? Nervous, she debated a moment, then grabbed her bag.

TEN MINUTES LATER she parked her grandfather's motorcycle in the shadows by the gold-tipped fence that ringed the square around Chapelle Expiatoire. Dense rotting-leaf smells filled the wet night. The Greco-Roman-style chapel, bracketed by stone arcades, mushroomed from the undergrowth, reminding her of ruins, an archeological discovery. The square stood over the ancient Cimetière de la Madeleine where, in 1793, Louis XVI and Marie-Antoinette were dumped in a mass grave after being guillotined at nearby Place de la Concorde. Later the royals were disinterred—their bodies were identified by the queen's garters, rumor went—and reburied in the royal Basilique Cathédrale de Saint-Denis. Aimée had always thought it was eerie passing by this chapel, with its famous history, but it was smack dab in the middle of the eighth arrondissement and the bus ran right by.

Elise's rue Lavoisier address—a mansion with a baroque plasterwork façade—straddled the corner and continued down both streets. How could people afford to live in these anymore? Most had been taken over by banks who, Aimée had read somewhere, sold the upper floors as flats. Sodden yellow-brown leaves gave off a damp odor of decay and clung to her boots. She pressed the button by the name Peltier.

"Who's there?"

She leaned close to the grilled microphone. "Elise, it's Aimée Leduc. I must talk to you. I came as soon as—"

"Not here," interrupted a woman's voice.

"Madame Peltier?"

"Not here."

Hadn't Elise just left a message? A gust of wind shook the few leaves off the trees over the chapel.

"Who's this?"

No answer. She didn't like this.

"I need to drop off what Elise asked me to bring." A lie, but close to the truth.

"This late?" said the woman. "Do you realize the time?"

Aimée didn't like having this conversation on the dank street. Or the tone of whoever this was.

"Elise asked me to drop this off. It's important."

"Come back tomorrow."

Like hell she would.

"Who is this?"

No answer.

"Then you tell Elise, who insisted I drop this off, why you won't let me—"

The massive carved door buzzed open.

About time.

The black-and-white, marble-tiled foyer, lit by a chandelier, led to a winding staircase wrapping an elevator padded with worn blue velvet and so small she held her breath as she squeezed in. The wire doors clanked shut and the shoe-box ascended.

It shuddered to a halt on the fourth floor. A fiftyish woman wearing a velour turquoise tracksuit stood on the landing, framed by another set of massive carved doors. Her chin-length black hair was lacquered flat to within a centimeter of its life. She looked wide awake as she sized Aimée up. "I'll take that," she said, holding out her hand for Aimée's report.

Aimée had professors harsher than her.

"I don't think so," said Aimée, barreling past her. "Elise?"

The theme song of *Dallas* came from a *télé* down a cavernous hallway of palatial moldings and wall sconces. But the packing boxes and crates lining the walls gave it a forlorn feel.

The woman caught Aimée's arm. "Wait a minute, you can't come in here."

The tall windows overlooking the park and the chapel dome were fogged in the November cold. A faint waft of musk and leather attested to the presence of someone else.

"Where's Elise?"

The woman's long fingernails raked Aimée's jacket. "I'm calling the police, young woman."

"Not before I do." Aimée shook off her grip. "What have you done with her?"

Shocked, the woman's eyes crinkled. "Done with her? What do you mean, child?"

"I'm asking the questions. Who are you and what have you done with Elise and her mother?"

The woman stepped back.

"Answer me."

"I'm the housekeeper. They left me to finish boxing up the apartment."

"Why?"

"Madame Peltier and Elise just left."

Left?

"So late? So where have they gone?"

The woman's mouth pursed. She said nothing.

Had she stumbled into a robbery scam?

"How do I know you're the housekeeper?"

"I've worked for the family for years." The woman tugged her pocket zipper. Nervous. "Elise and her mother took the car and left."

"Like I believe you?"

"Me? You barged in here, what right do you have?"

Aimée scanned the dark hallway. On the sideboard were stacks of envelopes and newspapers, and a sheet of packing instructions with the underscored headline: *For Denise*.

"When did they leave, Denise?"

"Let me see your identification."

Aimée flashed her faux PI license.

Surprise filled the woman's face.

"There's a difficult situation, didn't she tell you? It's vital I reach her. Where did they go?"

"She never mentioned someone would come here." Denise's thin mouth turned down. "I remember now. A Monsieur Leduc." She was thawing a bit. "I didn't expect someone so young."

"I'm his daughter. Now tell me, Denise, when did they leave?"

"Not long. Forty minutes ago? They left for the village."

Great. "Where's that?"

"I thought you were family. Don't you know?"

She wanted to kick this stubborn housekeeper in her

glaring track outfit. The turquoise didn't suit Denise's sallow color at all.

"It looks better if you help me, Denise."

Denise hesitated. Aimée heard voices down the hall.

"Who's here?"

"Only me, JR, and Sue Ellen."

Aimée never watched the *télé* but everyone in France who did had *Dallas* fever.

"But if Elise left in a hurry, didn't she leave a message?"

A shrug and shake of her dyed hair.

"I heard the police called."

"None of my business. It's supposed to be my night off."

Helpful, this Denise.

A loud buzz came from the hall intercom. Denise jumped.

"You're expecting someone?" *Les flics?*

But Denise dashed down the hallway to the door without replying.

Aimée took advantage of this housekeepers' preoccupation and scanned the crates for an address in the village. Nothing. On the sideboard she saw an old-fashioned leather address book, the kind her grandfather kept by the phone. Most people didn't put their own addresses in something they kept at home, but she thumbed it open to P. Only the plumber on rue d'Amsterdam.

She found a scribbled grocery list on the back of an envelope: onions, garlic, rosemary. Thank goodness Elise's generation was so frugal, never wasted a scrap of paper. She turned the envelope over to see it had been forwarded to the Peltiers in Paris from the village of Chambly-sur-Cher.

Aimée stuck it in her pocket.

"I missed her?" a man was saying at the front door. "*C'est terrible.* I left as soon as I could." His tone spoke of formal,

MURDER ON THE QUAI

aristocratic French. He shifted the overcoat from his arm
and she saw he held a briefcase. He was of medium height,
with a crooked nose and dark hair greying at the temples,
but he emanated a presence, a charisma, like a politician.
The type you noticed, Aimée thought, by their stance, their
bearing, a *je-ne-sais-quoi*. Whatever it was, he had it.

The housekeeper was murmuring something in his ear—
all Aimée caught was "that detective's daughter."

"I was supposed to meet Elise, too," Aimée lied. "Do you
know when she's returning, monsieur?"

His brow furrowed. "No idea." He set down his case to
shake her hand. "I'm Renaud de Bretteville. And you are?"

"Aimée Leduc," she said. "A relative."

"How did the performance go, Monsieur de Bretteville?"
Denise asked, her voice fawning.

"Typical dress rehearsal. Complete with a third-act stage-
set disaster." De Bretteville sighed. "Still so much to work
on." Turning to Aimée, he explained, "I'm performing and
producing a piece at the theater."

An actor—that explained the presence, and the sigh. "Let
me make tisane for your throat." Denise turned to Aimée,
her voice dismissive. "Leave the package with me, I'll see she
gets it."

No way she'd leave crime-scene photos and her report
with a nosey housekeeper.

"My contact's with Elise." Aimée pulled out her notebook. "Give me the Peltiers' country number."

This time, Denise complied, and Aimée wrote it down.

Despite Denise's second invitation to tea, Renaud de
Bretteville declined. Shot Aimée a look she interpreted as
the last thing he wanted. So she followed him down the stairs.

"You're Elise's friend, Monsieur de Bretteville?"

"A little more," he said, his deep-timbred voice echoing off the marble stairs. A stage voice. "And you?"

"As I said, we're related." She still didn't know exactly how. "Elise left me a message on the machine that she was afraid. Can you think why? Did she say anything to you?"

"On the phone? It's so hard to hear backstage." He shook his head as he hit a button and the massive front door clicked unlocked. She pushed it open. "I think she called during—*non*, after the last curtain call. Maybe an hour ago," he said. "I feel terrible I couldn't get away. Has something happened?"

"If you don't mind me asking, how well do you know Elise?"

Another sigh, then a bemused grin. "How well does any man know a woman?"

She'd overheard the busybody housekeeper whisper "detective's daughter" to him—no use keeping it quiet. Her father always said it's a fine line knowing when to reveal you're a detective and when to try to get them to open up by other means. Maybe she'd learn more by enlisting his help. "Monsieur de Bretteville, this concerns her father," said Aimée.

He paused, a serious look on his face. "Her father? Look, I suggested that if the police couldn't solve her father's murder Elise should hire a professional. She said she had a family member in the business. That's you?"

"Leduc Detective's my father's firm, but I'm helping." A swell of pride filled her. She'd never been taken as a professional before. Her shoulders straightened. "I'm following up."

In the patches of light she glimpsed his expression—curiosity in his eyes. "A bit young for this, Aimée? *Alors*, who am

I to say? The police sit back, do nothing. At least that's what Elise feels. It's been a month. What have you discovered?"

Like she'd fall for that and cough up hard-won information? "My job's asking questions," she said. "Who would want to murder Monsieur Peltier or his circle of friends?" She guessed that last part, but from Renaud's startled expression, she could see it hit the mark. What mark, she didn't know.

Suspicious, she watched him closer. Walking in the chilly, rain-freshened night air, their footsteps were muted on the wet leaves.

"I can't guess who would want to kill Bruno Peltier, and neither can the *flics*. Elise's so frustrated," said Renaud. "The inspector took me aside and told me they'd rounded up a suspect, but then his alibi checked out. Of course they can't share his ID or their investigation. For her peace of mind I said, 'If you don't think they're doing it right, talk to a detective.' But I figure you'd tell her the same thing."

"*Alors*, please, can you help me?"

"*Bien sûr*, in any way I can." He sounded sincere and offered to walk her to the boulevard where she'd parked.

As she tried to figure out what information she could get from him, he gestured to the Chapelle Expiatoire, fronted by four Doric columns splattered with pigeon excrement. "You know, every January the right-wing aristocrats celebrate a mass here in the deposed Marie-Antoinette and Louis's honor."

"*Vraiment*? I never knew that," she said. Let him talk, she thought. Draw him out.

"Elise's father made a point of telling me," he said.

Here was a way to push for more information about Elise's father. "Did you know him well?"

"*Pas du tout.*" He shook his head. "He supported our theater foundation. But supporting the theater isn't the same thing as being happy that your daughter is involved with an actor."

How old-fashioned. Wasn't Elise old enough to make her own choices? She must be practically as old as Aimée's father. Ancient.

"You're saying her father disapproved?"

"Old school, *tu comprends?*"

Hypocritical, too, this Bruno who frequented *boîtes de nuit* on rue de Ponthieu.

"When did you last see Monsieur Peltier?" That was too direct, so amateur. Yet how else could she find out? She wondered how her father would have handled it.

"Let me think." Renaud's condescending voice rubbed her the wrong way. "I'd just dined with the family on Sunday at home," he said. "We were announcing our engagement. That was the last time."

Engagement? "Congratulations," Aimée said, surprised. She had an idea, decided to take a shot in the dark. "Were his old friends at the party? You know, the ones he meets—I mean, met—every month?"

"There was a superb foie gras, that I remember. But the other guests?" He shrugged. "*Désolé.*"

She'd try another tack. "Can you remember anything else about the last time you saw Monsieur Peltier?"

"You mean at the dinner?" Renaud's brow furrowed. "It's terrible, but . . . I can only picture Elise. How happy we were. But now . . . it's tearing her apart."

"Can you give me the date?"

Renaud paused under the streetlight and consulted his calendar. The taxi stand stood deserted.

"October eighth. We dined early since I had rehearsal."

The night before his murder.

"If I'd only paid attention," he said. "But I gave Elise a promise ring and her mother seemed happy and her father, *alors*, happy in his own fashion."

A Noctambus, the rare and infrequent all-night bus, approached on the boulevard. "*Désolé*, this bus stops at my door. I have to catch it."

"Here's my card, Renaud." She'd found him to be a condescending showman at first, but now he seemed like a caring fiancé. A nice catch for Elise. "Please, call me if there's anything you can think of."

Renaud took it.

Her grandfather's comment on the Sten gun came back to her. She'd try one more time, fish for one more thing. "I wonder if that evening Monsieur Peltier mentioned anything about the past. Maybe the war?"

She sensed Renaud hesitate. Then he shook his head. "*Non*, but I overheard a remark at the theater benefit."

"*Et alors?*" Right away she wished she'd kept the impatience out her voice.

"Just gossip, really."

The bus pulled up. Doors opened and a few passengers stepped off. Renaud de Bretteville edged toward the bus door.

"I'm listening. Please, everything's important."

He paused, pulling out a bus pass. "You won't mention this to Elise?"

"Everything stays confidential," she lied.

"I heard a rumor that Bruno had made out well during the Occupation. That that's why he had the money to be a benefactor of the arts."

"You're saying Elise's father collaborated with the Germans during the war?"

"It's only an overheard conversation," he said. "Not for me to slander the dead. People made fortunes and no one asked questions then." In the bus's doorway he turned back to add, "No one wanted answers."

As the bus lurched away, she pulled on her helmet. She thought about Vortek's father, the Polish resistance fighter, and his story about executing collaborators in the Polish forests. She took a last look at Chapelle Expiatore's dome, the glint of the gold-tipped fence. It was time to call it a night.

CROSSING PONT MARIE, she shuddered at the memory of what she had seen earlier, not so many bridges away. Why would the police have contacted Elise unless this second murder connected to her father's? Of course it did. Afraid, Elise must have packed up her mother and left in a hurry.

Afraid of what?

That they were next?

Did that mean Elise knew who might be after her? Did she already know who'd killed her father? Had she withheld part of the truth when she'd come into Leduc Detective?

Or was it just that the grief and stress were too much for her, and she had decided to get away for a while? A second murder, the police calling in the night—it would have taken a toll.

On the Ile Saint-Louis she turned left down the quai d'Anjou and parked. She saw a light on in their window.

The Leduc family flat took up the third floor of a seventeenth-century *hôtel particulier* built on the island where once the king's cows had grazed. Inhabited now by aristos and old families whose descendants had inherited an architectural jewel but couldn't afford to redo the archaic heating and plumbing. She'd grown up with it, so she was used to it—used to keeping her coat on indoors in the winter, used to remembering to turn off the sagging chandeliers before switching on her hair dryer so as not to blow a fuse.

Over the years, rising humidity had dampened the three-hundred-year-old walls and warped the inlaid parquet floors. The eight-room apartment's walls were lined by smoky age-patinaed mirrors, granite fireplaces, and cracked marble busts that had been left to her grandfather. He'd told her the original owners had sadly taken a one-way trip in 1942. Now he bought lotto tickets, hoping to win enough to renovate the place.

Her shoulders sagged with tiredness. She crossed the cobbled courtyard, passed the glistening pear tree, and made her way up the age-worn marble stairs. Cursed when, as usual, the key stuck in the old lock. She kicked off her boots on the creaking wood floor of the foyer, hung up the jacket, and rubbed her sore finger with the blood blister. She heard barking.

Mon Dieu, he'd brought the stray home.

In the kitchen, a wet nose popped out of a little nest of blankets by the radiator. On the wood table, her grandfather had left a note: *Fed, walked, and needs love. See you in the morning.*

"*Mon pauvre.*" She picked up the little thing, a warm ball of now clean white fluff. "What can I do with you until tomorrow?"

Licks on her cheeks answered her. He had the pinkest tongue she'd ever seen. She nuzzled him back, held him for a while, trying not to think about the body she'd seen on the quai, thinking instead about her father and wondering why he'd kept back the truth about his trip to Berlin. Why the hell did her mother have a Stasi file?

A keening whine came from the little dog. Her grandfather's note said the puppy had already been fed, but . . . "Thirsty?"

She peered in the cupboard and came up with a chipped Limoges bowl she hoped her grandfather wouldn't mind her using. Filled it with Evian, which the dog lapped up.

Her own stomach growled. She turned on the radio to *jazz classique* and shoved yesterday's cassoulet in the old oven. She tore off a piece of baguette and uncorked the bottle of red wine on the table. Strains from a ballad from Miles Davis's *Kind of Blue* album. The melancholic notes matched the gusting wind outside the window, the leaden hanging clouds. Any minute it would pour.

She picked the puppy up again, felt his little bones shaking. He was warm and comforting in her arms. He barked.

"*Voilà*," she said. "I'm calling you Miles Davis for now."

SIPPING FROM THE glass, she moved the salt and pepper, spread out her notes and photographs on the table.

A cast of characters and a gruesome scene.

The oven's warmth heated the high-ceilinged kitchen, toasted her bare toes. Miles Davis warmed her lap.

Yawning, she closed her eyes.

She woke up to Miles Davis's barking, a kitchen full of smoke. Her eyes burned. *Merde*, she'd nodded off and burnt her dinner. She grabbed a mitt, pulled out the flaming cassoulet, dumped the charred contents in the sink. Its black edges sizzled in the cold water.

A perfectly good cassoulet fallen victim to her baking skills.

She opened the window, fanning out the smoke, her eyes tearing. A lone figure stood on the Pont Marie, silhouetted in the mist. She shivered, feeling paranoid. She wished her papa were here.

Chambly-sur-Cher · November 1942

THROUGH BINOCULARS GAUBERT watched the small regiment in Givaray loading antiaircraft guns onto a unit of convoy trucks. Heavy bombardment had continued that week along the rail lines in the occupied zone. Now the *Boches* looked like they were moving out.

Givaray was so close that he heard orders barked in German, even saw the lace curtains move at the cheesemonger's. Heard a baby cry from the kitchen.

On the morning of the executions, he heard the fusillade of gunshots. Sixty shot in Givaray while he'd sat in silent guilt. Word came the bodies had been dumped in a communal grave, not even a proper burial allowed. All week, he and the others laid low, expecting a knock on the door.

Good God, what had they done but engender a village of widows and fatherless children? His intentions of confessing and taking the blame got harder and harder as he imagined more victims. What if it happened here in Chambly and his son, Gaby . . . He couldn't finish the thought. How could he possibly make it up to the innocent victims? He'd had the idea to persuade Alain and the others to help him steal arms for the Resistance—he could get supplies to them through Fanny's brother—but he wasn't sure he could convince the others and pull off his plan for stealing guns from the gendarmes.

A soft knock at the back door. "Gaubert?" He recognized Alain's voice. "We're meeting in your barn."

Now? "It doesn't look good, you all coming here."

"It's dark. Bring some candles. Bruno got a telegram from Fanny's aunt."

"My wife's aunt? Why the hell is he in my business—"

"His mother works at the post. He saved you a trip, Gaubert."

Since when had Bruno become so helpful? Gaubert had been limping since the last war, but Bruno had never picked up his post for him before.

In his barn, the mare pawed the earth. He shoved an armful of hay into her feeding trough. Her breath steamed. A flickering kerosene lamp threw light on the three men huddled near the stall.

"Where's my telegram?"

Bruno opened his jacket pocket, took out an envelope of thin war-grade paper.

Gaubert read the few words.

Colt and mare fine.

He bit his lip. Read the lines again. Code for "arrived and safe."

How he missed his little Gaby, his darling Fanny. They needed warm clothes, needed to be in their own home, with him. But it was too dangerous.

Bruno pulled out his tobacco papers and pouch, rolled a cigarette. Gaubert knew there was something, apart from the tobacco, on the tip of his tongue.

"Is that all? What aren't you telling me?"

"The horse stumbled and Gaby broke his nose, Gaubert. But he's fine."

"What? How do you know that?" His little Gaby.

Bruno scratched a match. Lit his rolled cigarette and puffed. "The whole village knows they fled, that's what I'm telling you."

"Of course I made her flee. There've been executions . . ."

"Idiot, didn't you realize that if you sent them away it would look suspicious?"

Gossip. Rumor. Every step they took was being watched.

"We've got a plan, Gaubert," said Philbert, "and we want you to hear it. To agree."

"You're coming up with plans now?"

"We have to. It looks suspicious."

"What does?"

"You sending your family away. Everybody noticed."

"It's wartime. Germans are executing people in Givaray less than a kilometer away across the river, and you're telling me it looks suspicious that I want to protect my family? But what do you know about protecting a family? You still live with your parents—all of you. I won't have any of you tell me how to live, or that I can't keep my wife and son safe."

"What if Fanny lets something slip? Confides in her aunt? We're all in danger, don't you understand?"

"Danger? Blame Alain for pounding Rouxel's head in with a rock. You think the Germans won't look for him?"

He saw it plain as day. In their greed, all they were worried about was the damn gold they'd buried in his barn floor.

"Did you tell Fanny?"

Gaubert shook his head in disgust. "Didn't we agree? We're all dead men if word gets out. The village, too. It's never left this circle, has it? Or have you told your mother, sister, or cousins?"

Sheepish looks greeted him.

"You have? Who did you tell?"

They were all shaking their heads now. "No one, Gaubert," said Bruno, turning to the others. "We swear."

"Good. My family stays away until we move the gold."

Philbert nodded. "There are more like Rouxel, those roaming fascists from the *Parti Populaire*, just trumped-up gangsters . . ." He paused, looked at each one for effect. "If anyone in Givaray found out, they'd kill us faster than the *Boches* could."

Bruno blew out a stream of smoke that swirled up to the barn rafters. "My cousin at the station and my mother at the post keep me informed," he said. "They both heard that POWs are reconstructing the train lines, and the Germans are being pulled to Vierzon and Bourges to set up antiaircraft emplacements."

Big words for a chicken farmer who lived with his mother. But Gaubert had seen the Germans' movement through his binoculars.

"There's a big offensive in Russia, they're massing troops to the front." Philbert lowered his voice. "My uncle heard it on the radio. The BBC."

Listening to the BBC's *Radio Londres* broadcast was illegal.

"*Et alors?*" Gaubert said.

"A perfect time for our plan. We melt one gold bar and say—"

"That it fell off a German train in the bombing?" Gaubert snorted.

"Close." Bruno grinned. "My cousin saw furniture and paintings lying on the rails. Incredible things flung from the trains."

Looted in Paris by the Germans.

"Common knowledge, Gaubert. Whoever could helped themselves."

He'd heard. Now the French were looting their own.

"So we say a POW found a gold bar on the bombed tracks."

"A POW? They're all gone, *non?*"

"Remember those Polish POWs who repaired the train tracks last week?" said Bruno. "We could say one of them found it and hid it. If anyone asks, we can deny all knowledge, say the POW didn't give us exact details."

"Sounds thin," said Gaubert.

Bruno shrugged. Exhaled a rush of smoke. "We let Minou think it's equal cuts all around."

"Equal?" Alain spit in the dirt.

"Eight ways," Bruno said. "We say there're others who need to be paid off. So we get everything but one eighth, *tu comprends?*"

Minou, the blacksmith, was dim but not stupid.

"He's my second cousin," Bruno said. As if that made him trustworthy.

"For God's sake, Minou shoes horses and forges farm tools," said Gaubert. How naïve could they be? "There must be special equipment for melting gold. It's not chocolate. He doesn't have those kind of things."

"But the jeweler, Baret, would," said Philbert. "Your old comrade-in-arms, *non?*"

Gaubert looked at the other three men. Village leftovers: Alain, seventeen, a lug and too young for conscription; Bruno and Philbert exempted as agricultural workers on their families' farms. The existing male village population, almost decimated in the last war, were the disabled like him and those who were too young or needed on the farm, like these.

"Let me think."

"We need to do this now, Gaubert."

"I think better while I feed my cows."

In the pale moonlight, he pitched hay into the cow shed. The cows' soft mewling floated in the night air. His thoughts were filled with Fanny. How he wished he could talk this through with her now.

Part of him didn't want to touch this gold with blood on it; but his hunger threatened to overcome all his scruples. Alain, Philbert, and Bruno's greed shone through; they'd be like rabid dogs when their own hunger set in. Better to wash his hands of this as much as he could. Distance himself. Go to Fanny. Be a father to Gaby.

That was all well and good, but he couldn't undo the damage that had already been done, the reprisals. No matter how far from here he went, he'd never escape that cry of the cheesemonger's baby. The innocents murdered for four men's stupidity and greed.

They had to give the gold back. He remembered Rouxel's note, knew that someday, somehow the Germans would come back for the gold. The puppet Vichy government was a joke. It was only a matter of time until the *Boches* rolled over the flimsy boundary. They'd blitzkrieged into Poland, walked into Paris.

He decided.

Returning to his barn, Gaubert set the pitchfork down and nodded. "Agreed."

Philbert patted Gaubert on the back. "I knew you'd see reason." The others took up shovels.

"Only on the condition we move the gold."

"You're giving conditions?" Alain, already digging, sounded spiteful and childish. "What gives you the right?"

The right? This damn Alain, an overgrown boy with a pea brain. "Notice whose barn we're in? And whose family's in danger of being shot if it's discovered?"

"Wait a minute, Gaubert," said Bruno. "You're talking like you're the only one at risk."

"My wife and child, your families, the people of Chambly are as innocent as those across the river," said Gaubert, his face flushing. "Who deserves to be executed against the village wall and dumped in a common grave? It's our fault and we have to make it right."

"So getting ourselves shot would make it right? I don't know what you think—"

"At least I'm thinking." He took a breath. Had to get rational, explain it in a way these idiots would understand. "We need to distance ourselves, so if the gold is ever discovered it doesn't point straight to us."

All eyes were on him. He had to talk fast, now that he had their attention. "You saw Rouxel's note. Someday the Germans will come looking for that truck. They know."

"But they're leaving for the Eastern Front."

"Not all of them." Gaubert shook his head. "Do you honestly think whoever went to the trouble of loading a troop truck with gold bars has forgotten? What happens if the fifth German survived?"

Quiet except for the sputter of candles. Gaubert sensed a palpable fear vibrating in the barn. He had them now. "Or that a commander who suspected won't answer to the chain of command? Someone's neck is on the line."

"Gaubert's right," said Philbert. "It's chaos now, but for how long? Let's hide this in the old Bourgault vault in the cemetery."

Philbert, the wheat farmer, made sense when he put in the effort to think.

"Out there?" Alain chopped at the dirt with the shovel. "What if someone steals it?"

"From a decrepit, abandoned crypt? It's in the old section no one visits."

"Anyone could walk right in."

"Anyone who knew it was there, Alain. So far it's only us four."

"I agree with Gaubert," Bruno said. "*Alors*, if anyone tried to hawk a bar of Nazi gold, they'd be shot on the spot. We keep it away from prying eyes until we have the chance to melt it down."

But Bruno's inflection raised a sliver of distrust. They had something planned. Something Gaubert wouldn't see coming.

Paris · November 11, 1989 · Saturday, Noon

AIMÉE STUMBLED BAREFOOT into the toasty kitchen. Nodded at her *grand-père*, who poured her a steaming bowl of dark coffee and topped it with frothy hot milk.

"*Bonjour* to you, too," he said.

She mumbled *bonjour*, scrunching her toes against the warm, sunlit tiled floor. Bleary-eyed, she plopped two lumps of brown sugar in the coffee, stirred, and sipped. She sat and tore off a piece of baguette, slathering it with butter from a blue pot. Farm fresh, from one of her *grand-père*'s friends at the market.

Breakfast was peaceful in her father's absence, since the two men didn't have to sit reading their respective newspapers in stony silence. In the cavernous apartment, they usually managed to avoid each other. More and more, her grandfather spent time at his mistress's.

Her anatomy book sat on the table, next to her report with the photos arranged in a row.

Her grandfather hung up his apron and ruffled Miles Davis's ears. "Our Prince Charming has quite an appetite."

"Where did you find him, *Grand-père*?" She dropped the butter knife. "Dognapping's an offense, you know."

"Dognapping? Pah, an abandoned, hungry, homeless thing, shivering on the quai?"

"No doubt the owner's looking for him. Put up signs, *Grand-père*."

"Leaving him in such a condition. That's criminal. He needs a name."

"He has one," she told him. "Miles Davis."

"*Meels Daveez?*"

"Has a penchant for barking, too."

"*Vraiment?* I didn't hear him."

Of course not, he'd calmed down when she'd let him curl up on her duvet. She couldn't afford to get too close to him; he wasn't hers. Like so much in her life.

"*Et alors*, Meels Daveez burned my cassoulet, too?"

"*Désolée*, you know my culinary skills." She tried for an engaging grin, but it came out lopsided. She'd been so tired she'd fallen asleep again before she could clean everything up.

"Don't tell me you take care of your lab instruments like that?"

She winced. Couldn't go into that now. She dunked her buttered baguette in the milk froth, the crisp brown crust soaking up the sweet coffee. Rubbed off the coffee splattered on her anatomy book, pushed it aside with her palm.

Her *grand-père* pointed to the photo of the man's body in the water.

She shuddered. "Last night. I found him like that. Floating by the quai, the same spot where they found Peltier, our relative. I couldn't get it out of my mind."

"So this man took a bullet and got left for fish food, too?"

She gulped down a mouthful of *tartine*. Nodded. "Remember at Le Soleil d'Or, when the police Zodiac sped by on the river? All those *flics* near us responding to an emergency?"

Her *grand-père* pulled up the stool. Tore himself the heel off the baguette. "You've got my attention." He threw a crumb at Miles Davis, who skittered across the floor, his nails clacking like tap shoes. "Start from when you left me with *le petit prince.*"

She explained her conversation with the bartender, how things didn't add up, the terrible coincidence of Peltier's friends dining together the night before, the man's bloated body. She showed him the photos.

"Coincidence, Aimée? I don't think so. Sounds planned and methodical. The killer knew this circle of men meets monthly. He's knocking them off one by one. It's got hall-marks—conforms to the previous MO. Symbolic, I'd say, ritualistic."

"Or the killer's making it look symbolic to throw every-one off."

"You sound like your father," he said.

But she heard a quiet pride in his voice.

"Passionate, too. As I was at your age." Wistful, her grandfather played with the pepper grinder. "It's smart to view a murder case from different sides. Investigate until it leads somewhere—or nowhere—then pursue the next angle."

Aimée's hand slipped on the coffee bowl. "A murder investigation?" she choked. "It's not my case. Elise hired Papa to find Suzy. I stepped in. *C'est tout.* I'll finish the report and deposit the check."

How furious her father would be when he found out.

"Of course." Her *grand-père* nodded. Stood.

"I mean it."

"*Bon*, I'm late for a minor masters auction at Drouot. A steal if my bid wins."

Why did her hands quiver? Her gaze kept being drawn to the photo on the quai.

Her grandfather paused to look down at the photo again. "Aimée, you did notice the weapon, *non?*"

"The weapon?" She looked closer. "There's no gun, *Grand-père*."

"Come, come, you're more observant than that."

"I see candy wrappers. I noticed he is wearing a prosthesis."

Her *grand-père* nodded. "Anything else?"

"A water bottle."

Another nod. And then she remembered once overhearing some men at the police firing range talk about silencers.

"You mean that plastic bottle was used as a silencer? This Vichy mineral bottle?"

"And you don't call that symbolic?"

HER PAGER INDICATED one call. Her father? No, Martine, her best friend since the *lycée* who studied journalism at the Sorbonne. Martine could wait for a few minutes. She tried the Berlin hotel, heard a series of clicks.

"Hotel . . ." Fuzz and buzzing, then the line clicked off.

A bad connection. Had the falling of the Wall disrupted the lines? On her third attempt she got through.

"Herr Leduc, you say he has a reservation?"

"Hasn't he checked in?"

"I don't see his name."

"Please, can you check?"

In the pause, she heard the rustling of pages.

"Our register shows a reservation for Herr Leduc. But no check-in."

A frisson skittered across her shoulders. There could be a lot of explanations; her Papa had changed his mind, the train got held up. Or worse.

She called Gerhard's number. No answer, no machine. Great.

She suppressed her worry, finished her report.

Fortified by more coffee, she called the Peltiers' number, the one that Denise the housekeeper had finally coughed up last night.

A woman answered. "*Oui?*"

"Madame Peltier? It's Aimée Leduc."

"Who?" the voice quavered.

"My father, Jean-Claude, is Elise's cousin."

"So you say." Not only old but suspicious.

"It's true, madame. My father is her second cousin," she said. "Elise knew me when I was little. I expect you did, too."

"I'd have to think about that."

Now was her chance, an opening. "But you'd remember my . . ." She hesitated—this word she'd used so rarely. "My mother, Sidonie. An American."

"*L'Américaine?* That's so long ago. Pah, you're not bringing all that up again?"

Aimée's heart tightened. What did this woman know?

"Bringing up what, madame?"

"*Alors,* I'm busy."

Friendly, too. All the things one expected from family.

"Elise asked me to call." A small lie—a variation on the truth. "May I speak with her?"

"Why?"

Pause. "I missed you last night. You'd already left when I dropped by. But Elise left me a message that worried me. She sounded upset after the police got in touch with her."

"I can't talk now."

A rooster crowed in the background.

"Please take my number down. I must speak with Elise."

"I don't know if I should."

"Just write my number down. Tell her I found Suzy, she'll understand. Then it's up to Elise, okay?"

The woman listened. Aimée heard the scratching of a pencil as she gave her number.

"Are you all right, Madame Peltier?"

"It's the barn owl."

Aimée tried to make sense of this woman—a woman who, according to Elise, had shut down after her husband's murder.

"Has something happened, Madame Peltier?"

A sigh. "Hooting just like the night the *Boches* came."

The phone clicked off.

Chambly-sur-Cher · December 1942

THEY TOOK ADVANTAGE of the last moonless December night to camouflage the blacksmith forge's smoke. Philbert stood watch outside the forge at the wind-swept crossroads; the hot shoeing of Gaubert's horse would serve as a cover if the Germans came to enforce curfew. Gaubert's nerves were frayed; the Germans controlled all of France now—even if eighty-six-year-old Maréchal Pétain, hero of WWI, remained a figurehead leader of the puppet Vichy government—and he ached for his Fanny and little Gaby.

Perspiration dripped down Gaubert's neck as he stood in the smoke-filled forge. Transfixed, he watched the Nazi gold brick glow and soften inside the conical melting crucible. Alain and Bruno shoveled coke into the blazing brick furnace. Shadows snaked up the forge's arched brick walls. The anvil bore a worn engraved date of 1781, the year Minou's ancestors went into business. Nothing had changed since Gaubert's childhood, when he'd brought his mother's soup pot to mend; the rods, bellows, piled charcoal, and tongs had hung in the same places decades earlier.

"'A watched pot never boils,' you know the saying." Baret, the jeweler, shook his head of thick, prematurely white hair. Older-looking than his forty plus years, he'd been Gaubert's captain in the last war. He unbuckled a leather valise with his working hand. His other arm was wood attached to a hook claw, courtesy of the Battle of the Somme in 1916.

Gaubert's throat burned from the smoke; he couldn't shake the nagging cough from that freezing rainy night on the river. In the trenches men didn't last long when their lungs sounded hollow—hollow as two bells. They called this the clang of death.

A flurry of sparks burst from the embers, bringing a wall of heat.

Alain jumped back. "We could have baked bread in less time."

"Don't compare baking bread to melting a dense five-kilogram bar of precious metal," said Baret. "If everything goes well, this will take another few hours."

"We should just file the serial numbers and stamp off," said Alain. "That would be quicker."

Baret shot a look at Gaubert. *Children.*

"Filing that deep to remove the Reichsbank stamp? Twelve hours at least." Baret shook his head. "Use your impatience to work the bellows."

"And get caught red-handed by the *Boches* patrols?"

"Didn't you listen when I explained yesterday?" Baret's face was flushed in the heat. "Gold melts at a thousand degrees centigrade. We must maintain this temperature for hours in order to liquify such a solid mass. So either pipe down or help work the bellows. Unless you think you'd be better off with the Reichsbank stamp."

Alain wiped his forehead. "I'm not an idiot."

"He knows what he's doing, Alain, he's a jeweler," said Gaubert.

"Was," Baret said. "Now I've taken over my father's farm.

Good thing I kept my tools." With the hook on the end of his artificial arm, he lifted a wine bottle from his valise, placed it between his knees, and twisted off the cork with practiced expertise.

Gaubert wiped his own forehead, sweating in anxiety as much as in the heat of the bellows. He had so much to worry about. If it wasn't these three young idiots—grasping and impatient—then it was the German military demanding that Mayor Gaubert enforce the curfew, scale back farm rations, requisition farm animals. God knew how long this would last—or could last.

Meanwhile, Rouxel's mother bombarded him every other day, wanting to know where her son was. Alain had taken him from the shallow grave on the river and reburied him. Gaubert never asked where. Fanny's ardent letters begged him to leave the village and let someone else deal with the Germans—Gaby had tonsillitis after his broken nose. Gaubert couldn't stop thinking about them; they'd never spent Christmas apart. But it wasn't safe for him to go to them yet.

The worst was the guilt—every night hearing that baby cry across the river in that village of orphans and widows. It was all their fault.

The Germans hadn't forgotten. Right now their energies were occupied on the Eastern Front. But they would be back, Gaubert had no doubt. What then?

Baret gestured to Bruno. "Open my suitcase, take out the long-handled tongs, my carbon rod, the ingot molds—you want to arrange them on the bench. Then we'll need the fluxing agent and the charcoal mixture."

"What's charcoal for?" asked Bruno, lifting out Baret's tools.

"That's the next step, after the bar melts. Before we pour we need a lift-off agent so the gold releases from the ingot mold," said Baret.

Gaubert's draft horse munched hay at the trough. Shirts off, their backs glistening, he and Bruno shoveled in the coke and Alain pumped the bellows. Minou, at Baret's instructions, used the long tongs to shift the crucible and add the fluxing agent. They dripped with sweat and Alain hadn't stopped complaining the whole time. It had been his damn idea in the first place.

After half an hour, the brick still maintained its shape, but a shiny gold puddle was spreading.

"We need to raise the temperature or this won't melt by dawn," said Baret.

Seized by a fit of coughing, Gaubert grabbed his hand-kerchief in time to catch his phlegm. Bright red blood. His hand shook. He balled it up, stuffed it in his pocket.

"Enough," he said. "We're dead men." Gaubert caught the wall for support and turned to Alain and Bruno. "This gold's a curse. Innocent people have been murdered. The *Boches* are hunting us down. Time we dump it in the river where it belongs."

Alain glared. Threw down the bellows and strode over to him.

"Or do you want to die for it, Alain?"

"*Non*, I want to live on it, you fool," said Alain. He swung back his fist and punched Gaubert in the gut. "I won't throw it away."

Gaubert felt the air get knocked out of him, wrenching pain. His lungs fought to breathe. Coughing and sputtering, he grabbed the metal tongs. "Greedy bastard, you'll get us all shot."

Bruno grabbed at Alain, knocking Baret to the dirt floor. A free-for-all in the dense heat.

Philbert burst into the forge, breathing hard. "What in the . . . Stop! Didn't you hear my warning? There's a *Boches* patrol coming."

They'd been tracked down. One of the idiots must have blabbed. Gaubert and Baret locked glances. Right then he knew they would die. They'd escaped it in the trenches, but here and now the reckoning arrived.

An owl hooted in the neighboring barn. Then Gaubert heard thrumming engines, the gunning of motorcycles and German voices coming in through the open wooden door.

Place de la Madeleine, Paris · Saturday, 1 P.M.

THEIR OLD MEETING place had changed, like so much else. Heinz Felsen took a deep breath as he entered *le Foyer* in the vaulted basement of the Madeleine Church. Well-dressed volunteers staffed the restaurant, a glorified cafeteria that reminded him of the Dresden University student canteen.

The Foyer's proceeds funded homeless programs, according to the sign on the wall. Give that to them, Heinz thought, but the clientele was a far cry from the population he remembered the Foyer serving during the war. Then, it had been a soup kitchen; today, the homeless ate in their own reserved section, while at communal tables sat office workers, locals, aristocrats, some elderly on a budget. Quite a three-course bargain in this chic quartier. Aah, the French.

Armed with his newly purchased membership card and meal ticket, he walked to a table he remembered. His brown suit and serviceable East German shoes looked shabby even among the working-class types here. Self-conscious and uneasy, he realized anyone who looked twice would notice—it would be glaringly obvious to these sophisticated Parisians. The culture shock of being in the West for the first time in forty years hit him.

"*Bonjour, c'est libre?*" he asked the woman at the table, for formality's sake. She was seventy if she was a day.

"*Asseyez-vous,*" she said. Her white hair was back in a tight chignon; she wore a slash of coral lipstick and turquoise earrings—a style from the fifties that looked à la mode today. Still a stunning woman.

"*Bien sûr*, I'd suggest you pass on the rubber *poulet* and order the fish, Heinz."

He'd recognize her voice anywhere: gravelly and low.

He nodded. "*Merci, Madame . . . ah . . . ?*"

"It's Comtesse de Ribes de la Besson," she said, flashing a megawatt smile.

Perfect white teeth, not her own. Taut alabaster skin with a hint of makeup and faint expression lines around her mouth. His informer, whom he'd known as Marie Buvet in the bordello, had done well for herself.

"But you can call me Comtesse. As I imagine you know, it's important in life to reinvent oneself, *n'est-ce pas?*"

Message received, loud and clear. Heinz, no stranger to reinvention, nodded. "Understood. What do you have to tell me, Comtesse?"

"Important things come after dessert. Much better for the digestion, don't you think?"

An all-night train ride to watch the old hooker play grande dame? Yet he was hungry. It was always better to eat and then talk.

She'd gambled that he was still alive, would get her message and show up now that the Wall was coming down. She'd lured him here, hedging her bets he'd come. Now she reverted to their former protocol. More than forty years ago, he'd sat here, his black boots shined, his insignia glistening.

"You remember the last time, *non?* I see it in your eyes," she said. "We say Paris hides many sins. The past melts away."

"It's done wonders for you."

Her tone became matter-of-fact. "The sole meunière's passable."

It was ambrosia to him. Then the salad and a dessert, *fromage blanc* with a swirl of raspberries. The small strong coffee accompanied by that tiny chocolate square. He remembered now the French attention to detail and taste.

The lunch rush ebbed; only two other tables were still occupied. "We were so young—the parties, the champagne . . ." She looked around to see if anyone was listening. "All you bad boys." She pulled out her lipstick. "Our deal's still good, Heinz?"

Heinz nodded. "The world's changed, but my word stands."

"How's your French holding up?"

"My Russian's better."

She slipped an envelope over the tablecloth. Inside it was a newspaper clipping, words underlined. He nodded. How he'd taught her. Then another article clipped from *Le Parisien* with lurid headlines of a murder.

"That's background," she said. "Read it later. But notice this?" She pointed.

His hands went cold as he scanned the photos. "Give me the gist of what's not here."

She applied coral lipstick, blotted her lips with her napkin. Looked around again. "Monsieur Peltier is . . . I mean, was . . . from my quartier, a neighbor down the street. Wealthy, but who isn't around there? My niece saw this article about his murder and, my God, she's upset because she made her First Communion with the daughter, knows the family."

Heinz had forgotten how the woman gossiped. But then that's what he'd paid her for in the past. The Marie he knew had resurfaced.

She noticed his look. "*Alors*, Heinz, I'll tell it my way. Long story short, at Peltier's funeral, my niece hears he came from a village next to Givaray, where your brother was lost. See, I never forgot."

Heinz folded his napkin. Put it on the table. Irritated, he wished he'd thought this through before jumping on a train a day after the Wall fell.

"Sounds like a coincidence," he said. "It's not even the same village."

He'd seen the death notifications of his brother's unit— his brother was listed as missing in action, whereabouts unknown.

"I left the business, Heinz, but I didn't abandon my contacts." She tugged her diamond tennis bracelet, checked the clasp. "Recently, a German troop truck was found sunken in the river by Givaray. I know an old *commissaire* who told me that in Givaray sixty villagers were executed in reprisals by your lot. Even the priest's parents. No one in Givaray has forgotten or forgiven."

The reprisals for four soldiers murdered on the night Heinz's brother had disappeared. He nodded. He'd developed a theory, after years of researching in the military archives, that his brother's unit had been guarding a gold train en route to Portugal.

"Go on," he said. He almost snapped his fingers for coffee and service, almost barked orders at the waiter, when he caught himself. Not even here two hours and he could slide back into those old habits. He might have just walked away from a Gestapo interrogation in rue des Saussaies . . .

"Rumor is the mayor of that Vichy village was responsible for the reprisals," Marie was saying. "The village over the river where the Peltiers come from, Chambly-sur-Cher.

Only a kilometer away. It even made the Paris papers." She indicated the article he was holding. "That's why I got interested. Remember, Heinz? I promised I would follow up on anything I heard."

She sat silently while he read the whole of the newspaper article.

> *While engineers surveyed the Cher riverbed to reinforce dikes by the old Roman bridge, they discovered more recent history—a sunken German WWII convoy truck on the river floor by the mill. A far more intriguing war-era discovery than the usual shells and Nazi helmets. Old-time villagers of nearby Givaray insist the German truck links to the murders of sixty villagers who were shot after four German soldiers' bodies washed up on their bank in 1942. "They blamed us, but we'd never seen them before," said a sixty-year-old woman, Pascale Alfort, a teenager at the time. "Who'd be such an idiot? Whoever killed them never came forward." Another old villager who spoke anonymously said Alphonse Gaubert, then mayor of Chambly-sur-Cher across the Cher, had been rumored to be responsible for killing the German soldiers. Rumors continue to this day, according to the anonymous villager, that a fifth German soldier escaped.*

Escaped. Heinz's brother's body had never been found. But after all this time . . . "You're saying the mayor, this Gaubert, murdered my brother and the others?"

She shrugged.

"Where is Gaubert?"

"Dead for all I know. In the South of France?" Marie paused. "Is it possible your brother is still alive? In Argentina?"

Even with the Wall, Gottfried would have gotten in touch. Wouldn't he?

Or had he gone AWOL, been afraid to surface? Had he made off with that gold? Maybe over the years he'd bought a new identity and burrowed into another life. That's what Heinz would have done.

After all these years, he wanted closure. Could that be all there was to it—a dead end and a hollow feeling inside?

He couldn't accept that. Not yet. He'd follow this to the end or he'd never have peace.

"Don't you have something for me, Heinz?"

"Have I ever come empty-handed?"

He pulled out the missing persons reports dated 1954 and 1961. The copy of the POW and Red Cross list, the displaced persons camp in Poland, all with WHEREABOUTS UNKNOWN stamped in red. He'd kept them for years, wondering if this day might come.

"I still check that name every few years." He passed what he had over to her. "But that's the last record I found."

Her shoulders sagged, her eyes deep pools of longing. And for a moment he saw a vestige of the young woman she was—the heartbroken young woman.

"Who was it?"

She opened her lizard-skin handbag, took out her wallet. "Silly, but . . ." A much-thumbed black-and-white photo in a Plasticine case: a smiling boy in short pants with a side part in his hair. "Yves, my little brother."

Heinz nodded in understanding. He turned the pinkie ring on his finger, the initials worn away from years of remembering, like the one worn by his own little brother. At least she had a photo.

"You did include a train timetable here in the envelope?"

"And a ticket, Heinz. I knew you'd want to talk to the priest yourself."

Paris · Saturday, 2 P.M.

AIMÉE WORKED ON her histology report at the kitchen table, Miles Davis at her feet on the warm tiles. The kitchen was full of the yeasty smells from her *grand-père*'s rising brioche dough on the counter, where it sat in a bowl covered by a damp dishtowel. Outside the window, low-lying mist, like an old man's wispy beard, wound over the Seine. The gunmetal sky promised rain.

The phone rang. She hoped it was Elise.

"Weren't you going to call me?" said Martine.

"*Mais oui*, Martine." She'd forgotten. Oops.

"You forgot. How could you—"

"Forget your birthday? Never. In fact I'm wrapping your present right now."

Her eye caught on Miles Davis. She pondered how he'd look with a pink bow.

Martine squealed. "Don't tell me. But I hope it's what I want."

Good thing she'd doubled back and bought that one-of-a-kind silk scarf last week from the Saint-Germain boutique after Martine gushed over it.

"What's with your pager, Aimée? You never answer."

Where had she put the damn thing? She should check it for messages.

"Don't forget the party's Madonna-themed," Martine went on. "You're bringing Florent, of course."

She couldn't tell Martine that going to a party was

the last thing she felt like doing. "*Alors*, Martine, last night . . ."

"Tell me later. I'm counting on you." Click.

Looking at her notebook, she gulped. She had to finish her histology report and make the deadline today. She'd gotten one extension already, couldn't afford to blow this one.

And what could she do with the puppy nestling at her feet? He'd peed twice on the carpet this morning. She couldn't leave him here.

"*Allons-y*, Miles Davis, time to go to school, okay?" she said, not wanting to move.

In answer he jumped up into her lap.

Fifteen minutes later, the report as done as she could make it, she forced herself to stand and headed to her armoire. The Breton striped shirt and classic cropped cigarette trousers? Or pencil skirt and retro silk blouse?

Her fingers paused on the Chanel. The first treasure she'd found at the vintage stall at the flea market. Her hands had caught on the silk lining of something at the bottom of the bin. A Chanel jacket. *Un coup de foudre*, love at first sight.

"*Une classique.* Can't say I remember wearing that, wish I had," said the chignoned middle-aged woman at the flea market stall.

"How much?" Aimée asked.

The worn cuffs didn't detract from the jacket's simple, elegant line.

"Of course it goes with your cowboy boots; *un peu chic, très éclectique*." The woman smiled. "Those *authentique*?"

From her summer abroad in America looking for her mother, when all she'd come back with were the boots.

"*Oui*, from Houston." Courtesy of a desperate phone call to her father to beg for a money order. "May I try it on?"

And she did, in front of the cracked oval mirror, the stall's merchandise flapping in the wind around her. She surrendered to the silk lining. It breathed style, panache.

"For you, *mon enfant*, a thousand francs."

Her heart fell. "Not in my budget." She tried to bargain. "It's years old."

The stall owner's eyes narrowed in bargaining mode. "But never out of style. See, even with your jeans, the jacket adds *classe*. Trust Coco, I've always said. A little black dress or a jacket of hers takes you everywhere."

Eventually Aimée brought the woman down, but still it emptied her snout-nosed piggy bank. Couture, the woman insisted, meant hand-stitched work, fitted lines, something to wear for years—cheap at the price if you consider true quality. And at this price until it rots off my back, Aimée thought, feeling like a sucker all the way home on the bus.

From then on, she added a bit of Chanel if she found a piece at the flea market or consignment shop. Learned how to combine, accessorize with a scarf or old pearls. The goal was to look effortless and tousled, not too studied, spontaneous—the real chic, as madame insisted.

For Martine's party, she donned her cowboy boots, a silk T-shirt softer than skin, and the Chanel, then slipped into her lined leather overcoat.

In the courtyard, her breath fogged as she pulled her bike out from behind the old stable. With Miles Davis wrapped in his blanket in the straw bike basket, she double-knotted her scarf. Her pager beeped somewhere in her bag. She checked, but it wasn't her father or Elise. Annoying. Was the battery low again? She'd deal with it later.

She rode out of her courtyard onto the quai, over the damp leaves and along the Seine. At the corner she turned, narrowly missing the chestnut seller's cart. The aroma of roasting chestnuts and damp leaves—autumn smells—filled the street.

Ten minutes later, she was at *l'école de médecine*, passing the engraved wall plaque honoring doctors who had given their lives in the First World War. In the campus court-yard of Université Paris Descartes, Miles Davis watered the cobblestones. Aimée turned in her histology report and got a stamped receipt from the department secretary. By then her pager was beeping nonstop, piercing little shrieks. What appeared to be some kind of code in repetitive alphanumer-ics streamed across the small pager window. Had the thing jammed?

Miles Davis whined and pulled at his leash. Without a working pager, Elise and her father couldn't contact her.

"Isn't there an electronics shop near here?" she asked the secretary.

The secretary put her hands over her ears. "You need René."

"Who?" Aimée tried hitting the off button, but the power switch kept sliding. It fell off.

"The only one who understands these infernal machines."

Did she have time?

Piercing shrieks erupted again.

"That's breaking my ears. You need René," she said again. The secretary wrote down an address at one of the Sorbonne's science divisions and waved her away.

THE SORBONNE'S UNIVERSITÉ Paris annex in the rear of Palais de la Découverte reeked of damp paint and mildew. The "temporary" classrooms that had been lodged here since before the Second World War were lined with peeling notices, and there was an old bomb shelter sign—Abri—with an arrow pointing to the cellar. Aimée shivered in the cold warren of passageways. She passed through the student lounge with an upright piano and sagging sofas and found the computer lab, a few terminals bathed in the dirty pearlescent light streaming through tall windows.

The only occupant was a male dwarf with brown, curly hair. He wore a tailored wool coat and clicked away one-handed on a keyboard. With the other hand he popped glistening orange segments in his mouth.

"*Bonjour*, I'm looking for René."

"Pager problems?" he said, a deep voice for a small person. Absorbed in whatever program he was running, he didn't look up.

She set down her bag. Wished she could grab an orange segment. "So you're the pager wizard?"

"Depends. It'll cost if I can fix it."

She didn't care. "I'm desperate."

She noticed his goatee and big green eyes as he looked up and gave her the once-over. "You, desperate?"

In more ways than she wanted to admit.

"Interesting," he said.

Aimée shrugged. "Can you fix it?"

"Give me a second." He stood, flicked the pager over, pulled out the battery, inserted a new one, and attached a new power button.

Handsome little devil, she thought, noting his long torso, short arms, and muscular legs. Tried to remember the answer to last week's exam question—were achondroplastic dwarfs disproportionate and hypochondroplasia dwarfs proportionate, or vice versa?

He pressed the power button several times. Clicked messages. "Hmm. You're getting a message. It looks like what's called 'leeting.'"

"What's that?"

He grabbed a paper and wrote something down. "See, a code like this, using numbers to represent letters. So here 'loser' is 10ser. But this? 3838—well, the first part, 3838, means *bébé*. and the rest—that's saying *back off or else*. Looks like someone is threatening you."

A frisson rippled up her spine. "Who is sending them?"

René shrugged. "Want my help or not? Leave it and come back later. Or better yet, tomorrow."

"You're kidding, tomorrow? This *petite chose*?"

But René's attention was taken by two male students, one blond and gangly, the other in a jean jacket, striding into the room. Before she could ask how much fixing the pager would cost her, the jean jacket grabbed René's arm. She could almost smell the testosterone.

"You owe us, *petit*," he said. "Pay up."

"Your motherboard's beyond repair," René said. "Kaput."

"We want a refund."

"Didn't you understand when I said no refunds for work done?"

"Talking like a professional?" The blond laughed. "More like a pint-sized amateur." He shoved René into the corner.

She didn't like the feral look in the blond's eyes, or the way he pushed René. Bullies. "Leave him alone," she said. Miles Davis growled.

"Stay out of this," said René, shooting her an irritated look. "I don't need your help." Perspiration dotted his forehead.

Jean jacket looked her up and down. "Don't you have fingernails to file?"

Her damn pager erupted in more shrieks.

Torn, she wondered what to do. She couldn't stand by and watch the bullies beat René up. Her knuckles whitened, clenching the chair's back.

"Cough up this time or else . . ." Jean jacket lifted his fist, aiming at René's head. René caught his wrist, twisted his arm behind him, and shoved it upward in one move. So quick she almost missed it.

"Act funny and I break your arm," said René.

Jean jacket winced in pain. Nodded. René let go, shoved him forward. "Out, both of you."

Miles Davis broke off his leash, shot like a bullet, and bit the jean jacket's leg. *"Aïe . . . merde!"* Moaning, the bully tried to bat the dog away. "Pull that mutt off or I'll have animal control put him down!"

"Not before I put you down, *comprends?*" René grabbed the leash and pulled Miles Davis off. "Take this with you." He threw the bag with their motherboard after the two *mecs*.

When they had left, René said, "Why did you try to defend me?" His green eyes flashed. "Who do you think you are?"

Her cheeks reddened. She'd hurt his pride. Stupid.

"Two against one didn't seem fair," she said. Weak, it sounded so weak.

Not a scratch on him. "What you really mean is you didn't think a man of my stature could defend himself," he said. "I'm a black belt. Don't need some *bourgeois* Left Bank bobo like you to fight my battles."

"You proved that. *Désolée.*" Abashed, she averted her eyes. She rummaged in her bag among mascara tubes, her lab notebook, *ELLE* magazine, and her keys and found a treat for Miles Davis. "You're impressive, René. *Vraiment.*"

"So's your attack dog." René brushed dust from his shoulders.

"Him? He's a stray. I'm just looking after him for my grandfather."

Miles Davis's black button eyes were trained on Aimée.

"Could have fooled me."

"So how much to fix my pager?"

"I need a drink," he said. "Or two. Although I was going to go to the theater for the late matinee."

She checked her Tintin watch. Good God, Martine's party—she was late. The idea of going alone terrified her. A loser whose "boyfriend" was getting engaged to someone else this weekend.

"Drinks I can handle," she said. "Feel like a party? An exclusive one?"

His eyes widened. "Like a date?"

"Pushing it, aren't you?" Stupid—she needed his help. Grinned. "More lively than the theater."

He smiled for the first time. "Give me three minutes and your pager will be like new."

Now she had to put on a happy face for a party. She wished she could be spending her time tracking Elise down. Getting in touch with her father so she could tell him what had happened. Pursuing links to the second murder.

"Got any enemies?" René asked, studying her pager.

"No more than usual."

René snorted. "What does that mean?"

She pulled her compact from her bag and checked her makeup in the mirror. "I hand out my business card with the pager number like candy."

But her fingers shook as she freshened up her Chanel red lipstick. Everything crowded in on her at once, as if she were battling an ocean current, struggling to stay on the surface, to breathe—school, Florent, her father's lying about her mother and his secret trip to Berlin, the murdered man floating at the quai, the threatening pager message.

"I thought you were a student."

She nodded. "First-year med."

Hanging by her teeth.

"And you fix computers?" she asked.

"A sideline."

Miles Davis's tail wagged. She handed René her self-made Leduc Detective card. "Since taking a surveillance job last night, I've given out about ten of these." She thought about it; the clubs on rue de Ponthieu, Suzy, Marc, the bartender, the man working the café where she'd bought Suzy coffee, Elise's fiancé.

"How does a med student have time to do surveillance?"

"Got to earn my allowance," she said. He thought she was a spoiled rich kid. "Leduc Detective's my father's firm."

René's eyes popped. "Do you have a gun?"

"Not with me." It was home in the spoon drawer—the gun was last year's Christmas present from her grandfather. Looked like it was time to get it out. Brush up her skills.

By the time René had done his magic—something he referred to as ReFLEX Telelocator Numerical Protocol—and reset her pager, Miles Davis needed to water the plants.

GLINTS OF MIDAFTERNOON sun broke through black-and-blue-tinged clouds, revealing patches of indigo sky. The wet zinc mansards gleamed. The afternoon wind whipped the damp leaves around Aimée's ankles as she walked her bike above the quai, René at her side. After the first few minutes of walking with him, she'd stopped feeling so awkward about towering over René. About four feet tall, she figured. He kept pace; once he tripped, caught himself, and she pretended not to notice.

Now her eyes were drawn along the khaki-colored Seine to the spot under Pont des Invalides. Caught on the yellow crime-scene tape flickering in the wind. The execution spot.

Here, just behind the Palais de la Découverte.

Her mind returned to the night before: the blanketing mist, the police Zodiac's blue glow, the shouts, that piercing white light illuminating the dark red hole in the back of the man's head, the rag in his mouth.

Suddenly she had a powerful feeling that she had missed something. In the shock of discovery, something had eluded her—what was it?

"I've got to check something out."

René's brow shot up. "What about the party?"

"Only take a minute."

Ahead on the quai, wavelets buffeted the docked *bateaux-mouches* as a barge glided past. Passengers huddled in line, waiting to board.

"Don't tell me the party's on a boat? I get seasick."

She leaned down on the quai by the blocked-off area under the bridge's arch. The dark moisture-stained cobbles radiated a metallic damp.

"What are we doing here?"

"Anything here strike you as out of the ordinary?"

As an outsider he'd have fresh eyes. Not that there would be much left at the scene a whole day later.

René snorted. "Besides the crime-scene tape?"

Something flickered at the edge of her mind, but she couldn't quite capture it.

"Weird echoes down here," said René. He gave a shiver. "Spooky."

"You're right." She whistled, heard the echo bounce and play under the stone arch and over the curdling water. She studied the dim spot under the arch.

"Why did we come here?"

She'd pulled out the photo, consulted it. Tried not to focus on those dead eyes but instead on the shadows surrounding him on the quai.

"*Alors*, playing some game, Aimée? Either we go to the party or . . ." He paused. "I've got places to go."

If she didn't explain, he'd leave.

"*Désolée*. Last night I was standing right here when the police found this man. A waterlogged corpse."

René looked at the photo in her hand. Shivered. "Gruesome."

She nodded.

"If you wait here long enough, maybe you'll catch him," René said, finally. "The killer always revisits the scene of the crime."

She looked up in surprise. "And you know that how?"

"Agatha Christie."

Chambly-sur-Cher · December 1942

THE GERMAN MOTORCYCLES rumbled up the
road. Nearer and nearer. Any moment now they'd swoop
inside, discover the almost molten gold brick. Fear gripped
Gaubert—what could he do?

Minou grabbed a hunting rifle from the wall; Alain
leaned and pulled out his knife. Gaubert envisioned the
carnage—the German reprisals against the village, against
his Fanny and Gaby.

"*Non, non,*" he said, gasping. "Put those down right now."

Alain's eyes slit like a wild dog's. "I'll take care of them."

"Stop him, or we're dead," said Gaubert.

Rooted in terror at the approaching sound of the motorcycles, no one moved. Alain was about to lunge.

Gaubert grabbed the nearest thing, red-hot tongs, and
swung at Alain's ankles. Alain fell on the dirt, moaning in
pain. Then Gaubert punched him in the head like he'd
wanted to do for a long time. The idiot boy's eyes rolled
back.

"Do what I say, everyone," shouted Gaubert. "Now!"

"CURFEW, MONSIEUR?" GAUBERT hiccuped,
his fist around Baret's wine bottle. "*Mais oui,* we're warm
and toasty in here." Next to him on the floor an unconscious Alain, leaning against the bench; beside him
Philbert, Bruno, and the heavy-lidded Minou. Baret, his
back turned, was taking a leak against the back wall. They

all reeked of the wine Gaubert had spilled down their shirts.

The SS man in black jackboots gestured to his patrol, a motley, windblown quartet with dripping leather jackets. Water puddled around their boots on the dirt floor.

"*Die Franzoise, eh?*" He mimed drinking with his hand. The soldiers grinned. "*Ja wohl*, you drink yes and we manage your country."

Gaubert grinned. "We French enjoy life, join us."

The SS chief took off his moisture-ringed cap, exposing short blond hair and a large forehead. The Aryan ideal, Gaubert thought, and offered him the bottle.

"Drink?"

The SS waved off the bottle with a sniff of his nose, muttered "filthy peasants"—one German phrase Gaubert knew. His eyes narrowed, taking in the mare munching hay, the closed metal doors of the burning furnace. "*Was machen Sie hier?*"

"Nights when I get my horse shod need good wine. *S'il vous plaît,*" Gaubert insisted again offering the bottle. Nearby at the water trough, the mare neighed. Hot, so hot. Sweat trickled down the back of Gaubert's neck.

The SS man flicked a finger at his corporal. "You're a farm boy. Check if he's lying."

"*Ja wohl.*" The corporal hurried to the horse, paused, stroked the neck, patted each leg gently so the horse would lift its foot. "Newly shod, *mein Gefreiter.*"

The SS man nodded. The death's head insignia glinting on his collar. "*Gut.* Show me what's inside."

"*Comprends pas.*" Gaubert poked the unconscious Alain. "You understand him?"

"I said show me what's in there," the SS man shouted, pointing at the furnace. "*Raus!* Get up!"

Gaubert staggered to his feet, pain lancing his side, and grabbed the blackened gloves. Before he pulled the makeshift furnace door open, he gestured to the date on the anvil. Paused for effect. "Our old tradition, a custom on the longest night of the year. Solstice, *comprend?*"

One of the soldiers cleared his throat. "*Ja, mein Gefreiter, Wintersonnenwende*, solstice, the shortest day of the year. In Bayern we do it with—"

"I know," he said, impatient. "But they're hiding something. Open."

A strong fecal smell came from Bruno, shifting and moaning on the floor. He'd shit his pants in fear. A dead giveaway.

The SS man wrinkled his nose in disgust.

"Hurry up. Show me what's inside."

Gaubert pulled the door back and the SS man shielded his eyes from the blazing heat.

Then he shook his head. Laughed. "Horseshoes?"

"That's for good luck, we say . . . *viel Glück, non?*"

Beckoned by their *Gefreiter*, the soldiers came to look, crowding around the hot forge. Gaubert trembled, watching and holding his breath. Would it work?

The bunch of horseshoes were still cold in the glowing fire. Would it give them away? "That's our custom, we burn away winter with the old, make way for good crops in the new year." Gaubert turned his grimace of pain into a lopsided grin. Shrugged and felt a sharp stab from his rib where Alain punched him. Broken? His lungs seized up again and he doubled over, racked by coughing.

Gaubert pulled out his handkerchief stained with blood long enough for them to see. Blew his nose. "*Désolé.* Bad lungs. Tuberculosis." He gasped for breath. "The boys here, too."

Baret turned, his fly open, clearing his throat, then lapsing into a coughing fit.

"You shouldn't get too close," said Gaubert.

To a one, the SS and soldiers stepped back, nervous. Tuberculosis was frighteningly contagious. At least, he hoped they thought it was.

With another mutter of "filthy peasants," the SS turned on his jackbooted heel and ordered his men out, shouting about "quarantining the village."

"QUICK." BARET ZIPPED up his fly with the tip of his hook. The noise of the motorcycle engines faded. "Pull out the horseshoes. Get shoveling more coke."

"We can take our time, eh? They won't be back." Philbert grinned.

"But others will, Philbert." Gaubert leaned against the wall, shaking. "When Alain wakes, get him working."

"With a cracked head?" Bruno said.

"Nothing cracks his thick skull." Gaubert winced. "Now grab that rag and help me bind up my chest. And clean yourself up."

TWICE THAT NIGHT they had to re-pour the gold, a cherry-red-orange molten mixture, into the ingot molds. The laborious process took close to three hours. With nine more buried boxes left to melt . . . they had nights of work yet. It would be impossible, given the German patrols. They couldn't talk their way out of the same thing again.

In the early morning light, steam hissed from the cold water bucket as the last bar cooled.

After half an hour, they had ten ingots, like thick

chocolate bars, five hundred grams each. Heavy as half a country loaf of bread.

"*Voilà*," said Bruno, indicating the measured piles. "Bonbons for everyone."

"No bonbons for the orphans and widows across the river in Givaray," Gaubert said, voicing the thoughts that had been plaguing him since the night of the flood. "We're not going to get away with it forever."

"Gaubert, you worry too much," said Bruno.

If he didn't worry, how could he have gotten them this far?

Philbert wiped his hands. "We've got to plan a more efficient way to melt this down. And the hard part—Baret needs a travel permit."

"First I need a reason to travel."

"But it's perfect," said Alain, rubbing the knob on his temple. "Don't you need a new arm? That one's beat up, *non?*"

Gaubert shook his head. "Think, Alain. First Baret's got to find a willing contact who can take the gold."

"He'll need a cut for doing business," Baret said. "Remember that."

Alain spit. "How's that fair? We do the work and—"

"Any legitimate metals dealer would be taking a risk, Alain. Gold trade's been restricted since 1939, *comprends?* You expect a dealer to take a chance from the goodness of his heart? Wake up."

Gaubert nodded. "After the contact puts it on the market, it's just a matter of time until this SS bastard puts it together."

"Not unmarked gold on the *marché noir*," said Alain. "There are all kinds of things for sale—diamonds, paintings. That's the Jews' currency for escape. It's just knowing the right contact, eh Baret?"

"More complicated than that," said Baret. "We'll need

a willing dealer with assay equipment who'll take a reasonable cut. That might be hard to find. Get that through your head."

Gaubert thought of the danger fueled by greed. The gold wasn't theirs, no more than it belonged to the Nazis who'd plundered it.

"Give me my cut of this batch," said Gaubert. "Keep the rest, all of it—it's yours. I'm out of this."

Five pairs of eyes stared at him, all tinged with anger and suspicion.

"You're giving up your share in the rest?" Alain said finally.

"My gift to you," Gaubert said.

"What's the deal? What do you want?"

"My price? Never mention me and my family. I was never involved."

"You're afraid, Gaubert."

"Fear is healthy. Baret and I know that from the trenches. It keeps you alert. Alive. When this hell of a war is over, then you should sell. Just leave me out of it. *D'accord?*"

Alain snorted. "I don't trust you."

"That's rich coming from a man whose life I just saved. All of your lives."

"He's right." Baret nodded. Picked up a bar. "Each bar's worth a hundred thousand francs, give or take."

A hundred thousand francs? The men looked at one another.

"Mon Dieu," whispered Philbert.

Silence except for the horse's hoof pawing the dirt floor.

"Not just pocket money then," said Baret, his smile grim. "Wait until the war's over. Invest. God knows you'll have to launder the profits, hide it."

Morning light slanted from the forge's one window; the dying embers glowed faintly.

"Gold lust, it's a curse," said Gaubert. "It will ruin your every day . . . worrying, thinking, afraid, always looking over your shoulder. That's the price you'll pay the rest of your lives. It's not worth it to me. So I'm out."

"It's not that simple, Gaubert." Bruno shook his head. "You'd put us all at risk."

"Why?"

Philbert shot the others a look. "We owe you for last night. We won't forget. But we can't have you using gold which could be traced back here."

Gaubert would later wonder, if he'd relented and stayed with the group right on that dirt-floored forge, could he have changed what happened? But in that moment everything was decided for him.

"Papa?" A voice outside, drowned by cart's wheels rumbling over the stones.

"Gaubert!" called Fanny. Laughter. "We're home! My brother brought us. Gaby can't wait for you to catch the Christmas fish."

Gaubert stuck a bar in each pocket, strode out before any of the other men—exhausted, sore, and short-tempered—could stop him.

He never saw the looks on their faces.

Or saw, as he grabbed Fanny and Gaby in his arms and hugged them to him in the cold morning sunshine, the five men in the forge drawing from five pieces of hay. The man who'd drawn the short straw squeezed his eyes closed. Then he grunted and picked up the German rifle the sandbaggers had recovered from the truck.

"You'll have to do it tonight. On the riverbank."

Paris · Saturday, 4:00 P.M.

IN THIS QUARTIER below Parc Monceau, the crimson Chinese pagoda with jade roof tiles stood out like a red thumb, Aimée thought as she chained her bike.

"Your friend lives here?" said René.

"It's a surprise party . . ." She caught herself before adding, "planned by the birthday girl herself."

In the entrance hall, red lanterns dripped from the high ceilings and Madonna's "Like a Virgin" pumped from the speakers. They followed the music past red-lacquered screens festooned with lucky peaches to a black wood-paneled room where a trio of Martine's sisters shrieked the chorus. Shimmying and laughing, they waved to Aimée; each of them sported lace leggings, off-the-shoulder tops, jean jackets, and curly side-parted bobs.

René's green eyes bulged. "I've never seen so many mullets and shoulder pads in a pagoda."

Pink spirit lanterns, red peonies in black lacquer vases, sandalwood incense, and a giant gold Buddha completed the scene. Couples were dancing, embracing. She felt as counterfeit as the faux gold-painted Buddha.

"Finally," said Martine. Her hair had been gelled into blonde waves, and she wore a black mini, lace leggings, and short-heeled boots. She kissed Aimée on both cheeks with her maroon bee-stung lips. "Got a new boyfriend?"

Martine's voice boomed in the brief lull in the music.

Twenty or so couples and assorted guests turned and laser-stared. René shifted in his shoes.

She shot Martine a *don't go there* look and handed her the wrapped gift. "Happy *surprise* birthday, Martine."

Neda, who had been Aimée's nemesis at the *lycée*, said, "Love your accessories," looking pointedly at René and then Miles Davis—as if a dwarf and a dog were accoutrements. Everyone was looking at them. "Exotic. Your taste in men's changed since the *lycée*."

Aimée sensed René tensing up. She wanted to melt into the Chinese rug. Why had she brought him? This had turned awful. Cruel.

Beyond salvaging? Not while she still had breath. Gritting her teeth, she forced a smile and aimed a carefree laugh at Neda. "Meet René, a computer wizard. Absolute genius. And this is Miles Davis, whom I'm dog-sitting."

"I've never met a computer genius," said Martine, her mascaraed eyes widening.

René blushed. "Happy Birthday, Martine," he said.

"*Mon Dieu*, I thought the puppy was my present," said Martine, taking a drag of her cigarette. "So you're the two handsome new men in Aimée's life. Champagne?"

René nodded. "Why not?"

Martine winked. "Don't mind me, René. Welcome to the family."

Martine handed him a flute of fizzing champagne and kissed him on both cheeks. The next moment everyone's attention had returned to the champagne. Phew, Aimée thought, watching René relax.

The black lacquered walls around them were inlaid with gold lotus leaves. There was teakwood furniture everywhere.

"What is this place?" René asked.

"Monsieur Loo's pagoda," Martine replied. "Amazing, *non?* My uncle's on the board of his arts foundation. He suggested a *chinoiserie* theme."

Martine's extended family included a chunk of the aristos and old money at the party. Aimée saw a lot of them in this eclectic crowd of young and old, scattered amongst *lycée* friends and their dates.

Aimée had made her appearance; now she had to get to a phone.

"Do you know where I can make a call?" she asked Martine.

"Try my new present." Martine lifted up a grey brick-sized handset. Grinned like a satisfied cat. "The latest cell phone."

It was attached to a battery pack the size of Aimée's anatomy book.

"*Incroyable, non?* It fits in my Vuitton."

Just.

"But no one's been able to figure out how to turn it on," her uncle said, champagne in hand, joining them.

René's eyes gleamed. "Mind if I . . . ?"

Within seconds he'd switched on the power, pulled out the antenna, hit a button, and got a dial tone.

Martine kissed René again. "You're brilliant, René."

Martine made the first call on the new device—her coiffeur for an appointment. "How did we ever live without these? Your turn, Aimée." She took René's hand and danced away.

"LOVE SHACK" BLARED. Not again. Poor Miles Davis whimpered at the pounding beat. She wrapped her silk scarf around his ears, took refuge in a red lacquered room behind the golden Buddha, and consulted her now behaving pager. A number she didn't recognize. She punched it into Martine's phone.

"Allô?"

Aimée recognized Elise's voice. The connection crackled. "You sound far away."

"Comment?"

"Hold on." Aimée stood and walked around fiddling with the antenna until finally, at a teak-framed window, she got better reception. "Elise, we need to speak fast. I might lose the connection."

"You found Suzy?"

Aimée took a breath. "My report's ready."

Elise's voice rose in fear. "You tracked her down by yourself?"

"Yes, and spoke with her at length. She met up with your father the night he was—"

A gasp. "Suzy killed him?"

"Non, Elise. I need to go over the report with you. I'll explain." And learn what you know about my mother.

"Does she know who killed him?"

Fuzzing and clicks. Merde, this connection could cut out anytime.

"Listen, last night the police discovered the body of a man floating at the quai—murdered like your father. Was he your father's friend? Is that why you left the apartment?"

Pause.

"Elise, what's wrong? Why are you afraid?"

In the background a door shut. "I can't talk."

Couldn't or wouldn't?

"Elise, tell me the other men's names."

"Other men?"

"The men your father ate dinner with at Laurent every month," she said, exasperated. "I think this man . . . Can you hear me, Elise? They could be next."

"I'm counting on you to find Papa's killer."

This wasn't going how she'd planned. Hardly professional.

"Technically you hired us to find Suzy, Elise. I did."

"But you said Suzy met him. She knows," Elise panted. "You promised to find out."

She hadn't really agreed to find Bruno Peltier's killer. Shouldn't the *flics* have seen the pattern by now? Besides, Elise had wanted her father's help, not Aimée's. What would he say if Aimée pursued this? Did she really care right now, since he'd lied to her? One lie deserved another.

"How can I if you won't help me?" she tried again. "I need to know—was last night's murder victim one of your father's friends?"

She heard what sounded like a hand covering the receiver, a muffled a conversation. Couldn't make out the words.

"I've got an appointment," Elise said finally. "Talk to you later."

The phone had clicked off.

Elise was holding back. What was she afraid of?

LOST IN THOUGHT, Aimée stared at the chipped gold paint on the Buddha's back. Madonna's "Material Girl" was playing now. René was dancing with one of Martine's sisters, the one who was an editor at *ELLE*. Aimée pulled the report from her bag, opened it. Read through Elise's statement again. No useful names.

Elise seemed to want to blame Suzy for Bruno Peltier's murder, but Aimée knew that didn't make sense. She was also sure

Elise was hiding something. Before Aimée could do anything else, she had to find out the second victim's identity, verify her suspicions. She needed to find out if these other men were in danger, or if one of them was the killer.

If she could get the victim's name, she could cross-reference the photos she'd taken of the Laurent reservation page. The photos had all come out blurry except one, and that one was cropped, only half a page of names. Better than nothing. She'd start there. But first she needed to know who she was looking for.

No name had been released by the *flics*. But she did know a *flic*. Her godfather, her *tonton*, Commissaire Morbier.

Time to give him a call on Martine's latest *accessoire*.

Not in his office. After five minutes of wheedling and little white lies, she found out he was at the rue d'Anjou *commissariat*. According to her *plan de Paris*, which she kept in her bag at all times, that was a short bike ride.

She waved to René, who was dancing with Martine's sister. Dumped the cell phone by the Saint-Honoré cake and blew a kiss to Martine.

Outside, the wet streets glistened under the lamplight. She made good time on her bike with Miles Davis in the basket. The narrow *rue*, named for the Duc d'Anjou, whose brother became Henri III, formed an eighteenth-century mélange of small and grand *hôtels particuliers*.

In the courtyard, she chained her bike by the ancient blue police lantern and trudged up the stairs to the old-fashioned *commissariat*. An anomaly, lodged in a bourgeois apartment with wood banisters, stained-glass windows, and a parlor. According to the historical pamphlet sitting on the reception desk, Juliette Récamier, after whom the sofa was named, lived here, and the Marquis de Lafayette next door.

The place was permeated with the smell of sweat and fear
she recognized from every police station she'd been in.

She asked the policewoman at reception if she could see
Morbier.

"You have an appointment?"

She tried for an engaging smile. "I'm his goddaughter."

That and five francs fifty would get her a *café noir*, by the
officer's no-nonsense expression.

The frosted-glass door of a nearby conference room
opened, emitting tobacco smoke and laughter—and Morbier's unmistakable low voice.

"I'll just pop in," she said.

"Wait, you can't go in there," said the policewoman.

"Only take a minute." Aimée slid past before the policewoman could stop her. She recognized a few police hands
from her father's days on the force. His old card-playing
cronies: smiling Thomas Dussollier, whose daughter had
sometimes played with Aimée when they were small; Lefèvre
with his red-veined nose, who was stouter than she remembered. Lefèvre was a proud *Orléanais*, and it looked to
Aimée like he'd been enjoying quite a bit of his favorite
Orléanais beer, La Johannique, which was flavored with
local honey. He always brought it with him when he came
over to play cards; it was the first beer Aimée had ever been
allowed to sip.

And there was Morbier, his brown basset-hound eyes
registering his surprise. His jowls sagged and his thick lips
turned down in disapproval. An expression she'd met often
as a teenager.

"Shouldn't you be in school?"

"*Bonjour* to you, too, *Tonton*." she said. "Class is over, by
the way."

Dussollier kissed her on both cheeks. "Long time, Aimée. Before you start curing the rest of the world, I wish you'd start on my arthritis."

She grinned. "*Grand-père* says the same thing."

"*Bon*, I'll get in line." Dussollier and Lefèvre paused at the door. "Best to your papa."

She nodded, grateful. Not many men on the force would acknowledge him these days.

Morbier shook his head. Aimée noticed his thick, dark hair was silvering at the temples. He closed the dossier and nodded to the policewoman. "It's all right, Morgane," he said.

"You're Jean-Claude's daughter?" The policewoman cocked an eyebrow. "But I remember you doing your home-work after school, when I was a rookie."

Aimée grinned in recognition, noticed her stripes. "That's right. Made sergeant, eh?"

The phone rang. Morgane winked. "Say hello to your father."

"*Merci*, Morgane."

Aimée noticed a big blackboard with GUCCI HEIST writ-ten on it. Names—a few celebrities she recognized. "Big case, eh?"

He shrugged. "I'm assuming school's going well and you're studying for exams?"

As if she'd tell him otherwise.

"Fine. Could you do me a favor?"

"Favor? It's not a good time, Aimée. This isn't even my turf—Robbery pulled us over here and I'm stretched thin."

He ran all over the place. Always had.

"The Eighth is rampant high-end crime."

Who knew?

"Rolex watches nabbed, a Gucci heist off the

Champs-Élysées, boutiques and jewelry stores robbed in broad daylight. A highly organized gang."

"I'll be quick," she said. "Can you take a look at the report from last night's homicide—the body recovered under Pont des Invalides? I need to know the ID of the victim."

"Eh?" She heard surprise in his voice. A rarity.

"Only take a second, *Tonton*." She smiled.

"That's classified information, Aimée. What's it to you?"

"Didn't you refer Elise Peltier to Papa? This is for her case."

"*Attends*, Aimée. How does this go together?"

"Doesn't it? Or you think there's a random serial killer shooting old men execution-style on the quai?"

Cellophane crinkled as he opened a new pack of Gauloises. He scratched a match on the table edge, lit up. Took a long inhale. "Let me talk with your father."

Treating her as if she were still five years old!

"Papa's in Berlin. He asked me to follow up with you and find the man's identity," she lied. She remembered the joy of stealing his Gauloises when she was younger.

"*Quoi?* Don't you have exams?"

Couldn't he talk about anything else?

"*Bien sûr*, and Papa's got rent to pay. I'm helping out."

"Tell your father that information's under wraps, pending family notification." Morbier flicked ash. "He'll understand."

Fat lot of good that did her.

"Aimée, did you run this by your father?"

What her father didn't know wouldn't bother him. Plus he'd lied to her.

She nodded. "You referred Elise to us, Morbier. But we can't help her if we don't know the second victim's name."

They stared at each other. Blue smoke spiraled in a coil up to the high ceiling.

"How about just saying *oui* or *non* to some names, that work?"

"What in the world's gotten into you . . . ?" Pause. "Since when do med students have time for side gigs?"

"When it involves family," said Aimée. "Elise is my cousin." Another half-lie. She took out the list of names she'd pulled from the Laurent reservations book after ruling out one- and two-person parties. "Mondini, Guerbois, Pribault? Anything strike a bell?"

"What are we playing, *Questions pour un Champion?*"

The *télé* game show.

"More like a game where you tell me if you recognize the victim's name."

"And I'd do that why?"

"To assist Papa's inquiries and identify the next potential victim. That work for you?"

His heavy-lidded eyes narrowed. "And your father wants this information? Sounds like you do."

"Didn't you refer Elise Peltier to Papa? *C'est-ça, non?* We're just trying to do what you told her we would. She says the *flics* do nothing."

"Pah, there's a forensics slowdown. The *brigade criminelle* deal as best they can. She's a nuisance."

Should she try a personal plea? "Can't you do a small favor for your own goddaughter?"

"So I used to take you to ballet lessons," he said, exhaling. "So what?"

So much for that strategy. One for the minus column.

"Look, I'm in the middle of a robbery investigation. Full-on."

"What's new?" Aimée said, annoyed with him now. So stubborn. "Elise broke down in tears in our office, begging us. Her fiancé says a police suspect turned out to have an alibi."

"*Et alors*, the *brigade criminelle's* got to prioritize, but they're investigating and she's not helping by meddling."

"Can you help me or not?"

A sigh. He stabbed out his cigarette and the Ricard ashtray clinked into a water glass. She'd seen him do that a thousand times. Another sigh as he stood up. "No promises."

While she waited, she munched the crudités and *jambon cru* she'd pocketed from the party. Shared some of the ham with Miles Davis, who'd woken up.

"Who's this?" Morbier had returned with a stack of folders. Miles Davis licked Morbier's pointing finger. "Another of your *grand-père's* strays?"

She told him.

"*Meels Daveez?*"

"He likes you, Morbier. Can't you just tell me the victim's name?"

"How do I know? I grabbed the latest homicide reports. Takes time to go through them. So read me your list of names quick or we don't do this at all. I've got a meeting."

Better than nothing.

She read out the names she'd culled from the reservation log in the photo. "Mondini, Guerbois, Pribault."

Morbier thumbed the reports, keeping them out of her view. Shook his head.

"Dubois, Pepy . . ."

"Any with a B?" asked Morbier.

"Could be . . . " She pulled out the blurry photo again, but the angle of her hurried shot distorted the letters. "Would it be Ba . . . looks like B-A-R . . ."

"Baret?"

Had to be. Party of three. Two other names listed in the left margin—those names she could make out.

"That's him. He dined with an Alain Dufard, and Phil-bert Royant." She tried to contain her excitement at the discovery—after all, it could be a coincidence. The blurry name might be something else entirely; the second mur-der victim, Baret, might not actually be a friend of Bruno Peltier's, or have anything to do with him at all. But she remembered what her *grand-père* had said about coinci-dences—they usually weren't. "Those other two men need to be warned," she said.

"Warned?"

"What if they're in danger?"

"That's supposition, Aimée."

"A supposition you can't afford to ignore. Were Bruno Pel-tier's friends, whom he dined with the night he died, even questioned? Now it looks like a second man from that group has been executed in exactly the same way. I don't need a crystal ball to tell you the others might be next."

Morbier snorted. "Well, our crystal ball's called *evidence*." He gestured to the board. "This is how it's done. Piecing together solid evidence to build a case." Another shake of his head. "Now look. I have my hands full with my own cases. This isn't even my department. Belongs to the *brigade criminelle*, who have it under control."

Under control? Hadn't he hinted the case ranked low in priority?

"Now you tell your father he owes me."

Lichtenberg, Former East Germany
Saturday Morning

"YOU OWE ME this, Gerhard," said Jean-Claude Leduc, pulling his wool scarf tighter in the slicing wind.

Gerhard, his contact, put his hands deep in his coat pocket. Jean-Claude heard coins jingle.

"And my contact owes me," said Gerhard. He was an unusual-looking man, with high Slavic cheekbones, slanted eyes, and thick black hair. "You know how it works."

Favors begat favors here on the grey street in Lichtenberg, where the Stasi had their headquarters on the outskirts of Berlin. The prewar buildings were pockmarked with bullet holes. The HQ, a stark, oyster-grey concrete building, stood next to a weed-choked bomb site. It had once housed the main office of the Soviet Military Administration in Berlin; before that it was a Wehrmacht officers' mess.

"*Et alors?* I expected the documents ready and waiting for pickup. Like we've always done, Gerhard."

"My contact went out celebrating," said Gerhard. "He got drunk after the Wall fell, set fire to his Trabi. Expecting a Mercedes like everyone drives in the West." Gerhard grinned. And when he did, the Asian in him surfaced. The child of a Mongolian soldier and Prussian mother, he'd been conceived in the Battle of Berlin as the Soviet troops invaded. Gerhard never knew his father. After a long night of drinking, he once told Jean-Claude he doubted his mother knew him either. She'd been hiding in the basement when a Soviet Mongolian troop found her. His mother hanged herself when he was two. There were many like Gerhard, *Russenkind*, though Gerhard said no one talked about them. He grew up in an orphanage in what became the East.

Jean-Claude rubbed his hands. So damn cold. "Why is it you're just telling me now?"

"I'm not," Gerhard replied. "When your daughter woke me up in the middle of the night, I told her, too."

His heart caught. "She called you? Why? Something wrong?"

His little princess, worse than a squirrel after a nut.

"*Nein*. Not from what I heard. She was going to leave you a message at the hotel."

Jean-Claude hadn't had time to check in.

"What did you tell her exactly, Gerhard?"

Gerhard scanned the windblown street. "Your daughter? I said my contact went incommunicado, I think. She woke me up."

A man in a leather jacket walked by, stopped to greet Gerhard in Russian. Gerhard spoke Russian, German, French, and British English, the Allies' language of his childhood on the rubbled Berlin streets.

"Give me a little *trinkgeld* for my contact. You know, so he can get himself some schnapps for his hangover. Hair of the dog, you call it?"

Gerhard still surprised Jean-Claude with his inimitable Berliner gallows humor, cynical and irreverent. Not even the most hardened homicide *flics* he knew came close.

Reaching back in his overcoat pocket, Jean-Claude pulled out a handful of West German marks. "What else did my daughter say? You didn't tell her anything, give any names, did you?"

Gerhard's eyes narrowed as he looked over Jean-Claude's shoulder. "There's my contact, he's going in the gate. If I don't hurry I'll miss him."

Jean-Claude reached in another pocket and thrust a wad of American dollars in his hands. "Get it, Gerhard. Beg, borrow, steal, promise anything. I mean it."

Gerhard nodded. "Wait for me in that *Kaffeehaus*. The same one."

The wind whipped gusts of shredded paper and a yellowed *Berliner Tageblatt* down the street as Jean-Claude watched Gerhard go. The time was now, before Stasi officers shredded and burned their way through several decades' worth of intelligence files. They wanted to protect informants, hide government crimes, and cleanse the archives of any evidence that would be used against them. Or, in some cases, they wanted to sell the files to the highest bidder.

Walking through the Berlin streets, Jean-Claude felt the euphoria and confusion—all the rules and regulations were out the window. He had to make the most of the chaos as the Wall came down.

HE LINGERED A moment on the street. Felt a curious tingling up his neck, like a sixth sense. He turned around. Only vacant windows like hollow eyes, a man and a woman pushing a baby buggy across the windswept street. Their laughter floated on the wind.

His remembered pushing Aimée in a buggy like that. She'd been muffled up for a cold November. Sidonie's arm was in his, her other clutching a sketchbook, as they walked on the quai after her drawing class. He remembered stopping in the steamy, warm café. Sidonie's laughter at Aimée's look of delight as she tasted her first sip of *chocolat chaud*.

A bus pulled up, the couple mounted, and then it was gone. He was alone again on the grey street.

In the *Kaffeehaus*, a utilitarian establishment heated by a coal stove, he debated on a coffee. Went with the *bière*. With his change he went to the phone cabin by the dirt-streaked window. Seventies prefab blocks, anonymous and drab, were scattered between rundown nineteenth-century buildings.

He tried Leduc Detective. No answer; he left a message. Worried, he tried Aimée's pager. The phone ate up his coins before he could put in the hotel's number to retrieve his message.

What had Aimée been up to, calling Gerhard in the middle of the night? For now he put that aside as he sat at the gouged wooden counter. He had to keep the desperation at bay, to count on Gerhard succeeding, as he always had.

From force of habit his mind went to Monday's upcoming surveillance at Place Vendôme. Ticked off the boxes again, mentally checking each task. Each dreaded task.

A reminder had arrived in this morning's telegram with the message NO ONE EVER LEAVES. He'd thrown back, WATCH ME.

He pulled out Soli Hecht's card. Pushed it back and forth between his fingers. But why would Soli offer him a contact when Soli could go for Sidonie's files himself—as eager as he appeared for her Hezbollah connections? Or would he use Jean-Claude to do the work while he had bigger Nazi fish to fry?

Or . . . Sidonie was the Hezbollah contact and Soli planned on pressuring him to make her cough up the others.

He pushed a twenty-mark note across the counter. The walrus-mustached barman looked up. "Beer or change?"

"Both, *bitte*."

Coins in hand, he turned and saw the phone cabin was occupied. But from the corner of his eye, he caught a woman's face outside the window. Only a moment. And then, with that remembered stride, she was gone.

Could it . . . ?

"Forget the beer." Jean-Claude bounded off the stool, grabbed his coat and pushed his way past the heavy draft curtains, through the swing door, and out to the street.

He ran.

At the next street he saw people boarding a streetcar. The flash of a leg, that familiar slant of her shoulder. It was her. *Mon Dieu.* Sidonie.

He made himself speed up. The tram's doors were closing. He waved his arms, yelled for the driver to stop.

But it took off just as he reached the platform, panting and gasping for breath. He saw her profile, the hint of carmine lips, and then it was gone.

Paris · Saturday, 5 P.M.

SEARCHING THE PHONE book at the corner café, with Miles Davis sitting at her feet on the cracked mosaic tiles, Aimée found several listings for the men. After calling a number of them, she whittled them down to three and wrote the addresses in her lab notebook. None of these numbers answered or had an answering machine. She fumed. If only Elise had given her more information. But she was committed now; she couldn't stop.

She'd take the chance there would be a family member at home at Baret's house, given the tragedy. Or maybe Dufard and Royant were there themselves, offering condolences? At least it was a place to start.

She cycled past the Ministry of the Interior's side exit on rue des Saussaies. Whenever she passed it, she thought of the Resistance members who were tortured in its cells. Her father, who had been inside often, had described the messages and names scratched by fingernails into the walls. "What man did to man"—he'd said with a shake of his head—"under the cloak of Vichy . . . The ministry hid this for years."

No one talked about it then. Or now. One never knew what another person's past was, what he might have done during the worst days of the war, or what he might have suffered. Better not to know certain things about your friends, her father once said.

Behind the soot-darkened hulk of Saint Philippe du

Roule Church, she saw fragments of the old Roule village, famed for its goose market in the thirteenth century. At the Place Chassaigne-Goyon, once Roule's center, on the side of the church was an *allée* of wooden nineteenth-century storefronts. Any day it would fall to gentrification, but for now it held small shops. By a *crèmerie*, under a faded *boulangerie* sign, she spotted a miniscule café advertising international phone cards—specialty Asia. Here, in one of *les quartiers les plus chics* of fabulous wealth, this was no doubt where the help came to make phone calls home.

When she located Baret's address, a three-story limestone affair, she buzzed the tarnished button by his nameplate.

An older woman in an apron answered. The concierge.

"*Mais oui*, mademoiselle, I clean for Monsieur Baret, but he's out."

Out and he wouldn't be coming back.

"Does Monsieur Baret live alone or have other family?"

"Alone, as far as I know. Family? Outlived them, he once said."

She could rule that out. But she had to reach the two other men.

"Haven't his friends come by?"

The concierge shrugged.

"I don't mean to trouble you. When did you last see him, madame?"

The concierge rubbed her hands on her apron. Took a notepad with her shopping list out of her apron pocket. Consulted it. "Must have been two weeks ago. He's not here much these days."

She hadn't heard about his murder.

"He asked me to work today because I couldn't last week. I just got back from my sister's—"

"That's helpful, *merci*," she said, cutting her off.

"What's this about?" The concierge's brow creased in irritation.

Better lighten up or she'd lose this woman's help.

"*Désolée*, but I'm a relative of the Peltiers, his old friends. Just got into Paris, no answer at the Peltiers', and I've lost the numbers for *messieurs* Dufard and Royant."

"*Comprends pas*. How does that involve Monsieur Baret?" she said. She shifted her mop and took a step back into the foyer. "I'm busy, mademoiselle."

Afraid the concierge would close the door, she thought quick.

"*Zut*, I'm meeting them all for dinner and I don't know where," she said. "I'm stranded. Can you help me? Would Monsieur Baret's address book be handy?"

"A very private man, Monsieur Baret," she said. "Not my place to go through his personal items. I value my job."

The *flics* would be going through them soon enough. She felt guilty not telling the woman, yet if she revealed Baret's murder she'd get no link to the others.

"I understand. Any idea where he could be? If I can find him, I can ask him which restaurant."

"*Désolée*, mademoiselle. But the bookstore's right down the street. I'm sure it's all right for me to tell you that."

"I don't understand."

"The bookstore. Monsieur Baret used to run the place. He's still involved." The concierge stuck a rag in her pocket, stepped outside the door. Pointed. "*Voilà*, you can't miss it. The hunting bookshop."

Couldn't miss it? The shop was the size of a postage stamp, its dark red storefront hidden in the shadows behind the church. Librairie Dupont—*tout de chasse*. A hunting book

store, old shelves lined with both new and antique leather-
bound tomes on hunting and falconry. Aimée felt like she
was stepping into an 1880s lithograph.

"*Allô?*"

No answer. Aimée shouldered her bag, which con-
tained a sleeping Miles Davis. The bookstore foyer opened
to a wood-paneled reading room with flickering fire
under a marble mantelpiece. She wouldn't mind sitting
down. A perfect spot to study her anatomy textbook. But
she had work to do.

Further on was a stockroom with floor-to-ceiling books.
A cold, brisk draft came through the open back door. The
door to the back office was also half open, and a whirring
sound came from within.

"*Allô?*" She stepped into a state-of-the-art office—computers, boxes of floppy disks, a printer—a complete contrast to
the store's antiquarian ambience. No one here. An open
bottle of sparkling Evian sat next to a computer screen,
across which ran a fast-moving string of numbers and letters.

Familiar. She'd seen something like this before. Where?

Her gaze caught on a framed black-and-white photo on
the wall. It showed a group of young men standing by
a barn with a horse cart. Taken during the last war, she
figured, noting the men's clothes and the Vichy label on
the horse's feed sack. She thought of the plastic Vichy
bottle on the quai. Under the photo was a label that read
CHAMBLY-SUR-CHER. The envelope she'd stolen from the
Peltier apartment had been forwarded from Chambly-sur-
Cher.

Pinned to the corkboard was a typed agenda with today's
date:

Peltier estate
Baret
Dufard
Royant

The names from the Laurent reservation. A thrill rippled up her spine—it was all there, all the pieces she had puzzled out together in one place. It was almost too good to be true.

"Who are you, before I call the police?" said a voice behind her.

Chambly-sur-Cher · December 23, 1942
Midnight

WILD THYME SCENTED the cold midnight air on the riverbank. The Cher gurgled peacefully below Gaubert. So unlike that night more than a month earlier, the night of the flash flood, the gold bars, the dead soldiers who drifted from their watery grave. The truck still lay sunken beneath his dangling fishing line. What ever happened to the fifth German soldier, Gaubert wondered, but he pushed the thought aside for once, savoring the moonlight that silvered the alder leaves into shiny mirrors. He crumbled the chalky soil in his fingers. He'd concentrate on his family, being together with Fanny and Gaby for Christmas. Like always.

At this time of night, trout fed among the long, green river grass that flowed like hair in the current. On Christmas Eve, for a treat, Fanny would serve his catch, *merval*, the freshwater catfish, baked with garlic, a specialty of the Sologne region.

He'd already caught two silverbacks when he heard the rustling in the bushes. Starlings, he thought, disturbed by a squirrel close to their nests in the blackberry brush. But then branches crunched and someone grabbed him from behind— large hands jerked his arms back and bound his wrists behind him. He managed a garbled shout, but a dry cloth was stuffed in his mouth. His heart pounded like a hammer.

What was happening? The Germans? The fifth soldier, who'd floated away and now come back for the gold?

Muffled church bells pealed in the distance.

Gaubert heaved, gagging on the rag clogging his throat. Acid bile filled his mouth. He sputtered and gasped for air.

His head was slammed from behind and pain shot through his skull. He reeled, partly blinded by blood filming his eyes, and collapsed on the band of withered, blond grass stretching to the Cher. He wanted to plead for his life, but all he could do was shake with fear and hope somehow to bargain his way out.

The rag was pulled out of his mouth. Gaubert blinked tears and blood. The swallows twittered in the bushes as he crawled toward the glistening Cher.

"*Nom de Dieu*, the gold's buried in my barn," he cried. "Take it."

Gaubert felt the gun barrel against the back of his head. The last thing he heard was the metallic click of the trigger.

Lichtenberg · Saturday Afternoon

JEAN-CLAUDE LOOKED FOR a taxi. Nothing. Not even a Trabi in these godforsaken, rubbish-strewn East Berlin streets.

He'd seen the tram number and destination—Alexanderplatz. The last stop before the now crumbling Wall. Not much good, but a direction.

Sidonie could be staying in the East or West, no Checkpoint Charlie controls now. Ten to one she hadn't trusted him to come for her Stasi files, had taken the risk of coming herself.

He had to find her, to see her.

He kept going, crossing wide barren avenues intersected by small cobbled alleys, passing bullet-pocked buildings and vacant lots. Another tram came rumbling and the brakes screeched. He jumped on, his gaze trained on the passersby as it neared the center of town. He'd lost her. Again. Gone.

Paris · Saturday, 6 P.M.

A MIDDLE-AGED MAN stepped in front of Aimée, blocking her view of the computer screen and peering at her over drooping black-framed glasses that sat on his cheeks.

"What are you doing in here, mademoiselle? *C'est privé.*"

Mon Dieu—her gut wrenched. Staring at her on the corkboard was what could be the hit list. And this man, the killer?

Breathe, think, as Papa would, do not run scared. If this was Baret's bookshop . . .

"You're trespassing."

She racked her mind to come up with an excuse. Best defense is a good offense, he'd say.

"*Alors*, you didn't hear me call out?" she said. She hefted her bag, expelled air in irritation. "I know I'm late."

"Late?"

Play dumb and see what he knew.

"*Zut!* A Métro slowdown. What have I missed?"

She prayed her bluff would work. That he wouldn't notice her shaking hands.

He looked more irritated than nervous. "Who are you?"

She noticed now his white shirt with a black armband, an old-fashioned mourning tribute. He also wore celluloid cuff protectors. A real last-century bean counter, although she guessed he was only in his thirties. He didn't look much like a killer. But they didn't walk around with it stamped on their forehead, as her father often said.

"Monsieur Peltier's daughter, Elise, sent me. I'm her cousin." She neglected to say how distant. If this was the killer, she hoped her lie on the fly would protect her. "And you?"

"Mademoiselle Peltier never told me she had a cousin," he said. From his sneer, she could tell her youth counted against her.

"Calling me a liar now? How does that concern you anyway?"

"I'm going to call the police."

Merde, this wasn't working. "Go ahead. But check with Elise first." Aimée set her bag down on the nearest swivel chair, marking her territory. "I'm not leaving until you tell me what's going on."

He blinked. At least, she thought he did, but it was hard to tell with those glasses.

"I'll need to verify you're who you say you are," he said, his arms braided over his chest. Typical defensive posture.

She smiled. "And I'll need to do the same, monsieur."

He shifted on his high-gloss black shoes. "That's my desk." He pointed to a name plaque that read M. PINEL, DIRECTEUR FINANCIER. It stood next to a small photo of him in hunting gear holding a rabbit carcass.

She suppressed a wince. Dead animals—not her thing. She noted his muscles were visible under his shirt. If he'd murdered two old men, would he . . . ? She pushed that thought aside.

"Not so painful, was it?" She handed him her Leduc Detective card.

"You need more than a fake ID to prove a connection to Mademoiselle Peltier. I'd say you're fishing around for private corporate information. And a very clumsy effort at that," he said. "An amateur."

She hoped the flush burning up her neck didn't show.

"Well, since you've decided," she said, "let's get Elise on the phone and explain how obstructive and unhelpful you're being." She set her jaw. "Go ahead. Call. I'm wasting time and she's paying for my services. I charge by the hour."

His chin quivered. Doubt. Good.

Two minutes and several phone calls later, he hung up. "I'm unable to reach her and confirm your story."

What the hell was he so cagey about? No customers had come in while she'd been there. The place felt bogus. A perfect front for another kind of business—she thought of a case her father had worked on in Deauville, when a shop had been a front for a gambling den.

"Then we'll need to figure out how you can cooperate in my inquiry on a trust basis. Clarify for me your relationship with Monsieur Baret and his partners."

She didn't know that but took a guess.

"Relationship? I'm just an employee." Pinel sighed. "*Alors*, we cancelled the meeting out of respect for Monsieur Baret's passing. Everyone was informed."

What meeting? But instead she said, "You mean of Monsieur Baret's murder, *n'est-ce pas?*"

He swallowed. His Adam's apple strained at his starched white shirt collar. "The police notified me this morning."

"Doesn't he have family they'd inform first?"

He shrugged. "Maybe they did."

"You mean at the flat here on this street?"

"He lives . . . lived mostly on Place François Premier now."

So what meeting with Baret would Elise have known about? Unless the hit list was really the meeting memorandum—it did say AGENDA and had today's date.

"How did Dufard and Royant react to the news?"

"You'd have to ask them."

Aimée sat back down without an invitation. "Look, it's not my business what goes on here. That's outside my scope." She pointed to the black-and-white photo. Took a chance. "But two of those men were murdered. Royant and Dufard might be next."

"Like I said, you'd have to talk to them. I just work here."

"Where are *messieurs* Dufard and Royant?"

He adjusted his sleeve cuff. "I left them messages. Haven't spoken to them in a week." His pale complexion had flushed pink.

He was hiding something. Or lying.

The phone rang from the shop. "Now if you'll excuse me, it's time for me to work and for you to leave."

She stood and made a show of patting Miles Davis, settling him in her basket. Meanwhile she readied her camera, which she'd pulled from her bag. As the bean counter went to the door, his back turned for the first time, she took rapid photos, coughing to hide the clicks. On a last-ditch impulse, as she was following him out the door, she shuffled the closest floppy disk and stack of papers off the corner of the desk and under Miles Davis's blanket.

AIMÉE HUDDLED UNDER a blackened stone portico across from the bookstore, hidden by the church's shadows. It was 7 P.M. and the bookstore would close soon; when Pinel stepped out, she'd follow him. She didn't know what she would learn from him, but she had a hunch he might lead her somewhere.

She looked at the papers: the first was a spreadsheet, then what seemed like a draft of an article of incorporation.

Having the proper company name, she'd be able to locate their business license, shareholders, board, a tax ID—maybe a trail from there. One practical thing she'd learned in med school researching a boring pharmaceutical company.

Just then she saw movement behind the shop door. Pinel turned the OPEN sign over to CLOSED, peered outside. A minute later the lights went out. She pulled on her wool cap, leaned against the damp stone. Minutes passed, and still no Pinel. Night had descended on the dark street.

Merde, he must have gone out that back exit. She let Miles Davis finish doing his business in the gutter. A taxi, its light on, stopped in front of her where rue de Courcelles narrowed. One of its headlights was dimmer than the other. *"Non, merci."* She waved it off.

The door swung open, blocking her way out of the passage.

So persistent. She couldn't see the driver, but she intended to give him a piece of her mind. She reached forward to shut the door.

All of a sudden her arm was yanked sideways by a steel grip. Her forehead hit the doorframe—pain exploded in her temple. Her vision flickered. Another yank and she was being pulled inside.

"Let go of me!" Her aching head was pushed down into the passenger foot well, her lower half hanging outside. Screaming now, she couldn't see anything but the dirty floor mat. Somehow she curled her booted ankle around the doorframe, trying to pull back and leverage out with all her might. Her arms lashed out and her fingers caught something.

She heard a rip. She swung out her elbow, hit air. Pathetic. Then again—this time she heard a grunt.

A horn blared outside. If only she could get herself out of the car. Miles Davis barked. Another elbow jab found its mark. The grip loosened. Fighting the pain, drawing on her last bit of strength, she pulled loose. The taxi shot forward, and her legs were dragging on the cobbles. The engine whined. Somehow she shoved off the dashboard and tumbled out, the door swinging into her head. Again.

Brakes squealed and she found herself lying on the cobbles in a car's headlights.

"Falling down drunk this early?" An irate woman was silhouetted in the headlights' glare, her hands on her hips. "You young people!"

Aimée blinked, raising herself up on her elbow. Her head swam, her tights were torn, her knees were scraped raw. Her bag—had he taken it? It held her whole life. "Where's my bag?"

Miles Davis whined, pawing the cobblestone as he sniffed her bag where it lay on the pavement. She could have sworn he understood her.

"I almost ran you over," said the woman.

"That taxi driver attacked me," she said. "Did you get a look at him?"

"Attacked you?"

Like she'd lie about that. "Did you see the taxi number? Or the company?"

"Looked like one of those gypsy cabs."

Driven by con artists—on the sly with no taxi license. The damp cold seeped into her limbs, numbed her feet. She got to her knees, pulled herself up from the curb.

The woman gasped. "You're bleeding." Then she had her arm around Aimée's shoulders, helping her into the car. "I'm taking you to the *clinique*. There's one just a few blocks away."

"*Non*, take me . . ." She scrabbled in her bag for a card.

But everything was spiraling, going dark. Miles Davis was licking her face.

Givaray · Saturday Afternoon

HEINZ FELSEN EXAMINED the algae-encrusted remains of the German troop truck in the old garage. An empty, rusted shell. Disintegrated tires. Reeked of the river. "That's all?"

The garage worker, a young kid wearing jeans, shrugged. "*Alors*, I'm afraid you made a wasted trip."

"Where is the German soldier's burial site?"

The kid shrugged again. Looked bored. "Before my time."

Heinz concealed his frustration. Did his accent cause the yokels to put up roadblocks? He'd made the trip; he had to find out something. "Show me where you found it."

But the kid picked up a drill. "The river's straight ahead. Can't miss it. We dredged the truck right there in the deepest section by the mill."

No respect, this generation, Heinz thought.

The river's olive green-colored water flowed and swirled under a sky the color of tin. Whatever secrets it held, he could see no trace of them. Standing on the bank, gazing at the river and the village on the opposite bank, he sensed eyes watching him. His noticeable accent and age had drawn looks in this place. People remembered. It wouldn't do good to spend time here.

"YOU HAVE A *carte de visite*, monsieur?" asked the grey-haired woman about his age who'd answered the church rectory door.

He had several, but none this woman would appreciate.

The minute he'd opened his mouth and asked for the priest, Père Robert, she'd stiffened. His smile and his little bow hadn't fooled her. For a moment he thought she'd yell *dirty Boche* and slam the door.

"I'm sorry, not with me."

"If you write down your name, I'll let him know when he returns . . ."

"The *comtesse* told me to contact Père Robert."

"Come back later, monsieur."

Her face went blank. She was lying. Some things never changed.

But he wasn't here to interrogate her, just the priest.

He handed her Marie's old-fashioned *carte de visite*—an elegant, thick, pale-pink vellum—with her *comtesse* title. "I believe she arranged an appointment."

The woman took the card, then spit on his shoes. "No German enters this house of the Lord."

He met her gaze. "I'll wait."

Hate simmered in her eyes. She shut the door.

Heinz walked in the rectory garden, among its leafless trees and bare rose bushes. Below, the bank led to the river, where it crooked like a hairpin. Voices came from an open window in bits and snatches.

"Père Robert . . . *traumatisée* . . . your family . . ." was all he could catch.

Heinz noticed how the garden extended to the water's edge. His gaze caught on the flowing, dull-green river, how it swirled and eddied, lapping on the bank.

A while later, he grew aware of a presence. Turned to see a priest wearing a black cassock—a man in his sixties, white hair and a thin, long face.

"Hypnotic, *non?*" said the priest. "I watch the river for hours. Meditate."

"Père Robert. I'm Heinz Felsen."

"I know. He said you would come."

Heinz twisted the ring on his pinkie. "You mean, after all these years . . ." His throat caught, couldn't finish.

"I want to show you something," said the priest. "This way."

Paris · 7:30 P.M.

"NO RETINAL DAMAGE," said a voice close to Aimée's nose. White halos filled her vision—a probing light in her dilated eyes. "But we won't know the extent of your head injuries until we examine the X-rays."

Aimée groaned. Her temple throbbed, as did her shoulder, courtesy of the taxi door. Why hadn't she taken that self-defense class? There were too many classes she wanted to take—and too many she needed to take.

Another doctor had come into the small *clinique* room.

"What are you doing here?" the first asked. "I thought you were off this weekend."

"Plans changed," said the new doctor, consulting Aimée's chart. "Let me take over on this patient." He reviewed her file for another moment as he waited for the first doctor to leave. "A medical student should understand the potential gravity of a head injury. Shouldn't you know better, Mademoiselle Leduc?"

"Know better than to walk my dog on the street and get attacked?" she said, irritation rising. "*Attends*, how do you know I'm a med student?"

He gestured to her student ID and the *carte d'assurance maladie* clipped to her chart. She got a look at him for the first time: thin, middle-aged, blond hair whitening at the temples. Vaguely familiar—maybe he taught classes at her school.

"My son's a medical student at Université Paris Descartes, as well," he said.

Her pager started beeping on top of her coat. She reached, missed. It clattered on the examining table. The doctor picked it up, glanced at it, did a double take.

Pause. "And he appears to be paging you."

She froze. Wanted the earth to open up and swallow her. Now she remembered Florent saying that his father, a top surgeon, consulted at a *clinique* in the eighth. Just her luck. The father who, Florent had complained, insisted he follow in the medical family tradition.

But what was Dr. de Villiers doing here if Florent was getting engaged this weekend? Come to think of it, why was Florent paging her now, of all times?

"Why's my son paging you now?"

She shook her head. Winced. "I don't know."

"Let me guess—you're the one in that picture in his room?"

Florent's father saw her picture from that all-night party?

"From what I gather, you know each other well," said Dr. de Villiers. His thin eyebrows knit in disapproval, reminding her of how Mimi's were drawn on—the apple didn't fall far from the tree in this family.

Trying to cover up her shock, she shrugged. Her shoulder throbbed. "From what I hear, Florent's getting engaged." *And you and Mimi resent me for getting in the way.*

"Not today."

Hope fluttered in her heart. She couldn't help it.

"My aunt had a car accident. We've postponed the engagement party."

Hope flew off on wings. No wonder Florent was paging her. He assumed she'd be waiting and available.

A nurse stepped in with the X-rays. Dr. de Villiers studied them and clipped them on the lit board. "Good news,

Mademoiselle Leduc. The radiologist has concluded no cranial involvement," he said, in professional mode now. "You'll just have a lump." He pointed to the greyish-white image of her skull on the backlit screen. "See here. It's normal. But if impact had occurred three centimeters to the right, your orbital cavity would have been affected."

Looking at the image of a human skull, she thought of the details in Peltier's autopsy report, of the bullet entry hole at the back. The shot would have to have been fired at very close range for the stippling and gunshot residue evidenced on the autopsy. Similar findings would appear, she figured, on Baret's autopsy report, once they got around to it. But she hadn't seen any bullet casing on the quai—her photo was clear enough that she thought she would have spotted it if it had been there. This was different from the Peltier crime scene, where, according to the police report, they had found a nine-millimeter casing. What could that difference mean?

"How often, would you say, in a case of a close gunshot to the back of the head"—she pointed to the spot on the image of her cranium—"would a bullet lodge in the brain instead of exiting?"

"Excuse me?"

"What are the odds, would you say?"

"Is this for a class project?"

"It's a hypothetical question, doctor." All doctors like hypothetical situations. In such cases, they can't be blamed, held accountable, or sued. "Approximately what percentage of bullets shot from a distance of say this far"—she stretched her arms—"would exit and leave a casing?"

"You're quite something, mademoiselle." He shook his head. "That's not my area of expertise, and I'd need exact measurements. But in med school, when we did the forensic unit, I asked a similar question. I remember the forensic pathologist speaking of a total of maybe four or five cases of a bullet exiting the soft tissue of the brain. That's out of hundreds of cases he'd worked on."

Her pager went off again. Awkward.

"Bordeaux has an excellent forensic pathology department," said Dr. de Villiers. "You're bright, mademoiselle. You'd do excellent and succeed there, and transferring is easy. I'll smooth the waters with my old colleagues."

He wanted to get rid of her. So hypocritical, making it sound like he had her interests at heart.

"I could never leave Paris." Couldn't and wouldn't. She reached for her Chanel jacket. Slipped her pager in the pocket. "Why do I sense you're warning me off, Dr. de Villiers?"

"I'd say you're not the type to take second place."

He got that right.

"So you've been the one messing with my pager and sending me threatening messages?"

Gone and opened her big mouth again.

His shoulders tightened. "Threaten you? As if I have time for that, mademoiselle?" A muscle in his cheek twitched. "*Désolé*, my daughter gets carried away sometimes."

Mimi? She could believe it.

"But like I said, you're smart. You should see a wonderful opportunity opening up, I'd imagine. Florent is taken."

Cruel, too, Florent's father. His words stung. "You think it's me chasing Florent? It's the other way around."

There. Let the aristocrat chew on that.

"Be careful not to muddy your January exam scores," said Doctor de Villiers. "Everyone knows cheating's rampant. Any hint or allegation and an exam is void. To the point, mademoiselle, my old friends on the board at Descartes will think as I do."

"I hope that's not a threat," she said with more bravado than she felt. "My godfather's a *commissaire* in the police."

Fat lot of good that would do her. She grabbed her bag, slung it over her good shoulder, and ran out the door before she could hit him with it. The gall.

At the reception, she wheedled the duty nurse for use of the back office phone. The nurse, who'd been dog-sitting, was happy for a few extra minutes to shower Miles Davis with treats, and Aimée slipped behind the desk.

Her pager showed three pages from Florent. Screw him and his father.

Shaking, she dialed into the Leduc Detective voice mail as she downed a painkiller with several slugs of Evian. Blinked her dilated eyes—damn blurry vision.

A message from Elise, her voice trembling. "*Maman*'s had a stroke. I must see you. The last train from Gare de Lyon leaves at nine twenty-five."

Aimée grabbed her anatomy notebook and a kohl eye pencil, the closest thing to a writing implement she could find in her bag. She wrote down Elise's directions and checked her Tintin watch. Just enough time to leave Miles Davis with her grandfather and grab some clothes. Looked like she was leaving Paris after all.

THE BRANCHES OF an ancient pear tree, Aimée's favorite, spread a shadowy canopy over her courtyard back at home on the Ile Saint-Louis. The pear tree was one of the reasons she loved living here, despite the freezing, wet winters, the sputtering heat, the icicles which hung from her bedroom ceiling in years of record cold.

Miles Davis scampered beside her up the marble steps to the third-floor apartment.

"Ça va, ma puce?" Her grandfather stood, an apron around his middle, over the copper pot of something smelling wonderful.

She settled Miles Davis by the radiator. Took a breath, leaned against the counter.

"A run-in with a gypsy taxi."

"The fancy *clinique* called and said you'd had an accident. Before I could find my keys to come pick you up, they'd rung again and said you'd discharged yourself."

"No accident, *Grand-père*," she said. Shivered. "I was attacked by a taxi driver. I'm getting close to the truth about Bruno Peltier, that's why."

"Wait a minute, young lady. You'll tell me what happened."

She condensed it—the corpse's identity, the agenda at the hunting bookstore, how it felt like a front. She tried to keep the trembling out of her voice.

"So this gypsy taxi was a plant; you're being trailed by someone who wants to kill you and followed you to the bookstore?"

The way her grandfather put it opened her eyes. Scared her. The thrill dimmed. But she couldn't give up the chase. And wouldn't know any more until she confronted Elise.

He banged down his stirring spoon on the tiled counter. "Too close for comfort. Back off. Don't throw yourself in danger."

"That's why I'm going *à la campagne*."

"The countryside at this time of year? Don't you need to study? Aren't exams coming up?"

Not this again. Like she didn't worry about it all the time?

Her eyes welled. She didn't want to tell him. Wouldn't tell him.

"Your turn with Miles Davis, *Grand-père*. I'll return tomorrow."

She turned away. Wished her shoulders wouldn't shake. Wished she could stay in this warm, fragrant kitchen and feel safe.

"*Ah, ma pauvre.*" His big arms enfolded her. His wiry mustache scratched her cheek. "There's something else. What's really wrong?"

He tilted her quivering chin up with fingers smelling of tarragon. Stared deep into her eyes. She blinked and the tears flowed. She never could hide things from him for long.

"*L'amour,*" he guessed. "Picked the wrong one again? Ah, you take after me." He sighed. Hugged her. "In so many ways, *ma chère.*" With a deft touch, he dried her cheek with the edge of his apron. "It's that Florent, the one who's been calling all afternoon?"

"I hate him. He's getting engaged." She inhaled her grandfather's musky smell. "Can you believe it? Just my luck, his father treated me at the *clinique*. He warned me off Florent. Threatened if I don't transfer to medical school in Bordeaux, he'll make sure I fail the exam."

"One of those, eh?" Her grandfather kept his arm around her shoulder and guided her to the stool. "You did tell him your grandfather's retired *Sûreté*, and your godfather is a *commissaire?*"

She nodded. "Don't tell Papa, please."

He paused. "Never trust a doctor, Aimée. Hypocrites milking the system. At least with a criminal, you know where you stand."

Sometimes.

He took in her look. "Medical school's making you unhappy, *ma puce*. Maybe you should do something else. Something you feel passionate about."

He'd never pushed her, unlike her father.

"But I can't give up, *Grand-père*."

"You don't have to look at it that way, Aimée. *Vous allez trouver votre place*."

You will find your place. That common saying. But it made her think. Where was her place? What was she good at?

She looked at the time. Late—she'd miss the train. She ran her fingers through her spiky hair, smoothed it down. Winced at the pain in her shoulder.

"I've got to meet Elise."

"Not a good idea, Aimée."

"Until I do I won't know what's going on." Or about her mother, but she left that out. "No use trying to talk me out of it, *Grand-père*. I'm catching the train."

Her grandfather smoothed his mustache, a thing he did when thinking. "Did your father sign a contract with Elise?"

"She paid us a retainer, *Grand-père*." Under French law, institutional and archaic as it was, a PI's investigative scope was narrowly defined by contract. Aimée needed to get one to cover her *derrière*.

"What were you thinking?" said her grandfather. He shook his head.

She changed and threw in a change of clothes in her worn Hermès, along with another pair of boots, her makeup kit, the dossier of her notes, her surveillance log, the photos. She called a taxi. No gypsy taxi for her.

Her grandfather stood waiting for her at the door with her old school lunchbox, which emitted smells of rabbit with mustard sauce, and a contract form. "Take this. It's standard. Have her sign off and come home."

CLOSE TO MIDNIGHT, Aimée, in black leather pants and parka, gripped her bag and climbed from the short platform onto the third train, a diesel engine nicknamed Micheline, finally bound for Chambly-sur-Cher. Elise had painted an optimistic picture when she'd said two train changes. That was on days other than weekends, holidays, or August.

She breathed the acrid fumes and the tang of oil. At least the eyedrops had worn off. A nasal voice over the crackling loudspeaker announced timetable changes, then finally trumpeted their imminent departure.

Biscuit crumbs crunched under her as she sat down. She whisked the mess onto the floor. A young half-Arab man, headphones plugged into his ears over dark sideburns, escorted a bent, white-haired woman into the compartment. He seated her across from Aimée, sat down, then promptly ignored her.

The engine snorted, then chugged off. Aimée peered out the window, but only saw one track, a single-gauge line. What did they do when they met another train?

"Bertrand," the old lady across from her shouted.

No response. The young man's eyes were closed and his head shook rhythmically.

"Bertrand!" A roll to her Rs, typical patois of a *Berrichon*. The deep country of *la France profonde*.

She kicked him in the shin and he glared.

"Stick the eggs on top," she commanded, pointing to her shopping bag.

"*Oui, Grand-mère*," he said, and meekly complied.

Half asleep, Aimée watched the train zigzag past dark clumps that hinted at the lush forests she might see by daylight in the Sologne. They trundled through low-lying mist blanketing what she imagined were wheat fields. She caught glimpses of running deer beside the track in the engine's light. At the dirt road crossings, the train's piercing whistle scattered billows of startled night birds. Only a few hours outside of Paris, yet this region felt like another world.

The train finally chugged into Chambly-sur-Cher's white stone station. A line of washing hung limply between the rafters in the lit station house. The station mistress, in jeans, gold loafers, and a tight Lakers jacket, approached with a lit cigarette dangling from her mouth. With muscular arms she pulled the chute that swung the main track aside, then waved back to the engineer.

Aimée descended, relieved to have finally arrived. Her heeled boots crunched on the dusty gravel in front of the station. The way to the village was illuminated by a string of lantern lights. Her heart dropped—no Elise.

The old woman drew near, leaning on her cane. Her grandson had shouldered their large shopping bag.

"I'm visiting the Peltiers," Aimée said. "Know them?"

Her grandson looked up. "Who doesn't?"

"If you have trouble finding them, let me know." The old woman winked. "Everyone knows me."

"*Merci*, I will. Your name is . . . ?"

"Madame Jagametti," she said, spitting the Ts sharply.

Madame Jagametti, with her darkly handsome grand-son escorting her, shuffled down past Chambly-sur-Cher's old village wall, which was crumbling and plastered with faded circus posters. In some places bald stones were all that remained of the ancient Roman wall curving into the neighboring forest and beyond. The three-quarter moon illuminated rolling hills, slate-roofed farmhouses, and lines of cypress trees. The silver-green of a river snaked in the distance.

A battered blue Renault screeched to a halt by the row of bare-branched plane trees. The car door swung open and a large man lumbered out. He was in his fifties, his shiny bald crown ringed by thinning dark hair, reminiscent of Friar Tuck. His overalls needed patching.

"*Bonjour*, I'm Clément. Mademoiselle Peltier asked me to pick you up. I'm a friend of the family." He extended a large paw-like hand, which Aimée shook. "*Ça va?* Easy trip?"

His tone was light, but Aimée noticed his guarded look.

"Plenty of local color," she said and nodded toward the retreating figures of the limping madame and her grandson. Clément grunted and heaved her luggage onto the cracked upholstery of the back seat, which released a few chicken feathers. He climbed behind the wheel and ground the transmission into first gear.

Aimée gripped the door handle as the car lurched forward. Already she had a bad feeling about Clément's driving. From the way his mouth was screwed up, she could see it didn't come easily to him.

"I'm used to a tractor." He shrugged. "But driving is like riding a bike, *n'est-ce pas?* You never forget."

Aimée gave him a thin smile. She didn't have a car or want one, but she knew how to drive, more or less.

"Why didn't Elise meet me? Has her mother's condition worsened?"

Clément narrowly missed a late-night yellow mail van

that turned out of an alley. He shrugged. "Gone to the emergency room. That's all I know."

Sounded serious. But weren't all strokes? "Best you drop me at the hospital."

"That's all the way in Vierzon."

Vierzon? She could have gotten off before the last transfer—she'd be talking to Elise right now.

"Wouldn't it make it easier if I caught the train back to Vierzon?"

"The last one left an hour ago."

Great. So now she'd be stuck here for the night without getting answers from Elise?

Chambly-sur-Cher's main square was bordered by a late-century *mairie* with a limestone façade, the town hall, *la poste*, and a shuttered café, deserted in the night. Twisted, narrow streets radiated from the square, vestiges of a market town's medieval grid. The place felt lifeless, so unlike her grandmother's village in the Auvergne.

She might as well try to get what information she could from this Clément.

"You said a family friend—how do you know the Peltiers?"

"When hasn't my family known them?" he replied.

"So you're a local, a *Berrichon*," she said. "Then you know *messieurs* Baret and Dufard."

He hunched his shoulders. "Me, I live across the river in Givaray now, where there's work."

What had once been a thriving river town, Aimée imagined by the look of the many shuttered houses, had dwindled to an almost deserted village. The Renault passed a *boulangerie*, its windows lined with blue, white, and red bunting. Next door was an abandoned shopfront with several battered bicycles leaning against it.

Clément careened past the spurting marble fountain. She wished he'd take it easy.

"Almost there." Clément honked at a dog. "It's just around the corner."

The corner happened to sit at the edge of the village, down a stone-walled sliver of an alley. Maybe wide enough for a horse cart, Aimée thought. Fat drops of rain splattered the windshield, multiplied, turned the dirt into muddy rivulets. A downpour. Several times the car door scraped the old stone walls as Clément maneuvered, cursing under his breath. Finally he jumped out to pull open a pair of metal gates, which grated over the cobblestones.

Bare wisteria branches climbed the tidy two-story stone farmhouse—modest compared to the Peltiers' Paris apartment. Aimée caught dark-green shutters being pulled closed from inside. The rain poured as Clément hefted her bag out. Panting, muddy, and wet, they stood scraping their shoes on the mat until the carved wooden door opened.

A dark-haired woman, handsome although her face was webbed with fine wrinkles, shook Aimée's hand. Bony and thin, the woman had a surprisingly strong grip. "What are you waiting for, Clément?" she boomed. "No need for formality when you're being drenched. Come in!"

The woman pulled Aimée into the sitting room, stuffed with aging upholstered furniture. The cramped room, small and lived in, was lined with oil paintings—mostly pastoral scenes, amateur but skillful.

Provincial, all right. Who was this—the Peltiers' country housekeeper?

"Call me Honorine. I'm Clément's mother. Elise asked me to settle you in," she said. "Some warm milk before bed?"

Treating her like a baby? What in the world had Elise told them?

"*Non, Maman,* she'd prefer a tisane." Clément winked and left for the kitchen.

Aimée sank into a sagging armchair. "I'm confused. Elise called and insisted I come at once. And she's not even here." She looked askance at Honorine, hoping the woman liked to talk.

She did.

Over herbal tisane, Honorine recounted how she'd come to visit this afternoon and discovered an immobile Madame Peltier by the cellar stairs. *"Quelle horreur."*

With more probing, Honorine continued: *Mais oui,* such a tragedy, Monsieur Peltier. *Oui,* Royant and Dufard had family homes here in the village but lived somewhere else. Rarely saw them, but of course, when Elise returned, there was time to visit.

Time? Not in Aimée's schedule. Her own life was on the line. She needed answers.

The dull throb in her head wouldn't go away. Rain beat against the shutters.

"How far away are their houses?" she asked.

"Monsieur Royant's family house is next door and Dufard's is down the street," said Honorine. "Like I said, they don't live here."

"Where's poor Monsieur Baret's house?"

"Ah, that's not occupied much, either. He never comes."

Aimée stowed that fact away. Honorine seemed to be forthcoming. Time to amp up her questions.

"Does Monsieur Baret have relatives here?"

Honorine shrugged. Stuck her large hands in the loose pockets of her black cardigan.

"*Alors*," said Aimée, "I thought maybe his murder the other night was the reason Elise and her mother came here."

"What?" Shock painted the woman's face.

"Terrible. Shot on the quai, in the same spot as Monsieur Peltier."

Fear, almost palpable, emanated from Honorine. What was she afraid of?

"You didn't know?"

"Why would I know?" Honorine said, trying to sound dismissive. "He's a neighbor I haven't seen in ages."

The woman was hiding something. Aimée could smell it, as her father would say.

"But he and Monsieur Peltier were in business together, *non?*" She was going on a hunch, based on the meeting agenda she'd seen at the bookstore. "As well as the other two, Royant and Dufard?"

Honorine stiffened.

"Good friends, weren't they?" Aimée pressed. "They all got together in Paris every month to have dinner at their favorite restaurant."

Why was Honorine so quiet all of a sudden?

"But you must know about *les affaires*," said Aimée, nudging. "Do you know what kind of business it was?"

"You're tired." Honorine had shut down tight as a clamshell. She went to the door and pulled out an umbrella. "Clément will show you to your room."

CLÉMENT LED HER up polished wood stairs, down a hallway, and then down another before he opened a creaking door. Faded floral wallpaper, floor-to-ceiling windows overlooking the rain-drenched garden. A sunflower-print duvet covered the low wooden bed.

Aimée wondered if she looked as uncomfortable as she felt. Or as spitting mad. She'd come on a job, not on holiday, pressured by Elise, who wasn't even here. Elise, who stonewalled her at every turn.

And her head hurt.

"Clément, did Elise give you a message for me? The information I asked her about?"

"Me?"

Aimée's rain-soaked travel bag, which Clément set down, dripped on the wood floor. She grabbed a hand towel from the marble-topped dresser and wiped the floorboards. "Clément, I need your help. Can you tell me why Elise called me here? Or anything about the Peltiers' family business?"

He drummed his sausage fingers together. Shrugged.

Exasperated, she said, "Listen, this is important. Elise's father and another man, a Monsieur Baret, were murdered in Paris. The same way."

"He who pees in the wind wets his teeth." Clément's voice was so low she almost didn't catch it.

Her pulse jumped. She was wide awake now as the insinuation took hold. The answer lay in this village.

"How's that?"

"Everything's so complicated." Clément raked his thick fingers through greying hair. He was tongue-tied by indecision, she thought.

Aimée watched him, waiting. Don't fill the silence during questioning, her father advised, let them speak first.

"Elise is a good person," he said, finally. "I remember her as a little girl. She's stayed that way—sweet, innocent. Her parents sent her to school in Montreal—she's been away for years. Now she appears, scared and asking me for a favor."

She read it in his eyes: Clément was sweet on Elise.

She heard her father's voice—*Do whatever you have to do: cajole, flirt, empathize. Intimidate as the last resort. Just find what they're hiding. They're always hiding something.*

"Something happened here during the war, didn't it, Clément? That's what Peltier's and Baret's murder have in common, *non?*"

This was the first time she'd seen a man's mouth drop open in surprise. He nodded. "No one talks about it."

Score! she almost shouted. She was getting somewhere.

"What? What was it that happened, Clément?"

"You seem awfully curious for someone your age."

"Two men have been murdered, Clément. Men from this village."

Aimée saw a struggle in Clément's face. He'd picked up a polished stone shaped like an arrowhead from a collection on the shelf. Prehistoric silex stone tools—she remembered from a *lycée* history class. The Loire Valley had been populated long before the Romans arrived, before the Gauls were even tribes.

"Anything you tell me stays within these four walls," she coaxed, hoping she came across as trustworthy and confident. What would it take to reach this stubborn peasant?

Clément fingered the silex, a mottled greenish brown. His wariness seemed to get the upper hand and he silently shook his head. "You're a kid playing detective. And like all Parisians, you expect the world."

"*Alors*, Elise is family. My cousin. Can't you trust me? I'm useless to her if I don't know more background."

Clément hesitated. She needed to make up his mind for him.

She reached for her handbag on the old burl wood desk

and took a big breath. "I'm sorry for what I'm about to show you. Does it strike a chord?"

Clément stared at the photo of Baret's bound body against the quai. His big hands shook.

"Where did you get this?"

"More to the point, what if Elise is in danger, too?"

Perspiration beaded Clément's upper lip. That got to him.

"What is it, Clément? What are you thinking about?"

An intake of breath. "The old nightmare."

That's all he could say? Here she was, clutching at straws—so close she could smell it.

"What do you mean?"

He averted his gaze. Well, he wasn't going to open up. Time to try something else.

"Call me a taxi, Clément," she said. "I'm going to Vierzon."

She was leaning down to grab her wet bag when Clément spoke. "Wait." He pointed outside the window, to the rain-distorted mercury of the river. "It was Christmas, 1942. I was eight. I went down to the river and found the mayor shot in the head. There."

"Mon Dieu." Wide-eyed, Aimée sat down on the lumpy bed. Winced as her shoulder hit the wall.

She'd been eight when her mother left. It had marked her for life. How had his discovery marked Clément?

"Thought it was a dead animal at first . . . I'll never forget the smell. And the black flies. That day had turned warm for December, his body had been lying in the sun."

Aimée nodded, never taking her eyes off Clément.

"Later Papa yelled at me," he said. "He was mad that I had followed the men who found the body. They didn't know I'd tagged along to fish." Clément's jaw quivered. "I never understood why he got so angry. But it was the four men you've mentioned—Bruno Peltier, Alain Dufard, Philbert Royant, and the jeweler, Baret."

Aimée suppressed a gasp.

"And there was a fifth man, too, the blacksmith, Minou. He died at Liberation."

Aimée nodded in encouragement. "What happened when you found the body?"

"The men told me that Gaubert, the mayor, was *un traître*. That he'd been shot by the Resistance. After that, my parents wouldn't let me go out," he said. "Not even to school. Or to see my friends."

"So Gaubert was a traitor—why does that matter now?"

Clément shook his head. "Who says it does? Terrible things happened then. We'd hear shots at night, machine guns across the river in Givaray." His eyes moistened. "The Germans executed sixty villagers one morning." Clément shrugged. "My parents never talked about it. No one did."

"Sixty people executed, the mayor shot, and what—everyone goes silent?" She shook her head in disbelief. "I've heard villages are like fishbowls; everyone knows everyone's business."

"Don't you understand? Times were different. People shut up, kept their heads down. No one wanted to be next."

"Next?"

Clément shrugged again. His whole generation had such chips on their shoulders—always talking about how they'd gone hungry, worn wooden shoes stuffed with newspaper, how her generation wouldn't understand, blah blah, on and on. If she asked questions, she'd get a long sigh and a hooded look, a murmured *you wouldn't understand*. Their past only dribbled out in unguarded moments—a detail here or there when memory took over. Move on, she wanted to shout, the war ended more than forty years ago.

She would try again—ask him specific questions.

"Were *messieurs* Peltier, Royant, Dufard, and Baret involved in the Resistance?"

"I was a kid. What would I know?"

A kid, but not dumb or mute.

"But didn't you say they told you the mayor had been a traitor? That the Resistance had shot him?"

"Like I said, I was a kid."

She needed to ask him something more specific, try to draw him out. She thought back to Baret's hand, those prosthetic fingers. "Do you remember Baret? Would he have lost his hand or arm in the war?"

"Came from the next village, a jeweler. Lost his arm at the Somme, like my uncle. The villages were full of war-wounded when I grew up."

"What about after the war? Has something come out recently?"

Clément paused in thought. "There were things the grown-ups talked about when they didn't think we could hear."

"What did the grown-ups say?"

"Pah, the usual. The mayor's wife slept around, their son wasn't his, that the mayor had knifed the *Boches* over a black-market deal, or maybe he knifed them for making time with his wife . . . things like that."

For a kid he'd heard a lot.

Village gossip, a necessary evil since time immemorial. Gossip equaled currency, clout in the village. Sounded like this gossip's roots had taken hold and deepened over the decades. Still, why did it matter now?

"What happened to his wife?"

"She blamed the villagers for killing him. *Un peu fou*—you know, not right in the head. They locked her up in the loony bin, my mother said once. Never came out."

Convenient.

The rain lashed the window. A steady drumming pelted the roof tiles—a veritable downpour.

The mayor's story connected to Peltier and Baret's execution-style murders—she was sure of it, although she didn't know how. Either that, or someone wanted to make it look like it connected. And the gypsy taxi was involved. She shuddered thinking of it.

Someone was lying. Had lied for years.

A thought formed in her mind, indistinct.

"And their child?"

Clément shrugged. "A class clown, accident prone—that I remember. My mother pitied the boy. No clue what happened to him."

Aimée tried to make sense of Clément's words. "Why would someone want to kill *messieurs* Peltier and Baret in the same way the mayor was killed?"

"How should I know? You're not accusing me, are you?" said Clément. "Plenty of others saw the mayor dead."

"Then . . . why is this happening now?"

His face sagged. "There were some who made money in the war. That's what my parents said. What everyone says to this day—at least, the old ones who are still around."

Aimée turned this over in her head. "You mean wheat farmers who somehow made out during the war? Suddenly became wealthy?"

"Rich as Croesus, the old ones say," said Clément. "Whoever Croesus is."

"Croesus?" She searched her memory. "That's right, the legendary Greek—he's the wealthy king who first minted gold coins."

She saw Clément stiffen.

The phone rang downstairs.

"That's Elise." Clément hurried away and clattered down the stairs. She put on dry socks and her low-heeled Valentino boots and caught up with him. He was pulling on his overcoat.

"Elise's car's stuck in the mud," he said.

"I'll join you."

"Turn the heater on. I'll be right back." Then, in a blast of wet wind, he'd rushed out the door. She heard his battered Renault start up.

Great.

On second thought, she wouldn't mind warming up—and it was a good chance to delve into the Peltiers' past. With the place to herself and any luck, maybe she'd be able to find more about this corporation whose info she'd taken from the bookstore's sleek office.

She fiddled with the furnace controls until it rumbled to life and heat radiated from the floor vents.

Her stomach growled. Hungry even after the rabbit her grandfather had packed for her, she peered in the pantry. Flour, rice, salt—the staples, along with glass jars of Petrossian caviar, foie gras, Fauchon tins . . . a gourmet treasure trove. One of those big jars of caviar would cost more than the rent of someone's Parisian apartment.

She helped herself from the tin of Hediard truffle biscuits. Picked up a newspaper lying on the faded-green linoleum floor.

La Gazette de la Loire, dated this past October. It was

folded open to an article headlined DISCOVERY IN THE
CHER: GERMAN WWII CONVOY TRUCK FOUND SUB-
MERGED NEAR OLD MILL OF CHAMBLY-SUR-CHER.

Not that uncommon. Farmers found war relics all the
time, unexploded ordnance and even active toxic mustard
gas, left in fields since the First World War.

The military truck's ID had been tracked—it had been
bound for Portugal, bearing "recovered contents" of a German train, and had disappeared during a bombing raid on
Vierzon. In the article a Georges Ducray, a Givaray resident
who was quoted at length, insisted the sunken truck was
linked to the execution of sixty villagers by Germans in
1942.

This article was only a month old—why hadn't Clément
mentioned it?

After her snack, Aimée started snooping. The choc-
olate-brown file cabinets yielded little besides old wheat
crop reports. But according to these, Bruno Peltier's fields
belonged to a cooperative. How had he made all his money?

Outside the kitchen window a light shone in the opposite
building. Two figures were silhouetted against the curtains.
Even in the pounding rain she could make out their raised
arms. A fight? She unlatched the window hook a few centimeters. Inhaled the dampness, the scent of molding leaves.

The room across the way had gone dark.

About to turn back, she heard raised voices over the
splashing. What sounded like two men arguing. Was she
hearing what she wanted to hear, or had one of the men
said the name Baret? She leaned forward. Tried to hear, to
understand, catch a phrase.

Impossible in the pounding rain. Concentrate, she had to
concentrate. A glass shattered. *"Imbécile."* The slam of a door.

Then quiet, apart from the splattering rain outside.

She retraced her steps as she heard the grinding gears of the Renault. Ran upstairs to get a sweater from her bag, and to pop a painkiller. Back down in the warm kitchen, she found Elise huddled at the table. Clément had his arm over her shoulder.

Elise's tear-swollen lids, the rings under her wide-set eyes, her drawn, pale skin made her look as if she'd aged overnight.

Clément looked up, his brows knit. "Snooping around, kid?"

"Shush, Clément. Tell me what you've discovered about Suzy, Aimée."

"It's all in my report. Isn't that why you wanted me to come?"

"Your report? But I thought your father was taking this on—"

"Time's essential, Elise," she interrupted, afraid of where that was going. Worried she wouldn't get Elise enough in her debt to ask about her mother. "It's all here and with photos."

Elise opened the file Aimée put down on the table. Thumbed through, her fingers shaking.

"So Suzy's connected to my father's murder?" Elise said.

"Not that I found, Elise."

For a good fifteen minutes Aimée explained her surveillance report, detailing her activities up to her visit to the hunting bookstore and finding the agenda for the meeting.

"Eh, what's all this mean?" Clément snorted. "You solved nothing. Child's play."

Aimée seethed. He gave her no credit for all her work, much less recognized the professional quality of her documentation.

But Elise, not Clément, had hired her, and she'd delivered.

"If you'll just sign this contract, please. The job was to find Suzy and talk to her," she said to Elise. "I found Suzy and talked to her. It's all in the report. Now can we talk about my mother?"

"Mother?" Elise looked up, startled. "What do you mean?"

What did she mean? "But you knew my mother. Told me there were photos."

Elise expelled air from her mouth. "I met her once."

Aimée's stomach tightened. "What?"

"If you can call it that," said Elise. She uncorked a bottle and poured herself a glass of wine. "You know, we never kept in touch. Your family had the nerve to shun us over Papa's uncle's illegitimate son. A baby who died."

Hadn't her *grand-père* hinted at this? Yet how was she related exactly?

"That's nothing to do with my mother, Elise."

"I met her once at a *resto*. You were in a stroller." She shrugged.

"But you said there were photos. You knew she was an American." Desperate, she was desperate.

"A big argument, that's what I remember. Years-old saga of the Leducs against the Peltiers, your grandfather's complaints about the baby's mother and support." Elise shrugged. "Your parents left."

"But you led me to believe . . ."

"Sorry, Aimée, I didn't want to bring all that back up. Everyone stormed out. *C'est tout.*"

Aimée's shoulders sagged in exhaustion. Defeat. She'd been so foolish to hope. She stuffed the bitter pill down.

"Renaud told me you met him last night. He's coming here—wants to help."

"Then I'm finished here," said Aimée.

"Please stay, Aimée. *Désolée*, good job, you found Suzy. You've done better than the police."

She had that right. And look where it got her—attacked by a taxi driver and stranded in a country downpour.

Elise shook her head. "Forgive me, but stay, please. I don't know what to do now. My mother is so unwell. She keeps saying the fifth *Boche* came back."

"*Boche?*"

Clément nodded. "That's what we called the Germans behind their backs. There were other names, too—Fritz, Kraut, a Hermann. The worst was a *chleuh*."

The fifth German? Another war connection? Aimée thought of the German reprisals, the sixty dead. "Does this figure in the murder of your father and now Monsieur Baret?"

"I don't know."

"Someone followed me to the bookstore tonight and attacked me, Elise. It's dangerous."

"Attacked you? *Mon Dieu*." Elise's hand flew to her mouth.

Aimée explained what happened. "But Royant and Dufard, Elise, they're next. You need to talk with them."

"But it's too late."

Aimée gasped. "You mean . . ."

"They pulled out as we drove in."

Late again.

AFTER CLÉMENT LEFT for the night, a distraught Elise had uncorked another good Médoc, and her words had flowed like the wine. She had told Aimée about her childhood boarding school in Montreal, how she'd stayed in Canada for university and then taught economics. She had only come back to France permanently two months ago, when her father had insisted she return home to run the family investments.

From what Aimée could understand, that's what the meeting was about—to incorporate the shareholdings this group of men held together. After her father's passing, the aging members wanted her, with the accountant's assistance, to assume daily operations out of the bookstore which they owned jointly. But Elise had passed out before Aimée got the full story.

There were still so many questions to answer. There were still two men in danger and a dangerous killer on the loose. Aimée had the headache to prove it.

She couldn't leave this undone—she had to figure it out one way or the other. So she'd come up with a course of action while Elise slept.

First thing Sunday morning, she tried the hospital. Madame Peltier remained under observation and couldn't be disturbed, or so the nurse told her. A shame—Aimée was certain the woman would have been able to answer some of her questions. She must have known something about her husband's affairs.

She gave it another try, called the hospital, this time pretending to be Elise and asking for the ward directly.

"But I just spoke with you, didn't I?" said the nurse.

Great. "Look, I'm sorry, but it's important. It's vital that I reach Madame Peltier."

"And I told you she's taken medication. Impossible. Doctor's orders: she's not to be disturbed."

Click as the nurse hung up.

Next, she left messages at the Berlin hotel—still no answer from her father. Had he found her mother's secret Stasi files? Would he tell her if he had?

She changed the bandage on her smarting knee, donned her boots, wrapped a wool scarf around her neck and headed to the river bank Clément had pointed out.

Those feelings she'd been suppressing took over. The anger. How her mother hadn't been there to cuddle with her in the window seat, reading stories and stroking their old *chat*, Émilie. The birthdays and graduations marked by her mother's absence—Aimée's classmates winged by beaming parents while Aimée stood alone, her father inevitably arriving late from a stakeout.

No time for a pity party. Feeling sorry for yourself gets you nowhere, her *grand-mère* would say; put one foot in front of the other and move on.

Her mother had. Never a word, a photo, a message.

After her mother had first left, their old neighbor Madame Bouvier would invite Aimée over for *chocolat chaud* every month, and she put out paper and pencils so Aimée could draw pictures, write stories about her day. Madame Bouvier said she loved hearing her stories and shared them with a lady who lived far away and missed France. Aimée did her best to make the stories funny.

One day she'd gone to Madame Bouvier's as always and a man had answered the door. A man who spoke French with a strange accent. Madame Bouvier had left, no idea where she'd gone, he said. And what did she talk about with Madame Bouvier, what did they do together?

Something made Aimée lie. Oh, we just talked about my piano lessons, she said. Madame helped her with mathematics sometimes. She ran away when the man asked her where she lived.

The chill brought her back to the Cher riverbank. She walked in the drizzle, searching for the spot where Clément had found the mayor. Bullfrogs croaked and her boots sank in the spongy loam and sodden birch leaves. She doubted she'd find any trace after forty years. Still, her father always insisted on revisiting the crime scene—to put yourself in that time and place and imagine. Her imagination stalled on this damp, overcast morning.

Here on the riverbank in 1942, the mayor, Alphonse Gaubert—rumored to be a German collaborator, a traitor—had been shot in the head execution-style. More than forty years later, two of the four men who'd found him had been murdered in the same way on the quai in Paris. A symbolic reenactment, a message?

Clément, then a young boy, the eyewitness—she'd put his name in the suspect column, along with Dufard and Royant, the survivors who'd fled. But in her head, she could hear her father asking why. What was the present-day motive?

Her mind went back to last night. Elise, in her wine-induced rambling, had mentioned Madame Jagametti, the woman Aimée had met on the train. Aimée hadn't been able to get anything further from Elise before she'd passed out. Better find out what the connection might be. One more try before she caught the train back home.

Bertrand, the grandson, answered Madame Jagametti's door. Aimée guessed she was a few years older than him.

"*Bonjour.* May I speak with madame?"

He took in her cowboy boots, leg warmers, the long shearling coat and smirked.

"*Grand-mère*'s at church."

"*Bon*, I'll wait."

She wiped her boots on the mat, stepped inside before he could stop her. She spotted the open books on the kitchen table and the Tetris showing on the *télé* screen. She realized she'd caught him playing video games instead of studying. Good, a way to get him to talk.

"Studying for *le bac* is a real grind. I almost had to take it twice."

He stared at her. "You don't look like most Parisians who come down to mix with the peasants."

She laughed. His envy was as obvious as the brand-new Converse sneakers he wore. "Parisian rats like me go for the dark side, *mon ami*. I'm here to try to find out about an old murder that happened here during the war. That's what I want to ask your *grand-mère* about."

He shrugged. Bored.

"Don't suppose you've heard anything?"

"Why should I tell you if I did?"

She glanced around the house. A few expensive pieces—a period chair in the sitting room, in the kitchen a sparkling state-of-the-art stove. A pile of records by the high-end stereo. Heavy metal mostly, and Styx. She shrugged. "Maybe you'd like tickets to the Palladium next week. Styx."

"That's sold out." His bored look evaporated.

Aimée pulled out a card from her worn Vuitton wallet and flashed it. "My old classmate Stephan works there. He always finds me a ticket if I ask him."

Bertrand's eyes popped. "*Vraiment?*"

"Do me a favor and I'll do one back."

"Like what?"

"Tell me what you know about what happened here during the war. Has your grandmother ever talked about it?"

"They talk all the time, the old folks, when they're playing *belote* or drinking at the café. You think I listen?"

Bertrand, she figured, didn't want to appear uncool.

"But if you did?" She put Stephan's card down on his homework. "Should I call Stephan for a ticket?" she said. "After I sit down and you tell me what your grandmother knows? Or should I just go talk to her at the church?"

He shook his head. "She'll lie. They all do. Pay homage to the Peltiers, the aristocrats."

"Then this better be good, Bertrand."

He pulled out a chair, gestured for her to sit down. He offered her a Carambar from a pile by his mathematics book. She unwrapped the paper twisted around the caramel and glanced at the comic inside.

"I'm listening."

"There's always been this thing—we can't offend the Peltiers. Never talk about the dark times. But the villagers do."

She ran her tongue around her molars, checking for caramel. "What do you mean, the dark times?"

He rubbed his fingers together. Money. "They've paid off my *grand-mère* and her friends for years."

Surprised, she sat up. "For what?" And why was he

revealing this to her? Unless those Styx tickets meant more to him than his grandmother.

"Silence is *golden*," he said meaningfully.

The second time gold had come up since last night.

"I'm tired of platitudes and riddles." She tapped Stephan's card. "Give me something or this goes back in my wallet. Who's paying whom to keep quiet about what?"

"Listen," he said. "My parents died in a car accident when I was twelve. I came to live here. My clothes, my extra lessons, my tutor—all paid for by the grace of the *seigneur*— not God, but Peltier. There are regular deposits made into *grand-mère*'s bank."

"But what leads you to think she's covering something up?"

"Secretive, her and all her friends. At first I thought they were Freemasons."

"So what exactly is it that your grandmother knows that Bruno Peltier has paid her to keep quiet about all these years?"

His brows knit. He blinked. He was trying to play cool, but he was nervous, she realized.

"She won't know what you tell me. I promise, Bertrand."

"There was a traitor, a collaborator during the war. A villager killed him."

"Old news. You mean the mayor who was killed by the Resistance?"

"That's just the story. After a bottle of *eau de vie*, though, my *grand-mère* would tell you how the mayor was honorable, that the others stole his share, had his wife committed and made his kid disappear."

That corresponded to Clément's words.

"Share of what, Bertrand?"

He checked his watch. Shrugged uncomfortably.

"Does it connect to the reprisals in Givaray in 1942, the sixty people executed, this German truck that's been found?"

Bertrand stood up and parted the lace curtain. Checked his watch again. "I don't know, but I know where we can find out."

She followed him into the kitchen. By the pantry he pulled open a cellar trapdoor in the wood floor. "After you."

Did she trust him?

"My *grand-mère* doesn't believe in bank deposit boxes. Keeps stuff down there."

"Stuff like what?"

"You interested or not?" He glanced at his watch again.

She nodded, pulled out her penlight. Shook it until the thing lit.

She wished she had René's martial arts skills. But that didn't stop her from stretching the truth. "Don't get ideas, I do judo."

The dark cellar was lined with canned goods, jam jars, crocks of preserves, some dated as far back as 1975, others from last season.

"Enough food to feed an army here," she said.

"She's afraid of going hungry, like during the war. As if that would ever happen." Bertrand latched the trapdoor from the stairs. "A sickness, that old war mentality."

Aimée passed a card table covered with a red-and-white checked cloth. On top were a pack of cards, and full tins of foie gras and truffles. A kerosene lantern, chintz-covered armchairs. A vaulted stone underground refuge.

"Gourmet taste, eh?"

"The old fogies gamble for goose liver, can you believe it?"

Expensive goose liver.

"Why bring me down here?"

"The houses connect by tunnels dug during the war,"
said Bertrand, "from the barn near the river."

Aimée thought. The barn. Somehow this was important.
"Whose barn?"

"The murdered mayor's barn. Been for sale for years."

"Tell me what the men stole from the mayor, according
to your grandmother."

He never answered. A high-pitched voice was calling him
from upstairs.

"Bertrand! I know you're down there. Why aren't you
studying?"

He put a finger to his lips.

"Get back up here."

"Wait here," Bertrand said to Aimée. "She'll get mad if she
knows I showed you this place." He scurried up the wooden
steps. "Give me two minutes to get rid of her." The next thing
she heard was the trapdoor closing.

Panic prickled her skin. She was stuck. Stupid to trust
him. Idiot, what had she been thinking?

The jolt of fear caused her to perspire in the dank air.
Caused her shirt to stick to her back. How could she get
out? Bertrand had said the tunnel led to other houses.
Shuddering in the damp, she hitched up her bag. With her
penlight marking yellow rays over the stained earth walls,
she made her way. She didn't know what she was looking
for, but Bertrand's grandmother and her village cronies felt
safe down here in this hidden lair.

The bank deposits, the inexplicable wealth, the villagers'
silence all spun in her mind.

Was there some kind of treasure buried down here?

Farther on she found a wormholed door with a shiny new
lock. Above it was a faded sign: ABRI—an old bomb shelter.

Curious, she pulled her lock-picking set out of her makeup bag and got to work. Japy, her father's friend the thief, had taught her to pick locks the summer she was fourteen.

Jiggle here, toggle there, squeeze, et voilà.

The wormholed wooden door creaked open. Behind it was an old-fashioned storm door with another lock. A tougher one. She groaned. No wonder it had seemed easy. More security than the Banque de France.

Perspiring from anxiety despite the chill, she fanned herself with the newspaper from the Peltier's kitchen. Tried toggling with a slim hook and pressing down with the double-ended straight pick. The whole time she listened for noises, for anyone coming down here.

No one. Only a steady *drip, drip* in the distance.

The kid probably got wrapped up in his computer game. Or his grandmother had wrestled him down to study.

On the fifth try the lock yielded. Her penlight shone on stone walls as she descended more wooden stairs, breathing in the earthy, mold-tinged smell.

A niggling uneasiness crept up her neck. She had no right to be breaking into the old bomb shelter—did she? She didn't even know if there was anything down here worth finding, despite the grandson's implications. Maybe he was playing a game; maybe she should forget this and turn around and get the hell out of here.

Her eyes spied another door, a key set hanging from a nail. Might as well investigate since she'd climbed down here. And then she saw the thin orange thread in the door jamb.

She'd seen that in a spy movie—a trick to mark if someone had entered. With her tweezers she removed the thread and stuck it in a crack in the wall.

The key turned in the well-oiled lock.

She hit the cracked porcelain light switch and stepped into a past era. The wartime shelter, buttressed by wood beams, was clean and freshly dusted. The vaulted stone cellar ran a quarter of the length of what she figured was the street above. She explored, noting an old charcoal stove, canned food, framed black-and-white photos on a tidy notary-style desk. Plastic Evian bottles were the only concession to the present day.

Someone had been down here very recently. She caught a whiff of *muguet*, lily of the valley—the scent her mother wore. For a moment her mother's laugh floated in her mind, low and silvery.

The smell drew her to a desk, where she found a handkerchief embroidered with a T. On a notepad was written *Baret, Peltier, Royant, Dufard*. Those same names—a hit list?

The drawers held a tin *pastille* box of photos, a Clairfontaine ledger with amounts entered in old francs, a leather-bound diary held together by a rubber band.

She removed the band and thumbed open the diary. Pages of blue ink, still vivid, with entries in sections from 1942, 1943, 1944.

She thumbed back to the front page. Ninette Minou's diary. That name . . . why did she know it? And then she remembered—Clément said the blacksmith Minou had been one of the men to find the mayor's body by the river, that Minou had died at Liberation.

In a photo similar to the one she'd seen at the bookstore office were the same men, and a younger version of Madame Jagametti. Beautiful. Was she his sister? Cousin? His widow, who'd remarried?

Fascinated, she sat down on a creaking wood chair, set down the photo and started reading.

Pasted on the first page was a picture of three teenagers swimming in the river. The photo was labeled *Thérèse, me, and Minou on my birthday* and showed a young Madame Jagametti, a freckle-faced Ninette, and a stocky, short man.

Dear Diary, you are my birthday present from my best friend, Thérèse, today, August 14, 1942.

So Madame Jagametti—Thérèse—had kept her best friend Ninette's diary. But why?

Aimée read through the wartime descriptions of how Ninette's mother scraped together a chocolate crème cake, trading Minou's horseshoeing with the chicken farmer for eggs. Normal teenage entries that went on for pages—crushes on the postman, black-market cotton her mother sewed into a dress for her, the kittens born in Thérèse's cellar. A life of a young girl—unremarkable apart from the German soldiers in the occupied zone across the river who eyed her when she went swimming. Little line drawings of cats filled the margins. A yellowed picture of a movie star Aimée had never heard of cut from a magazine.

A sweet girl, Ninette.

Aimée skipped to November. Now Ninette's entries expressed horror at the executions across the river. Four dead German soldiers had washed up on the riverbank. Everyone lived in fear. Ninette's parents feared letting her go outside or to see Thérèse. The baker was spreading a rumor that there had been a fifth German soldier who had gotten away—that he would come back for revenge.

Aimée paused as she read that. Her heart was racing.

Dated December, after Christmas, was an entry about how Ninette had woken up at night and overheard Minou telling their father he'd been melting gold bars. He wasn't supposed to tell anyone—it involved those four dead German soldiers and how Alain, Philbert, and Bruno were afraid of the people in Givaray. How the Resistance shot the mayor but her friends didn't believe it.

Aimée pulled her coat around her, rubbed her hands together for warmth. Read more. How did this connect to why the men were being killed off now?

In 1943 Ninette's entries concerned how daily life got harder. In January, the Germans occupied the town. Minou was angry all the time, always shouting at her. She wrote about her mother's TB.

Later, in the spring, Ninette wrote about how Philbert Royant, Alain Dufard, and Bruno Peltier paid people good money to dig tunnels for bomb shelters. Everyone was grateful for their generosity—the wheat harvest had been ruined and the winter was hard. No one was asking where the money came from, but Ninette thought Minou knew. Ninette didn't help with the tunnels—she worked replanting the fields. She heard noises from the cellars at night, but she was supposed to pretend not to hear.

Aimée paged ahead to 1944. In August 1944, at Liberation, only one entry:

> *Dear Diary, I should be happy—the Allies are coming, people are dancing in the street. But they murdered Minou—the greedy bastards—in cold blood. Took his share of the gold.*

Her jaw dropped.

Angry and devastated, Ninette had wanted the truth remembered, and she had put it all down here. Aimée flipped ahead;

there were still pages of feverish writing. A thought curdled her stomach: Had Thérèse Jagametti been paid off for hiding the incriminating evidence in her best friend's diary? Had she been using the diary to blackmail the conspirators?

Cold air wafted as if from an open window. Or from the door above? Someone was coming. Shuffling footsteps, not the kid, Bertrand.

Quickly she stuffed the diary into her jacket just as an old man with a silver froth of hair burst into the shelter. Huffing, he shook his cane at her, smiling. He was stout and square in his cashmere coat, full-faced, with the red-veined nose of a drinker.

She stared at the photo of the men she'd set on the desk and then back at him. "Monsieur Royant, I presume."

He blinked. His blue, rheumy eyes teared in the cold.

"Close. I'm the one next to him."

"Dufard?"

"And you're Peltier's brat. Good job, kid." He stuck out a Monoprix plastic bag. "Fill that up with everything in the desk, and don't slam the door on your way out."

Was Dufard the killer? Her heart beat so hard it almost jumped out of her chest. The pieces flashed in front of her—the men in the picture, the gold, the mayor murdered on the bank.

She tried to make sense of this—two of the four men had been murdered. Wasn't Dufard in danger? Or had she read this wrong? Like an idiot, had she put herself in front of the killer?

She stood. Eyed the door to escape. "Don't you realize you could be next? You and Royant." Keep talking and get to the door. "Peltier and Baret's murderer is ready to tick your dance card." That old phrase of her grandmother's had popped into her head.

A muscle in Dufard's jowly cheek jumped.

"I need you to give me everything you've found, young lady."

She needed to get out of here. "I'm afraid not. Elise hired me."

"And paid you well for it, I know." He grinned. Stepped in front of the exit, blocking her. "Haven't you figured out we've been following you, *mademoiselle la détective?*"

Old men had her under surveillance and she hadn't even known? Talk about amateur. "Following me?" Now the centime dropped. How could she have been so stupid? "So you had a gypsy taxi attack me outside Baret's bookstore last night. Now you're here to finish the job."

Surprise crossed Dufard's face. What she took for fear. Then it was gone. "What? No. I drove Elise's mother to the hospital yesterday afternoon. Elise was a basket case, so I had to do the paperwork to get her mother admitted."

Easy enough to check. Though she didn't like him, she believed him. "Why follow me, then? Didn't you know this shelter was here all the time?"

"Did I?" Dufard scanned the desk. "Let's say I'm tying up loose ends I didn't know about."

Loose ends? Had he assumed Madame Jagametti kept valuables—or the diary—in a safety deposit box?

"What's so important to you?" Aimée squeezed the diary tighter under her arm. Shivered. "Has this woman been blackmailing you and the others?"

"We had an understanding. Always have. As I said, loose ends."

"Why didn't you just come down here yourself and take them?" She bit her tongue before adding, "They're *your* tunnels."

"I heard you're smart. A medical student. Too busy to worry about what you don't understand. So let's keep it that way." He shoved the crinkled Monoprix shopping bag toward her. "Keep earning your *fric*."

Fric, slang for money—a kid's term at his age? This old man trying to act *au courant* sickened her.

"Empty the drawer in here like a good little girl."

Like hell she would. "Do it yourself," she said, backing toward the wooden steps.

Dufard's cane shot out across the doorway. "Not so fast, young lady."

Should she kick it away, knock over an old man? Outrage battled with fear inside her. "Stealing a woman's war mementos—that's criminal."

And even worse criminal activity was alleged in the diary. Part of her didn't want to believe this old man and his cronies were murderers, war profiteers who had corrupted the village. The other part—reason, deduction, and her gut—knew it only made sense.

"You've saved me time." Dufard stepped closer, pulled out a long-handled flashlight and a wad of cash. "Glad Elise found you to lead us to what we needed."

Her insides wrenched. She felt she'd been socked in the gut. Used, she'd been used by Elise, sucked in by a family sob story to lead these old crooks to what they were looking for. Naïve.

Her father had been right.

Tired of waiting for her to act, Dufard was pulling out the drawers and scooping the contents into his Monoprix bag. Without an *excusez-moi* he'd reached in and riffled through her bag on the floor.

"Who's after you, Dufard?"

"You have no idea, *chérie*. Open your pockets."

"Why?"

The diary was wedged tight under her armpit. She could overtake this old man—kick him in the shin or balls . . .

As though he had read her mind, he stepped back.

"Popular girl," Dufard said, picking up her pager and scanning the numbers. She'd put it on mute. "So who's this calling you all the time?"

She had to put him off track, get out of here before the diary slipped out of her armpit.

"My ex-boyfriend."

He threw her pager against the stone wall, shattering it into pieces which he picked up and put in her hand. "This should stop him for a while, *chérie*. Royant," he yelled up the stairs, "get the car started! We're getting out of here!"

He tossed the wad of cash into her bag. Throwing money at her as if it could make this all go away.

"Alain, what's taking so long?" Fear quavered in the reedy, old voice that came from the tunnel above the old bomb shelter.

Despite the bravado, these old men were scared. Maybe there was someone they couldn't bribe anymore.

This stank. Hurt, anger, and disgust made her want to kick herself. Or do serious damage to the old fart.

Up in the tunnel, his colleague Royant was smoking a cigar. He was fatter and wider in a camel-hair coat. A long, white comb-over—a ladies' man, he must figure himself. Dissipated *roué* to her. But something cunning, too. Sharp. He reeked of *pastis*—that licorice smell on top of the cold dank of mildew made her gag.

"She delivered." Dufard puffed up the steps. "Let's go."

Such a damn smug look on his fat, jowly face. These old

men were cockier than teenagers. What the hell did they plan on getting away with—and how?

Time to act on a hunch and hope it burst their bubble. "Haven't you forgotten about the fifth German?"

The Monoprix bag dropped. Photos and notebooks scattered on the dirt floor, kicking up dust motes in the flashlight beam. She'd struck a nerve.

Apart from the dripping water and the fat one's breathing, silence.

"You know, that missing *Boche* who never washed up. Back when the sixty villagers in Givaray were shot—the German reprisals."

"Ancient history." Dufard got down on his haunches, shuffled things hurriedly back into the bag. "Long gone."

"Not according to Madame Peltier," she called after them as they took off down the tunnel. But what else did Madame Peltier know?

THE WHOLE TIME she'd been investigating she'd felt so smart, so organized, documenting her work, thinking about what her father would do. And in the end she'd failed—been an unwitting stooge.

Idiot. Should have listened to her father in the first place. But she'd never tell him that.

She retraced her steps, surprised to find the trapdoor open. The Jagametti kitchen was warm and full of the aroma of coffee. Madame Jagametti, whom she'd shared the train compartment with, was hunched over the kitchen table, holding ice to her eye.

What in the world . . . ? And would this woman start yelling at her for trespassing?

"*Pardonnez-moi,*" Aimée said, searching for excuses.

"Bertrand . . ." She didn't want to get him in trouble. Nothing for it but to be direct. "Madame, I apologize for intruding, but is this yours?" Aimée pulled out the diary.

A spark of surprise flitted across her dark brows. "*Pas du tout*. It's Ninette's. She's long gone, it doesn't matter now."

"But I think it does, madame. You've kept it for years. You knew Ninette wanted the truth remembered. Wasn't she your best friend?"

She gave a harsh laugh. Shrugged.

"What happened?"

Rain pounded on the windows, wind shook the bare-branched trees outside.

"Ask those two who stormed into my kitchen and did this to me. Your employers." Her lip trembled. She emanated fear and helplessness.

Aimée shivered.

"Not my employers. Elise Peltier hired me—I have nothing to do with those men. Please, I'm asking you."

"I don't want to talk about the past."

"Where's Bertrand?"

"Pac-mania, that boy has," she said. "Since you weren't invited, I can't ask you to leave. But I expect you to."

But this was the person she'd come to see. She couldn't just walk out.

"*Désolée*, madame. Can't you help me? Help me under-stand what happened here in the war that's still so important now?"

Madame Jagametti's thin mouth turned down in defeat. "Open secrets and closed mouths, *comprends*? It's about men leading double lives and a village that protected them."

Aimée sat down uninvited. Should she take the woman's hand to show she was sympathetic? Would the woman even let her? She reached for rough, calloused, arthritic fingers. Madame Jagametti shook her off. Bad idea.

"Please, just go."

But she couldn't give up.

"I will, madame, but you were Ninette's best friend," said Aimée. "*Et alors*, you know more than anyone, I imagine. You're the only one who can explain how what happened in the war led a bunch of wheat farmers to live in the exclusive quarter of Paris."

Madame's arthritic fingers clenched. "What's it to you? You're working for them."

"No, I'm not. Elise used me."

"*Tant pis*. You're surprised? Consider it a life lesson, young woman. In life you buy a ticket and take the journey."

Aimée shook her head. "It's not what you think. *Vraiment.*"

"You don't know what I think, mademoiselle."

She'd have to tell the woman the truth. Gamble on getting it in return.

"My father, a detective, didn't want us involved," said Aimée. "Elise asked for my father's help finding a woman involved in her father's murder. Or so she said. My father didn't want to take the job. But I went against his wishes and took the job. I never knew this before, but we're distantly related to the Peltiers. Elise told me she remembered me when I was small."

The rest she recounted in a brief version. She had to get as much info as she could before this distraught woman kicked her out the door.

"*Désolée*, I didn't mean to trespass and pry, but—"

"Of course you did. You talked my grandson into helping you. Not difficult." A sigh.

Her friend Stephan's card had disappeared from the table.

"He hates this place and everyone who lives here. Resents them."

"Sounds like he resents how they treat you, Madame Jagametti."

"*Alors*, mademoiselle, I'll tell you this for free. Farmers and peasants don't trust banks. In the Peltiers' case, they bought one."

"A private bank?" Aimée needed to read further in the diary. She took a guess. "Funding it with the stolen Nazi gold?"

"What does it matter now? They paid everyone off to shut up." Madame Jagametti's bitterness had found a release— once she opened her mouth, it all came out. "Ninette wrote down what happened. Minou, her simpleminded brother, the blacksmith . . ." Madame Jagametti sighed. "The things he told her."

"All those innocents murdered to keep things quiet." Aimée nodded. "How does it involve Gaubert, the mayor? How did the Resistance executing him figure in this?"

"Someone told you that?"

Aimée nodded again.

Madame's deep-set eyes were far away. "Didn't buy it then, and I don't buy it now."

"Why's that?"

"A decorated Great War veteran with a bad leg whose wife's brother was a Maquis?" Her thin mouth hardened. "Gaubert a traitor? Never." She took out a handkerchief with that *muguet* smell. Readjusted the ice at her temple.

"I haven't seen Alain or Philbert in ten, twelve years. *Connards*. But it seems they wanted to tie up loose ends." She gave a brittle laugh.

"Loose ends as in blackmail? Ninette's diary gave you enough leverage for them to come to an 'understanding,' that it?"

Would this prick the old woman's conscience?

"And you can prove that—that they paid me and others off, *mademoiselle la détective*? I don't think so. *C'est fini.*" Madame Jagametti's face shut down.

Aimée's mind clicked, remembering the meeting agenda she'd seen in the hunting bookshop office. These four old cronies had been on the verge of some kind of business undertaking . . . maybe something to do with their private bank? What if the murders of two of the partners nixed whatever deal they'd been planning? Was the murderer trying to sabotage that?

"Why do you think it's all coming back up now? Breaking into your house, taking your things—they could have come any time in the last ten years, couldn't they? Why now, when two of them are dead?"

"Like I know?" She gave a small smile. "I remember those men as simple farmers, hotheads, greedy, couldn't see beyond their noses. Yet shrewd. Paranoid, too."

Matched what she'd seen of the two old men.

"Still, madame, they were smart enough to invest," said Aimée. "They own apartments in *le triangle d'or*, near the Champs-Élysées. Their neighbors are aristocrats and sheikhs."

Madame Jagametti shrugged.

"If it were me," said Aimée, trying to prompt her, "I'd hire a savvy financial advisor to help me invest in property, businesses—to protect the assets and hide them."

"Me, I just wanted to give Bertrand a good future."

She tried another tack. "Could Peltier and Baret have

been murdered for revenge? Is someone hunting them down?" She waited. Only quiet and the ticking of the old clock on the kitchen wall. "I mean revenge for the executions in Givaray—feelings resurfacing after the German truck was found?"

Thérèse Jagametti's mouth sagged and the years showed on her face. *"Un massacre."* She shook her head. "All those innocents—my teacher, the priest's parents, so many. I wondered—everyone did—what we'd have done if that had happened here, and it scared me. Scared Alain, Bruno, and Philbert, too. Terrified them, that's why they moved away."

She shrugged.

"But who wants to kill the goose who lays the golden egg?" Madame Jagametti pulled her sweater around her shoulders. "My guess is those old rats are just keeping true to form, greedy to the end and killing each other off."

On the way to the door, Aimée noticed the Sèvres porcelain pieces, the good Turkish rug. Was Madame Jagametti one to throw stones when it came to greed? Maybe she had convinced herself that it hadn't been blackmail, that she had accepted gifts as thanks for turning the other way?

Aimée paused, her hand on the door handle. "One more question. Wasn't there a fifth German soldier whose body was never found?"

"So they say," Madame Jagametti said. "Now shut the door on your way out."

Berlin · Sunday

THE CRISP BERLIN air sliced cold below a cloudless sky. Harsh sunlight shone on another weed-choked bombed lot. Still so many bombed sites and run-down buildings, Jean-Claude thought, pacing by the Bäckerei-Konditorei.

This place affected him—it was as though the Cold War had frozen the city in the 1940s. He remembered growing up in the Auvergne countryside after the war. Gaunt farmers with no crops to plant. How he and his friends played on an old Allied tank left over from some battle. All that was gone now.

But here, men of his father's generation who'd survived the war were reminded daily. The younger generation had grown up in rubble. God only knew how difficult it had been for the hungry, defeated city to be occupied by Ivans. With the Wall down, the former East was exposed like a raw, open wound.

Gerhard's contact had delivered. Now Jean-Claude had the incriminating reports, the files on Sidonie that Interpol and the Hague would never see. Nor would they ever see the names of Sidonie's contacts in Hezbollah. He'd destroyed them.

His fingers folded and unfolded the card Soli Hecht had given him. Checked the time. Soli's contact was late.

A telegram had arrived just as he was leaving the hotel. The Hand enlisted him for another job after Place Vendôme. But he had Sidonie's records—no one could hold them over him or Aimée now. He was done. Decided. After this last job, he wouldn't let them get away with it anymore.

A flash of brown tweed—Soli was beckoning from across the street, by the long wall on Schönhauser Allee. He suddenly disappeared into what Jean-Claude realized was the old Jewish cemetery. Soli liked his cloak-and-dagger tactics. He better have brought his contact.

Half-sunken, lichen-covered tombstones carved in German and Hebrew sprawled forgotten under a carpet of orange and yellow leaves. How had Hitler missed this, he wondered.

"Always the picturesque with you, Soli," said Jean-Claude. "Afraid I don't have time for off-the-beaten-track Berlin."

"Nor for its ghosts, Jean-Claude?"

"I'd say that's all that's left, Soli." Jean-Claude couldn't help but notice a tiny, blackened tombstone—tiny for a child. It was dated 1873.

"You're telling me? I grew up across the street. The building's gone. A whole world lost."

"So you came for *la nostalgie?*" he said. "Where's your contact, Soli? He should be on time."

Soli looked around, motioned him toward a clump of peeling birch trees. A yellow-leafed canopy roofed the walkways. Peaceful, quiet. No one here would make any noise. They couldn't.

"I'm your contact, Jean-Claude," he said as they walked.

"No surprise, Soli. I figured as much."

"So let's finish negotiations, as you said on the phone."

Jean-Claude took out the envelope and handed it to Soli. A black, satin-shiny crow landed on a tombstone. The taker of souls, they said in the countryside. The crow stared with its yellow eyes.

"That's all?" said Soli after reading it. "Sidonie's name on a terrorist training camp roster from the seventies? That's old news. I want fresh. Don't hold out on me, Jean-Claude."

He'd come up with a plan. "For now, Soli. My contact's contact worked at the Syrian desk. Later he transferred to the Lebanese-Palestinian section. My contact only found out last night and he's gone back for 'specifics.' You know how it works, Soli."

"How convenient. Specifics like what?"

"This terrorist Abbas Musawi, the Hezbollah raid in the Bekaa Valley—that interested you, right?"

Big fish.

Soli took off his glasses, cleaned the lenses with a hand-kerchief. Would he take the bait? "Musawi's in your wife's network?" Soli asked after a minute. "Or the other way round?"

Jean-Claude squeezed the mark coin in his pocket. Willed his breath to slow, and his eyes not to give him away. Lied as he'd always lied for her. "That's why I had to cross-reference. Her only contact with him was in Syria. Everyone went through that camp. Don't tell me you don't know that." Keep talking, he had to keep talking, keep Soli satisfied. "Aren't you retiring, Soli? So I imagine you'd like Musawi on a platter for a coup de grâce. Out in a blaze of glory, that interest you?"

"I wouldn't put it that way, Jean-Claude. Old dogs like me, we finish the job, c'est tout. Furnish me Musawi's intel when your contact delivers and we're done."

"And what do you have for me, Soli?" His heart pounded.

Soli handed him a plastic shopping bag from KaDeWe, the upscale department store.

"Zut alors, what's this?"

"Everything discovered on my end."

Jean-Claude riffled through: reports, index cards, surveillance documentation. The last dated two years ago.

"Only this?"

"Her file's been cherry-picked."

"By whom?"

"The cousins, of course—MI5 and across the pond. But you knew that would have happened unless you got there first."

He had. Sworn to get there first. His stomach churned. He stared at Soli Hecht. Plumbed his eyes, almost black in their deep sockets, half a lifetime of suffering in them. Soli was telling the truth.

Jean-Claude opened his wallet. Soli laid his gnarled hand over it. Shook his head.

"But I owe you Soli. I keep my word."

"Better for me if I collect in the future. I will collect. *D'accord?*"

WHY DID HE dread that more than a simple payment? Jean-Claude stood by a tumbled tombstone, leaning against a slender tree. The sun's haze lingered over the cracked black-granite mausoleums. The crow, like a sentinel on the tombstone, basked in the slanted rays.

Despite Aimée's complaints, he knew she had it in her to become a doctor. Carve out a career, a profession—be invulnerable to her mother's past. But as her father, he had to make sure.

He rubbed a gloved hand over the peeling birch bark, lost in thought. Hadn't he survived her teenage rebellion years—the boys, the parties, those damn expensive cowboy boots from Texas? All the things he'd done for them to get by. The things he said he'd never do. *Bien sûr*, he'd survive her travails in medical school. Patience. He had to remember she was a kid facing grueling courses, competition, all kinds of pressure.

A shadow passed in front of him, blocking the sun. The scent of *muguet* he remembered so well. A delicious shiver traveled up his spine. Took him back to that summer day when he'd almost arrested her at the demonstration on the Left Bank.

His heart beat fast. He felt the blood pumping through his veins. His gaze lingered on the shadowed leaves, postponing that moment he would look to see if it really was her. As long as he delayed he could believe it was Sidonie . . . and when he did look, and saw her standing there in a dark wool coat, he melted once again.

"You beat me, Jean-Claude," Sidonie said. "I can't have you using those files against me. No matter how you feel."

That fractured French, that accent, that curve of her leg.

"Not against you, Sidonie," he said, his voice thick. "I kept my promise. For once think of your daughter."

She blocked the light, filled the sky—like she always had. "Who says I don't? You know nothing of me now."

Had he ever really known her?

And then Sidonie sat down and pulled him next to her. Her hair was different, black sunglasses masked her eyes. Tanned, she looked thinner. The carmine lipstick was the same.

Still a beauty. *Ma belle.*

"Living on the lam suits you, Sidonie."

"How many years has it been, Jean-Claude?"

She knew. So did he. To the exact month, day, and the hour when he'd gotten her out of the French prison. But she'd never looked back.

"More than a few."

Why was he so weak? Why did he want to take his wife in his arms—even just once? Erase everything, pretend none of the past had happened—her betrayal, how she left them with a big hole in their lives. Left his daughter without a mother.

"I'm running on borrowed time, Jean-Claude," she said, her voice reedy. Alert, she glanced around. "Please, you swore."

"And you swore you'd never come back."

"Haven't I kept my promise? Stayed away?"

His gut wrenched. So easy for her. She hadn't changed.

"You're assuming these files—"

"Are mine. And explosive if in the wrong hands. You promised, Jean-Claude. Swore to me."

She read him so well. Yet still couldn't trust that he'd find and destroy them. She'd come to save her own skin. Hurt, he wondered why he'd even worried about her.

"And I've spent most of my life lying for you, Sidonie."

"Did I ever ask you to lie?"

He threw up his hands. "So you wanted Aimée to know about prison, the terrorism, the extortion?"

"Unproven. But the truth, that's what I've wanted to tell her."

"You mean to salve your conscience—" *Merde*, everything came out so judgmental. Priggish.

"Wrong," she interrupted. "To save you."

"That's all you wanted?"

Her warmth against his arm traveled through his whole body.

"What I want doesn't matter, Jean-Claude," she said. "I'm facing a sham trial, Turkish prison. I signaled you because of your contacts. I knew you could get hold of what I couldn't."

"Not if you're valuable to the CIA. Don't underestimate yourself."

"Meaning?" Her voice raised in accusation. So like Aimée.

"Let me see your eyes."

She paused. Sensed his weakness the way a shark scented blood. "Will you tell me about her?"

Aimée, her daughter, and she couldn't even say her name. As if she had ever acted like a mother.

"Don't pretend you care. Or have shown any interest in all these years."

"Trouble in med school?"

Shocked, he pulled back. "How in God's name . . . who told you?"

"She's doing it to please you. She's young, Jean-Claude. Don't push her."

He wanted to shake her. "Where have you been in Aimée's life? What gives you any right to say she—"

"Thinks that's what you want?" Sidonie shook her head. "She's not even twenty. Remember how you were? She's afraid to disappoint you. She adores you, Jean-Claude."

Shaken, he looked down at the yellow leaves. Was he pushing Aimée too hard—ignoring her doubts, not listening to her?

Sidonie took off her glasses. Those huge almond eyes, so like Aimée's—blue now, she must wear contacts. He had to ask her the question that tormented him. The one that still woke him up in the middle of the night. Made him think of her every time he caught a whiff of *muguet*, or saw lily-of-the-valley blossoms—her favorite—at the flower shop on his way home. Or saw a woman resembling her on a Paris street. Pathetic. But he had to know.

"Where did you go, Sidonie? Another man, some cause? . . . just tell me. That's all I want to know."

Sidonie's long fingers knit together. Silence except for the rustle of leaves.

"Don't you owe me, for all that I've done for you, my renegade terrorist wife?"

He left out the black deals he'd made to free her from prison. The price he still paid now. Doing one more job when he returned to Paris.

"It hurts to say, Jean-Claude. You're right." Sidonie leaned back. "Call it a pebble that grew into a snowball. Mistake after mistake. I was coming back, Jean-Claude . . ."

"What do you mean coming back?"

"As usual, to meet Aimée when she came back from school, but I'd brought posters to the antiwar rally and it turned ugly. Violent. Before I could leave, protesters in our group got hurt. They wouldn't go to the hospital. They were from the wanted Haader-Rofmein group, I learned later."

The German terrorist gang of the seventies. Political when it suited them.

"I got caught up in it before I realized who they were."

"Why didn't you leave?"

"You think I didn't try? The leader shot a policeman, things spiraled. We were on the run and it turned into a manhunt. The next thing I knew, we'd been smuggled over the border into Switzerland. Wanted. My face was the only one the authorities didn't know—so they made me drive when they robbed clinics for medical supplies. That implicated me and put me on the run, too." She shook her head. "Maybe you don't believe me."

He did. But maybe he wanted to believe her.

The crow cawed. Leaves rustled. "After prison what did you do?"

"The deal you arranged, getting me out, had strings, Jean-Claude."

"Strings?"

"They wanted me to *stay* useful to certain people." Her eyes, those eyes bigger than Juliette Gréco's, drifted to the sky.

Jean-Claude's mind raced. "To play both ends and set up your old cohorts?"

"Close enough. That was the rest of the deal, they didn't tell you. That or do time in a maximum-security prison in upstate New York. But now I have a new identity. Once I destroy the evidence, I won't need to run and hide anymore." She played with her sunglasses. "I won't have to be 'on the road.'"

That damn beatnik bible she gave him when they first met. Did she mean come back?

He wished he didn't want that to be true. Why did he want her—for them to be together again, the three of them? Crazy.

"Your hair's long, Jean-Claude." She'd leaned forward, her arms touching his. "Remember when I used to cut your hair in our first apartment? That top floor overlooking the canal and only space for a bed?"

Hungry, he pulled her close. Her kiss burned his lips. He held her hard, tight, and felt her warmth fill his arms.

A horn blared twice.

She pulled back and ran her hand over his face. As if memorizing it. "I have to go."

A dreamer, sucked in every time.

"You always have to go, Sidonie." He felt the lingering warmth of her. "The Mossad wants your contacts."

She nodded. "I know."

A pause.

"Jean-Claude, I'm not asking you to wait for me, but . . . if . . . you decide . . ." Her voice quivered in the clear air. "I'll never hurt you again."

And then she'd gone, the *muguet* scent fading. The crow, he realized, had disappeared. Flown off with Sidonie's soul.

TOO LATE, HE started after her, running through the dry fallen leaves. His foot caught on an exposed tree root, and suddenly he was facedown on a lichen-laced slab.

By the time he'd picked himself up, ignoring the pain and blood dripping from his knee, he heard a car door slam. He ran faster, panting, and got to the stone gate in time to see a car pulling away across the street. A dark-grey foreign sedan in a street full of Soviet Trabis. The only ones who drove those worked at embassies. A car like that only belonged to *les Américains*.

"DUFARD AND ROYANT called you my bloodhound?" said Elise. "I don't know what they're talking about."

In the house, Elise paced on the rust-maroon carpet that reminded Aimée of dried blood. A tension thick as wool hovered in the over-upholstered salon.

Uneasy, she watched Renaud add logs to the fire, his overcoat beaded with rain. His car keys lay on the table and he was muttering about the damn Paris traffic.

Aimée had shown Elise Ninette's diary. "I'm afraid it puts your father, all of these men, in a bad light."

"That all happened during the war," said Renaud, standing up and brushing ashes off his knees. "Difficult times. How do you know this diary's authentic?"

The smell told her. "Take a whiff. That's old paper. And be careful of the silverfish." Aimée took out the ten or so photos from her pocket and spread them on the table—black-and-white village scenes, the boulangerie, children, dogs, men playing *boules*. "There's your father, Elise, and the mayor who was shot. See the names written there."

Aimée recognized a younger Royant and Dufard, without their double chins and large girths from years of good living. Suddenly, she was tickled by the thought that there was something familiar about the mayor's face. What was it?

"May I?" Renaud picked up the photo and stared.

Aimée nodded. A blurred scene showing Dufard, Peltier, the mayor, and a young boy holding the mayor's pant leg.

"Apparently, some people remember him as an honorable man. A hero of the Somme," said Aimée. "Madame Jagametti doesn't believe he turned traitor or collaborated with the Germans."

Elise's chin quivered. "So she thinks my father did?"

Out for himself, maybe. "Not my call. But I don't think this is about collaborating with Germans. It's about stealing from the Germans. Gold, the diary says. Maybe there was art, valuables, I don't know. But these men paid off the village to keep quiet."

"What do you mean keep quiet?" Elise said.

"Madame Jagametti for one," she said. "Ask Clément, he'll tell you."

Wasn't Clément sweet on Elise? Could he be jealous of Renaud, her fiancé—did that play into this? But she'd think about that later.

"Tell me what, Aimée?"

"Elise, somehow this connects to the Givaray memorial to the sixty executed in reprisal for the dead German soldiers. See?" She showed Elise the October newspaper article she'd found. "Look at this about a sunken German truck linking back to the soldiers."

"How? I don't see a link." Elise shook her head. "That's years ago. My father was murdered last month."

"But if he and the others were involved . . ."

Aimée waited, trying to guess how much Elise knew, and how much she was in denial about.

After a few moments, Elise sat down on a damask chair. "All of a sudden, two months ago, my father wanted me to take over the business. He insisted I give up teaching and come back to take over. He was incorporating all their interests—Baret, Dufard, and Royant's. They'd all agreed on it.

They were business partners, not enemies or rivals." She picked at nubs on her sweater sleeve, rolled them between her fingers. "There was supposed to be a formal meeting of the board—a signing of papers . . ." Her eyes were tearing.

"But your father was murdered before the meeting."

"It was postponed. But then the next meeting was cancelled when . . . " Elise's mouth dropped open. She'd put it together. About time for the economics professor. "I hadn't suspected until now," said Elise. "But what if Royant and Dufard really wanted total control? Killed him, then Baret, all to put me out of the picture?"

Aimée wondered. A possibility. "Speak with the *flics*, Elise."

"And say what?" asked Elise. "They haven't listened to anything I've said yet. There's no proof of anything—the gold, the executions—it's just theories and a sob story in a diary. The woman can't even spell."

Private diaries weren't written for snooty grammarians.

"Or you're worried this might bring attention," said Aimée. "An investigation into how farmers bought apartments in the exclusive *huitième*? And set up a private bank with gold?"

"Who's seen this Nazi gold?" Elise shook her head. "Long gone if it ever existed—that would be opening a basket of snakes. Bring Holocaust survivors and their children with claims for restitution, compensations." She pointed to the newspaper. "Does it say what this truck transported? Whose gold? I don't see that."

She had retained Leduc Detective to learn the truth about her father. But Elise, the daughter of privilege, wasn't so interested in the truth when it threatened her comfort, it seemed.

Elise thumbed through the photos. Her eyes somewhere else. "Papa looks so young. Here, that's Mama. Look, the horse I fed when I was little. The draft horse. Then we moved away."

And then Elise threw the diary in the fireplace.

Aimée yelped. "What are you doing? That's not yours! You can't burn the proof!"

"Lies."

The flames licked the worn leather. Aimée grabbed a poker. Her attempts to retrieve the diary only pushed it deeper into the flames.

"But it could explain what's happening now—"

"All lies."

The fire smoked, crackled, swallowing the yellowed pages in moments. Renaud caught Aimée's arm. With a whoosh the old diary pages curled, turning a burnt orange. "Let the past go."

Too late now. *And the guilty got away. Again.*

Elise was gathering the photos, but Renaud stopped her. "Why throw these away, Elise? It won't change anything. You'll lose memories."

Elise bit her lip. "*Bon*, I'll keep the photos. Then I'll confront Dufard and Royant, the liars." She took a key ring from the bookcase. Swearing, she fumbled with the key until she'd unlocked the biggest drawer. "This will hold them. Keep them safe."

Elise pulled an old wood box with leather handles onto the desk. Her hands shaking, she set each black-and-white photo inside, one by one. Tears were streaming down her face. Renaud rubbed her back, trying to calm her.

"You've upset Elise enough," he said. "I think you should go."

Aimée's eye focused on the box. "What's that?" Aimée rubbed her fingers on the box's wood side. Dark soot, like charcoal, came off.

"What are you doing?" said Elise.

From this angle, in the slant of winter light, she'd seen something embossed. A design.

"It's dirty, let me clean it off for you." Aimée rubbed with her scarf. Spit on her scarf and rubbed again. Ancient black shoe polish, by the smell and smudge of it. "Your father's box, that right?" Aimée asked.

Elise nodded.

She turned the now semi-cleaned box to reveal what she'd scrubbed and found.

Swastika. *Eigentum der Reichsbank.*

"Nice size for gold bars."

ON THE MINITEL in the Peltier's hallway, she looked up the number of the man in the newspaper article. Called and arranged to meet him at the train station. She shouldered her bag and walked through the damp lanes, avoiding puddles in ruts made by old horse carts. Breathed in the rain-freshened air to clear her mind, put her questions together.

A few shops were open. She passed the *boulangerie* in the town square, the one she'd seen in the photo. Little had changed in fifty years except for the posters of Johnny Hallyday headlining at Bourges, the Armistice ceremony commemorating the Great War. She envisioned the old guys with medals at the square, the doddering few veterans of *la Grande Guerre*, as they appeared every November. Sad, so sad—their eyes filled with memories and their numbers dwindling every year.

"Mademoiselle Leduc?"

"*Oui?*" She turned in the station hall to see a man peering over his newspaper as she stood in the ticket line. "Georges Ducray?"

He folded his newspaper, nodded.

"The reporter I spoke to had a lot more years on him than you."

She caught the implication—she was too young to take seriously. She'd lied and told him she was a freelancer from *Le Parisien* interested in his allegations in the article.

"But the reporter never followed up on my information," said Georges Ducray.

Good. Now she'd have an in.

"That's why I came, Monsieur Ducray. I appreciate you meeting me." She needed to question him before he asked why the story hadn't been picked up by a national paper like *Le Parisien*. Or complained how a big city ignored the provinces.

Think, she had to think like her father. Ask the right questions.

Ducray—short, barrel-chested—was fortyish, with tight, greying curls like a wire-brush helmet. A red-embroidered train club patch on his jacket lapel. "You'd be better off catching the 12:04 at Vierzon straight to Gare d'Austerlitz."

Mon Dieu, not one of those train enthusiasts. One of her father's colleagues, obsessed with railroad minutia and loco-motives, had dragged her as a teenager to his model train club under the Gare de l'Est. Grown men, she'd thought in disgust, playing with toy trains.

"The Vierzon line's direct and quicker," said Ducray.

A slight hiccup-like sound ended his phrases. A drinker? This early in the morning? She groaned inside.

Maybe this had been a bad idea.

"Otherwise you'll wait forever," he said.

"Still, it gives us time to talk," she said, pulling out her anatomy notebook. She gestured to the benches. "I'll take notes."

"What if I give you a lift, show you something en route?"

A few tipples of *vin rouge* and keen to get her in a car?

As if sensing her hesitation, he pointed to his chest. "Asthma sufferer. Side effect of my new medication gives me the hiccups."

No whiff of *vin rouge* and he seemed steady on his feet.

She pulled out the newspaper clipping. "I've got a story to write," she said, lying her heart out. "A story my editor won't accept without facts. These theories you're quoted saying—every little thing requires backup evidence." At least that's what Martine, who was studying journalism at the Sorbonne, complained about.

"Driving to Vierzon takes thirty minutes, give or take." He pulled out an old rail map with X's marked in red. "I can show you everything I've researched. The German truck recovery site, the river's course then and now, logistical problems."

She snapped her bag shut and stepped out of the ticket line. "Lead the way." An odd tour guide, but it worked for her. "Any basis to support your allegation that the sixty villagers executed in 1942 were related to a German truck bound for Portugal?"

"I thought you'd never ask," said Ducray, lifting the glasses hanging from a string around his neck onto his face. They got into his old Peugeot. He handed her the map, ground the car into first, and shot out of the parking lot. "Hold on, Mademoiselle Leduc."

AFTER CROSSING THE bridge to Givaray, Ducray turned onto a muddy road and let the engine idle on a small bluff. Across the river lay Chambly-sur-Cher, and a stone's throw away, a crumbling water mill. Aimée caught a whiff of damp manure drifting from over the river.

"Let me set the scene, that's how you say it, *non?*"

She winced. A crackpot? "In the movies maybe, Monsieur Ducray. Unless you've got facts, I haven't got a story."

Or a suspect who'd murder old men with shady links to Nazi gold.

Shouldn't she feel like an imposter, playing two roles, neither one very well? But she enjoyed playing reporter, giving herself a script and getting this train obsessive to cough up real details. Better than in the movies.

"Why are you so interested in this?" she said. "What's driving you?"

"I was a baby when my father was executed with the others," he said in a flat voice, emotionless.

The car engine idled. Ducks in a V formation rippled the river's gunmetal-grey surface. Georges Ducray had the perfect motive for revenge.

"When the war ended, I was two or three, but I still remember the German's black boots. We didn't go hungry, because this was farmland, and my mother ran a cheese shop. But I was never full."

She understood the difference. Nodded.

Ducray pulled over, reached in the back seat for a folder. He showed her photos; one titled *La ligne de démarcation à douaniers* with a sentry booth at the bridge crossing, the French border guards wearing *képis*, a pregnant woman, a beret-wearing man with her pushing a bicycle.

"Our only family portrait," Ducray said, a sliver of emotion.

He continued, matter-of-fact. "My uncle was a *cheminot* at Vierzon station. I've loved trains since I was a kid, gobbled up everything to do with them."

She nodded again, praying this went somewhere. That she could make Ducray's story come out.

"He always said the rail lines were bombed the night before my father and the villagers were shot."

She hadn't heard that before. Maybe it was in the damn diary Elise burned. "Go on."

"The Germans routed trains to Spain and Portugal via Vierzon—it's still a hub between north and south," said Ducray. "Because of the bomb damage on the tracks, the Germans deployed troop trucks to recover stock from stranded rail cars. The commandant requisitioned the trucks from the garage where my uncle worked." He paused. "There was a flash flood that night of the bombing. The river overflowed the banks there—in Chambly-sur-Cher. Where the missing truck was found, in the deepest part of the river, by the mill."

She looked around. "Wasn't this the demarcation? Are you saying the truck was in the unoccupied zone—illegally?"

"You're quick." Hiccup. "There's no access from our side. See?" He pulled out another map from his pocket. "Here's the river now. I marked in yellow the old course of the river in the late thirties from an agricultural map, and the barge routes. See, it's changed course—that was after the flash flood in 1942. The only way the truck could have ended up in the river by the mill was from the Chambly-sur-Cher side. There's no other way. Not even the mill has access."

She saw that. Her gaze caught on water grass under the surface, waving hypnotically like a woman's long hair.

"But that could have happened any time during the war. How could you match it to the requisitioned trucks?"

"All the records exist in the train station cellar," he said. "I know it like the lines in my hand. The logs, the garage requisitions." He handed her a stapled bunch of photocopied pages. "The recovered truck engine number matches one of the trucks that was requisitioned that night," said Ducray.

It made her think. "But given your scenario, okay, the passing truck would have been seen by the border guards."

"Just ask the retired butcher," said Ducray. "All hands were busy sandbagging the banks. Still, the wheat fields flooded. Guards were busy in the storm and with the RAF bombing."

An answer for everything, this Ducray. She wondered about him—his thoroughness raised red flags for her. His eagerness to set the record straight bordered on obsession. Besides, he had a potential motive for murder—revenge for his father, if he'd linked the German reprisals to the men who'd seemed to profit from the missing gold.

But he was a trove of information. She might as well see what else she could get out of him.

"The four German soldiers who were murdered—were they ever identified?"

"We know the serial numbers had been taken off their uniforms," said Ducray. "Presumably the Germans have identified them in their records."

"Have you checked that out, too?"

He hiccuped. "*Non*, that's all in Paris. I don't go to Paris."

"Why's that?"

"One time on a school trip, I got lost for hours in the

Louvre." He gave another shrug. "Call me provincial, but it frightened the hair off me. Never want to go back."

True or not, she stashed that thought for later. Didn't want to burst that suspect theory yet. She nodded and smiled. "You're not the only one. I've gotten lost in the Louvre, too. And I'm *Parisienne*."

He started back toward town. "We need to get moving for you to make the train."

In the back of her mind something niggled. Ducray braked to avoid a mud-spattered spaniel. She wondered how Miles Davis was doing.

As he flashed his signal to pass a tractor, her eyes scanned the Chambly-sur-Cher riverbank, the bridge, the old mill. She remembered Bertrand's words. "Is that the mayor's barn over there? It's for sale?"

"It's abandoned. The sale sign's been there for years."

But it was so close, literally a stone's throw from the river. She used her kohl eye pencil to sketch the scene before her.

"I'll take you through Givaray," Ducray said, "past my shop."

It was an old-fashioned cheese shop, train set in the window.

"Does the window in back overlook the river?" she asked.

"Like to see?"

She nodded.

Inside, the young woman behind the counter smiled at her as Ducray spread the beaded curtain to lead Aimée through to the living quarters. Bare-bones, clean; worn, functional furniture—so unlike the Peltiers' luxurious house, or Madame Jagametti's quarters with its tins of foie gras and truffles.

"May I?" she opened the window to the damp but fresh air. The warble of a bird carried over the gurgle of the river.

She heard the tractor engine turn off, the farmer in conversation with his neighbor.

Amazing. But whatever Georges Ducray's mother or father had heard from over the water had died with them.

Back in the car, they passed a limestone wall with a memorial plaque to the sixty villagers who had been executed. "Shot right there?"

Ducray nodded. "They only put the memorial up a few years ago. I don't know why. Gone is gone, my mother said. After it was finished, people didn't talk about the war—it wasn't something they wanted to relive."

But Thérèse Jagametti's words—how Alain and the others were afraid of Givaray—sounded in her head. "People would want revenge, I'd think, after a massacre of innocents."

"Move on with life or the past haunts you, the priest would say."

"But look at Chambly-sur-Cher. It's almost deserted, lifeless. Were those people broken by the war, when Givaray has somehow moved on, despite the tragedy?"

Ducray expelled air, shook his head.

"Any theories about who killed the German soldiers? Rumors?"

"If so, I didn't listen."

"*Mais* soldiers murdered, reprisals taken out on your village—*bien sûr*, people must have talked. Any gossip? Anyone ever find out?"

"I thought journalists couldn't use hearsay. Facts and evidence, you said." He grinned, throwing the words back in her face.

"You got me, Georges. Eh, but just between us?"

He shifted into second. Checked the rearview mirror. "There's been a German here asking questions."

The *Boche* Madame Peltier saw—just before she had a stroke.

"We've got twenty minutes or so, *non?*" She pulled out her anatomy notebook. "And I won't quote you—I'll just say an anonymous source. And along the way, I need to buy some tape."

SHE JUMPED ON the train, threw her bag up in the rack, and settled in with her new roll of tape to repair her smashed pager. Once she'd reinserted the battery, *voilà*, the thing worked. Wonder of wonders.

She kicked her boots off and started reading Ducray's file of information. Immersed, she barely noticed the glow of a November sun laying a russet orange over the rolling green fields, or the lulling *schwa schwa* of the wheels over the tracks. Two impressions stayed with her: Givaray, a bustling village, and Chambly-sur-Cher, lifeless—as if poisoned. Poisoned by the past. Shouldn't it be the other way round?

She reached in her pocket for the photo she'd pocketed from Elise's collection. Youthful Dufard and Peltier with the mayor, Gaubert, and the little boy.

Her pager showed a number. She didn't know it.

When the train stopped in Lyon, she jumped off onto the platform, ran to the pay phone and dialed.

"*Oui?* Who's this?"

"It's René . . ." The rest of his answer got muddled amid the loud speakers. Passengers rushed to the train, dragging children and suitcases.

"René, can you meet me at Gare d'Austerlitz in half an hour?"

"Make it forty-five minutes, upstairs at le Train Bleu in Gare de Lyon."

The train conductor blew a whistle.

"René, but that's not—"

"Le Train Bleu. Upstairs. I want breakfast."

Breakfast this late? But he'd hung up. The train to Paris was pulling out of the station with her notes, the damn file. She took off, jumped over an old woman's suitcase, pumped her legs. Leapt onto the train car's steps as the train gathered speed.

"Let me get this straight." René's short legs dangled as he leaned forward. He looked around, sipped his fresh-squeezed orange juice. "Sabotage?"

She whispered, "*Non*. I just need info on a company called Foundry, Inc. I thought you could use your computer skills to help me find what I'm looking for. You know, use your computer to get into their computer—people can do that kind of thing, right?"

Pause. His folded *Le Monde* sat beside his late breakfast: croissant, orange marmalade, *yaourt de nature*, and a stiff double espresso. The front page was hoopla about the opening of I. M. Pei's pyramid at the Louvre. "You mean hacking? That's illegal." René pulled a laptop out of his briefcase. "Shame on you, trying to lead me into a life of crime. Why don't you do it yourself?"

She would if she could. And if she had a computer. "Why, when I can ask an expert like you?"

"Who said I'm an expert?" He sipped his orange juice.

"Your card does, in case you hadn't noticed." She pulled out his card. "Says you can rebuild a computer, rehab motherboards. So you should be able to weasel into them too, *non*? How about deciphering a floppy disk?"

René set down his glass. Shrugged. "I'm expensive."

Playing hard to get? "So you keep saying. And worth every franc, I'm sure." She pulled out the floppy disk she'd taken from the bookstore. Checked the time. *Merde,* she had a biology study group! She signaled the waiter with the long white apron for the check.

"What's that?" René was peering at Ducray's thick stapled file.

"Railway manifests. I need to figure out what stock the Germans were bringing in from Portugal in 1942." She pulled out her worn Vuitton wallet. "Talk about a headache."

"Wolfram."

She blinked. *"Eh, c'est quoi ça?"*

"Wolfram ore, also called tungsten. The German army plated tanks with it."

Did he know everything, this man of short stature with the liquid green eyes?

"A history buff, too? I'm impressed." She leaned back in thought. "Did they pay Portugal in gold?"

"Bien sûr. The only way Salazar would do business. Gold up front shipped in trains and the return-trip boxcars filled with tungsten." He adjusted his tie.

She pulled out Ducray's old rail map. Studied it.

"So according to the checkered history," she said, "would-be Nazi gold, plundered from murdered Jews, would leave occupied France on trains bound for Portugal's tungsten deposits via Spain?"

"More or less." René nodded.

That meshed with Ducray's findings.

"After the war," said René, "rumor goes, Nazis escaped through Allied hands on these same tracks."

"One problem solved," she said.

"Any more?"

"What ever happened to the fifth German?"

"Now I could sink my teeth into something like that. Sounds like that thriller I read. A Ludlum."

"So we agree on your price . . ."

"I said I'm expensive. That's all. I won't decide until you tell me what the hell it's all about. Then I balance the risk."

Cautious, smart, stubborn, a kick-ass machine. He pissed the hell out of her. She'd like to work with him.

"I can't prove everything yet," she said, "but in a nutshell, in 1942 during a flash flood, five German soldiers in a troop truck recovering gold from bombed-out train cars get lost. Some farmers from this village, Chambly-sur-Cher," she pointed to the map, "plus maybe the village mayor, murder the five Germans, or so they think, empty the gold out, and dump their truck in the river. Four German soldiers wash up in the village on the opposite bank, Givaray. The Germans shoot sixty villagers in reprisal."

She took a breath.

"That's a nutshell?"

"There's more. The Chambly-sur-Cher mayor is executed later, supposedly by the Resistance. But now, more than forty years later, two of the four remaining farmers who took the gold have been murdered. Copycat style—just like the mayor's execution."

René raised his pudgy hand. "*Dites-moi*, how does this involve the fifth German?"

"Madame Peltier, the first victim's widow and my distant relative, suffered a stroke. She said the fifth German has come back. Meanwhile, a man with a German accent has appeared, wanting to see this old truck." Aimée gave him the rundown of her visit to Chambly-sur-Cher. "For years these men bribed the villagers to keep quiet. Meanwhile they left the village for residences in *le triangle d'or*. And now Elise, Madame Peltier's daughter, is afraid the two other farmers are trying to prevent her from assuming control of Foundry, Inc. as all had agreed."

René whistled. "They melted Nazi gold, laundering it through their company, Foundry, you're saying? Reminds me of something Balzac wrote—behind every great fortune is a crime." He inserted the floppy into his Compaq SLT-286 laptop, a model she'd lusted after. "And what do you want from me, exactly?"

Doubt hit her. Did she want the only extended family member she'd ever met slapped in the face with more of the ugly truth? How could she make Elise face the kind of person her father had been? The murders he'd been involved with, the lies. But wasn't he also a victim?

Fragmented loudspeaker announcements called out train departures. "The 15:07 to Limoges . . ." Get back to the task, her father would say. Focus. Follow up. She'd need René's help to learn more about Foundry.

But she was done, wasn't she? Her paying job was over. And hadn't Elise used her, trading on a distant family tie, suckering her in with talk about Aimée's mother?

But Aimée's gut said Elise was the one being used. It was only instinct, not something she could formulate into coherent thought, but Aimée couldn't shake the idea that Elise wasn't one of the perpetrators here—and that if Aimée didn't help her, she might become one of the victims.

The mouse was out of the hole, as her *grand-père* would say, no stopping things now.

"Ground control to Aimée," said René, waving his short-fingered hand in her face. "You back on the planet?"

Aimée pulled out the wad of francs Dufard had stuffed in her bag. Peeled off several five-hundred bills. "Hope you take blood money."

"What?" René's eager eyes clouded.

"Squeamish?" A heaviness filled her. "I guess I want Elise to know the truth. Where the fortune came from and what she's signing on for. Once we show her, it's her decision."

René hadn't picked up the bills. Stared at them, crumpled and dirty in the low afternoon glow coming from the high windows.

"Do it for the Givaray families whose sixty innocent relatives were slaughtered in revenge for a crime they didn't commit." She shivered. She pushed the photos across the table. "All Georges Ducray has to remember his papa by is an old photo. It's different when you meet a human affected by this."

"You're making this personal, Aimée. Looks to me this Georges Ducray's a possible suspect. "

"Maybe you're right, René. Still, can you just let a murderer steal the gold those sixty innocent people died for?"

René was staring at the photo of Dufard, Peltier, the mayor, and the little boy. "They were executed, too?"

"*Non.* This photo is from Chambly-sur-Cher." She told him what she knew about each of the men in the picture.

"There's something familiar about that man, the mayor," said René. "Too bad it's blurry."

René shrugged. "Puzzles intrigue me. Still, without more info, this is a wild-goose chase."

"Plenty of meat to chew on here, René. I know someone who knows someone at the *mairie*'s archives."

René's brow knit. "*Alors*, it's pro bono. I don't care for blood money." He handed the cash back. Checked his laptop. "The disk's files are encrypted. I need to open it with a program back at the computer lab."

"*Merci*, René."

She glanced out the door at the station clock, whose hour hand was on the 4. Late, so late already.

René stuck his laptop inside his bag, stood up. Grunted. The laptop had to weigh close to ten kilos. "Contingent on one thing, Aimée."

What now?

"Next week you're taking me to Martine's sister's party at *ELLE*."

Paris · Late Sunday Afternoon

AIMÉE RUSHED UP the stairs of Pâtisserie Viennoise, a student haunt on narrow rue de l'École de Medécine. She loved the homey, wood-paneled old-style Viennese bakery. The butter smells. And its pastries.

Her study group, at a back table, had gathered their books and were already breaking up. "Late as usual," said Serge, the group leader. "*C'est fini.*"

Merde.

There was Florent, blond hair tousled, wearing a wool scarf she recognized as the one she'd forgotten in his apartment. Her insides wrenched as she watched him help a woman into her jacket. His new fiancée? Talk about throwing it in her face.

"*Désolée*," she said to Serge. "Here's my section summary, I'll get copies to the others."

"We've covered the section already. Handed out exam study questions."

Already? How could she catch up?

"I saved you one." Serge handed her a stapled sheet. "We're eighty percent sure of the exam questions."

Stunned, Aimée scanned the sheets. "Don't they call this cheating?"

Serge's eyes clouded behind his thick lenses. "Your boyfriend had already shared copies before I got here. Ethics matter little to first years. You do anything to make it into second year. You know that."

"Report him, Serge."

"I did once. Like that made a difference."

It made her sick. One of her fellow study groupers stashed the paper and winked at her. How could this be fair, or make for a good doctor?

"You think it stinks?" said Serge. "Just wait until the exam."

"So only those students in the right study group will have a chance of passing? How do you go along with it?"

"I don't. But I've wanted to be a doctor all my life. I'd rather fight to be a forensic pathologist than battle an archaic medical system." Serge shrugged.

Just as corrupt as the *flics*—where only the inner circle got the leg up. No wonder her father had been glad to leave the force.

She turned on her heel.

Halfway down rue de l'École de Medécine, she felt a hand on her shoulder. "What's the hurry, Aimée?"

Florent pulled her close before she could stop him. His warmth, that smell of his—a trace of musk and lime—were so familiar it was hard to push him away.

"Where's your fiancée?" she blurted. Stupid. She wished the cobblestones would crack open and swallow her and her big mouth.

"That's not important." He brushed her hair from her eyes. "You're important." He pulled her into the doorway of a bar, kissed her hard.

By the time she came up for air, his arms had circled her under her jacket. "We're going here for a drink and you'll understand why."

She caught her breath. "What's to understand?"

He grinned. That smile in his eyes almost melted her. "It's you and me. *C'est tout.*"

"I don't think your father agrees with that. Or that I do."

Florent's smile faded. "I'm not going to let him ruin my life."

"*Alors*, make him stop ruining mine." She pulled away, checked her vibrating pager. "Got to go."

"I've worked it all out." Florent grabbed her hand. "My family has an apartment in Bordeaux. Two hours away. We'll see each other every weekend."

Worked it all out. As if he and his family had decided the course of her life?

"*Un nid d'amour*, a love nest? What, you'll keep me as your *maîtresse*, that's what you're thinking?" She laughed. "*Incroyable.*"

"I'm your bad boy, *non?*"

Not her kind of bad boy.

A little girl in a blue coat holding a doll pointed at them. "*Maman*, he's a bad boy, he said. Will he get in trouble?"

Her mother, a trench-coated blonde, steered her down the cobbles. "Don't point, *ma chère*."

"Florent, it's 1989," she said. "Royal mistresses were acceptable back in *le grand siècle*. History has moved on."

"What's the difference, though, really?"

Her mouth dropped open.

"My family is descended from the House of Bourbon," he said. "There's my title to consider."

Like anyone cared about that anymore. "Join the eighties, Florent." She shook her head. "Maybe you're descended from royalty. I'm descended from outlaws. And outlaws don't give a damn about titles." She pecked him on both cheeks. "Chew on that, *mon prince*."

She smiled to herself as she strode away.

She ran all the way to Odéon Métro, down the stairs, and made it to the platform as the number 4's doors were closing. She changed and exited at the small Place de l'Europe, a starburst of streets with names of European cities, radiating out above the tracks of Gare Saint-Lazare. Once the busiest part of Paris, Place de l'Europe had been the subject of twelve of Monet's canvases—Aimée had had that fact drilled into her by her art teacher in school. It had been a question on their test. Monet had even persuaded the railway to stoke extra coal so that he could paint the effects of belching steam—graphite grey when trapped inside the station, pearl and cloudlike against the sky.

The neighborhood that Hausmann had built opened to wide, tree-lined boulevards. Plastic bags whipped in the wind and caught in the riveted supports and railings of an old aboveground depot. Bourgeois mansions dotted the pointed roundabout—still well maintained, but no one lived there anymore. Now they were art foundations, an educational institute.

Scarf flying, jacket flapping, she hurried across the normally busy rue de Rome, the music district. The street was closed to traffic today due to roadwork, or maybe a demonstration—there was always something. She passed the shop where *grand-père* used to buy her sheet music, the violin makers, her piano teacher's apartment with its trailing ivy, and the music conservatory. Strains of a cello drifted from a window.

Her teacher, Madame Sisich, used to hand her a raw egg to hold in her cupped palm, instructing her to keep her hands positioned just so when she played. She'd broken the egg once, but never again.

Madame's son, Blaise, worked in the documents archive section in the *mairie* of the eighth arrondissement. Thank God he'd returned her call—if anyone could help her locate the paperwork for Peltier's private *banque*, Blaise could.

"It's crazy today, Mademoiselle Aimée," said Blaise Sisich, kissing her on both cheeks. He wore a navy three-piece suit, and brushed back his brown hair to show that widow's peak hairline that fascinated her as a child. He'd always shared Flavigny mint drops from a blue tin with her after lessons. "There's a reception for our remaining Great War veterans today, following the Armistice celebration. That's the only reason we're open. Hurry, I've got to get upstairs."

In the *mairie*, a nineteenth-century *hôtel particulier*, Blaise led her through what had been the carriage entrance and garden where wedding shots were taken after a ceremony in the *salle des mariages*. She hurried behind him up the marble staircase to the *ancien fumoir*, the old smoking salon, now the deputy's office.

Piles of papers, files everywhere, smelling of moldy, mildewed paper. She bit her lip. "What happened in here?"

"We had a minor flood. Most of those records you requested should be here. Somewhere."

In this mountain of mildewed paper? More than the usual reams of bureaucratic paperwork. Daunting.

"What if it's damaged? That's if I can even find it."

Blaise shrugged. Dusk hovered outside the rectangular window. "Remind me again why I am letting you into the archives?"

"These?" She handed him Café Crème cigarillos in a brown-and-white box, his favorite Henri Wintermans brand from Holland.

Blaise grinned. "My wife would shoot me. *Merci.*"

"Any way to point me to *la liste électorale* and business licenses?"

"Here and here." Two paper mountains on a marquetry-inlaid desk.

Narrowed it down a bit.

"I close up this wing in forty minutes."

"Then I need to hurry."

She pulled up a worn Louis XVI chair and got to work. Ten minutes into a behemoth stack of CVAE, *la cotatisation sur la valeur ajoutée des enterprises*, she'd found the Foundry file.

At least the ancient office had a fax machine. She paged René with the number printed on the black rotary phone. A moment later, the high-ceilinged office echoed with ringing.

"*Allô?*"

"Found it, Aimée?"

"Think so. What's your fax number? I'll fax the pages over."

He gave it to her. "Stay on to make sure it goes through."

She hit his number, fed in the pages, and heard a corresponding rumbling and grinding.

"Came through," said René. "What's this Banque Lazare on the floppy?"

"Their private bank, according to what I've found."

"I'll see if I have what I need to access a site and poke around Foundry. Meanwhile, find the bank's business license."

She used the fax machine to copy the sheets while she sorted through two hundred business license folders. The eighth arrondissement was the business district, *le quartier des affaires.* There was Banque Lazare—the tax number, the shareholders.

Voilà.

By the time Blaise returned, she'd faxed René, made a rendezvous to meet tomorrow, restacked the files, and stuffed the copies in her bag, which was heavy with Georges Ducray's info.

"*Merci,* Blaise," she said.

"Got what you needed?"

"Let's hope." After he locked the door, they walked down the marble staircase, now lit by the huge tear-drop crystal lamp.

He clicked open the Café Crème cigarillo box. Offered her one.

"Don't mind if I do."

DARKNESS BLANKETED THE street. Tired, her bag hanging heavily across her chest, she dreamed of bed and Miles Davis's little wet nose. Still another two blocks, then two Métro changes. She paused to light the cigarillo. Felt a jolt to her lungs.

No one was out this Sunday evening. The small *commissariat* in the *mairie* was dark too. She heard clinking cutlery, a radio newscast from a window. Brrr. Looked around for a taxi. Nothing.

A ripple of unease traveled down her back.

She pulled her leg warmers up to her knees, puffed on her cigarillo, and put on her headphones. ZZ Top launched into "She's Got Legs." She kept step to the twanging guitar, eager to reach the Métro and get off the deserted street. The drumbeat pounded. At first her mind didn't register what it meant—a sailing shard of glass splintering into diamond dust at her feet. A gunshot had shattered the window of the building beside her.

Her reflexes kicked in. She dropped the cigarillo and dove behind a parked Mercedes, pulled off her headphones and crawled, peeking to see where the shot came from. The revving of an engine, a metallic whine as a bullet scorched the car hood ahead of her.

Someone was trying to pick her off.

No one even looked out their window. Damn, the shooter was using a suppressor.

A taxi's blue light shone ahead by the stairs to the rue du Rocher overpass. She slung back her bag, scrambled to her feet, and ran. Her breath came in spurts, her heels wobbled. Why hadn't she worn her high-tops?

That taxi looked familiar. Looking back, she could make out a dark figure inside pointing something at her. Dumb move number two.

She zigzagged, veered right. Pumped her legs as fast as she could. The taxi careened toward her. Shots pinged off the stone wall, erupting in limestone bursts. Why wasn't there traffic, a bus? Other people? But then she remembered the road closures.

The quartier felt like a crypt. Her crypt.

She made the staircase, ducking as she ran up. That cab couldn't follow her here. Safe, she'd be safe if she made it up to rue du Rocher.

Panting, sweat running between her shoulder blades, her lungs straining, she regretted that cigarillo. At the top she grabbed the railing and struggled for breath. Dark windows looked down on her. Two options: run uphill toward Parc Monceau or downhill to the Métro at Saint-Lazare. She chose the latter. Headlights loomed, a car raced toward her. The gypsy taxi had swung around and come gunning up the wrong way on the one-way rue du Rocher.

Out for her blood.

The street-level window ahead of her was grilled. Nowhere else to go before the car gained on her. With no time to think, she pushed the door's buzzer, pushed again.

Several green garbage bins stood near the street lamp, so she kicked one and then another into the street. Anything to slow the taxi down. Over the screeching of the taxi's brakes, the door buzzed open.

Thank God. But not for long.

An old man in a flannel robe shook a fireplace poker at her. "*Quelle emmerdeuse*, you've no right to making a racket, waking the whole—"

Like she had time for this? "Call the *flics*, *grand-père*, report the gypsy taxi outside."

"Why?"

She stumbled in past him, slammed the door. "He's trying to kill me, that's why. Now make the call and jot down his license plate number."

Pounding came on the door.

"*Vite!* Where's the way out?"

He pointed.

She ran through his house, past garbage bins reeking of yesterday's fish, out into the moonlit walled courtyard. She was surrounded by period details, wrought-iron balconies—a picturesque trap.

The old liar. Back in the foyer she searched for the cellar door. *Bien sûr*, right behind the pungent trash. Locked.

She heard the front door click open.

She overturned the trash, ran like hell. Pounded the courtyard door of the next building. *"S'il vous plaît."*

A buzz and it opened. "Up here, quick." A woman wearing a silk dressing robe, beat-up wool slippers, and a copper saucepan on her head beckoned.

Not thinking twice, Aimée ran up to the landing. The apartment, all in pink pastels with swag draperies and old-fashioned Japanese screens, was redolent of an old-lady lavender scent.

"It's the *Boches*, they've come back, *non?*"

Go along with her. Aimée nodded. "I need to get out, madame, can you help me?"

"Won't be the first time," she said, picking up a silver-tooled musket that looked like it last saw action in the Napoleonic wars.

Slamming of doors, footsteps coming from the courtyard. Her heart pounded. She couldn't wait it out—what if the old man hadn't rung the *flics?*

"Madame, which way?"

"Through here." The galley kitchen opened to a dim, narrow landing. "Take the *escalier de service*. My grandmother snuck the Communards out here to escape the Prussians."

The crazy madame's thin mouth cracked in a laugh, her face a web of wrinkles. Aimée had never seen such an old woman. Her voice, at odds with her face, had the high pitch of a young girl's.

"Take the steps to the cave, left door and the tunnel leads to . . . I don't remember, it's been so long." The woman put a rusted long-handled key in her palm. "Don't worry, when the *Boches* come I can handle myself."

Did every member of this generation fear the Germans would come back?

The *escalier de service* led to the cave. The key turned in a creaking, water-rotted door. Once inside she pulled out her penlight. A slime-covered tunnel. Scurrying sounds, splashes. Long, greasy tails slithering in the muck.

Rats. The size of bunnies. A bite from one of these . . . She couldn't think about that—only about escaping. Her mind went back to the tall double doors by the outside stairs, some water station servicing *les égouts*, the sewers under the rue du Rocher. If she could work her way there, she'd exit on the adjoining street. Right where she'd come from.

The damp metal stairs corkscrewed down to a narrow walkway over gushing water smelling of sulphur and worse. Light shone from a glassed-in office where two men smoked. Hard at work as usual, these public employees of *le service de l'eau de* Paris.

Careful not to slip, she crouched and crab-walked her way past the glass. At the tall, dark green metal doors, she slid a bolt back. Winced at the loud screeching and slipped out the door. She scanned the street for a taxi—none. She ran.

Paris · Late Sunday Night

SHOT AT. CHASED. She couldn't count on being lucky the next time. There wouldn't be a next time if she didn't find the murderer. Even after taking a hot, steamy bath, she'd drifted off to wake up shivering.

Couldn't sleep.

She checked outside the window overlooking the quai for a watcher, a glowing tip of a cigarette, an idling taxi with the windows fogged up. If he was there, she didn't see him.

The clock showed 3:00 A.M. Miles Davis was nestled on her duvet, and her grandfather's snores issued from his back wing. An empty bottle of champagne on the table—no sense trying to wake him up. She gathered her father's wool bathrobe around her, pulled on thick socks, and paced. Streaks of light glimmered from the quai-side lamps over the rippling Seine. Everything crowded in her head; her hands jittered. Even the *tilleul* tea didn't calm her nerves.

What would Papa do?

She checked the answering machine. No message. Dialed into Leduc Detective's answering machine. Only a message left yesterday from his secretary—still in bed sick with *le rhume*.

Nerves eating her up, she tried to think. What had she missed? What didn't add up?

Note everything, no matter how small or seemingly insignificant, her father would say. If an investigation stalled or got stuck, he'd go back over his notes. Reread them and tease out, with a fine-tooth comb, whatever didn't make sense—a detail uncorroborated, an alibi that should be rechecked.

And when that failed, he'd sigh and go back to the beginning.

She took out Georges Ducray's stapled file, the copy of the report she'd given Elise, her notes from her anatomy notebook. Crawled back in bed with Miles Davis, pulled up the duvet, and started reading, underlining and circling words.

Paris · November 13, 1989 · Monday Morning

BY THE TIME the copper light of dawn crept over the mansard roofs and pepper-pot chimneys across the Seine, her head was swimming with it all.

Miles Davis whined. Sniffed her sleeve. A telltale sign he was about to leave a puddle on the floor.

"At your command, fluff ball."

Throwing on her leather pants and a mohair Sonia Rykiel sweater, she grabbed a wool scarf and duffel coat and slipped into her ballet flats. A quick check of the suitcase-sized fridge revealed the sum total of a second bottle of champagne, this one still full.

What could she feed the poor thing at this time of the morning?

Miles Davis watered the pear tree in the courtyard. His keening told her he wanted a walk on the quai.

"New route today," she said, leashing him up and going out the back way, so narrow her shoulders rubbed the old stone. A thick plank door let them out on rue Saint-Louis en l'Île, the main artery of Ile Saint-Louis.

At this time of the morning, in the spreading hint of

dawn, buildings were still in shadow, and little moved or stirred. She smelled baking bread from the *boulangerie*. Wary, she walked, keeping an eye out for a taxi, any trace of suspicious movement. Only a sleepy street overlaid with mist. She needed to clear her head. Breathe in the crisp air, let Miles Davis scamper and do his business.

At the tip of the island, she came across a couple, laughing, arms around each other, on their way home. Some party, she thought. For a moment she wished she'd just stayed at Martine's party, forgotten about Elise and her broken phone call.

"Aimée."

Stiffening, she turned to see Paul, the Ile Saint-Louis butcher, loading his truck. "I've got that order for *le vieux*. Mind taking it before I go to the market? I'm helping my son out today."

All the butchers in Paris knew her *grand-père*.

In the shop, Paul came out from the back wiping his hands on his apron. "A little something for the pup—fresh horse meat, eh? They love it."

Miles Davis stood up on his hind legs, pawing the cabinet.

"See, I told you." He handed her the lamb wrapped in white paper for her grandfather and a special white-waxed-paper packet for Miles Davis.

"I didn't bring my wallet, Paul. Can you put it on the account?"

A nod. "*Alors*, let's see . . ." He'd gone behind the register. On a long sheet of butcher paper taped to the back wall, he wrote *20 francs* under LEDUC. He noticed her look. "State of the art, eh? My son says I need a computer. Pah, a quick glance and I see it all at once."

Aimée stared at it. It was like a map of the island: who
ate what and when, who owes how much. She had an idea.

"Paul, roll me out some extra butcher paper. Add that to
our account."

IN THE KITCHEN, Miles Davis inhaled the horse meat,
licked his chipped Limoges bowl clean. Aimée munched the
hot brioche she'd cadged from the bakery, swept the flaky
crumb from her lip, and added another name to the butcher
paper she'd taped to the wall. Sipped an espresso, strong
and lethal, she'd made from grinding the last coffee beans.

Under *Persons Involved—Suspects?* she'd written a list:

>   *Suzy*
>   *Gypsy taxi driver*
>   *Clément*
>   *Georges Ducray*
>   *Bruno Peltier*
>   *Alain Dufard*
>   *Philbert Royant*
>   *Baret*
>   *executed Mayor Gaubert?*
>   *Thérèse and Bertrand Jagametti*
>   *Elise Peltier and Renaud de Bretteville*
>   *Marc from the resto*
>   *Madame Peltier*
>   *Pinel, the accountant*
>   *the fifth German*
>   Under *Motive:*
>   *gold*
>   *control of bank?*
>   *investments and property—greed*

revenge for the executions in Givaray?
ritual murder, or just made to look that way?

Under that, a rough timeline:
   December 1942—Alphonse Gaubert murdered
   October 9, 1989—Bruno Peltier murdered
   November 9, 1989—Berlin Wall falls
   November 10, 1989—Baret's body discovered

Nothing spoke to her yet. She added method:
   Sten gun
   bound extremities
   rags
   9-mm bullet casings

What wasn't she seeing? She stepped back and thought. She needed the whole picture.

So she mapped out the locations much as her anatomy professor had diagrammed the central nervous system—he'd called it the geography of the body, explaining how the brain and spinal cord connected the entire body through cause and effect. She sketched a rough diagram of Chambly-sur-Cher, the river, the mill, Givaray, the Peltiers' house, Gaubert's abandoned barn, Madame Jagametti's house with its cellar and tunnel, and approximate locations of Dufard's and Royant's houses. She added Georges Ducray's cheese shop and his X showing the discovery site of the German troop truck, and a big X for the Vierzon train station. Interesting, she thought, how the rail line threaded the whole damn area like little neurons attached to a spinal cord.

She took an old blue marker and drew lines connecting

the names to locations. A blue spider web appeared. Miles Davis sat attentive, his paws crossed, eyes never leaving her.

"What do you think, fluff ball?"

He cocked his head.

Nothing jumped out. She dunked her brioche and downed the espresso. Keep going, somehow she'd see a pattern, or a multiple connection that would point to the killer.

Next she drew a circle for Paris, inside it a triangle for *le triangle d'or* in the eighth, and sketched dots for Le Gogo on rue de Ponthieu, the resto Laurent, the quai under Pont des Invalides, Baret's, Peltier's, Royant's, and Dufard's addresses, the hunting bookshop, and Banque Lazare.

What was she missing?

She taped up the murder-scene photos Vortek had developed, the photo Elise had given her of Bruno, the wartime snapshot of the men in Chambly-sur-Cher. Mulling it over, she stepped back to see the big picture.

She heard the phone ring once before her *grand-père* stumbled into the kitchen. "*Ça va, ma puce?*" He kissed her. "*Mon Dieu,*" he said, glancing at the butcher paper on the wall before picking up the phone. "*Allô?*" He handed her the phone. "Morbier," he whispered. "Sounds serious."

She grabbed it. "What's happened, Morbier?"

"Meet me at the *commissariat* on rue d'Anjou. Now, Aimée."

Commissariat on rue d'Anjou, Paris
Monday Morning

"WHAT'S SO IMPORTANT, Morbier?" Aimée's chest heaved. She'd skipped anatomy class and run up the *commissariat* stairs two at a time.

"*Bonjour* to you, too, Aimée," said Morbier. "*Assieds-toi.*"

On edge, she couldn't sit. Placed her hands on the desk.

"Last night the old coot called it in, *non?* The gypsy taxi on rue du Rocher? Did you find the killer?"

Morbier's perplexed expression became an irritated one. "*Écoutes*, Aimée, I'm telling you this for your own good . . ."

He hadn't found the killer. Her heart sank. "I was shot at last night and—"

"Shot?" Morbier shook his head. "We'll get to that in a minute. There's something you need to know." He shot a look at the door.

Shining her off? Fuming, she sat down. Ancient Sergeant Timset, long overdue for retirement, shuffled in bearing two demitasses of steaming espresso, a file under his arm. She hated how he surveyed her legs.

"*Commissaire*, here's the communiqué with the telexed photos."

"*Merci.*" Morbier took the file and an espresso, and waved him out after Aimée had taken hers.

Aimée plopped in two brown sugar cubes, stirred with the tiny spoon while Morbier scanned the file.

"*Bon*, Aimée, *c'est entre nous.* The Chambly-sur-Cher *gendarmerie* responded to a call this morning in the Sologne region near the Loire Valley. Two men were found bound, gagged, and shot in the head, on the Cher riverbank."

She gasped.

"The report came in to us because the victims reside . . . resided in the eighth arrondissement. Their names were Philbert Royant and Alain Dufard."

Her mind spun. Only yesterday old Dufard had turned nervous when she mentioned the fifth German. When she'd asked him who was after them, he'd fluffed her off.

She didn't know what to make of their murders—the attack on her and how it connected. But it did.

Chewing her lip, she pointed to the photos in the file. "Can I see?"

"Not pretty, Aimée."

"I read *ELLE* when I want pretty."

"Not supposed to . . ."

She shoved away the thought that Morbier was sharing this with her because he wanted something. She took the folder.

On the riverside by the mill, two figures were slumped behind crime-scene tape. Royant's gag had slipped and glistened with vomit, his mouth a rictus, frozen in a scream. Dufard's head was cocked sideways, a look of cold fear caught in his dead eyes.

Horror-struck, she covered her mouth. Yet hadn't she suspected they were next? Tried warning them?

When she found her voice, she said, "Just like Baret and Peltier. I told you they were in danger." She stared at the photo. "All four were murdered in a ritual style. It's symbolic."

Her mind went to Clément—his obvious feelings for Elise, the fact that he'd discovered Mayor Gaubert's body, shot just like this, back in 1942. Now he was the only man who had been on the riverbank that day who was still alive. But Georges Ducray had a more obvious motive for revenge, if he thought these men were responsible for the execution of his father and the others in the village.

"It smells like revenge," Aimée said. "Either for the sixty villagers who were executed by the Germans in 1942, or for the mayor who was supposedly shot by the resistance."

Morbier sighed. "More fantasy, Aimée? First you think you've been shot at—"

"Nazi gold, Morbier," she interrupted. "The four executed old men—Peltier, Baret, Royant, Dufard—they stole it from German soldiers, who they murdered, melted it down, ignored the German reprisals, shot the mayor to keep it quiet. There's proof."

Morbier shook a Gauloise out of its cellophane packet, scratched a kitchen match on the desk's edge. Lit up, inhaled, sat back and exhaled a plume of smoke.

"Proof which I'm sure you intend to furnish," he said. "Leaving your fantasy aside for now, how do you explain this? It was found in Dufard's wallet."

He slid a faxed sheet over the table, wedging it under her demitasse. It showed her faux PI business card and what appeared to be a torn paper fragment with the words *Aimée Leduc 11:00*.

Merde! Who in the hell would have written that? Unless it was one of the old men who'd followed her, or the killer to implicate her.

"Oh, that?" She couldn't deny it, had to tell him some version of the truth. "Yes, yes, I saw them. Sometime in the morning. But I didn't give him my card. You should be looking for suspects in the village they come from."

"This playing detective needs to stop, Aimée."

Playing detective?

"Morbier, I'm getting close. The killer drives a gypsy taxi—check the call-ins last night on rue du Rocher."

Morbier stabbed out his Gauloise in the overflowing ashtray.

"Some old fart on rue du Rocher reported an intrusion, another insisted the Germans were coming." Morbier sighed. "And for now I'm going to close my eyes to this. Pretend they didn't report a girl fitting your description." He leaned forward. "Your father wouldn't appreciate this, Aimée. I helped because . . . *zut*, because of the family connection."

"You were the one who referred Elise to us, remember?"

"Yes, and this has gone way further than I ever recommended. The *brigade criminelle*'s working their end. I referred the woman to get her off my back and make some business for your father. You should be studying and leaving this alone."

She thought of her father—the last she'd spoken to him was when he'd been rushing for the train. "Papa hasn't called from Berlin. I'm worried."

A knowing look filled Morbier's deep brown eyes. "He doesn't want to know about this silly playing detective. And he won't."

"Four men murdered ritualistically—that's silly? I don't know why you're not following up on what I've found."

Morbier crumpled his empty pack of Gauloises, threw it in the bin. Missed. Pulled another from his pocket. "If your father won't put his foot down, I will. Time you listen to sense."

"Sense?" She flushed. "Papa's in Berlin searching for my mother's records. He lied to me about why he was going. Won't even reply to my calls. Are you in on it too?"

"Little fool, he's protecting you. Why can't you get that through your head and leave all that alone? You're a medical student—someday your real business card will say Doctor Leduc. How proud you'll make him. Me."

Her throat caught. She wanted to make her father and Morbier happy. She did. Yet she heard *Grand-père's* words—*you take after me*. He'd said her only duty to her family was to be passionate in what she attempted.

She'd tried. But she knew she'd had enough. Couldn't stomach it anymore.

"*Bien sûr*, medicine is difficult, Aimée," said Morbier, striking another match. "Stick to it. You're smart, you'll make it. Nothing worth doing doesn't have its potholes."

Her father said the same thing.

"You'll be using your skills to treat those in need. It will be a secure income, rewarding work. You'll spend your life surrounded by esteemed physicians."

She dropped her demitasse spoon. "Like I want that. Medical school and the esteemed physicians are as corrupt as the *préfecture*."

Morbier examined the cuticle of his left thumb. Danger signal. "And you know this how, Leduc?"

From Morbier, that counted as an insult. "Since when am I 'Leduc'?"

"As long as you talk to me like those I put in lockup—all attitude and mouth."

She swallowed. "You don't understand. Why don't you ever listen to me?"

"*Classique*. That's the line of poetry they all quote."

She slammed her fist on the table, scattering papers. "Four old men murdered—two I warned you about—and you rake me over the coals? Instead of treating me like a child, why don't you investigate the case? I've done all the work, put the pieces right in front of you."

She stood, grabbed her bag, and wheeled around, bumping into the leering sergeant, who was hovering at the door. "Bad day in school, mademoiselle, or that time of the month?"

She almost slapped him.

"I'm keeping this file in my desk," said Morbier, reaching for the phone. "No tantrums, Leduc, or you'll get a spanking."

MORTIFIED AND SEETHING, she kicked the bollard in the courtyard. Wished she had Morbier's head to drop-kick instead.

Her stomach knotted. She'd been shot at and did he listen? *Mais non*, dismissed with a warning of a spanking, as if she were five years old.

She'd show him—all of them. The killer was on the loose, and she was going to stop him. Stop him before he stopped her.

THAT PHOTO MORBIER had shown her of a bound Dufard and Royant with the old mill in the background haunted her. Twinges of guilt rustled like the plane tree leaves on the quai. Had she stirred up Georges Ducray to revenge? Or Clément, who'd said . . .

He who pees in the wind wets his teeth.

Hopefully René had found something she could use. She needed to get to the bottom of this. Money, she had to trace the money.

Would she trace the money to Elise?

Behind the Palais de la Découverte, she passed through a crooked stone arch. René was waiting for her on a bench in a garden whose entrance she'd passed a million times and never known existed. A weeping beech and a pond with a waterfall, all sheltered below the street, quiet but for the sound of water. The leaves had changed—brown, copper, and orange. Evergreens, bamboo, and maples surrounded them. Carp fed at the surface among water lilies, leaving trails of glistening silver bubbles.

"Private investment banks are a league of their own, Aimée."

"Tough security at Banque Lazare?" She hoped it wasn't more than he could handle.

"Break-ins are easier when you have the dial-in bank number. Which you handed me."

"I did?"

"Going on the assumption that Pinel, the bookstore's *directeur financier*, would access the bank's computer directly through a dedicated line, I found the bookstore's leased line on one of those transfer orders with the bank account number."

"How did you break this? Did you need a password?"

"No, that's too hard. Did it the easy way and analyzed the floppy. I knew what kind of programs they were using and how to crack them. It's a pretty routine bit of cryptanalysis."

All geek to her but she nodded.

"Pretty obvious *crib*."

"*Crib?*"

"Crib means routine stuff, like a predictable series of numbers." René sat up straighter. Happy to show off, she could tell. Fine by her. "I knew the first couple of bytes from the files copied onto the floppy probably come from a Lotus 1-2-3 spreadsheet. A standard for accounting data. They all have a beginning in common. I used several trial keys, the *crib*, until the program fell over like a dead canary." He gave a proud little smile. "I did it the easy way."

He called that easy?

René handed her a printout. "Here you see the shareholders, board member percentage holdings from off the floppy disk. That what you wanted?"

Yes and no. This told her Elise reigned as financial queen—her family holding eclipsed the other men's family share holdings, and she was now the only living board member. Mentally, Aimée underlined Elise in the suspect column.

But it didn't tell her the source of the money. Or prove it came from Nazi gold.

"Any luck from what I found at the *mairie?*"

"That gets interesting. The business license dates back to 1946, the year the four same men purchased the bookshop. But it incorporated under the business titled Foundry as of the sixties."

"They wised up, hired a financial advisor," she said. A spiked chestnut pod crunched under her feet. Brittle and dry—like her investigation. If she could call it that. "Say they'd melted the gold, traded in gold futures and bundled it up in this private investment bank. Any way I can trace this fortune back to the gold?"

"Time travel?" René shrugged. "Or a confession?"

"A little late, René. All the conspirators are in the morgue."

"*Alors*, firms keep ledgers. Maybe there is a double set of account books?" René raised his hands. "I'd say either Elise Peltier's next or she engineered it."

Neither a good prospect. She hated to admit it, but it looked that way.

"Or the fifth German."

"You're back to a Ludlum thriller," said René, pulling a *tartine* out of his bag. "Even if there were a phantom fifth German, why would he come back now?"

She liked bouncing ideas off René—no judgment, no bias. He actually tried to help, unlike Morbier.

"The Wall just came down. Say he's been stuck in Germany and now he can return to exact revenge."

René tore his *tartine aux jambon et fromage* in half, handed it to Aimée.

"*Merci.*" Delicious. She hadn't eaten since the brioche at dawn.

"That doesn't explain the murder of Baret, a month before the Wall came down." Good point. "But put that aside for a minute. I don't buy that it's revenge. Not with gold involved." René chewed. "Greed more like it. Say the fifth German returns for the gold after all these years, extorts a payoff, blackmail."

"Why kill his golden geese?"

"The men refused to pay up? Or like a *tontine* scam—remember in that movie with Lino Ventura? What if there is no fifth German—they're killing each other off, last man standing keeps the big payoff?"

Thérèse Jagametti said the same thing. "But who's left standing now?"

"Who knows?" Suddenly René hit his forehead. "That's right. I knew he looked familiar."

"Who?"

"The man in that old village photo you showed me. He reminds me of an actor I saw in a performance a few weeks ago—the name escapes me. One of those theaters on rue des Mathurins, just up from the chapel where the monarchists congregate."

Her mind perked up. Renaud de Bretteville? "Chapelle Expiatoire. Elise lives right across from it. Remember the play?"

"Which one was it? I've seen so many lately. Maybe I still have the ticket stub . . ." René rustled through his wallet. "*Mais non.* Oh well. The photo reminded me of him, that's all. Life's funny, eh?"

A coincidence? Never in an investigation, her father would say. Build your case by wearing down your shoe leather, getting statements, checking out each detail. If it doesn't pan out, file it away because that detail might just come back to bite you.

And the most important advice: if it niggles at you, go scratch that itch.

RIGHT NOW HER itch was Banque Lazare, the private investment bank. Not for the likes of her—one needed a minimum of a million francs to open an account. The no-nonsense lobby breathed wealth, all white marble and understated bronze accents.

She asked to speak to the bank officer who dealt with Foundry.

"Do you have an appointment?" the receptionist asked her.

"Mademoiselle Peltier sent me," she lied. "I need to speak to the account manager before the police do." How easy this lying had become. Aimée flashed her PI license.

The receptionist blinked and checked something on her screen. "Your name again, *s'il vous plaît?*"

"Aimée Leduc."

"The account liaison is Madame Fontaine, but she's out until this afternoon."

"I didn't want to disturb her, but it's urgent."

"*Un moment.*"

But it was more than *un moment* before the receptionist, who made several phone calls, explaining the situation each time, said "Understood" and passed over an address on a piece of paper.

"Madame Fontaine's at Théâtre des Mathurins. She can spare you five minutes."

At a theater? Another coincidence?

"It's around the corner from the department store Printemps."

Aimée knew it well.

THE SKY WAS a dove grey, amber traffic lights gleamed on the buildings. She kept to broad Boulevard Haussmann—the business hub of the upscale, yawn-inducing commercial section of the eighth arrondissement. Buses and bicycles passed; office workers on break smoked on the pavement. A few cafés, shops, and the characteristic Haussmannian buildings—limestone façades and wrought-iron balconies.

On the sidewalk, near Place Saint-Augustin, she noticed the weekly wine-tasting signs under the awning of Les Caves Augé, her *grand-père*'s favorite wine shop. She peeked inside, inhaled the musky oak-barrel smells from one of the oldest wine merchants in the city: the nineteenth-century dark-wood interior patinaed with time, still crammed from floor to ceiling with every kind of wine, aperitif, liquor. The owner had laughed when her ten-year-old self said it belonged in the *Guinness Book of World Records*. "More like in a Balzac novel," he had said. "Balzac lived just up the hill, you know. They say he'd nip down here."

She hurried past Berteil's washed-out yellow façade, a boutique for old-lady types who think they're *très sportives*, according to Martine. A block further was Square Louis XVI with its dark foliage and shadowed vaulted stone, an overgrown ruin-like appearance in the middle of Paris emitting damp leaf smells. She turned on rue de l'Arcade. A few minutes later she stood in the foyer of Théâtre des Mathurins.

The playbill windows were empty. *Merde.* She had no clue if it was the theater René had mentioned. Inside the Italianate lobby—deserted apart from the nymphs carved overhead—she caught the sound of someone talking inside the theater. Shrieks from a microphone.

A woman with a sleek bob stood on the stage giving directions in a cut-glass accent. *Très grand bourgeois.*

"Madame Fontaine?" Aimée asked when she finally got her attention.

The woman nodded to the sound-crew tech, a bored twenty-something who sucked a hand-rolled cigarette. "Ah, the bank called me, but, mademoiselle, I can give you five minutes only." She called to the sound-tech crew, "Adjust the mic volume, *s'il vous plaît.*" She said to Aimée, "Give me *une petite seconde.*"

Aimée wondered at the woman's focus on the situation here—whatever it was. The stage was vacant apart from an armchair, a side table, and a microphone apparatus. Madame Fontaine realigned the chair with a stage mark.

"We're preparing for a talk in our *philosophe* series. *C'est immense*, standing room only when the big hitters lecture. Eat *à la* brown bag—something I saw on New York's Wall Street—you know, get your culture at lunch." Madame

Fontaine was clearly impressed with herself and her trendy, forward-thinking copycat ideas. "Banque Lazare sponsors this little series," she said, "our *petit bouillon de culture*. I'm easing the transition since Monsieur Peltier's passing. It was a priority to him and to the bank that we stand by this important piece of culture."

Benefitting from a nice tax write-off too, Aimée figured. But that fit in with the theater foundation reception that Renaud mentioned Bruno Peltier sponsored. Rich people loved tax write-offs that made them feel like they were contributing to a cultural legacy.

Madame looked at her pointedly. "Now if that's all?"

Where were the five minutes?

"I'm here about an investigation into the Foundry corporation and its ties to the bank."

"That's confidential. I only discuss bank business with clients."

Aimée scrambled to come up with something to get the woman to talk. "But madame, why's that?"

The woman's face had turned stony. "Silly of you to come and waste my time."

"Then you'll deal with the police, who have questions," she lied. "Didn't the bank tell you Elise Peltier hired me?"

"Get authorization in writing." She waved a dismissal and returned to readjust the microphone, obsessed with her flurry of minutia.

Stupid, what had she expected? A forthcoming banker? As if they existed.

Frustrated, Aimée looked around for playbills of upcoming performances. In the lobby, a short man in overalls with a cigarette hanging from his mouth stood over a box of electrical wires.

He shook his head at her query, the long ash of his cigarette threatening to fall on the theater's mosaic tiles. "Playbills go up this afternoon."

She didn't know for sure this was the theater René had meant, anyway. She'd try the theater next door.

But before she left, she'd take one more shot.

"Do you know Renaud de Bretteville?"

The electrician nodded. "He's the troupe director. Those photos in the side foyer are all his productions."

"What's he like?"

"Eh? He's an actor." He shook his head and ash drifted to the floor. He rubbed it out with the toe of his shoe. "Like a lot of actors—at ease everywhere, at home nowhere."

A philosopher, this electrician. But she could learn something.

"You mean kind of lost?"

He lifted his tool kit. "Except of course when he's on stage. He's a real *bête de scène*, a born actor."

That and ten francs would get her an Orangina. So far, her trip here had been a waste.

In the red-velvet-wallpapered side foyer, she scanned the glass displays of former productions: a maquette of the theater used in the 1890s for seating, old programs, photos. An illustrious history boasting the plays of Camus, Baudelaire, Beckett . . . on and on. Bored, she searched the photos, spotting Renaud in different roles—a cavalier, a pirate. In one production, as part of an ensemble piece, he wore *sabots*, the wooden clogs worn in the countryside. Her *grand-mère* had a pair.

It wasn't a coincidence—the actor René thought looked like Mayor Gaubert must have been Renaud de Bretteville. Renaud, who appeared to be in his forties or fifties, looked very much like the executed mayor had in the old photo. She searched in her bag for a comparison, then remembered she'd stuck the photo on the butcher-paper outline.

Her arms tingled. Eerie. How could that be?

What were the chances—a Parisian actor with an aristocratic name and a mayor murdered in a village during the war?

She had to find out.

A FEW BLOCKS down narrow rue des Mathurins, Aimée's pager vibrated—Elise? She retraced her steps to the corner café, ordered an Orangina, and hopped downstairs to the phone cabin.

But it was a hoarse, cigarette-infused voice she recognized as Suzy's, asking to meet. Why Suzy? Why now?

She bounded up the stairs, almost plowing into a waiter bearing a tray of Ricard, threw ten francs on the counter and left, her Orangina untouched.

She took a shortcut through Passage Puteaux, a sleepy, glass-roofed passage with a *bar à vin*, lines of flowerpots, and a forgotten feel. Two short blocks later, she walked into the old Marché de la Madeleine, the vaulted stone entrance partially obscured by the starred hotel next door. What had once been a covered local fruit, produce, and flower market now was a characterless courtyard, home to a few lunch spots, mostly Asian, for office workers in the modern buildings behind. She found Suzy smoking.

"About time, kid," said Suzy, smiling. "I'm in a hurry and doing you a favor."

In a hurry for what, Aimée wondered.

"Because you liked the Chanel No. 5 sample, Suzy? Or because you're afraid?"

Suzy's grin faded. She wore a faux fur bolero jacket with shoulder pads, a leather pencil skirt, and dark glasses. "Just listen. Then make of it what you will. You never heard this from me."

Aimée took out her notebook and uncapped her kohl eye pencil. "I'm all ears, Suzy."

"Rue de Ponthieu's protected by the Corsican gang. Everyone knows this. Grandmothers and even the *flics*."

Her mind went back to Morbier's chalkboard diagram in the *commissariat*—the high-end robberies.

"But the Corsicans got upset because there's a gypsy taxi that's been playing out of bounds."

Aimée shivered. The same driver who'd attacked her twice, no doubt. "Playing out of bounds—you mean not paying protection money?"

Suzy took a puff, exhaled. "Among other things, but it's *pas de respect*. This gypsy taxi driver's causing problems on the gang's turf."

"*Et alors?*"

"The Corsicans want the gypsy taxi."

"What's that to you, Suzy?"

"Do you know who I work for?" Suzy looked around. "Listen, kid. The Corsicans feel if one gets away with it, others will follow."

"You work for the Corsicans, Suzy?"

"Not officially and I'll deny it. Everyone who works on rue de Ponthieu has to butter their bread, if you know what I mean."

Aimée tried to digest that.

Suzy exhaled a plume of smoke.

"*Attendez*, you said gypsy taxi on their turf," she said, thinking back to the other night. "So you're saying the Corsicans suspect the gypsy taxi driver of . . . what?"

Suzy shrugged. "The old geezer, Bruno—the one you asked me about. The driver might have used his cab to kidnap and kill him. Maybe some others, too." Tossed her cigarette, stubbed it out with her toe. "That's the rumor."

"Do they know the driver's identity?"

"Like they tell me, *chérie?*"

"Did you lure Bruno to Laurent the night he died? Are you involved with the taxi driver?"

"Bruno invited me, remember? But I split. Good thing, too."

And Aimée believed her. Suzy was afraid of the Corsicans.

"Still, I don't get it, Suzy." She did but wanted Suzy to spell it out.

Suzy pulled out the Chanel No. 5 sample Aimée had given her, spritzed it on her wrist. "Before the Corsicans launch into a full turf war, I'm whispering in your ear, asking if you have any leads on the old men's murderer. My job's to provide tips, *compris?* They'd like to make an example of whoever did this."

And leave the *flics* out of it?

Disappointed, Aimée shook her head. "I need leads myself. I got shot at last night and . . ."

"That was you?"

"You heard?"

Suzy gave a little nod. Took out a compact, checked her lipstick in the mirror. "A warning, kid. If you find him first, turn him over to the Corsicans. That's how it's done."

"How it's done?" Aimée's mouth went dry.

"Welcome to the real world." Suzy snapped her compact shut. "Make the call. My neck's on the line here. My boss wants information." She handed Aimée a card from the club.

Bile rose in her stomach. "Suzy, get the hell out of this. Leave that club. You're smart, you don't have to . . ."

"I'm smart so I'm alive, *tu comprends?*" Suzy's bravado didn't match the quiver in her voice. "Like it or not, you've joined the big league. Wise up."

"Wrong. I'm employed by the victim's daughter."

"Look at it anyway you like, *kid.* Just make the call."

And then Suzy had gone in a cloud of Chanel No. 5.

A SUDDEN BURST of rain pelted the old glass market roof. Thrumming like her nerves. She was caught in a web. Whichever way she turned, it twisted tight around her.

The Corsican gang controlling the quartier wanted to catch the murderer to keep street cred, enforce their turf. Anything with Corsicans meant bad news, her papa always said. So, in theory, catching the murderer would stick her between a rock and a hard place: Turn him over to the *flics*, who'd done little and would claim credit? Or to the Corsicans, to be made an example of?

Who were they to pressure her?

Cross that bridge if and when you come to it, she could hear her father say. Still, her stomach cramped in fear. What the hell had she gotten into?

She needed to stay out of the gypsy taxi driver's crosshairs long enough to find him.

BACK AT HOME, rivulets of rain streaked the kitchen window overlooking the pewter Seine. Miles Davis snuggled on her toes, warming them. His tail, the color of bleached cotton, squiggled like a question mark.

Questions, questions, that's all she had looking at her butcher-paper chart. She read through the printouts René had given her. Bank structure, shareholders, numbers—all eye-glazingly boring. How could she convince Elise that Nazi gold had funded her family apartment, her schooling in Canada? Who knew what else?

Then again, as René pointed out, Elise could either be in danger or behind all this. She struggled with the idea of Elise hiring her if she'd murdered her own father. Yet from the get-go Elise had fixated on Suzy, and had proved unhelpful at every step, avoiding Aimée's phone calls, missing their Chambly-sur-Cher rendezvous, burning the diary. Would she have paid a sham retainer to hide her tracks?

The back-up floppy and bookstore paperwork raised questions. Huge sums earmarked for an account—René had flagged these with a red pencil. Did Elise have a partner to help her—maybe her fiancé, Renaud? Or gone in cahoots with the bean counter, Pinel?

Her father said, if you can't convince someone of your way of thinking, or prove your point with fact, the best thing to do is to raise doubt. Doubt slivers friendships, erodes trust between couples—it's corrosive and powerful. She'd raise doubt.

Her nerves jangled at the ringing phone piercing her thoughts. Miles Davis's ears perked up. Could it be his owner, calling the number on the announcements she'd persuaded her *grand-père* to post on the quai?

"*Oui?*"

Loud static, a buzz, then a clinking sound, like a coin dropping in a pay-phone slot. "Aimée?" her father's unmistakable voice.

"Papa, you've worried me." Relief washed through her. Then she remembered he'd lied to her. That she was mad at him.

But she wanted to tell him what had happened, how

she'd messed everything up, gotten in over her head. Rushed headlong and hit a wall. Should she admit how incompetent she'd been?

"I got what I needed, Aimée."

Her heart stopped. "You found her files? *Maman*'s files?"

"How did . . . ?" Clicks, more static. "Say nothing."

"But Papa . . . "

"I'm hanging up."

He used to joke, if I ever hang up on you, it's because the phone has ears.

Their line was tapped. The clicks. The static.

Buzzz. The line went dead.

Fear hit her. Her big mouth again. Yet how was she to know? Why hadn't he told her the truth in the first place?

I got what I needed.

Was her mother in danger? Or dead?

FROM THE HALLWAY came the sound of a lock turning. Her *grand-père*'s cough, shoes scraping on the creaking hardwood floor. Miles Davis barked, leaped off the duvet and scampered to the hall.

Pulling her father's cashmere cardigan around her, she slipped into wool socks and ran to greet him. He stood with his raincoat glistening, a large, square brown-papered package in his arms.

"Another painting? Where will this one go?"

"*C'est magnifique*, Aimée."

He always said that.

He unwrapped it. A black-and-white sketch of a figure leaning over a ballet *barre*. "Masterful strokes. Unsigned but probably an early Degas study. A steal at Drouot, so I had to."

She sighed.

Another find at the auction house. He had a whole library full of them. Even in their cavernous seventeenth-century flat, there was no more room left for new acquisitions.

"We're going to Giverny . . . the gardens."

"In the rain?"

"You know she paints the garden *chaque saison*. Arguments don't work with her."

His mistress.

"Take care of your cough," said Aimée.

"Only if you let me bring *Meels Daveez*. He needs exercise."

"He's not ours. You shouldn't get attached."

A snort. "No one's ever called, eh? Face it, he's ours." He leaned down and ruffled Miles Davis's fur. "*On y va*. She's waiting in the car."

"Now?" Aimée had so much to run by him. She wanted to get his take on the suspects whose names she'd written on the butcher paper. A horn honked.

"We'll stay at the auberge tonight. Don't worry, I'll bring the pooch back tomorrow." Her *grand-père* grinned. As if reading her thoughts, he took her hand. Squeezed it. "You're thinking, at my age? But life's only worth living if you live, *ma puce*."

He pulled her close, hugged her, his scratchy mustache on her cheek.

"Don't do anything I wouldn't do," she said.

He set the drawing on the hall *escritoire*, grabbed Miles Davis's leash and another scarf from the rack. Winked.

"Oh, I will, *ma puce*."

The door shut and she was alone.

A IMÉE   REREAD   THE   bookstore accountings page by page, comparing transaction sums with the account numbers René had red-penciled. It was mind-numbingly tedious. But she found all the links she could have hoped to find. She was sure now—or as sure as she figured she could be—there was a dormant account, like a reserve, which had gone for review prior to a sell transaction. It must hold several million francs.

As she was about to call Elise's apartment, a rumbling came from the fax on the desk in her room.

> *Plans changed. Now meet me at the apartment, I'm waiting.*
> *Bring your report so I can pay you. Elise*

What could Elise mean? She'd already given Elise her report, gotten her retainer. Odd. She tried calling the apartment number. Busy.

A trap? Still, she needed to ask Elise about this huge transaction.

Her father's old adage about *flics* working in pairs to cover each other's back sounded in her head. With her *grand-père* and father out of the picture, she needed backup if she'd even consider going to Elise's.

Better tell someone, just in case. She paged René. Waited. No answering call. Was she overreacting? She felt silly. Did she really think Elise might be dangerous? In league with the gypsy cab driver? Her instincts told her no, but her instincts had been wrong about so many things.

She changed, pulling on stovepipe jeans, her nautical navy-and-white-striped *marinière*, her Roger Vivier ankle boots—a last-season bargain from rue Saint Honoré, just waterproofed at the cobbler's—and topped it all off with her motorcycle jacket. Wool cap and gloves for the raw November wind. She stuffed the papers in her big leather *sac*.

She heard the phone, ran and caught it on the sixth ring.

"Aimée?" René's voice wavered, horns blared in the background. Sounded like a pay phone on the street. She pictured him straining on his tiptoes to reach the receiver. How high a public phone must be to someone his size.

"Sorry, René. Listen, I'm going to thirty-four rue Lavoisier to get answers from Elise . . ."

"*Quoi?*"

Poor René. "Thirty-four rue Lavoisier. Remember that if I don't . . . "

The phone cut off.

She tried Elise again, just in case. Busy.

In the courtyard the rain had left puddles among the cobbles, the veins of rain pooling in the cracks reflecting the overcast sky. Pigeons cooed as she biked along and she almost hit a slow-moving seagull who'd swooped over the quai on Ile Saint-Louis.

All the way she wondered why Elise had faxed instead of paging her. The fiscals she'd been looking at bothered her. Why had the bookstore requested the new review prior to the sell transaction? Most of all, she wondered if Elise had even ordered this transaction. Was Elise part of an elaborate money-laundering conspiracy, one that had escalated to murder? Or was she someone else's pawn, or future victim? What exactly did she need Aimée for? What was Aimée riding toward?

Back again now for the second time today by the park enclosing Chapelle Expiatoire. An overalled worker swept leaves in the running gutter. Behind him lay an open manhole with a sign: ATTENTION—TRAVAUX DES ÉGOUTS.

She chained her bike to the rain-wet metal fence under a gold fleur-de-lis.

The massive blue door of Elise's building opened to her buzz. She stepped inside the black-and-white-tiled foyer.

A taped sign on the elevator read OUT OF SERVICE and below it a handwritten note: *Aimée, I'm down in the garage packing the car. Level 1.*

Didn't she have a housekeeper for that?

Aimée listened at the door leading to the underground garage. Quiet apart from the ticking of the timed light. She reached in her bag for her Swiss Army knife. Palmed it and felt along the stucco walls as she wound her way down. As she reached the bottom, the light went out.

Merde. Only the lit exit sign from above the metal fire door. She pulled the handle, hit by a wave of cold, concrete-scented air. Several cars were parked under the dim lighting.

A Mercedes had its trunk open, a carryall bag on the ground. About to call out for Elise, Aimée noticed the car parked next to it. A taxi.

She stifled a gasp, ducked down and crab-walked around the Mercedes. LA VILLE written on the side—the gypsy taxi?

Scraping sounds and voices came from the cellar adjoining the garage. Horrific thoughts filled her mind—Elise abducted by the gypsy taxi driver, tortured? Worse?

Should she run back upstairs and get help?

An older man wearing a work smock—the concierge, she figured—appeared at the stairs of the cave, stooped under something heavy he was carrying.

"Monsieur, where's Elise Peltier?"

"Eh, who are you? Why did you come down here?"

"I'm her cousin," she said. "There was a note on the elevator to meet her—"

"*Vraiment?* I'm loading up her car."

None of this made sense.

"So she's upstairs?"

"Took a taxi," he said.

Aimée's blood froze. "How long ago?"

"Half an hour?"

"Did you see the taxi?"

He shrugged. "Didn't pay attention. She and the *monsieur*, that nice one, said they'd be back."

"You mean her fiancé?"

He shrugged again. Her thoughts raced. What about the impending bank transaction? Now that all the old men were dead, was Elise making a run for it with all their money? Moving a secret stash of cash and jetting back to Canada, maybe?

It all fell into place—Peltier's daughter had been out of the country for years, far away from any whiff of conspiracy; she'd studied economics, bided her time until . . .

Could Elise really have murdered her own father and come to the Leducs for help in covering up her crime?

Only one place where Elise could be—a place with an online connection to the bank.

BACK ON HER bike, Aimée pedaled as fast as she could toward Saint Philippe du Roule Church. Eight blocks and two traffic jams later, she chained her bike in the narrow passage hugging the old soot-grimed church. The place where the gypsy taxi driver had trapped her and pulled her inside his cab. She was shaking. She didn't know how she'd do this, how she'd confront Elise on her family's turf.

The FERMÉ sign hung on the bookstore door.

No doubt Pinel, the obstructive *directeur financier*, was in on it with her.

Dusk fell early in November and few people waited at the bus stop facing the church. A choir practiced and melodious voices drifted from the open church doors. She remembered the bookstore's back door, the yard and trash bins she'd glimpsed behind it. It gave her an idea. Baret's apartment was several doors down. Would the concierge remember her?

She was about to buzz the door of Baret's building when it opened and a young man with a toddler rushed out. "*Excusez-moi,*" he said. Smiled and held the door for her.

A piece of cake. So far. She stepped inside and held her breath. No one. The concierge's loge was dark.

She hurried through the courtyard to the old stables, now garages. Now what? Climb atop the shed roof and shimmy over the stone wall? She suspected Baret had used a back entrance connecting the yard to the rear of the bookstore for discreet access. Like her father always said, master crooks keep it simple.

She delved into the ivy cascading over the wall, pulling apart the strands, and then she found it. A door.

A shove and it scraped open to a dirt walkway behind the shed in the next back courtyard. A minute later she'd skirted the mulberry bushes and was looking in on the back of the hunting bookstore. Lighted and empty.

Disembodied voices singing in Latin from the church drifted and disappeared. She shivered—not from the chill.

Had she read this wrong, jumped to conclusions? Would she be caught at any moment for breaking and entering?

A figure flashed by the window, disappeared into the

office. Aimée crept closer, moving behind the door. Tried the handle. Locked.

But the moisture-warped side window yielded to her nudge, centimeter by centimeter, until she could slide her forefinger in to shove the handle up. As she did, she popped her blood blister. Pinched it to stop the bleeding. Great.

A moment later she'd squeezed through the window and shut it. Logs smoldered in the fireplace of the back reading room. A few charred sheets of paper curled. Burning more evidence?

Warm, the place was so damn warm. Perspiration trickled down her neck. Her motorcycle jacket was stifling. Her nose was runny from the cold.

The ringing of a phone from the interior office. She edged closer.

". . . don't you see . . . ?" Elise's voice.

See what? She sucked on her damn finger and crouched to peer around the bookcase. One hunched step closer and she'd get a view . . . The wooden floor creaked.

"Finally," said Renaud, turning to her and beckoning. "Join us."

Caught. She straightened up, stepped inside the bright, halogen-lit high-tech office.

"What's going on, Elise?"

Elise sat on a swivel chair at the desk before a computer. Her mascara was smudged around her red-rimmed eyes. Her hair was flat, and she wore the same pantsuit she'd worn yesterday.

"Why did you fax me to meet at the apartment, Elise?"

Elise looked up at Renaud. "Tell her."

"That you set me up, Elise? Used me to lead Royant and Dufard to their murder?"

Elise's wide-set eyes teared. "No, you're wrong."

"They're out of the picture, so you'll control this financial empire," said Aimée, scanning the humming machines. "This empire your father built on Nazi gold."

From the smile on his face, Renaud approved. He applauded.

"Bravo," he said. "See, Elise, the med student's got part of it right."

Her heart thudded.

"I won't sign, Renaud. I don't believe it. You'll have assets—"

"When we're married?" he interrupted, harsh. "Poor Elise, you don't understand. That's not the point." His face hardened. "Sign."

Elise reached for the phone, her hands quivering. A sob. "I can't."

And then Renaud had grabbed Aimée's arm, yanked her around, and put her in a choke hold. She felt the cold metal of a pistol in her temple.

"I won't miss this time," he said.

Aimée's knees wobbled. Idiot, she'd put it together wrong. He'd been after the old men's money, picked them off, and planned to marry Elise for the empire.

"Non!" Elise screamed.

Aimée's tongue stuck in her dry throat. Renaud's grip tightened. She sucked air. It felt like forever, but it must have lasted only seconds before he shoved her into a swivel chair, keeping the gun trained on her.

"So what's the point, Renaud?" she gasped.

"For someone so smart, you don't get it, do you, med student?"

"Put the gun down, Renaud." Elise's voice quavered.

"What universe have I lived in the past few months? This whirlwind affair, your proposal . . . Where's that sweet man I met, Renaud?"

"You saw that man because that was the man I wanted you to see." Renaud's black eyes stared like the pit of a dark soul.

Always the actor.

"Now get signing the final trust assets into my account."

Aimée knew there was more to it than that.

"Why now, Renaud?" she managed. "Why kill the old men? Why not just wait for them to die, take over gradually, legally?" Her neck stung, her mouth as dry as cardboard.

"What's your connection to the Chambly-sur-Cher mayor, the man in the photo? His name was Gaubert. He was shot as a traitor by the Resistance."

"He wasn't a traitor."

"That's right." Aimée nodded. "An honorable man, Madame Jagametti said. He was your father, *non*? And it's you in this photo, hiding behind his leg? You're taking revenge."

Elise's face drained to a chalk white.

"Your papa killed mine like a dog." Renaud's voice changed to that of a young boy. A sad, high pitch. "It's only right he and the bad men got back what they deserved." He bobbed his head up and down. "That's right, don't you think, Elise?"

His childish voice—how he changed like a chameleon—sent shivers up her spine.

Elise's mouth quivered. "You're Gaubert's son? How can that be? I don't understand you, Renaud."

"Pretend," said Renaud, in the little boy voice. "That's what I'm good at, *Maman* said. Always pretend, she said, so I'd survive."

He never took the gun off Aimée.

"In the hospital *Maman* said I must keep pretending, make everyone believe I'm someone else. I'm so good at it, she said. So I promised." He shivered. "I never saw her again. A man took me away. He was wearing Papa's coat. Told me if I ever talked, he'd dump me on the road and I'd go hungry with all the lost people. So many lost people in the war."

Renaud cleared his throat. His voice adult now. Explanatory in tone. "I've had to act parts my whole life, Elise. I've never had a real home to live in, a real place to belong, because your father killed mine."

A schizophrenic? A deeply damaged person, that much she knew for sure. The hair rose on the back of her neck.

"Can you see me as Avi, the Jewish orphan at Liberation, adopted by 'loving parents' who made me learn Hebrew and have a Bar Mitzvah?" Renaud glanced at his watch. He was waiting for something or someone. "I pretended, hoping *Maman* would visit. But she hanged herself in the lunatic asylum. I found that report years later." His words came out matter-of-fact, hollow, his face expressionless. "In Paris, I was a natural for the conservatory, a stellar acting student."

Aimée's hands curled in her pocket around the Swiss Army knife she'd taken from her bag. He wanted to talk, he wanted her and Elise to know. Dramatize his story. But of course he was an actor, over the top. He'd left messages, pointers, a trail to be figured out—she only saw it now. Stupid. The murders had been staged ritualistically: the Sten gun, the Vichy bottle, the gags—like a scene.

"Greed, your father's and the others' greed—that's what killed my papa. This isn't about the money, Elise. I'm over fifty, yet a few months ago I discovered my true vocation—revenge."

Aimée watched him. He had perfect pitch, perfect timing, he was performing and they were the audience.

"My parents raised me as *un Juif*," said Renaud. "Of course I took a stage name. When they died this year, I put the apartment up for sale and cleared out their cellar. That's when I found *Maman*'s letter. They'd hidden it. They were supposed to give it to me when I was eighteen, but they didn't. She wrote down how your father shot Papa and melted all the gold. The same way they shot Minou, as that stupid Ninette said."

Renaud leaned down so he was at eye level with Elise. Smiled. "To think if I hadn't found *Maman*'s letter, your father would have gotten away with everything."

He cocked the trigger at Aimée's head.

"I've engineered the bank to fail, the empire to crumble. All I need is your signature, Elise."

Just like that? Wasn't it more complicated?

"Don't shoot her, Renaud. I'll do it. Take what you want." Elise grabbed a pen, scratched her signature.

Aimée's cold fear battled with guilt for having doubted Elise. She didn't believe Renaud intended to let them live, no matter what Elise gave him.

"Sign each of the six copies, Elise." Renaud's tone was almost conversational. He directed his attention at Aimée now. "Just think, I could have been your age when I discovered the truth about my parents' past. It could have changed my whole adult life."

That struck a chord. "So you're the only one with family secrets, Renaud? My American mother abandoned me when I was a little girl, and my father lied to me about who she was."

Renaud's flat stare scared her.

"Elise, my father didn't want anything to do with your case. But I helped because we're family. It was selfish, okay, but I wanted to find out about my mother from you. That's why I helped you. Now I'm going to get shot for it?"

"Ah, the young—so self-absorbed, so dramatic," said Renaud.

"With a pistol to my head, why not?"

Renaud slapped her. "Shut up." He turned to Elise. "Your father shot mine because my papa had a conscience." With a thunk, Renaud dropped a gold ingot on the desk with his free hand. "Like a chocolate bar, *non*? That's how my mother described it in her letter."

Transfixed, Aimée stared at the gold, the dull sparkle, the scratches of time marking it. She imagined its origins and shivered.

"Think where this came from. The jewelry of *déportés*, their gold fillings." She shook her head, sickened. "What do you mean your father had a conscience, Renaud? He took stolen gold, then let people die to keep his secret. It's tainted."

"*Non, non*, you don't understand. But who cares? That's not the point. I'm telling you, *Maman* wasn't the type to hang herself over a broken heart. They killed her."

Aimée understood. And wished she didn't.

"Gold lust, greed—did it ever make your father happy, Elise?" said Renaud. "Paranoid old men living *dans le luxe*, keeping mistresses, dining at four-star restaurants and always looking over their shoulders. Afraid I'd gotten away and would come back." He smiled. "*Et voilà*, I did."

Elise shoved the signed forms back at him, mascara tears smearing her cheeks. "I had no idea, Renaud. My parents sent me to boarding school in Montreal." She wiped her face. "When I returned home, I found a paranoid father and a reclusive mother. Strangers." Elise shook her head. "Even if what you say is true, this won't make it right. Or fix the past. Revenge gets you nowhere."

"Oh, it will get me a lot of places."

"Take all of it, Renaud. It sickens me."

He checked his watch again. "Ready to fax these on the secure line to the bank, Elise?" Renaud smiled. An adult doing a business transaction. "Then we're done, *d'accord?*"

Done? Aimée bit her lip, couldn't ignore the tremor in her stomach. The panic spreading through her. "Elise, he'll shoot us both."

Elise dropped the papers over the desk. "Renaud, I don't believe a man I love, who loves me—"

"He shot your father in the head, Elise." Aimée clutched the Swiss Army knife in her pocket.

Elise's eyes darted back and forth. "But Renaud, you'll let her go."

"Fax the documents, Elise."

"Okay, okay, just let her go."

"You won't get far, Renaud." Perspiration poured down between her shoulders blades. So damn hot. If only she could bat that gun out of his hands . . .

"Think so?" Renaud laughed. "I pretend for a living, med student. There's no detail I haven't taken care of."

"I know so, Renaud. You missed one big detail—the Corsican gang running rue de Ponthieu and the quartier. You ticked them off, big time, playing a gypsy taxi driver. They want to take care of you their way."

For once he looked surprised.

"Money won't buy you out of that." She tried inching closer on the chair, just a few centimeters.

"Look at what it bought the old men out of for forty years," said Renaud. "They had a good run."

"In my bag's a number I'm to call if I find you."

"I don't think you'll make that call."

"Don't have to." Time for a lie. "I was tailed coming here tonight."

Renaud slapped her again. Her cheek stung. "Such a pain in the ass since day one. Damn loose cannon. An interfering brat playing detective. You should have stuck to medical school. Now that career option's over, I'm afraid."

"I'd make a terrible doctor," she said, willing him closer. "I have a bad bedside manner."

Renaud's short bark of laughter unnerved her. "A comedian, too. So many talents wasted."

Closer, he'd edged closer now. A few more centimeters, that's all.

"Why did you encourage Elise to hire us and risk discovering the truth?"

"The playwright's oldest trick in the script," he said. "No one ever suspects the perpetrator to hire a detective." He sighed, then squealed for effect. "The audience gasps at that plot twist every time. "

The man was enjoying this, for God's sake. He'd play out his revenge, act his part and kill them both.

She'd sprung the knife's blade release open in her pocket as he laughed, aiming at his kidney. If she could get close enough, she'd stick the blade through the thin inner pocket lining. Damn, this was a good jacket, she hated to ruin it.

Upset and scared, Elise shot her a *what do I do* look! Then Aimée's eyes rested on the power strip under the desk near her feet.

Think, think . . . she had to come up with something.

Or they'd be dead and in the taxi trunk within five minutes. She worked her booted toe toward the power strip connecting several cords. The red power button at the opposite end.

"Pinel called, didn't he? I heard the phone ringing. He's on his way, Elise."

"Nice try," said Renaud, pushing Elise to the fax machine. "Pinel's tied up in the closet. I'll deal with him later."

Merde. How could she stop him? She'd only get close enough for him to put a bullet in her head if she rushed him with her short-bladed knife.

"If you think you'll get away with leaving a body in the closet . . . "

"No one knows I'm here. Or who I'll be when I leave."

His words chilled her. Stupid, she'd given René Elise's home address. Desperate, she racked her mind.

"I've heard there's a German asking questions." She worked her toe forward to one of the outlets. "An old man. Is he the fifth German?"

"Shut up."

"In Ninette's diary, she wrote that only four bodies washed up. They never found the fifth soldier."

"Liar."

"If Elise hadn't burned the diary, I could show you. Right, Elise?" She kept talking. "Your mother was afraid he'd come back—that's why she made you drive to Chambly-sur-Cher."

Tears welled in Elise's eyes. "She saw him on the riverbank, she kept saying. He's back. It gave her a stroke."

Her toe couldn't shove the cord off. Too tight. But if she could time it right and kick when he wasn't looking . . .

"The Wall's down, the fifth German's come back, hoping for his piece of the pie, Renaud."

The phone rang, piercing the air. Two, three rings.

"That's the bank, answer it," said Renaud.

Elise nodded, her eyes wide with fear.

But it didn't happen how Aimée thought it would. Elise picked up the phone and screamed. Galvanized, Aimée kicked the outlet hard and half the room went dark. The computers and fax machine sighed. Died. Renaud rushed forward, grabbing Elise and the phone.

Aimée lunged. Her knife connected to something soft, then hard in Renaud's side. Elise was screaming. Aimée twisted the knife and heard a groan of pain. Felt his hand around her neck, squeezing her windpipe. Choking, she was choking. Sucking for air.

Then she heard a shot.

Mon Dieu. Elise?

The hand let go. Gasping and breathing hard in the shadows, she grabbed whatever she could with her left hand, the answering machine, yanked it from its cord and whacked his face.

A light flickered on. Then another as a backup system kicked in. Renaud was on the floor, he wasn't moving. Catching her breath, she knelt down. His carotid artery wasn't pulsing either. Her hand came back sticky. A chalky gunpowder residue hovered in the air.

"Elise?" She heard sobbing. "Are you hurt?"

Elise had curled up in a fetal position beside the fax machine. The pistol by her ankle on the floor.

"We're damned," said Elise. "Cursed."

Aimée pulled herself up. Reached for Elise.

"I shot him." Elise's shoulders heaved. Her breath came in gasps. "Shot him like my father shot his."

———

"So Elise Peltier claims self-defense, Aimée." Morbier stood at the crime-scene tape, a glaring yellow in the night illuminated by the red and blue police car lights on the cobbles.

"So it's not Leduc, anymore, *Tonton?*"

Morbier shrugged. "You all right?"

She rubbed her neck, nodded. "*Bon*, better believe her. Otherwise I wouldn't be here. You'll find his gypsy taxi somewhere nearby. The old Sten gun in the trunk will match the ballistics, no doubt. Somewhere, too, a letter from his mother about his father's murder and the Nazi gold—"

"Oh, we found some gold all right," he interrupted. "Blood on it in more ways than one, I imagine."

"So sad, but . . ." Aimée paused, wouldn't say she'd told him so, even though she wanted to. That would be childish, *non?* "Have fun with the Corsicans. They contracted out for him. Just keep my name and Elise's out of it, *d'accord?*"

"Issuing orders now, Aimée?"

"Please don't tell Papa. I'll tell him myself, in my own way." She had a lot to tell him, like her decision to quit medical school, but she'd have to steel herself for that.

"As long as you hit the books," said Morbier.

The last thing on her new to-do list. Morbier wouldn't say it, but she'd proved she wasn't bad at this. She'd proved it to him, to all of them, but most importantly to herself. She'd made mistakes, *bien sûr*, but her investigation had felt right.

Elise stood shivering with a blanket over her shoulders near the back of the ambulance. Pinel was being carried on a stretcher.

"In an investigation isn't it important to tie up as many threads as possible?" she said. "The fifth German's a loose thread."

"Ah, the ignorance of youth, as if you knew as much as you think you do," said Morbier, lighting a Gauloise. The orange tip glowed. "In 1957, according to the *gendarmerie*, a fifth German soldier was discovered in a shallow grave by the river at Givaray. The priest had given him last rites and buried him, so they said."

"How does that figure . . . ? Wait, didn't the Germans execute the priest's parents? Is he the same priest?"

A shrug. "*Alors*, if there's more, that's between him and God. But it seems his brother just claimed his body."

"His body?" she said. "How could they tell?"

"A matching pinkie ring."

Paris · November 14, 1989 · Tuesday

JEAN-CLAUDE LEDUC STEPPED from the second-class car onto the platform at Gare de l'Est, lugging his valise. He hadn't told Aimée when he'd be arriving. He'd page her to call—the only secure way he could avoid their wiretapped phone.

Damn the secret security branch who monitored him. A decade had passed but the nastiness continued.

After finishing today's job, he was meeting the Ministry contact. Washing his hands. Blowing the whistle.

Passengers milled on the platforms under the dirty, grey glass roof; a loudspeaker announced train departures in a nasal voice amidst the usual clatter and bustle.

By the time Aimée rang him back in the phone booth, he'd snagged an espresso and several *gougères*, cheese puff pastries. Starving. That German food, so heavy, didn't agree with him.

Two rings. He picked up in the cabin.

"Aimée?"

"You're in Paris, Papa, I can tell by the number. At the station?"

"And no time to talk. The border's so crazy, the train was five hours late."

He heard her take a breath. That little intake he so loved. "What is it, Aimée?"

"Did you find her files?"

He sighed. Weary. So weary of lying.

"I found *her*."

Pause. A baby cried on the platform, pigeons pecked at the *gougères* crumbs near his feet.

A gasp. "Does that mean what I think it does?"

"We've got things to discuss." He glanced at the station clock. "*Merde*, I'm late. You did reserve the van?"

"It's in your name at the garage by Gare du Nord."

The same garage he always used.

"Pick me up at the corner on rue du Louvre, Papa."

"Don't you have class?"

"I'm coming with you. Papa, I have so much to tell you. But first you're going to tell me—"

"No time, Aimée. The surveillance got moved up. I don't know why. I need to get the van in place."

"Papa, I'm dropping out of medical school."

"What?" Nice bombshell to drop on him. But when did she do what he expected of her? Or listen to him? *Mon Dieu*, but he had a level-three surveillance in Place Vendôme, and he had no time to spare. Doing the dirty for the last time, and then he was out of it.

"Not now, Aimée. We'll talk when I get home."

"But Papa, I'll meet you there."

"Listen to me for once. Just once."

But she'd hung up.

AIMÉE RAN TO the courtyard and found her bike tires flat. Her pump was nowhere to be found. *Merde*. She jumped on the Métro at Pont Marie and got off at the Tuileries. She hurried, turned up rue de Castiglione, and ran under the arcades. Past the designer boutiques, gypsies hovering near tourists—running faster, her scarf flying behind her.

So much to tell Papa—so much for him to tell her.

She crossed rue Saint Honoré, her heart racing. *Bien sûr,* he'd be mad at first, but he'd understand why she couldn't go to medical school, she'd convince him. They'd work together, she'd earn a real PI license. And her mother . . . that flicker of hope burned into a flame.

He'd found her.

She was alive. Blood pounded in Aimée's every vein.

Alive. Her mother was alive. He'd found her.

That had to mean she was coming back.

Lungs bursting, she reached the Place Vendôme—the Ritz, the Chanel boutique, the jewelry stores all surrounding the cobbled square and the iron pillar built by Napoléon commemorating his victories, melted from the battle cannons.

Her Papa's van—she saw it, parked near the column—white, anonymous like a service vehicle. He'd be inside, using the long-range camera for surveillance, recording the cars, the stream of people. Waiting for his target.

Like so many times before. The usual.

As she was about to step off the pavement, a blinding flash erupted into a white-yellow fireball of light. The explosion shook the soles of her feet, ran up her legs, her whole body. A pressure wave sucked and then released her with a hot blast, singeing her eyebrows.

She stumbled back, then felt as though she'd been lifted off her feet. She was flying. When she came to—seconds or minutes later, she didn't know—she was a few meters away from where she'd been standing. Her back had hit a stone bollard; a sharp pain coursed up her spine.

And she saw billowing smoke, people running, their mouths open as if they were screaming. But she couldn't hear a thing. All she knew was her mouth was dry, her throat burned from the smoke. Coughing, she pulled herself up. Smelled burned flesh.

Non, non. Somehow she ran. She was screaming "Papa, Papa!" but she couldn't hear herself.

The van's door handle came off in her hands. Searing heat. The lenses of her father's glasses lay shattered on the cobblestones. His foot, still in his shoe, beside it. A howling wail came up from inside her. She was crying and reaching for his—his—but people were pulling her back. Firemen were hosing the cobbles down. And then she knew no more.

Acknowledgments

MANY THANKS TO Dot, Max, Barbara, Heather and Susanna. For all the wonderful help from Bill Whetstone, jeweler and gemstone expert *magnifique*, cat *maman* Jean Satzer; Marc Weber, the founding curator, Internet History Museum; the patient and generous techmeister Allan Schiffman. *Merci*'s in Paris go to: Guy Pradines, Police Judiciare 8th arrondissement; Stephané Pervieux of the Brigade de Répression du Proxénétisme; incredibly generous Arnaud Baleste; JC Mules, former Brigade Criminelle; Thierry Boulouque; Dr. Christian de Brier; Ancien secrétaire général et cofondateur de la Compagnie nationale des Experts de Justice en Criminalistique. Toujours Anne-Francoise Delbegue, Dr. Philippe Bray, Carla Bach, Berdj Achdjian, Jean Abou, Christophe, Martine, Mary Kay Bosshart, Celia Canning, and dear Julie McDonald. To Andi and Isabelle who took me to "Chambly" and Colette and the late Jacques Gerbault, who shared his story. Always to James N. Frey, wonderful Katherine Fausset, Bronwen, Rachel, Rudy, Amara, Abby, Paul—the whole Soho family, and Juliet Grames, editor extraordinaire. Jun and my son, Tate, without whom nothing happens.

Continue reading for a preview from the next
Aimée Leduc investigation

MURDER
IN SAINT-
GERMAIN

Paris, Jardin du Luxembourg · July 1999
Tuesday, Early Morning

THE BEEKEEPER ROLLED up his goatskin gloves, worried that the previous day's thunderstorm, which had closed the Jardin du Luxembourg, had disturbed his sweet bees. He needed to prepare them for pollinating the garden's apple trees, acacias, and chestnuts that week. Under the birdsong he could already make out the low buzz coming from the gazebo that sheltered their wooden hives. As he approached, he passed gardeners piling scattered plane-tree branches, their boots sucking in the mud.

What a mess. On top of the cleanup, he had a beekeeping class to teach here this afternoon. The buzzing mounted—had a hive been knocked over in the wind? As he adjusted his netted headgear, he felt a lump, something squishing under his boot.

Pale, mud-splattered fingers—a hand. Good God, he'd stepped on a human hand protruding from the hedge surrounding the apiary. Horrified, he stepped back, pushed the dripping branches of the bushes aside. He gasped to see a woman sprawled in a sundress. One hand clutched her swollen throat; buzzing bees, like black-gold jewels, covered most of her body.

Even before he'd shouted to the gardeners for help, he knew it was too late.

Paris · Tuesday Morning

AIMÉE LEDUC'S BARE legs wrapped around Benoît's spine as his tongue traced her ear. His warm skin and musk scent enveloped her. Delicious. Early morning sunlight pooled on her herringbone wood floor.

She didn't want him to stop. A sniffling cry came over the baby monitor. *Non.* The cry grew louder.

"Yours or mine?" Benoît sighed.

She'd know her daughter Chloé's cry anywhere; these were the cries of Benoît's niece, Gabrielle. "Yours."

One of the phones on the floor beeped. He looked at her again.

"Mine," said Aimée.

Benoît nuzzled her neck, disentangled himself, and found his shirt. She reached from where she lay on the duvet to the pile of clothes on the floor and found her cell phone.

A voice mail. Unknown number. She dialed in, heard the tone, and waited. "It's Dr. Vesoul." A clearing of the throat. "Our patient, Commissaire Morbier, went into emergency surgery. We're calling the family. He was asking for you."

Aimée's heart scudded. A knifelike pain wrenched her gut. Morbier. Her godfather . . . the man responsible for her father's murder.

The man she'd gotten shot two months earlier.

The man who had taken her to ballet lessons when she was a child. The man who'd lied to her for years.

Go hear him lie again? Never, she told herself. Kept telling herself that as she slipped into the work outfit hanging in her armoire—a black pencil skirt and white silk blouse—and as her shaking fingers struggled with the straps of her Roger Vivier sandals.

BRONZE SUNLIGHT STIPPLED the worn tiles on the kitchen floor. Miles Davis, Aimée's bichon frise, licked the spilled milk under Gabrielle's high chair. Holding her *bébé*, Chloé, on her hip, Aimée handed Benoît a freshly brewed espresso. He responded with a long kiss on her neck.

She would have liked that to go on forever. His scent lingered in her hair. "Tonight?" she asked.

"I've got meetings."

Benoît, a Sorbonne professor, tall and dark haired, lived across the courtyard at his sister and brother-in-law's. Stretching a long weekend, they'd asked him to babysit. His niece, Gabrielle, shared a caregiver, Babette, with Chloé. The babies were only a month apart in age.

"Playing hard to get?" she whispered. Stupid. Why couldn't she set boundaries, as the *ELLE* relationship article counseled? Keep him wanting more, not pull Gabrielle's uncle into her bed every night.

"Look for me around eleven," he breathed in her ear. His hand slipped into her blouse and traced the edge of her lace bra. "I'll bring the champagne; you provide the chaos. And wear that."

He waved goodbye to Gabrielle, seated in her high chair, and greeted the arriving Babette, who chattered about her upcoming Greek vacation. Aimée sat eight-month-old Chloé in the high chair next to Gabrielle's—like two peas in a pod; she never got over that. Chloé mashed a raspberry in her pudgy fingers, then smeared it on the stuffed bunny Morbier had given her at her christening.

For a moment, Morbier's face flashed in Aimée's head. She wanted to throw the bunny in the trash. But as she eased it from Chloé's sticky hand, the baby emitted a little cry. *"Désolée, ma puce."* Aimée tossed the favorite bunny into the hamper.

She could do this, couldn't she? Pull off being a working *maman*. She'd scored with a sweet caregiver for Chloé and a hunk who lived just across the courtyard.

She flipped open her red Moleskine to her to-do list, half listening to Babette's vacation chatter. A handwritten phone number glared up at her. Morbier's handwriting. Her insides trembled. Her godfather's presence was everywhere in her life. She pictured herself at his deathbed, imagined his accusations. Felt a beat of pain and drew a deep breath.

One thing at a time. Compartmentalize. Her goal these days was to put things into mental boxes, deal with the non-priorities later. Hopefully, by the time she got to the most unpleasant item, it would have gone away.

She picked up Chloé and inhaled her sweet baby smell.

"Give *maman* a *bisou*," said Babette, folding diapers by the window and puckering her lips.

Chloé cooperated with a raspberry-scented slobber. Her daughter's grey-blue eyes were so like those of Melac, the girl's biological father, and reminded Aimée of him every day. Melac had a new wife, and he and Aimée had a custody truce—life was good, wasn't it?

For a moment, in her sunlit kitchen, with the Seine gurgling below the window, Babette's bustling faded away.

All Aimée wanted to do on this muggy July day was sit back down and play with her rosy-cheeked Chloé. Forget about the day ahead . . . and Morbier.

Her phone rang in the hallway.

"See you tonight, *ma puce*." She blew a kiss.

At the coatrack she grabbed her trench coat, found her phone in her bag, and hit answer.

"*Allô*, Aimée? It's Jojo Dejouy. Got a moment?"

An old *commissaire* who'd been a colleague of her father's—and Morbier's. Not now of all times.

"*Oui*, can I call you later? I'm off to work . . ." She held the phone against her ear as she hurried down the marble stairs, grooved with age, to the ground floor.

"Morbier's asking for you, Aimée. I thought you should know."

First the doctor and now Jojo. She wanted to yell, *Leave me alone!*

"Not a good time, Jojo. *Désolée*." She shooed a stray black cat out of Chloé's stroller, parked next to Gabrielle's by the stairs. Brushed off the cat hairs.

There was silence on Jojo's end of the line. Aimée stepped over the courtyard's puddles. She held the phone between her shoulder and ear, dumping her bag in her motor scooter's basket.

"I know how you feel about Morbier," he said finally.

Like hell he did. She checked the spark plug. Kicked the tires. Good enough.

"There's not much time," said Jojo. "If you don't hear him out, I think you'll be saddled with more guilt than you feel already."

Guilt? "That's not the word I'd use, Jojo."

"It's for your sake that I called, not his," said Jojo. "It's you who's got to live with the consequences. Like I do. Never leave things unsaid, Aimée. Come to terms with Morbier."

"*Alors* . . ." Her heel skidded on a fallen pear from the courtyard tree. Crushed on the cobbles, the fruit emitted a sweet scent.

"Wait, Aimée." Jojo's voice rose. "Your father meant a lot to me. I didn't show it when they kicked him off the force. That was wrong. To my last day, I'll regret that. But I know you're a bigger person than I am. You find the good in people. You're generous, like your father."

Aimée wiped her heeled sandal on a cobble. "Got to go, Jojo."

"You're afraid of his accusations?"

"I've as good as killed him."

"The CRS shot him, not you. Morbier's an old dog," said Jojo, "been around long enough to know the score."

She hung up. Grabbed the handlebars of her faded pink Vespa so hard her knuckles hurt. Couldn't she put the past aside for once and get on with today?

Yet she'd known Morbier all her life. She wondered what her father would have done.

A mist filled the quai, the plane-tree leaves rustled, and a siren whined as she gunned over Pont de la Tournelle to the Left Bank.

Find the good in people? Generous? She didn't feel generous.

But maybe she did want to hear whatever Morbier had to tell her. Could she face Morbier? Or would she end up kicking herself later? Would she regret it even more if she didn't hear him out?

At the traffic light beyond the quai, she turned left instead of right, heading toward la Maison de Santé du

Gardien de la Paix, the pale brick police hospital that bordered the Latin Quarter. Of those who went in, half made it to the country rehab clinic; the rest came out in a box.

The gathering clouds promised more rain after yesterday's storm. The humid heat was like a blanket lying over the streets. What she wouldn't give for a whiff of breeze. Her damp collar stuck to her neck, her fingers trembled, and she almost turned around.

Perspiration dried in the cleft of her neck. She'd come this far. Determined, she hurried up the hospital stairs. A few minutes, that would be all. She'd hear what Morbier wanted to tell her, then go.

Cool antiseptic-laced air met her in the old-fashioned wood-paneled lobby. Near the reception desk, she caught sight of Jeanne, Morbier's middle-aged girlfriend. Jeanne leaned against the wall, her hands covering her face. Too late?

The disinfectant odors couldn't block the smell of two old men on Aimée's left, each standing with the support of a walker. "Good job. Take another step. We're almost there," said a perspiring young nurse. Aimée recognized one of the men—Philippe, from her father's old *commissariat*. A haggard face now, one side of him drooping, drool hanging from his chin.

Sobs came from another corridor. Aimée shuddered and stepped back. Her fault, all her fault.

Jeanne saw her and beckoned.

That cold, wet night came back to her—Morbier reaching for what she thought was his gun, her signaling the SWAT team, the shots, the blood, all that blood, Morbier wheeled into emergency surgery.

Guilt, sadness, and anger washed over her.

Aimée couldn't push that scuffed door open. Couldn't face his dying. She shook her head at Jeanne, felt a tear course down her cheek, and turned around.

"Aimée, come back," yelled Jeanne.

A minute later, she'd jumped on her scooter and taken off.

Tuesday, Late Afternoon

AIMÉE CHEWED A paper clip as she stared at the computer screen in her temporary office at the École des Beaux-Arts on the Left Bank. She was in a former seventeenth-century cloister, overlooking the Cour du Mûrier with its Chinese mulberry tree. The steel of the minimalist Danish chair bit into her hip as she ran scans of the art school's database system.

There, with birds warbling from the courtyard, Aimée monitored eye-glazingly boring accounts, checked the interface and server IP logs. Slog work, but lucrative; she counted herself lucky for the contract with the prestigious crème de la crème art school. This was the bread-and-butter computer security work her detective agency survived on. She'd been referred by her best friend, Martine's sister, an editor at *ELLE*. It was the third time Sybille, *la directrice*, had hired Aimée.

Only rarely did a low conversation drift up from the garden; the classical statues were abandoned in their painted arcades. The school was deserted of students for the summer; the few staff on the premises were those jurying fall student submissions. Aimée stifled a yawn and reached for the fizzing glass of Perrier by the screen. Behind her lay a sun-drenched back terrasse, covered with ivy, hidden and intimate—not a bad job perk.

What a place to work, she thought. Almost the heart of Saint-Germain-des-Prés here by the Seine and surrounded by historical monuments.

Aimée checked her phone for messages. One from Babette, as usual—she was diligent about updating her. Chloé had eaten her yogurt, and the girls had gone down for a nap.

She imagined her Chloé in the crib, light from the window dancing on her blanket. Safe. That's how Aimée got through the day—check-ins with Babette, a little babble time with Chloé in the afternoon.

No more calls from Jojo. A wave of relief mixed with guilt passed over her. She rechecked the configuration options, the database scan—all in order—and finished up running the system's daily maintenance.

She grew aware of a shadow just before a man sat down next to her. The air stirred, and she caught a scent of something she couldn't put her finger on. Chemical, medicinal, oil based?

"Jules Dechard," he said, introducing himself. She recognized the well-known art history professor and critic. He was lean, russet haired, thin faced, tanned. He looked healthy for an academic. But then, what did she know? Benoît was an academic, too, and Aimée certainly found him fit enough.

Jules Dechard leaned forward. "Sybille says you're discreet."

"Discreet" meant many things. None of them good.

"Do you have a problem with your computer, Professor Dechard?" Probably he wanted her to scrub his hard drive—the usual request. She doubted he wanted to discuss the current art scene.

"Mademoiselle Leduc, I want to hire you."

Hire her? She toyed with the paper clip. "That could bring up a conflict of interest with my contract here,

Professor Dechard. I'm afraid that would prevent me from working for you."

"It's personal." He was staring at her Gigabyte Green nails.

What kind of problem could he have? A cheating wife? A son kicked out of a prep school? "My scope's limited to computer security."

"I know you can help me. I've read about you."

Who hadn't? Morbier's shooting, the ministry corruption, the widespread police fallout. *Paris Match* was having a field day.

"It's a simple job, Mademoiselle Leduc." He pushed a folded yellow Post-it into her palm. On it, in neat, slanting handwriting, was an email address, *aft@agt.fr*. "Computers mystify me. I'm old school. But I'm trying to collect any emails to and from this email address. Quite easy for you, I'd imagine. Maybe there's just some simple way you can check the whole . . . what's it called, the server? Collect all the emails from this sender? Even if they have been deleted—there's a way to do that, *non*?"

She could do that in her sleep.

She smiled. "I'll fax you a contract from the office."

Dechard laid his hand on her arm. Clammy. He slipped a wad of franc notes into her open secondhand Hermès bag. A large wad of franc notes.

"Keep it between us, please," he said. "I'm counting on your discretion. Cash and no accounting."

Strange. René would kill her—he hated working off the books. But for such a simple job, maybe she didn't need a contract. "All right, Professor. I will compile any emails that came in to you from this address and check in with you tomorrow."

"Not emails that came in to me," he said, lowering his

voice. "In fact, please do not search for emails to me. I need to know who else at this school has been receiving emails from this address."

He was spying on his colleagues, and he thought he'd enlist her? As if she would jeopardize her contract. "*Désolée*, Professor, but I cannot help you. Email is private."

"I assure you it's not," Dechard said. "This is a Ministry of Culture–funded institution. Any correspondence undertaken under the school's name should be free and available to the public."

Aimée thought about that. She wasn't sure what he said was correct, but she was sure taking a private contract to hack staff members' emails for another staff member would cause her nothing but trouble.

"I'd like to help you, but . . ."

"You're worried you'd get in trouble. But I guarantee that won't happen. Sybille, the directrice, recommended I ask you to help with this. She's my sister-in-law. Besides, nothing I'm asking for would violate ethical considerations."

Aimée hesitated. "If Sybille suggested I do this, she should ask me herself."

"Check with her to verify if you must," Dechard said. "But please be discreet. Tell no one but Sybille."

The wad of money would probably cover childcare, the office rent, for months. Maybe even a few days away on *vacances*. If Sybille approved, how could Aimée say no? But something about this felt off to her. Why was Dechard so insistent on secrecy? What was he hoping to find evidence of? Usually these types of jobs involved an extramarital affair, or some other love-life indiscretion. Was Dechard married? He didn't wear a ring. Or was this something else entirely? A rivalry with another faculty member? She'd heard academia was cutthroat.

She'd talk it over with René—they'd return Dechard's money if they had to.

"I'll see what I can find," she said.

In the early evening, Aimée stepped out onto the narrow street leading away from the Seine. The heat had barely cooled even as the shadows of the seventeenth-century building lengthened. No taxi in sight and a scorching three blocks to the Métro. Forget the bus with traffic at a standstill. Only a ten-minute walk if she hurried through Saint-Germain. But before she could even cross the street, the sky opened. Late July was nothing but heat, showers, and tourists here on the Left Bank.

She ducked back under the glass marquise awning. Above her, rain drummed in three-quarter time. She belted her trench coat and debated unfurling the umbrella to battle the sheeting warm rain. *Mais, non.* Caught, she'd wait it out.

Aimée's grandfather Claude used to complain that the Saint-Germain he knew in the old days had disappeared. It had tipped beyond the reach of the working class, the students and artists who used to populate the quartier. She knew Oscar Wilde had died in a fleabag hotel near the school, penniless and alone, rumored uttering the line "Either this wallpaper goes, or I do." Today the fleabag was a boutique hotel, and the streets surrounding it were chock-full of antiquaries, art galleries, and prestigious publishing houses. Claude had been in love with an artist's model who had posed at the École des Beaux-Arts— before he'd met Aimée's *grand-mère*, he'd assured her—and his nostalgia for that time had colored his thoughts, she suspected. Saint-Germain was a shadow of its storied past, her *grand-père* would tell her, a far cry from what it had been when Delacroix, Picasso, and Manet had lived here. Café les Deux Magots, where de Beauvoir and Sartre once wrote all day nursing a single coffee, had quadrupled its prices for tourists.

Still, in her time here back when she was a premed student, she'd loved Saint-Germain's bustling street life. The tiny art-house cinemas, the rue de Buci market, the bistros, the old cellar jazz clubs that closed at dawn. Change was inevitable, and Saint-Germain mixed old and new—like where the surviving fragments of a twelfth-century wall built by King Philippe Auguste had been repurposed into part of a parking garage.

As quickly as it had begun, the rain stopped. She started down rue Bonaparte and paused, startled to see a familiar face beckoning her from a *café tabac* doorway.

Suzanne Lesage—Melac's former undercover partner, head of an elite undercover counterterrorism squad. Suzanne, blonde and fit, had always looked sharp, and today's outfit proved no exception: flared gaucho pants, a crop top, metallic sandals, and gold hoop earrings. Usually dry and cool as a cucumber, Suzanne had rings under her eyes.

"*Quelle surprise,*" said Aimée. "So you just happen to be on rue Bonaparte?"

There was no such thing as a coincidence with top cops like Suzanne.

"I see you're back in shape after your *bébé*," said Suzanne, kissing Aimée on both cheeks—the customary *bisous*.

"Chloé's eight months now. Got one more kilo to lose," said Aimée, ruing the previous day's *tarte aux abricots* at the pâtisserie. Despite the shadows under her eyes, Suzanne's face, makeup free apart from red lipstick, looked fresher than her own in the humidity. Aimée's mascara had clumped in the heat, her eyelashes sticking when she blinked.

"Your partner told me you'd be here, Aimée. Working at École des Beaux-Arts."

Her partner René?

"He said you'd be delighted to offer assistance in an investigation."

The traitor.

"*Un café?*" Suzanne gestured to her table inside.

Acid roiled in Aimée's stomach. She hoped she wasn't getting mixed up in another sting operation.

Suzanne ordered, then lasered in on Aimée. "Do you remember that favor I did for you, Aimée?"

Aimée nodded. Her heart pounded. What was Suzanne about to ask her to do?

"I'm calling it in, Aimée. You owe me."

Join the club, she almost said. Juggling work and childcare demanded all the favors she could call in and then some. Still, Suzanne had helped her out when she'd been desperate—Suzanne had used her professional connections and put her own career on the line to help Aimée track down a kidnapper when Zazie, the daughter of the proprietor of the café below Aimée's office, had gone missing.

"Of course, Suzanne." Wary, Aimée wondered what she was agreeing to.

"This is strictly between us, *comprends?*" Suzanne checked her phone. "I trust you, but I can trust no one else right now." Then her face broke into a small grin. "Plus I know where you live. *Un moment.* I've got to take this call."

While Suzanne paced in the street on her cell phone,

Aimée plopped two brown sugar cubes in her demitasse. She stirred, uneasy, wondering what this was about. In the mist, a bus pulled up in front of the Carrefour across the street, disgorging dry passengers who were promptly replaced by damp ones. She inhaled the scent of Saint-Germain: a whiff of perfume from a passersby, cigarette smoke, the smell of butter wafting from a boulangerie.

Suzanne sat back down. Thin lines creased the bridge of her nose. "*Alors*, it's crazy right now. I've been called in; a car's going to pick me up in five minutes. So I'll make this quick. I need your help."

Aimée nodded. "Why the cloak-and-dagger?"

"No one must know we've talked. It's off the book, Aimée."

"Unofficial?"

Suzanne looked around. "I'm not speaking to you as an officer now. I'm a mother too, okay?" She leaned over the café table. Her thick, stylishly blunt-cut hair swung over her shoulders. "Last night I stopped at my local *café tabac* to get my Loto ticket, like I do every Monday." Her voice had dropped to a whisper. "I saw him, Aimée, in line at the counter." Her hand twitched on the demitasse handle. Aimée realized Suzanne was shaking.

"Saw who?"

"I saw a ghost."

OTHER TITLES IN THE SOHO CRIME SERIES

Sebastià Alzamora
(Spain)
Blood Crime

Stephanie Barron
(Jane Austen's England)
*Jane and the Twelve Days
of Christmas
Jane and the Waterloo Map*

F.H. Batacan
(Philippines)
Smaller and Smaller Circles

James R. Benn
(World War II Europe)
*Billy Boyle
The First Wave
Blood Alone
Evil for Evil
Rag & Bone
A Mortal Terror
Death's Door
A Blind Goddess
The Rest Is Silence
The White Ghost
Blue Madonna*

Cara Black
(Paris, France)
*Murder in the Marais
Murder in Belleville
Murder in the Sentier
Murder in the Bastille
Murder in Clichy
Murder in Montmartre
Murder on the Ile Saint-Louis
Murder in the Rue de Paradis
Murder in the Latin Quarter
Murder in the Palais Royal
Murder in Passy
Murder at the Lanterne Rouge
Murder Below Montparnasse
Murder in Pigalle
Murder on the Champ de Mars
Murder on the Quai
Murder in Saint-Germain*

Lisa Brackmann
(China)
*Rock Paper Tiger
Hour of the Rat
Dragon Day*

*Getaway
Go-Between*

Henry Chang
(Chinatown)
*Chinatown Beat
Year of the Dog
Red Jade
Death Money
Lucky*

Barbara Cleverly
(England)
*The Last Kashmiri Rose
Strange Images of Death
The Blood Royal
Not My Blood
A Spider in the Cup
Enter Pale Death
Diana's Altar*

Gary Corby
(Ancient Greece)
*The Pericles Commission
The Ionia Sanction
Sacred Games
The Marathon Conspiracy
Death Ex Machina
The Singer from Memphis
Death on Delos*

Colin Cotterill
(Laos)
*The Coroner's Lunch
Thirty-Three Teeth
Disco for the Departed
Anarchy and Old Dogs
Curse of the Pogo Stick
The Merry Misogynist
Love Songs from a Shallow Grave
Slash and Burn
The Woman Who Wouldn't Die
The Six and a Half Deadly Sins
I Shot the Buddha
The Rat Catchers' Olympics*

Garry Disher
(Australia)
*The Dragon Man
Kittyhawk Down
Snapshot
Chain of Evidence
Blood Moon
Wyatt
Whispering Death
Port Vila Blues
Fallout
Hell to Pay*

David Downing
(World War II Germany)
*Zoo Station
Silesian Station
Stettin Station
Potsdam Station
Lehrter Station
Masaryk Station*

(World War I)
*Jack of Spies
One Man's Flag
Lenin's Roller Coaster*

Agnete Friis
(Denmark)
What My Body Remembers

Leighton Gage
(Brazil)
*Blood of the Wicked
Buried Strangers
Dying Gasp
Every Bitter Thing
A Vine in the Blood
Perfect Hatred
The Ways of Evil Men*

Timothy Hallinan
(Thailand)
*The Fear Artist
For the Dead
The Hot Countries*

(Los Angeles)
*Crashed
Little Elvises
The Fame Thief
Herbie's Game
King Maybe
Fields Where They Lay*

Karo Hämäläinen
(Finland)
Cruel Is the Night

Mette Ivie Harrison
(Mormon Utah)
*The Bishop's Wife
His Right Hand
For Time and All Eternities*

Mick Herron
(England)
*Down Cemetery Road
The Last Voice You Hear
Reconstruction
Smoke and Whispers
Why We Die
Slow Horses
Dead Lions
Nobody Walks
Real Tigers
Spook Street*

**Lene Kaaberbøl &
Agnete Friis**
(Denmark)
*The Boy in the Suitcase
Invisible Murder
Death of a Nightingale
The Considerate Killer*

Heda Margolius Kovály
(1950s Prague)
Innocence

Martin Limón
(South Korea)
Jade Lady Burning
Slicky Boys
Buddha's Money
The Door to Bitterness
The Wandering Ghost
G.I. Bones
Mr. Kill
The Joy Brigade
Nightmare Range
The Iron Sickle
The Ville Rat
Ping-Pong Heart
The Nine-Tailed Fox

Ed Lin
(Taiwan)
Ghost Month
Incensed

Peter Lovesey
(England)
The Circle
The Headhunters
False Inspector Dew
Rough Cider
On the Edge
The Reaper

(Bath, England)
The Last Detective
Diamond Solitaire
The Summons
Bloodhounds
Upon a Dark Night
The Vault
Diamond Dust
The House Sitter
The Secret Hangman
Skeleton Hill
Stagestruck
Cop to Corpse
The Tooth Tattoo
The Stone Wife
Down Among the Dead Men
Another One Goes Tonight

(London, England)
Wobble to Death
The Detective Wore Silk Drawers
Abracadaver
Mad Hatter's Holiday
The Tick of Death
A Case of Spirits
Swing, Swing Together
Waxwork

Jassy Mackenzie
(South Africa)
Random Violence
Stolen Lives

Jassy Mackenzie cont.
The Fallen
Pale Horses
Bad Seeds

Francine Mathews
(Nantucket)
Death in the Off-Season
Death in Rough Water
Death in a Mood Indigo
Death in a Cold Hard Light
Death on Nantucket

Seichō Matsumoto
(Japan)
Inspector Imanishi Investigates

Magdalen Nabb
(Italy)
Death of an Englishman
Death of a Dutchman
Death in Springtime
Death in Autumn
The Marshal and the Murderer
The Marshal and the Madwoman
The Marshal's Own Case
The Marshal Makes His Report
The Marshal at the Villa Torrini
Property of Blood
Some Bitter Taste
The Innocent
Vita Nuova
The Monster of Florence

Fuminori Nakamura
(Japan)
The Thief
Evil and the Mask
Last Winter, We Parted
The Kingdom
The Boy in the Earth

Stuart Neville
(Northern Ireland)
The Ghosts of Belfast
Collusion
Stolen Souls
The Final Silence
Those We Left Behind
So Say the Fallen

(Dublin)
Ratlines

Kwei Quartey
(Ghana)
Murder at Cape Three Points
Gold of Our Fathers

Qiu Xiaolong
(China)
Death of a Red Heroine
A Loyal Character Dancer
When Red Is Black

John Straley
(Alaska)
The Woman Who Married a Bear
The Curious Eat Themselves
The Big Both Ways
Cold Storage, Alaska

Akimitsu Takagi
(Japan)
The Tattoo Murder Case
Honeymoon to Nowhere
The Informer

Helene Tursten
(Sweden)
Detective Inspector Huss
The Torso
The Glass Devil
Night Rounds
The Golden Calf
The Fire Dance
The Beige Man
The Treacherous Net
Who Watcheth

Janwillem van de Wetering
(Holland)
Outsider in Amsterdam
Tumbleweed
The Corpse on the Dike
Death of a Hawker
The Japanese Corpse
The Blond Baboon
The Maine Massacre
The Mind-Murders
The Streetbird
The Rattle-Rat
Hard Rain
Just a Corpse at Twilight
Hollow-Eyed Angel
The Perfidious Parrot
The Sergeant's Cat: Collected Stories

Timothy Williams
(Guadeloupe)
Another Sun
The Honest Folk of Guadeloupe

(Italy)
Converging Parallels
The Puppeteer
Persona Non Grata
Black August
Big Italy
The Second Day
of the Renaissance

Jacqueline Winspear
(1920s England)
Maisie Dobbs
Birds of a Feather